Rhapsody

Lauren E. Rico

Rhapsody by Lauren E. Rico

Copyright © 2016 Harmony House Productions

Cover design by: Florida Girl Design Inc. www.gobookcoverdesign.com
For permissions contact: Lauren@LaurenRico.com
Visit the author's website www.LaurenRico.com
ISBN-13: 978-0-9974303-4-9

The Music of Rhapsody

The musical selections mentioned, both in passing and in detail throughout this book were carefully selected to complement the mood of each character and to reflect the tone of the of the story at that point in time. If you have the opportunity to listen to some of the selections as you read, I think you'll find the music adds an entirely new emotional depth and dimension. Happy reading and happy listening!

-Lauren

HAYDN: STRING QUARTET OP.76, No.4 "SUNRISE"
JS BACH: SUITE No.6 FOR UNACCOMPANIED CELLO
JS BACH: SUITE No.1 FOR UNACCOMPANIED CELLO
(ARRANGED FOR FRENCH HORN)
ELGAR: VIOLIN CONCERTO IN B MINOR, OP.61
DVOŘÁK: PIANO CONCERTO IN G MINOR, OP.33
WHITACRE: THE RIVER CAM

For Ma Mére

Prologue: Jeremy

Watching my father die isn't nearly as entertaining as I'd hoped it would be. It's kind of cliché, actually. Even in the throes of death, the stupid son of a bitch is underwhelming. He's clutching at the collar of his shirt, trying to pull it free of the buttons that are causing it to strangle him. His face is a darkening red, and his frantic eyes are getting larger by the second. His breath is coming in labored wheezes.

The one thing I do find interesting is the fact that not once has he reached out to me, mouthed to me, or begged me with his eyes to help him. That's probably because he knows I'd laugh in his oxygen-deprived face. He won't give me the satisfaction. Oh, he did try to get to the phone on his own, but he just couldn't quite crawl across the floor. Gee, too bad. I could have reached it just by stretching out my arm.

I must admit I didn't come here looking to kill the guy. But when I realized he was headed toward a heart attack or stroke or whatever the fuck this is, I was only too happy to help him along. I have a way of getting under people's skin when I want to. And I *really* want to.

He's squirming now and his lips are starting to look blue. When I see that his eyes are starting to roll into the back of his head, I squat down beside him. I can tell there isn't much time left and I want to make sure the last words he hears on this earth come from my mouth.

He gasps in one last breath as best he can and tries to focus on me. I smile and put a hand on his shoulder, as if to comfort him.

"Don't you worry, dad. Mom won't be too far behind you. I promise you, I'll make sure of that."

And then he is gone.

Prologue

Matthew

They call it 'The Magic Hour'—a small window of time just before sunset, when the world is bathed in a warm, sepia glow. Right now, this perfect light is cast across the back lawn of the North Fork Children's Home, as I watch my bride make her way toward me. I'm waiting for her at the point where the earth falls away into the steep, sandy bluff below. Behind me, the inky water of the Long Island Sound is dotted with sailboats, some wafting lazily, others picking up speed as their sails expand with the salty breeze.

That same breeze just catches the hem of Julia's dress so that it billows out around her—making her appear as an angel floating toward me. Adding to the illusion is the way the light in her auburn hair creates a gentle halo around her perfect, porcelain face. Her left hand holds a small bouquet of wildflowers, while her right is wrapped in the arm of the man who is giving her away. Dr. Sam Michaels couldn't look more proud than if he actually was her father.

All around us there are children. There must be two hundred of them lining the path that Julia is walking, throwing rose petals at her as she passes. They are of all different ages, backgrounds and ethnicities. What they have in common with us, and with one another, is that they will spend some part of their childhood in this place.

"It's like we're all family, Matthew," she reminded me. *"I want them there, participating, witnessing. I want them to celebrate with us."*

And now, as the flowers fly, and the tiny North Fork Children's Home band honks away on Mendelssohn's *Wedding March*, I see that she was absolutely right.

From next to me, the Reverend Caldwell pats my shoulder supportively, but I hardly notice because I cannot take my eyes off of Julia. She crosses the long patch of soft green grass to the very spot where we sat as children, looking out to the water and planning our lives together. When, finally, she's standing only inches in front of me, Dr. Sam takes her hand and puts it into mine, patting the two, as if he can adhere us for eternity.

"She's yours to watch over now," he says softly, seriously.

"She always has been," I reply, without even looking at him.

Julia is even more breathtaking up-close. I see now there's a wreath of tiny white flowers and ribbon on her head. And, for the first time, I notice that she's barefoot. This makes me smile. She makes me smile.

"You look... amazing," I whisper.

She blushes as she gives my hand a squeeze, and we settle into our positions. Dr. Sam steps back behind us, and the Reverend moves in front of us.

"It is my great honor to join together today in holy matrimony a pair of souls who were united a long time ago. Matthew, Julia, I remember you clearly from your days here at the children's home. You were inseparable companions, protectors and confidantes for one another. You assuaged the pain of mutual loss and found the strength to build a life together out of the ashes of your earliest days. Never before have I felt more confident in a union, for you are already devoted to one another. You have already sacrificed for one another. You have already weathered some of the worst trials a human being can endure and yet, here you stand before me, your belief in the goodness that exists in the world still strong enough to give you hope for the future. Please face one another and join hands."

We do as he says.

"Julia Victoria James, will you have Matthew as your lawfully wedded husband? Will you love him and cherish him and stand by his side all the days of your life?"

"I will," she responds softly, her emerald eyes affixed to my brown ones.

"Matthew David Ayers, will you have Julia as your lawfully wedded wife? Will you love her and cherish her and stand by her side all the days of your life?"

They're the two words I have been waiting to utter for what seems like my entire life. It's all I can do to keep myself from shouting them.

"I will."

Dr. Sam pulls the pair of matching gold bands out of his pocket and hands them up to me.

"Matthew, please put the ring on Julia's finger and repeat after me. With this ring, I thee wed."

I do as I'm told, and we repeat the process in reverse with Julia slipping the band on my finger.

"Julia, Matthew, I am so happy to pronounce you husband and wife."

From behind us, there's the huge eruption of applause and catcalls from our witnesses. I glance over my shoulder at the crowd of young people who have congregated to watch the spectacle.

"You may kiss the bride!" the Reverend yells above the jubilant noise.

He doesn't have to say it twice. I pull Julia into my arms and plant a long, deep kiss on her lips. I pick her up and twirl her around as she throws her head back and laughs. I've never been much of a romantic, but I just can't seem to help myself. The way she looks, the way she sounds, the way I feel at this moment...I think she just might be an angel after all.

Part One

Chapter 1

Brett

It's hard to describe the sound that the human body makes when it hits a stationary object at a high rate of speed. My mind registers some cross between a 'thump,' a 'splat' and an 'ugh,' as I go flying out of the back seat of the cab and slam into the solid, Plexiglas partition that separates the passengers from the driver. Equally disturbing, is the smacking sound my head makes as it hits the armrest of the rear passenger door on my rebound journey. Now, I'm lying, face-up, staring at the roof of the car.

I'm jolted out of the eerie silence by a sudden explosion of noise. It's as if all hell is breaking loose around me. There is yelling outside of the cab, the drivers are screaming obscenities at one another. How did they get out of the cars so fast? I can hear excited conversation just outside of my door, but I can't lift my head enough to see anything out of the window. Horns are honking relentlessly.

"Open the door and help him!" I hear someone say nearby.

"Nah, man. You ain't supposed to move someone when they been in an accident."

"Has anyone called an ambulance?"

No one replies to that question.

For once, I had decided to splurge on a cab after one of the Walton Quartet gigs. We hadn't even cleared the intersection, when a box truck ran a red light, T-boning us. I try to lift my head, but I feel a rush of tears wash down my face as I do.

"Move!" demands a woman's voice close by. "Will you please get out of the way?" She's closer now, and more irritated.

Without warning, the car door swings open, and my head drops off of the armrest. I flinch with the expectation of hitting the metal jamb, but I don't. My head barely moves an inch. I try to see what's happening behind me, but at this angle, the late afternoon sun pours in, temporarily blinding me. I squeeze my sore lids shut against the glare.

"Hey. Hey there. Can you hear me?" It's a soft female voice. I think maybe the same one who told everyone to move.

"Yes, I can hear you," I mutter.

"Open your eyes," she commands.

I do.

The bright light is blocked by her head, hovering closely over me. I squint and try to make out her features, but she looks so dark against the backlight of the sun behind her. Not to mention the way she is leaning over me from the outside, she looks like a floating head with no body attached. That can't be right, can it?

"What's your name?" the head asks.

"Brett. Brett Corrigan."

"Hi, Brett. I'm Maggie. Listen to me, you've been in an accident," she says slowly, as if I'm an imbecile.

"No shit," I murmur. I think I can make out a smile on her shadowy face, but I'm not certain.

"Okay, good! You remember what happened. Are you in pain, Brett?"

I start to nod, and the tears flow again. Dammit!

"Hey, hey, don't try to move. We need to keep your neck straight until the ambulance comes, okay?"

"I don't think anyone called..."

"Don't you worry about that, they're on the way," she assures me. "Where does it hurt, Brett?"

I think about this question and a quick mental inventory gives me the answers. "My head. My face."

"How about your arms or your hands or your wrists, Brett? Did you try to brace yourself when you hit the partition?"

Oh, shit! Did I? One bad break and my career is over. I try not to panic as I assess the state of my limbs and digits. Finally, I take a deep breath and speak again.

"No. I don't think so. It happened so fast, I didn't have time to brace. Just my head hit and then I flew back."

Either my eyes are adjusting, or her face is lightening, because now I can make out the soft outline of her cheeks and jaw.

"Maggie?"

"Yes?"

"I can't stop crying."

I think I see her brow furrow, either in concern or confusion. Maybe both. "You're not crying, Brett. You're bleeding."

I'm about to say something when another head pops into my line of vision. This one is bigger.

"What the fuck, Maggie? You should have waited for the ambulance to come!"

Oh, I don't like this head at all. This head sounds like a dick.

"John, make yourself useful and find me some tissues or a towel or something so I can wipe some of this blood off of his face. And make sure it's clean!"

Dickhead lingers for a second before receding.

"Boyfriend?" I ask and am surprised to hear I have a slight slur now. If the girl notices, she doesn't mention it.

"Date," she says with a hint of disdain.

"First?" I ask, trying to focus on her as the pain behind my eyes intensifies.

"Second," she says. "And last."

I don't think I was meant to hear that last bit—it's barely a whisper under her breath.

"Here, I've got some napkins from the pretzel truck," I hear him say as a hand is thrust into view.

Maggie takes them from him with her right hand, still using her left hand to cradle my head. She presses the stack gently, but firmly on my forehead.

"Oh, fuck me!" I howl. "That hurts!"

She shushes me quietly. "I know," she murmurs. "But you're bleeding a lot and I want to try and slow it down."

From somewhere in the distance, I hear the squawk of sirens. "Those are for you," she informs me.

I can hear the sound of dickhead's voice nearby, but I can't quite catch what he's saying. Maggie has turned her head slightly toward him and now I can make out a halo of curls around her head.

"You know what?" she hisses quietly out the door behind her, "I'm done. Take your theatre tickets and shove them, John. And while you're at it, you can shove my phone number, too."

Ouch. Dickhead got a beat down in public. I wonder if his head hurts as much as mine does right now.

When she turns back toward me, I can see her smile. Sort of. Everything's a little hazy at the moment. The ambulance is very close now, blaring its horn as it tries to make its way through the gridlock this accident has undoubtedly created.

"Any second now, Brett. I think they'll probably secure your neck with a collar and slip a back board under you."

I moan, suddenly alarmed. "Do you think I hurt my spine? Isn't that why they do that?"

She's shaking her head and the hair shakes with it. "No. I don't think so, but we don't want to take any chances, right?"

I can hardly hear her now.

"Brett?"

And why is it getting so dark in here?

"Brett?" I hear her ask a little louder this time.

"*Brett!*"

Chapter 2

Maggie

The man I'm looking at in this hospital room looks substantially worse than the man I was looking down on in the car just two days ago. His nose is swollen and bent too far to one side. There are tufts of cotton stuffed up into his nostrils, and the gash on his head, the one that gushed all over me, has been sewn up in large, jagged stitches, a la Frankenstein. But the worst of it are the two perfectly black eyes. Jesus. This guy looks more like he was hit *by* a cab, instead of while *inside* of one.

I can see and hear the steady rhythm of his pulse as he sleeps, his chest rising and falling gently. The only other piece of furniture in this tiny room is a plastic, yellow chair. It doesn't look as if it's going to be especially comfortable, but it's what's available, so I pull it a little closer to the bed and sit myself down. No, not comfortable at all.

From inside my bag, I pluck one of several file folders, and my favorite pen. I start flipping through pages, reading evaluations and reports on a fifteen-year-old girl who has run away from three foster homes in two months, each time returning to the vacant apartment where she last saw her mother. The mother who packed up her things and moved out while the girl was in school. She's just one of ten new cases assigned to me this month, and hers is the least tragic of the bunch.

I sigh and shake my head. I haven't been a social worker for very long, but already I've seen enough to last me a lifetime. Still, I wouldn't trade it for any other career. I can't help myself, I've never wanted to do anything but help people who can't help themselves.

Now, I consider this guy in front of me, all banged up and bruised. Surely there's someone who cares about him. But, then again, maybe not. When he was staring up at me that night in the back of the cab, blood streaming down his face, he was trying to sound tough, like a smartass. But there was just something in his eyes that told me differently. He was scared, and alone.

I make notes in my file for another hour, watching in silence as an array of nurses pop in to check on his vitals, make notes in his chart and inject drugs into his IV line. They smile at me vaguely, assuming, I'm sure, that I'm some relative, or maybe a girlfriend. I'm thinking I'm going to drift off to sleep myself in this stuffy room when I hear a low groan from the bed. His hand feels around on top of the covers, for the call button, I'm guessing.

"What do you need?" I ask, jumping up at his side.

"Water," he whispers hoarsely, barely opening his eyes.

On the tray table next to his bed, I find a filled pitcher and matching plastic cup. I pour the water out for him, plop a straw into the cup and hold it up to his mouth so his parched lips can wrap around it. The water is gone in an instant.

"More?" I ask.

He nods, and we repeat this process two more times until, at last, his thirst is sated. I return to the yellow chair and give him a few seconds to adjust to consciousness again. Finally, he turns his head, stiff in a cervical collar, towards me slowly, squinting through bloodied eyes.

"I'm sorry," he croaks, "but do I know you? You don't work here do you?"

I shake my head and offer him a smile. "No, I'm Maggie."

He looks perplexed, so I elaborate. "I was there with you. I held your head in the car."

"Oh, *Maggie!*" he says, his face lighting up. "The angel head!"

"Excuse me?" I laugh. "Angel head?"

"Yeah, the way you were leaning over me. You looked like this free-floating head. And the way you were backlit, it was like you were an angel or something."

It's probably just the drugs talking, but I'll take that as a compliment.

"Sorry," he continues, "I didn't recognize you from this angle."

"And I didn't recognize you without all the blood," I quip back at him before realizing that he doesn't need to know how bad he was back there. "Looks like you got pretty beat-up in the back of that cab, huh?"

"Yeah, well, next time I'll stick to the subway," he mutters.

I chuckle.

"How long will you be in here?"

"Doctor says I should be clear to go home tomorrow morning," he says, reaching out for the cup again. I get to it first and hold it for him. When he's done drinking he looks up at me intently. "Thanks for helping me. I was really out of it after the accident."

I wave a hand at him dismissively. "I'm just glad you're going to be okay."

"I'm sorry I ruined your date."

"Hah!" I snort. "Are you kidding? You got me out of a three-and-a-half-hour play about the Civil War. Specifically, the women who collected the dead southern soldiers."

"Huh," he says, clearly searching for some appropriate response to that. "Well, I guess that could be interesting if you're into history..."

"It's a musical."

"What?"

I nod at him. "You heard me. Complete with a tap dance number."

Suddenly, Brett bursts out laughing. He's gasping and wheezing and wincing all at the same time and I can't tell if it's out of pain or amusement. Both, probably.

"Oh, no way! You—you're making that up!" he accuses.

"I wish I were! Brett, believe me when I tell you that your accident saved my date's life. I'm sure I would have killed him by the time the night was over," I inform him with a smile.

He joins me in the laugh, which quickly fades into an awkward pause. Better tell him what brought me to his hospital bed before he thinks I'm stalking him and calls for security. I reach down to the floor besides me and hold up the black case for him to see.

"I thought you might be missing this," I say.

Brett's eyes grow wide at the same time as a huge smile crosses his swollen face. I've never seen anyone look so relieved to see anything in all my life. "Oh! Oh, thank *Christ!*" he gasps. "I've had the nurses checking in with the police every hour trying to track it down! I thought it'd been crushed or stolen or something!"

Whatever this thing is, it's important enough to him that I think he might just cry. Before we get to that point, I pull the tray table across his bed and set the case down on top of it.

"Is it okay?" he asks, looking up at me, his expression turning anxious.

"I don't know, I didn't open it. Why don't you have a look?"

Slowly, he unzips the cover and pops open the latches. I hold my breath right along with him as he lifts the lid slowly, in tiny increments, trying to get a look, without having to witness the potential horror all at once. But, inch-by-inch, it becomes clear that his beloved instrument has survived the crash in one piece. When the top is all the way up, he pulls out a large violin, holding its beautiful, delicate wooden body gently as he examines it.

"Amazing," he mutters to himself. "It's perfect. Not so much as a crack in the varnish."

"Wow. That's really beautiful," I say reverently, moving closer to get a better look. "It's worth a lot of money, isn't it?" I ask.

In an instant, his entire demeanor changes. He puts the instrument back in its case and snaps it shut sharply. Then he glares at me. "Yeah, well, if you came here looking for a little reward money..." he starts to say.

I feel my face scrunch up, brows knitting together, mouth tightening and nostrils flaring. "Excuse me?" I ask him in a deadly whisper. "Is that what you think? That I've been holding your precious violin for ransom for the last two days so that I could squeeze a little cash out of you?"

"Well, yeah, kinda..." he says uncertainly. "What am I supposed to think? You just show up here out of nowhere... and it's a viola," he corrects me with a sniff.

"A what?"

"A viola," he repeats, more civilly this time. "Like a violin, but bigger. Lower pitched."

Seriously? This is what's bothering him at this moment?

"Well, that's nice and all, but you've got it all wrong, buddy," I say returning to my chair and stuffing papers back into my bag. "I grabbed the case and your messenger bag from the back seat after the ambulance took you away. I figured you didn't want the cabbie, or someone from the junkyard making off with them while you were in here. I would have brought it to you sooner, but they kept telling me you couldn't have any unrelated visitors. I finally got the okay today. Clearly I shouldn't have bothered," I huff as I sling my bag over my shoulder. This is the thanks I get for letting this guy bleed all over my favorite blouse?

"Wait," he says, holding out a hand. It's pulled back immediately by the IV line that he's tethered to. "Dammit!" he exclaims, trying to untangle himself from the tubing.

Oh, for goodness' sake...

"Hold on, hold on," I say, not bothering to disguise my irritation as I come around to the other side of the bed and help him to extricate himself. As soon as he's sorted, I start toward the door.

"Well, if you'll excuse me, I hear there's a guy in the ICU with a clarinet. He's on a respirator, so it should be easy pickings..."

"Hey, wait, come on," he calls after me, "Don't be like that. Come back... Please!"

His change in tone catches my ear and I stop, turning to face him. I raise an eyebrow and level my best glare on him.

"What? Did you want me to stick around so you can file a police report?" I ask, putting my hands on my hips.

He closes his eyes for a few seconds and rubs his temples against what I'm sure is a massive headache. Oh, hell. This guy just got his eggs scrambled, and I'm being a bitch.

"I'm sorry," he says when he opens his eyes again. "I was just so worried about it. When the police didn't have it, I was sure someone had stolen it. I didn't mean to be such a dick," he offers sincerely.

No, he didn't. That's plain to see. I sigh and move closer to him again. "I wasn't fishing for anything. Not a reward, not even a 'thank you.' I just thought maybe something that valuable shouldn't be sitting around your hospital room. I was going to suggest you call your mom or your girlfriend or someone to hold onto it until you're out of here."

"No girlfriend," he says a little too quickly. I'm surprised to find myself pleased by that statement.

"Oh. Well, is there someone else?" I offer. "I could drop it off somewhere if you want. That is, if you trust me with it." I just can't resist getting one last dig in. He pretends not to notice, probably because he knows he had it coming.

"You really wouldn't mind?" he asks me, more than a little incredulously. Ah, another jaded New Yorker, I see.

I give him a half smile this time. He'll have to earn back the whole one. "I really wouldn't mind. Just give me the information and I'll drop the viola, and your bag off on my way home."

He pulls the pad and pen from the tray table in front of him and jots down the information. "This guy, Joe Dancy, he's my boss. If you could leave it with him, I'd be really grateful, Maggie," he says as he hands me the slip of paper. I glance down at it and nod.

"Please, let me at least pay for your cab fare," he says, trying to make up for acting like a total ass.

I smile and start to chuckle. "Yeah... like I'm ever getting into a cab again after what happened to you? I mean, have you looked in a mirror lately?"

He shakes his head and smiles.

"Well, you've got me there," he says.

Chapter 3

Brett

"**Y**ou're going to sue aren't you?" Joe Dancy asks over the open refrigerator door as he puts away the groceries he's brought me.

I shrug from my couch of convalescence. "I don't know about that. I wasn't wearing a seatbelt," I say, recalling a lecture on the topic of public transportation and seatbelts delivered to me by the ER doctor. He returns to the living room and hands me a glass of ginger ale. "Thanks, man. I can't tell you how much I appreciate all this. I don't think I should be seen out in public just yet."

"Yeah...I don't think so. Have you seen yourself? You won't be fit for human consumption for at least another week or two." He chuckles. "*I* can barely stand the sight of you right now!"

"Okay, the part where I just said thanks? Yeah, I take that back."

He smirks. "Well, then I'll just take that thing back home with me," he teases, hooking his thumb over his shoulder toward my viola case sitting by the door. I roll my swollen eyes at him. "And speaking of the priceless treasure, who was that captivating young lady who dropped it off at my apartment?"

I wondered when we were going to get around to that.

"Captivating? What, are we in the 1950's? Jesus, Joe, you're not *that* old...are you?"

His turn to roll eyes at me. "Fine. Who was that hot piece of ass that dropped off your viola at my apartment?" he rephrases with a smirk. "Like that better?"

"Yeah... not so much when you say it." I laugh. "What did she say to you?" I try not to sound like I'm too interested.

"Nothing. She just called and told me what happened to you, then asked if she could stop by and leave the viola and your bag with me. She was standing in my lobby a half hour later. She a friend of yours from McInnes or something?"

"Nah. She was there when I had the accident. She talked to me until the ambulance came. Then she showed up at the hospital with the viola. I asked her to leave it with you."

I omit the part about accusing her of holding it for ransom.

Joe nods, thoughtfully. This guy has got the worst poker face I've ever seen.

"What?"

"Oh, nothing. She was just, you know, very..."

My head is throbbing right now, and I have no patience for this shit. "Christ, Joe! What? Spit it out!"

"Badass."

"That's it? That's the word you were searching for? Badass?" I ask incredulously.

He nods with a knowing smile. "Yes. Exactly. Badass. I was with that girl for all of three minutes, but I could tell she's a spitfire, that one. Reminds me of my Mary when we were first dating."

"Well, we're not dating. I didn't even recognize her when she turned up at the hospital. I don't even know what her last name is, Joe."

I hadn't realized that last part until just now. But I guess it doesn't much matter.

"I don't know, Brett. Nice smile, nice ass, feisty... I think she might be *just* what you need."

"Yeah, well, thanks for the love advice, Joe. I'll take it under advisement," I say, making it clear this particular conversation has concluded.

He sits back in my tattered old armchair, and I catch him eyeballing its well-worn armrests. I have to suppress a laugh. Joe has a thing for high-end, hideously uncomfortable furnishings. I wonder what he thinks of my Salvation Army Store find?

"So, how's Jeremy? Have you heard from him recently?"

"No, not a word," I say. "But I'm sure he's seduced half of Europe by now." I chuckle.

Joe smiles politely, but I can tell there's something on his mind. He's brought up the topic of my brother for a reason. "So… I have friends in Paris, Jacques and Heléne. You may have heard me mention their names. Anyway, they were at his recital on Saturday night, and it wasn't good."

"He didn't play well?" I ask with surprise. I've *never* known my brother to give anything short of a stellar performance. He may be a dick, but he's an exceptionally talented dick.

"Oh, no, no, that's not what I meant," Joe says quickly, waving his palms at me. "There just weren't many people there."

"Really? I thought the Kreisler winner's tour always got a packed concert hall."

"It does. Usually. But there have been a few articles in the local papers there. The Europeans take the Kreisler Competition almost as seriously as they take the Tchaikovsky Competition. But there's been a lot of criticism in the press about how things were handled after Cal Burridge's death. Not just the competition Director and board itself, but also the police investigation."

No one has actually been able to prove that my brother had anything to do with the death of Cal Burridge, but that certainly hasn't stopped people from speculating. Runner-up takes over for conveniently deceased winner. Anyone with an axe to grind, or a conspiracy theory to spread would have enough to latch onto there.

Still, it might have all blown over had Jeremy not fucked over his then-girlfriend, Julia James.

Matthew, Julia's roommate and self-appointed protector, was out for blood when Jeremy dumped Julia in the cruelest possible manner right before she took the stage for her final Kreisler recital. When she lost to Jeremy, Matthew went to the police, claiming Jeremy had poisoned Cal. And, when that didn't work, he started a campaign to spread the rumor across the country, to every orchestra, ensemble and conservatory that might potentially employ my brother.

Now, Joe leans forward in the armchair. "There's a certain contingent of the musical establishment—both here and abroad—that feels Jeremy may have had a hand in Cal's death. The Kreisler recital tour is being boycotted and I can already tell you beyond a doubt that no orchestra is going to hire him. I just thought you should know what's been going on while he's been on tour."

So, Matthew's plan has worked, then. Jeremy's reputation is shit abroad as well as back here in the US. I'm having trouble formulating a response because I'm not quite sure what Joe is getting at here. Or maybe it's more like I'm afraid of what he's getting at here.

"Joe, is this your way of telling me that I'm fired?" I ask bluntly.

His eyebrows scrunch together in confusion and then arch high in surprise. "What? No! No one wants to replace you. I just thought you should be aware of what's been going on over there. I wasn't sure how much of that your brother would share with you and I thought you had a right to know. Okay?"

"Okay..." I say, still not convinced. "How far back is my convalescence going to put us for the upcoming tour?"

"Not too far off," he says, clearly relieved to change topics. "We'll take this week off and see where you are next week. If you're not up to it, we'll start working the new piece without you. I have no doubt you'll be able to get up to speed quickly. We're not due in Philadelphia for more than a month, so there's time yet."

I nod, happy to have his assurances but feeling like a wuss for needing them in the first place.

"You going to be okay here by yourself for a while?" he asks.

"Fine. Especially since you were kind enough to lay in supplies for me. Hell, I live above a pizza joint so I'm not going to starve! The question is whether or not I'm going to go out of my mind, stuck in this apartment for a whole week. Or more." I shudder at the thought that I might need more than a week on this fucking couch. "Now I'm kind of wishing I splurged for the upgraded cable package." I laugh.

"Oh!" he says, jumping to his feet. "That reminds me! Mary sent a stack of DVD's for you. Let me get them from the kitchen." He returns with what is, indeed, a stack. There are easily twenty movies in his hands. Joe starts to flip through the cases. "Let's see here, we've got the Godfather, parts one, two and three. Alien, parts one, two and three. Back to the Future..."

"Let me guess," I cut in. "Parts one, two and three?"

He shakes his head. "Nope, sorry. Mary only liked the first one." He chuckles as he sets the stack next to my TV. "I'm sorry to shove off so soon, but I've got to teach a lesson uptown in less than an hour."

"No, please, Joe. I'm really grateful you came by."

He grabs his keys from my coffee table and starts toward the door, but then he stops and points to the viola case. "You really should track her down, you know. She's the one you owe a serious thank you to, I mean, you could be waiting for that thing to pop up on e-bay right now."

"Goodbye, Joe!"

"Yeah, yeah..." he mutters as he closes the door behind him.

Once he's gone, I get up slowly, knowing that the room will start to spin if I don't, and make my way to the bathroom. As I wash my hands, I examine my face in the mirror. It's still hideous. Worse, actually, than it was in the hospital. Now there are bruises all over. The whites of my eyes are still bloodied, although, luckily, my vision is much better. Now, if I could just shake this headache.

Back in the kitchen, I refill my ginger ale and am about to collapse onto the couch again, when I decide to take a detour. Setting the glass on the table, I unzip, unclasp and open the case to reveal my viola. It still looks good. I start to close the lid when I spot something. Next to my rosin is a tiny white card. I pick it up and read 'Margaret M. Collins, LCSW.' So her last name is Collins. LCSW. Something with social work, I think. Which would make sense since this is a business card for Child Protective Services. I take the card and set it out on the table for use at a later time. Joe's right, I owe the girl a thanks. But that's going to have to wait. Right now there's a bottle of Percocet with my name on it.

Chapter 4

Maggie

I'm up to my elbows in paperwork at my desk when Marisol sticks her head in my office.

"Maggie, that guy is on the phone again."

"Just put him through to my voicemail, please," I mutter without even looking up.

There's no response, but I can feel smoky-shadowed eyes watching me. I can also hear the snap of bubble gum. Finally, I look up, one eyebrow raised in irritation. "Marisol, I've got to figure out where to place this kid in the next hour. What *is* it?"

Her giant hoop earrings move from side to side with her disapproving headshake. "He has your office number, you know. He could just call the voice mail if he wanted the voice mail. But he wants to talk to you."

I stare at her for a long moment. "Please, please, please, just send him to voice mail or take a message. I don't have time for this—or him right now."

She shrugs nonchalantly. "Not my problem," she mumbles under her breath just before she closes my office door a little too hard.

A few minutes later, I hear the familiar chime of my email inbox.

I glance at the sender's address, go back to my notes and look back up again. "What the...?" I mumble out loud to myself as I spot the message from **#1Viola@WaltonSQ.org** and scroll down for the rest of the message.

```
Dear Maggie,
    I know you're at your desk, busy saving
the world, but I was hoping you might take a
night off from feeding the hungry, clothing
the naked and housing the homeless so I can
thank you properly for your help at the
accident. And for saving my viola from the
pawnshop. I'm thinking drinks tonight.
    Best, Brett
```

I roll my eyes, but I can't help the snort that comes out. I start to type a reply.

```
Dear Brett,
    I'll have you know I have never in my
life put clothing on a naked person. I did,
however, once run a coat drive. As far as I
know, all those people had at least under-
garments on. As for assisting you at the
accident and holding onto your viola, your
thanks is all the thanks I need. And you're
welcome.
    Sincerely, Maggie Collins
```

I go back to the file in front of me, thinking he'll get the hint. He doesn't. Another chime comes in under a minute.

```
Dear Maggie,
    I apologize! I never meant to imply that
```

```
you liked to get your hands on naked people.
For future reference I'll take note of the
fact that you prefer dealing with people in
their underwear. If you agree to meet me for
dinner, I'll come in my boxers.
     Yours, Brett
```

I let out a frustrated groan then I think for a second before typing again.

```
Dear, Mr. Corrigan,
     Please do not go anywhere in just your
boxers or I will be forced to have you taken
into   custody   for   psychiatric   evaluation.
Again,  while  I  appreciate  your  desire  to
thank me, consider it done. No need for us
to meet again. Ever.
     Sincerely, Margaret M. Collins, LCSW
```

I don't even bother taking my eyes from the screen this time. The reply comes in an instant. It's short and sweet. And obnoxious.

```
At last! A woman who understands my desires!
How about a weekend in Atlantic City? —B.
```

Jeez! This guy just will *not* take the hint. I'm about to start writing a more firm response when my thoughts—and my typing—are interrupted by another incoming message. It has only one word in the body of the email.

```
Please?
```

I'm reminded of the tired, earnest way he said 'please' in the hospital when he was trying to keep me from leaving in a huff. Now, I stop, take my glasses off and rub the bridge of my nose. After a long moment and an even longer sigh, I put them back on.

```
Okay. But just coffee. No Atlantic City. And
if I hear so much as a rumor that you're
going to show up in your underwear, I'm
gone.
```

A nagging little voice in my head warns me that I might just live to regret hitting 'Send.' I do it anyway.

* * *

"What? No, not you! You came to the rescue of a total stranger on the street? I'm shocked, I tell you! *Shocked!* "

"Will you cut it out?" I plead with exasperation. My sister Randi is nothing if not sarcastic. I'm not sure how much to tell her about my email exchange or my agreement to have coffee with this guy. That being said, she's a whiz at all things social and I *am* sure I'd like to pick her brain on some of this.

"Ugh, fine! So, let's get to the important question..."

"Yes," I assure her, "he was okay. He looked awful but mostly he was just bruised and banged-up."

"Jesus, Maggie! You know, you've been single for way too long," she says.

"What does me being single got to do with anything?" I demand.

"The important question, *Margaret Mae*, is whether or not your patient is *cute!* " she explains slowly, as if I'm dimwitted. I guess where romance is concerned, I kind of am.

"Alright then, *Miranda Michelle*, if you must know, he was cute. I think. It was hard to tell... with the blood and all..."

I hear her groan in disgust all the way from our family home in Connecticut. As far as younger sisters go, she's not half bad. A pain in the ass, for sure, but she's an invaluable resource for this kind of thing. The kind of thing I suck at. Romance. Dating. Guys. I'm hopeless with all of it, as she never lets me forget.

"Okay, so, what do you know about him?" she asks.

"Uh...not much, really. Just that he doesn't have a girlfriend, and there wasn't anyone who came to the hospital to see him. No family or anything. I had to drop his stuff off at his boss's apartment."

"What does he do for a living?" she asks, going down her patented 'Guy Feasibility Checklist.'

"I don't know. Something to do with the viola."

"Viola? What the hell is that?"

"Some kind of an instrument. Like a violin, but lower, I think." I try to remember what he told me about the thing before he accused me of holding it for ransom.

"Okay, so we think he's cute and we think he's a musician. Any other distinguishing facts I need?"

"Need for what?"

"Need to Google him," she says, the sound of her keyboard now audible in the background.

"Hey! No! Don't do that..." I demand. I've managed to avoid the temptation of looking him up online myself, I don't need Sister-Snoop-A-Lot poking around for me.

"Just a sec..." she says, ignoring me, as usual. "Oh! Hey now..."

"What?" I ask, suddenly interested. "What is it? What did you find?"

"Huh..." She murmurs to herself.

"Randi! What?" I whine.

"Okay, Brett Corrigan is twenty-eight-years-old. He attended the very prestigious McInnes Conservatory—Jeez, even I've heard of that," she interjects then continues. "Looks like he's played in a lot of Broadway shows. Now he's the violist for the Walton String Quartet."

"Why does that name sound so familiar?"

"Shit. Well, probably because they've won a dozen Grammy's in the last twenty years. They've been featured in more than twenty film scores... wow, Maggie, this guy's a big deal in classical music! They tour all over the world and they're the official string quartet in residence at the Tanglewood Festival. Remember how Mom and Dad used to take us there every year when we were little?"

"Oh, yeah! I'd forgotten all about that. Why did they stop?" I ask, searching my brain for the memories.

"Because we told them we wanted to go to cheerleading camp instead," she says flatly. "Didn't know a good thing when we had it, I guess..."

"Hey, speak for yourself! I didn't go to cheerleading camp," I object.

"No, right. You went to... what was it? Oh! Camp Cunnilingus!" she snorts loudly.

"Camp Connetquot! Jesus, Randi, get your head out of..." I stop, realizing no good can come out of the rest of that sentence.

"I'm sorry? Get my *head* out of *where*, Miss Cunnilingus Camper?"

She's laughing so hard that she snorts.

"Alright, alright," I groan. "What else do you see about the viola guy? And if you say that word again, I'm going to come through the phone and strangle you!"

"What word? Oh, cunni-"

"Randi!" I screech into the phone.

"Fine. Jeez, you're such a prude. Okay. So, according to Wikipedia..."

"Wait, he's got his own Wikipedia page?"

"Yup. Apparently being a member of the illustrious Walton String Quartet gets you there. Uh...Okay, parents are Daniel and Trudy Corrigan of Owl Bridge, Illinois. Owl Bridge? Really? That's an actual place? Anyway, he has one sibling who, apparently, is important enough to have his own page, because there's a link to his name. Hold on..."

I hear her clicking, and then silence as she reads. And reads. And reads. "Randi? You still there?" I ask, sure my crappy cell phone has dropped the call.

"Yeah, hold on a sec, Maggie," she says, distractedly.

I don't like how serious her tone has become all of a sudden. I wait another minute until she speaks again.

"Okay, well, his brother is Jeremy Corrigan. Does that name ring any bells?"

"Yeah, it does, actually. But why?"

"Well, he's that musician who was accused of poisoning his competitor in that big contest last year..."

"Oh, wait! He played the trumpet or something, right?"

"French horn," she corrects me and continues. "He was suspected of putting peanut oil on the guy's mouthpiece so he could take his place in the competition. They could never prove it though, and Jeremy ended up winning the whole thing."

"And *that's* his brother?" I ask, shocked and a little uneasy with this new bit of information.

"Yup."

"This is why I don't Google people, Randi. I don't need to hear rumors about the guy's family. Rumors that probably aren't even true..."

"Oh, please, you're a social worker, Maggie. You, of all people, know what kinds of insane shit people do. Brett sounds like a catch, but the brother... I don't know. That's just enough speculation to make me nervous," she says to me with concern. "If I were you, I wouldn't go chasing after this one."

"Randi?" I begin sheepishly.

"Yeah?"

"It's a little too late for that. He's already come chasing after *me*."

Chapter 5

Brett

My face returns to me in stages—the bruises fading from a dark purple, to a bluish gray, to green and yellow. My nose slowly shrinks back to its normal size, and miraculously appears to straighten itself out. The 'Franken-scar,' while far from invisible, has morphed to a nice shade of pink and looks considerably better now that the stitches are out. After two weeks, Maggie Collins doesn't even recognize me when she walks past me, standing in front of the coffee shop.

"Hi... Maggie?" I say, coming up behind her and touching her shoulder lightly as she hauls the door open.

She turns, surprised, and peers at me curiously through Buddy Holly glasses. Even though she's expecting to see me, it takes her a second to realize who she's looking at.

"Brett!" she exclaims with a bright, happy-to-see-me smile. I notice for the first time that two perfect dimples accompany the smile.

"Thanks for agreeing to meet me after I was such an ass at the hospital."

She waves away the thanks and the pseudo-apology.

"I didn't do anything anyone else wouldn't have done," she says softly, her cheeks pinking up.

I follow her inside the coffee shop, which is a dark, cool oasis on a hot summer afternoon. For the most part, she looks like I remember from my morphine haze. She's tall with long legs and, as Joe pointed out, a very nice ass. Her hair is a mass of dark curls that frame the bluest eyes I've ever seen.

"So," I say, once we're settled in a quiet corner, "I was thinking that since we didn't exactly meet under the best of circumstances, maybe we could start over again?"

I flash her my most charming smile.

"I'm Maggie Collins," she says, extending a hand to me across the table. "You must be Brett."

Her hand is warm and soft. I shake it gently. "I am. Nice to meet you, Maggie. Come here often?"

Now she rolls her eyes. "Seriously? That's what you're going with?" she asks.

I shrug. "Hey! Cut me some slack, will you? I have a head injury!"

"You *had* a head injury," she corrects in a teasing tone, "but I'll let it slide this time."

A young waitress comes over to the table. "Coffee? Tea?" she asks, chewing gum and looking bored by us already.

"Yes, please," Maggie begins. "I'd like a soy chai latte, please. Extra hot."

The waitress nods and jots it down on her pad. "And you?" she eyeballs me from above where I'm sitting.

"Uh... dark roast, with lots of milk and two sugars, please," I say.

Maggie holds up a finger for the girl to wait a second. "Oh, come on. You're in a real coffee house, why not try something you can't find at the corner bodega?"

"I'll have you know my bodega has an excellent dark roast," I say with faux seriousness. She smiles. The waitress rolls her eyes and snaps her gum.

"Uh, well, you know I'm a little out of my depth here," I say, craning my neck to see the chalkboard menu on the wall. I can hear the waitress tapping her foot impatiently.

"He'll have a latte, two sugars, please," Maggie jumps in. "Also, some of those little shortbread cookies."

Once we're alone again, she leans across the table and puts a hand on my forearm.

"I think you're going to like it. But if you don't, I promise I'll buy you whatever dishwater coffee your heart desires, okay?"

"I make no promises," I say noncommittally.

She smiles.

I smile.

We look at each other awkwardly. Okay. What now?

"So...tell me about the...what is it? The viola?" she asks.

I'm grateful for the topic and I jump onto it like it's a life raft.

"Oh, you're not the only one. Most people think it's a violin on steroids. But it's more than that. The viola is like..." I stop to think about the best way to describe it to her. "It's like the middle child of the string section."

She's looking at me strangely. "The middle child? How's that?"

"Well," I start, "the violin is like the oldest kid. It gets to do everything first. It gets the most responsibility and the most attention because it gets all the flashy solos. Then there's the cello, it's like the easygoing, mellow third child. It takes the lead when it wants to, and chills when it doesn't want to. Everybody loves the cello."

"Huh..." she starts, but I hold up my finger for her to hang on. I'm really proud of this analogy that I've pulled out of the ether, and I'm not quite done with it yet.

"And then, there's the viola. It's in the middle, trying to be heard. Fighting for a chance to distinguish itself from its siblings. Most people don't even notice it's there, but they'd miss it if it were gone."

"Ohhhhh my," she says slowly. "You've really given this some thought, haven't you?"

"I know it sounds a little nutty, drawing that parallel, but you won't forget the viola now, will you?"

"Well, you've got me there," she agrees with a smile.

"So that's me. Since you don't know what a viola is, then I assume you're not a musician."

"Oh, no," she says quickly. "I don't have a musical bone in my body. We found that out the hard way when I was in junior high. I saw Music Man and I just *had* to play the trombone."

"What happened?"

"Whenever I practiced, the neighborhood dogs would come running down the street and start howling in front of our house. It was ugly. And loud."

"You, or the dogs?" I ask.

"Both," she grins as she rolls her eyes. "So, I gave up my dream of being one of the seventy-six trombones in the touring company of Music Man and went a more traditional route."

"That being..."

"I've just finished up my Master's degree in social work."

"Oh no! Tell me I didn't just divulge my 'Viola as Middle Child' theory to a shrink!" I exclaim with faux dismay.

"Afraid so, my friend," she says, nodding solemnly. "I'll send you the bill in the mail."

I smile, but then the awkward silence settles over us again.

Listen, Brett, I'm easy." I can't help myself, I cock a lascivious eyebrow. "Not like that!" she says in a scandalized whisper, giving me a light slap on the wrist. "What I mean, is that I'm easy-going. Relax! If we don't hit it off, we don't hit it off. No harm, no foul. Just have a cup of ridiculously expensive coffee with me."

As if on cue, the waitress returns with two steaming cups and a plate of small round cookies. I survey the milky brew in front of me. I guess I'm obligated to at least try the stuff before I order a real coffee. A manly coffee that smells of wood chips and dirt.

"Well, here goes," I mumble unenthusiastically and take a tentative sip. I don't know what I was expecting, but this isn't it. I'm pleasantly surprised by the subtle layers of flavor. "Hey, this isn't too bad. In fact, it's really good," I say from inside the mug.

She looks pleased. It's a good look on her.

"Okay," I say when I finally stop sipping the latte thing. "So now that you've finished your Masters, what's the next step? Will you go into private practice as a therapist, or what?"

"I'm not totally sure yet. My emphasis is on adolescent counseling and I'm working for Child Protective Services in Brooklyn right now. There's a lot of work to be done in this city. In this whole country, in fact."

"I'll bet," I snort, a little too loudly.

She tilts her head to one side slightly.

"What does that mean?" she asks with a confused little smile.

I shrug. "Oh, you know. I'm just tired of hearing about how bad the economy is, how people are being downsized or are upside down on their mortgages. Get a job already! I manage to keep one. You managed to get one. What's wrong with people?"

She sits back in her chair and tilts her head a little, as if she's trying to work out whether or not I'm kidding. She starts to say something but stops herself, takes a deep breath and starts again.

"Well, that's a little...pessimistic, don't you think?"

"I don't know about pessimistic," I say, swirling the coffee at the bottom of my cup so that it forms a mini-vortex. "Realistic, maybe."

"Yeah, well, I tend to come into contact with people who have some serious needs. A lot of children—"

"And that's another thing," I pipe up, suddenly reminded of a conversation Jeremy and I have had before. "Why do people have children if they can't afford them? Why do I, as a taxpayer, have to be responsible for bringing up someone else's kids?"

She clears her throat. "Well, it's not always that cut and dried, Brett. Don't get me wrong—there are definitely people out there who scam the system. But, there are plenty of others who have very real problems. The kinds of problems that have kept them from the kind of opportunities that you and I have had."

"I haven't had any more opportunities than anyone else," I counter.

The smile is gone, and I'm not quite sure what it is that I'm looking at on Maggie's face right now. But whatever it is, I don't think it's a good thing.

"Oh, really? Because I imagine you had a warm bed to sleep in every night when you were growing up, not to mention at least one hot meal a day." I start to say something, but she shakes her head. "No. I'm not done yet. I imagine you had lessons to learn that fancy pants viola of yours. Maybe you even got to go to college to study it. I could be wrong, but I'm going to go out on a limb and assume you'll have a roof over your head tonight and the money to buy yourself a coffee in the morning..."

"Hey!" I start to object, but she's not having it.

"Brett, it's people like you who make my job so difficult. People who think that the poor are the problem in this country. The poor are not the problem. *Poverty* is the problem."

"Oh, well now you're just being dramatic," I say, waving a hand at her dismissively.

Without warning, Maggie Collins stands up. She opens her purse, pulls out a twenty and places it on the table.

"Hey! Hey, come on now. You're not going already are you?"

I get up as well and she offers me a tired smile.

"I'm really glad I was able to be there for you when you were hurt. And I wish you all the best, Brett."

I throw up my hands toward the ceiling.

"Oh, c'mon, Maggie," I coax, "we're just debating. You know, a little verbal sparring! Please, don't go so soon."

She considers me for a long moment before answering.

"What I want to know is, what happened to that guy?"

"Guy? What guy?"

"That guy in the emails. The sweet, funny guy who made me laugh. What happened to him? Because *that's* the guy I came here to meet." Maggie shrugs. "Too bad he never showed up."

And with that, she walks her perky little ass and floppy mound of hair right out of the coffee shop door. I'm standing there, looking like an idiot, eyes glued to the spot where she was just standing.

The waitress comes by and plucks the twenty off the table.

"I'll just keep the change, shall I?" She laughs as she walks away.

Wait...*what?*

What the hell just happened here?

Chapter 6

Brett

I process best when I walk. I process second-best when I drink. So I spend the next few days licking my wounds from the ill-fated coffee date by walking the streets of Brooklyn, getting to know each of the hipster bars, pubs and clubs which have popped up on every newly-gentrified block of my neighborhood.

Three days later and I'm *still* trying to figure out how everything went to shit so fast. And, more importantly, three days later and I have no idea why I even care so much. I mean this is hardly my first bad date. I usually just chalk it up to a lack of chemistry and move on. But jeez, the look on her face. I try to close my eyes against it, but my mind still conjures the image of Maggie Collins looking at me with so much disdain that it makes my stomach churn even now.

I've tried to call her a few times, but she hasn't returned any of my messages. And I doubt she will. Not that I have a clue as to what I'd say if she did. By the time I return to my dark and empty apartment on this particular night, I'm tired of thinking about it. Except, my apartment isn't dark. Or empty, for that matter.

"Holy shit!" I gasp with a start when I see my brother sitting at the dining table. "You scared the fuck out of me! What are you doing here, Jeremy?"

"What, not happy to see me?" he counters with a faux hurt tone.

I think my heart is going to pound right out of my chest and I actually have to work to steady my frantic pulse.

"Seriously," I rasp, "why are you here? I wasn't expecting you home for at least another month yet."

"The Germany concerts were cancelled," he says flatly.

I try to look surprised even though Joe has already given me the heads-up on this little bit of news. "What? Why?"

"There was a boycott. Can you fucking believe it? A boycott! Stupid Euro-trash prima donnas didn't like how the competition went down, so they refused to buy tickets. After low attendance in Spain and France, they decided to pull the plug on the rest of the tour."

"How can they do that? You signed a contract!" I ask, knowing it's in my own best interest to be indignant on his behalf.

"That's what I said. Then they paid me out. But dude, that is the *least* of my problems right now."

He gestures to the table in front of him, which I now notice is littered with torn envelopes and their entrails. Presumably this is the stack of his mail that I've been piling up in his absence. I take a seat across from him and survey the mess. "What's wrong?"

He picks up a letter and begins to read it to me.

"Dear Mr. Corrigan, thank you for your interest in speaking at the International French Horn Convention. At this time we have booked all of the available slots so, regrettably, we are unable to extend an invitation to you at this time."

"What? I thought that was a done deal!" I object, with genuine shock this time.

"It *was* a done deal!" he hisses. "And who else would do the keynote? I just took the highest honor in classical music!"

"Holy shit, man..." I mutter, picking up the letter that he has just thrown down on the table.

"I'm going to call those assholes tomorrow. They're not going to make me an offer and then rescind it. There's been entirely too much of that going on lately, and it's going to stop. Now."

Before I can ask what he means by that, he picks up another letter and reads.

> "Dear Mr. Corrigan, We regret to inform you that you have not been chosen for the final round of auditions for Second Horn of the Seattle Philharmonic…"

Holy shit. Again. *'We regret to inform you'* are five words my brother has never seen in one sentence in his entire life.

"Maybe they think you're overqualified for second horn?" I suggest.

He looks up at me. "Yeah well, I thought that, too. Until I opened this one from the Houston Chamber Symphony." He waves it at me.

> "We had many qualified applicants and were only able to take a handful for the live auditions. I'm sorry to say you are not among them… "

"Oh, yeah, and then this little gem from New Orleans," he continues.

> "Dear Mr. Corrigan, Thank you for your application but at this time we are unable to offer you an audition…"

I recognize the Detroit Philharmonia logo on another letter sitting next to him. "Detroit, too?" I ask, but I can already see the answer on his face.

"Oh, Brett, I have saved the fucking best for last," he informs me, picking up the final creamy, textured page with a flourish.

"Dear Applicant, we regret to inform you…"

He stops there and I'm glad. I don't want to hear anymore.

"*Fuck!*" he yells as he clears the entire table with one long swipe of his arm. The mail scatters onto the carpet, taking his career plans with it.

"Jeremy, man, I'm so sorry…"

"Screw sorry. I'm pissed and there's no way in hell I'm going down without a fight. I'm going to go see Glenn Garibaldi and I want you to come with me."

Glenn is Jeremy's lawyer. His very sleazy but very good lawyer. What he lacks in tact and finesse, he makes up for in blackmail, threats and dirty tactics. He was able to keep the Kreisler Committee from revoking my brother's gold medal.

I nod that I'll go along with him and, temporarily placated, he changes the subject.

"Any sign of Julia or Matthew?"

"Nope," I say, not bothering to mention that I haven't exactly been on the lookout for them.

"So, you haven't come across either of them since I've been gone? Or heard anything about them?" He sounds a little suspicious.

I shake my head. "Uh-uh. Not a thing. They've gone to ground."

"Well, I'm back now and I'm going to turn over every fucking rock until I find the one they've crawled under."

"Do you really want to waste your energy on those two?" I'm hoping to point him in a different direction, but it's no use. My brother is like a dog with a bone.

"This, Brett, this right here," he begins, gesturing to the rejection letters scattered across the floor, "this is all because of them. They launched a smear campaign that has me black-balled with every major orchestra in the country. If Matthew Ayers thinks he can fuck around with my life—my career—and get away with it, he's going to find out real fast how mistaken he is."

I know my brother well enough to know that he means it. Now, for the second time in less than thirty minutes, I ask myself why I even care. And, for the second time, I am stumped for an answer.

Chapter 7

Maggie

"Oh, no, no, no. He did *not* say that to you!" Randi marvels as she sips a glass of wine with me on the deck. "Good for you for just leaving like that. What a douche bag!"

"Randi!" our mother calls from the kitchen. That woman has hearing like a bat.

"Sorry, Mom!" she calls back to her while rolling her eyes at me. "What an insensitive fuck wad," she corrects herself and shoots me a wicked smile.

Three... Two... One...

The door swings open with a creak and Mom sticks her head out. "Miranda! You were not raised in a brothel! Now tone down that pirate mouth, young lady!"

The door slams shut with a smack before Randi can reply. We look at each other and burst into loud peals of laughter until we are wheezing and holding our sides.

"Brothel?" I howl.

"No! *Pirate* mouth!" Randi yells back with a cackle.

"I can hear you!" comes Mom's voice from the kitchen.

"We know!" Randi and I holler in unison.

Three... Two... One...

Again, the door swings open, but this time Mom comes out onto the deck to join us. With a wine glass of her own, she sits next to me on the glider.

"Was it that bad?" she asks me.

"Kinda," I mutter.

Our mother is a smart woman. And I mean seriously smart. She's a Nuclear Program Analyst with a specialization in Nuclear Survivability. What that means, in a nutshell, is that she figures out ways for humans to survive in a hostile nuclear environment. Oh, and she also makes a mean Barbie birthday cake.

"So, that's that then," Randi says. "I'm guessing you won't be hearing from him again anytime soon."

"Oh, no," our mom corrects her between sips of Chardonnay. "I'm guessing she's *already* heard from him."

I look at her and shake my head. "How do you do that?"

She shrugs. "I'm your mother. I just know these things."

"Bullshit!" Randi chuckles from her lounge chair. "She saw his text pop up on your phone while you were in the bathroom!"

"Mother!" I kick her gently with my bare foot. She grabs it and pulls it into her lap.

"Seriously, Maggie, I do know you. Sometimes, better than you know yourself, I think. If we're even having this conversation, then you're still interested," she informs me.

"No. Uh-uh," I disagree, wagging a finger at her. "How could I be? The guy pretty much trashed my profession—my beliefs!"

"Maybe yes, maybe no," Mom says cryptically. I wait for some clarification but it doesn't come.

"What the fuck, Mom?" Randi asks before I can.

Another scowl for the pirate mouth.

"All I'm saying is that the young man you helped in the car, the one you had those phone conversations with was someone who... intrigued you. You were drawn to him. And you're not drawn to many men, my sweet, fickle daughter."

I want to object, but I can't, because she's absolutely right.

"He may not have shown you his best side on that first date, but I'm not so sure that was his side at all," she explains. "When people spew that kind of vitriol, it's often because they're getting it somewhere else. They parrot a strong opinion that they don't necessarily share because they feel insecure. They want to sound educated and informed. They want to impress. I think that could be the case with your young man."

I open my mouth to say something, and then close it again. I'll be damned. And here, I thought *I* was the one with the deep insights into the human psyche.

"But, Mom, he knows she's a social worker. Why would he come at her with that kind of crap? He must've known it would piss her off," Randi argues.

"No. He didn't," I say quietly. "He was really stunned when I got offended. I think if he could have stuffed it all back into his mouth, he would have."

As my mother nods, I watch her long black braid slide up and down her back. "He's heard it all somewhere before, and, apparently, he's heard it often enough, that he can probably recite it word for word. I'm guessing that Brett has someone with some strong political opinions in his family. Maybe ultraconservative parents..."

"The brother!" Randi exclaims, smacking her forehead with the palm of her hand. "Holy shit! It's the psycho brother!"

Now my mother looks between the two of us, the alarm clear on her face. "What psycho brother?" she demands.

I fill her in on the information we dug up online. She listens thoughtfully, occasionally nodding or clicking her tongue in disgust or sighing heavily. When I finish, she swishes her wine around the globe of the glass and takes a long, slow sip. "I remember reading about that when it happened. The boy who died was from here, you know. Trumbull, I think. Such a tragedy." My mother sets her glass down and starts to rub my foot in her lap. "Sweetheart, you have a big, big heart. That serves you very well in your profession. But, what serves you even better, are your instincts. I have never known you to be wrong about someone—whether or not you knew it yourself."

"What does that mean, Mom?" I ask, defeated and frustrated by this entire conversation.

"Margaret, you already know who this man is. You probably knew it within the first five minutes of being with him at that accident. Whatever it is that he's saying—or *not* saying—now isn't aligning with what you already know to be true about him. So, why is that? Why does a man who you obviously believe to be decent and kind, start acting like an entirely different kind of a person? That's the question you need to be asking yourself."

Randi and I are both staring at her now, stunned by her insight.

"Damn, Mom, you should be the therapist," Randi murmurs and my mother bursts out laughing.

"Oh, no! I'll leave that to your sister. She's the one with the gift. She's the fixer."

"Fixer?" I ask. I've never heard her say that before. I don't even know what it means.

"Ever since you were a little girl, you've been able to look at someone and see into them. Good, bad, scared—you always manage to sense what a person is holding inside of their heart. And then, you try to fix it. That's who you are, my love. A fixer of hearts and a mender of souls."

"A fixer of hearts and a mender of souls," I repeat back to her, distracted by what I see in my mother's heart right now. Not that *it* needs fixing. True love never does.

Chapter 8

Brett

Joe Dancy is looking at me expectantly.

"Well?"

"Well, what?"

"Did you call her?"

I've told him the whole sordid story about my crash and burn at the coffee shop. "Yes, Joe, I've called her. She won't return my messages. And I've texted her, too. Same thing. Radio silence. The girl doesn't want to see me again."

"But you want to see her?"

I shrug. He raises a skeptical eyebrow. "Okay, yes," I finally admit to him...and to myself. "Yes, I want to see her again, though I have no damn idea why. She made me feel like shit."

His skepticism fades to a knowing smile. I briefly entertain the idea of slapping it off his face, but then I remember that he's my boss. And my friend.

"Listen, Brett, I chased Mary around the Oberlin campus for nearly a year before she agreed to go on a date with me. She had no interest in being with a musician—told me we were all a bunch of lazy, no good bums and she had no intention of marrying one. But I was relentless. I showed up outside of every class she had. I called her over and over again. Still, she wouldn't give me the time of day. I brought her flowers, candy...hell, I even took out an ad in the school newspaper asking her to go out with me. I did everything I thought I needed to do to get a girl."

I can't help myself, the thought of Mary making Joe run around campus with balloons and flowers has me grinning from ear to ear. I never realized she was such a hard ass!

"Okay, so, what finally won her over? Because obviously you did something right or you wouldn't be married today."

He looks down at the floor and up again at me, the smile turned suddenly self-conscious. "Yeah, well, it took me a while to figure out that what *I* thought I needed to do to get the girl and what *she* thought I needed to do to get her were two totally different things."

"Okay, Mr. Cryptic, what the hell is that supposed to mean?"

"I can't tell you that."

"Why? Is it like some big secret?" I sneer.

"No, you idiot," he laughs at me. "I mean, it's different for everyone. I can't tell you because what Mary wanted then and what Maggie wants now are two very different things. Best advice I can offer is that you show her who you really are. I wasn't a lazy, no good bum and I had to prove that to her. Based on what you've told me about that date, I'm guessing Miss Maggie thinks you're some politically outspoken know-it-all who has no respect for the work she does. That's not who you are, Brett. So go prove that to her."

I give him a tight nod. "I'll think about that, Joe. Thanks, man. Now, if you'll excuse me, I promised my brother I'd meet him at his lawyer's office."

I sense rather than see a hardening in Joe's demeanor. "So... does that mean he's going to fight the Kreisler Committee over cancelling the tour?"

I make a point of suddenly needing to look for something in my bag, so I don't have to see the expression on his face. "Uh, no, actually. Turns out you were right. He threw his name into the hat for four different horn spots around the country and he wasn't offered a single audition."

Joe puts a hand on my shoulder. I look down at it then up at him. I don't know why I expected him to gloat, when what I see in his eyes is sheer kindness. And, if I'm not mistaken, a little concern.

"You know it gives me no pleasure to be right about something like that, don't you?" he says as if reading my thoughts. I nod silently. I have no clue why this is such a hard conversation to have. "Brett, be there for Jeremy. Just don't..." he pauses to consider his words. "Just don't let his problems become yours. You two share the name Corrigan and I'd hate to see you caught up in something that has nothing to do with you."

Well, that's certainly easier said than done.

✱ ✱ ✱

"I'm sorry, Jeremy, I just don't see any way around it," Glenn Garibaldi says as he waves the four letters in his hand.

"How can they not allow me to audition?" my brother asks his lawyer as we both sit across from him and his cheap pressboard and wood-veneered desk.

I glance at my phone nonchalantly, hoping to get a return text or email from Maggie. I've sent her a new batch just in the last hour since Joe and I had our little talk. I suppose I should take the hint. But the more I think about it—and her—the more I don't want to.

"They don't have to allow anyone to audition," Garibaldi is explaining. "It falls to the sole discretion of the audition committee to decide who they'll hear perform live. I've checked it out, man. There were two-hundred-and-fifty-three applicants for the one spot in Seattle. Only *twelve* were invited to audition. All of them already hold full-time positions in smaller orchestras or teaching positions at colleges. Jeremy, you're technically still a student."

"Yes, but he's the Kreisler Competition gold medalist," I insist. "That's got to count for something."

Glenn takes off his glasses and wipes them with a cloth, his beady little eyes squinting as he speaks. "You both know as well as I do that the win is no guarantee of a job. You also know as well as I do *exactly* why this is happening."

We do. The thing is that the Kreisler gold medal was supposed to be Jeremy's quick ticket to the top. And my brother can become very agitated when things don't go the way they're supposed to go.

"Well, it seems to me we should be able to accuse them of some kind of bias against me," he hisses.

"Why? Because they've opted not to invite a reputed-murderer to come and play for them? Jeremy, I can file motions and make threats, but at the end of the day, you're just wasting your money. I say take the cash settlement the competition paid you, finish your degree and give things a little time to blow over."

"What about a defamation claim?" he asks, ignoring the lawyer's advice.

"Against who?"

"Matthew Ayers and his buddy—what's his name?"

"Ruggiero. Tony Ruggiero," Glenn replies. "He's the PI for Clay-comb and Ryder. I tell you, Matthew Ayers must have some deep pockets because no one at that firm, Tony included, comes for upwards of five-hundred-bucks an hour."

"So? Does that mean we can't go after him? They've been telling orchestras all over the fucking country that I was involved in Cal Burridge's death."

"And were you?" the lawyer asks, putting his glasses back on and leaning forward. As far as I know, this is the first time he's ever asked. "No, no. Don't tell me," he backpedals, waving a hand at us. "I don't really want to know. I mean, I do. But I don't."

I can see Jeremy considering whether or not to strangle this guy with his soup-stained tie.

"I do have one bit of good news for you, though," he says, trying to get my brother into a less violent frame of mind. "The Kreisler Competition office contacted me last week to let me know they're going forward with the gala at Carnegie Hall. So, they may have pulled the plug on the European performances, but you'll still be the headliner at the Kreisler Gala next month."

"So that wasn't cancelled with the rest of the tour performances?" I ask.

"Nope. It's the only part of Jeremy's contract they didn't buy out. I think they're banking on morbid curiosity to fill the hall."

"What the hell is that supposed to mean?" Jeremy demands.

The lawyer shrugs.

"Just that people love a good, juicy scandal. My guess is that the Kreisler International Music Competition realizes that your name on the Playbill will sell enough tickets to make up for what they lost in Europe."

"Are you shitting me?" Jeremy asks.

"What? You don't want to do it? I thought you'd love the idea of performing at Carnegie Hall."

"I do. But now my reputation is in the shitter and now they're going to use that to sell tickets and make money? That's fucked up, Glenn. How can you *not* make something of that in court?"

"Look," he replies, tapping a pen on his legal pad, "slander and defamation are very hard to prove. I can go down that road too if you want. But discrimination is a whole other ball of wax. Especially now that they use those screens on stage so the committee can't see who's auditioning. These days, it's the best man or woman no matter what their age, gender, sexual preference, political affiliation..."

"Hell, if you'd at least gotten an audition, they wouldn't even have known it was you," I observe. "I guess that's what they were afraid of, though. That you'd be the best player and they'd be stuck with you."

Jeremy's head whips toward me so fast that I recoil. "Holy shit, you're probably right, Brett," he says, excitedly. Then he turns his attention back to Glenn. "If I *could* manage to get onto the audition roster at one of these places, they wouldn't even know it was me performing. And, if I'm the best, they *have* to hire me, sight-unseen. Does that sound about right?"

Glenn considers this for a moment and nods. "Theoretically, yes. That's *if* the committee agrees that you are the best performer. You'd have a one in twelve chance of winning the spot. And once they offer it, they can't rescind it without having a very ugly legal battle on their hands."

Jeremy smiles.

"Oh, I'm a big fan of ugly, Glenn. A very big fan."

Chapter 9

Maggie

"These came for you..."

I know Maria, the office manager, is standing there but I can't see her. Her entire head is obliterated by a huge bouquet of flowers. And not just any flowers, either. These are irises of the deepest, darkest purple I have ever seen. There must be three-dozen of them, and they must have cost a fortune.

She puts the vase on my desk and hands me the tiny white envelope that accompanied them, then waits expectantly as I pull out the tiny white matching card.

"It's him again, isn't it?" she asks with a knowing expression.

I don't answer her, just slip the card back into the envelope and put it into my desk drawer with the others.

"Why don't you put these out in reception?" I suggest. "That way everyone can enjoy them."

"Girl are you crazy?" she asks, hands on hips and long neck craning as she scowls at me. "You know Marisol is allergic to everything. You ever heard her sneeze? It's enough to blow the roof right off this place!"

I have, in fact heard Marisol sneeze. Sometimes she sneezes so hard that the gum she's perpetually chewing comes flying right out of her mouth. I hold up my hands in a gesture of surrender. "Alright, point taken! I'm sorry I suggested it!"

"You should be! That boy spent a pretty penny on those buds right there. And if I'm not mistaken, those are your favorites aren't they?"

She knows they are. But how does he? A cold wave of nausea washes over me. Who's been talking to Brett Corrigan about me, and what, exactly, have they been telling him?

"Maria, do you think we have a mole in the office?" I ask, suddenly horrified by the possibility.

She looks over her shoulder, closes the door behind her and faces me again. "Maggie, last week he sent you red velvet cupcakes from the Magnolia Bakery. Your favorites. Three days later, it was those stupid finger puppets of Sigmund Freud and Carl Jung that crack you up so much. And now this? Hell, yes I think there's a mole in this department! Somebody's been feeding that boy information about how to get on your sweet side!"

I sit back in my chair hard and consider this. On the one hand, it's a betrayal—not to mention creepy—that someone I work with would give out my personal information. On the other hand, I have to give Brett points for ingenuity and effort. But who in this office would do that? And why?

And then it hits me like a bolt of lightning. I nearly come across my desk at her. "Maria Rodriguez! You *didn't!* " I hiss.

She regards me coolly. "Maybe I did, maybe I didn't. But let's just say, sometimes a girl needs a little help to see what's right there in front of her face."

"Oh? And what's that?" I ask unable to hide my irritation over this violation of my privacy.

But Maria doesn't flinch. In fact, she puts her palms flat on my desk and leans in so close that I'm only inches away from her flawless pink lip-gloss. "Maggie, I haven't seen anybody who needs to get laid more than you. Why not give the boy a chance to nibble on *your* cupcakes and smell *your* pretty petals?"

I think I'm going to yell at her. I think I'm going to tell her to mind her own goddam business, but when I open my mouth, I'm astounded by the loud, piercing cackle that comes out. Maria smiles and starts to laugh along with me until there are tears streaming down both of our faces.

"Oh! Oh, God!" I gasp, trying to catch my breath. My sides ache with the effort.

"Uh–huh. Now *that's* what I want to hear coming out of your mouth!" Maria says, pointing at me and nodding. "Go on now, call that little music boy and tell him to stop playing with his own instrument because you need help getting yours in tune."

As I eat lunch at my desk a few hours later, I swivel my chair around so I can people watch. I spot a nanny as she tries to corral her young charge, but the little girl is determined to get out of her stroller. On the other side of the street, a businesswoman walks at an impressive clip in impressive heels while talking on her cell phone and sipping an impressive green smoothie. I recognize a group on the corner as tourists. They're all wearing the same garish neon green t-shirts, presumably so they can keep track of one another. They look ridiculous as they pose for selfies, trying to get the Brooklyn Bridge in the background

The thing about my job is that it's really easy to get sucked up in the day-to-day. Abuse, addiction, depression, helplessness, hopelessness. I spend so much time trying to fix what's irreparably broken, that I sometimes forget that there are healthy people having healthy relationships out there.

Maria was right. I do need to get laid. Or, at the very least, I need a good date. Someone who'll make me laugh. Someone who'll hold my hand during the scary part of the movie and let me steal his dessert after I've finished eating all of mine. I don't need rich or drop-dead gorgeous or even a brain surgeon. I just need a kind and decent man who will love me for who I am, quirks and all. And sexy doesn't hurt either. So far, this guy is nowhere in sight.

As I nibble on my chicken salad sandwich, I consider Brett Corrigan. He seemed to have some potential. That is, until he opened his mouth. First in the hospital with the whole viola fiasco, and then again at the coffee shop. Maybe my mother is right, maybe his brother is a bad influence on him. But even if that's true, it opens up a whole other can of worms.

I spend a good part of my time sitting at this desk, weighing options. And rarely can I find a clear answer. Most of the time, it just comes down to which is the lesser of the evils. I don't like it, but I do it. I put possibilities on a scale in my mind and see if the pros outweigh the cons.

At this moment, I put Brett and his positive attributes on one side of the scale: He's hot. He's funny. He has an interesting job and I think maybe an interesting personality. On the other side, I heap his faults: he can be obnoxious and judgmental. He either believes in extreme social viewpoints or he's heavily influenced by someone who does. He has a brother, somewhere out there, who may or may not have been involved in someone's death.

I sigh heavily and dump the remnants of lunch in the trashcan. I'm tempted to throw the irises in there, too, but in the end I just move the vase to the windowsill behind me, so I won't have to stare at it all day. Nope, I'm sorry, but my love of pretty flowers and cupcakes does *not* outweigh my concerns about Brett Corrigan.

The scales have spoken.

Chapter 10

Brett

Fingers are snapping in front of my face.

"What?" I ask, irritated. "What do you want, Jeremy?"

"Hey, don't get all pissy with me, I've been talking to you for five minutes and you aren't even listening. What the hell's got all your attention? Porn?"

I slam the top of my laptop closed so he won't see the results of my Google search for Maggie Collins. "Yeah, porn," I repeat unenthusiastically. "What were you saying?"

He sighs in exasperation. "I was saying that I might have caught a break in my search for Matthew and Julia."

"Oh?"

"Yeah, one of the McInnes cellists, Tamika Wright, told me that she saw Julia on Dr. Sam's calendar for summer lessons."

I sit back in my chair and consider this. "Does Tamika make a habit of looking over Dr. Sam's calendar?"

I see a sly smile creep across his lips. Christ, not another one! Where does he find these girls? "Is that who you had in your room the other night?" I ask.

He shrugs and his smile brightens. "Yeah, hard to miss her right?

She's a moaner. But so fucking hot. I'd have done her even if she couldn't get the info for me..."

"Ugh..." I groan, dropping my head into my hands.

"Oh, come on, Brett! Grow up will you?"

I look up again and glare at him "Really? You're telling *me* to grow up, Jeremy? Dude, you won. You got the gold. You beat Julia fair and square. Why can't you just let it go? You're wasting energy on a girl who doesn't mean anything to you."

"*Why?* Are you kidding me? You know damn well why!"

I can only shake my head. It's like trying to reason with a toddler. "Alright, man. Whatever. So what's next then?"

"Burger Depot."

The unexpected response practically gives me whiplash.

"Burger Depot? The place in midtown?"

"Yeah, I've been dying for that burger they make, The Juicy Lucy. It's a patty between two grilled cheese sandwiches. I've got to work out all the disgusting European food from my system with some good old artery-clogging American beef. C'mon, I'll even buy."

Something tells me I'm going to regret this, but damn if the Juicy Lucy doesn't sound good right about now.

* * *

"Do you hear that?" Jeremy asks me over his shoulder as I trot to keep up with him.

I do, in fact hear it, if *it* is what I think it is—one of Bach's *Solo Cello Suites*.

I should have known better than to trust the son of a bitch. We're not at Burger Depot at all, we're on the second floor of the McInnes Conservatory, nearly deserted between summer sessions. My stomach is growling and I'm getting more and more irritated as I realize that my girl Juicy Lucy is less and less of a possibility.

Everyone knows that the Bach Suites are a favorite of Julia's and now I'm sure Jeremy is thinking he's struck gold when he hears the music wafting through the hall. I'd love nothing better than to just turn around and walk right the hell out of here, but I know that no good can come from a meeting between my brother and his ex-girlfriend.

"Come out, come out, wherever you are..." he calls softly in a singsong tone.

"Jeremy, what are you going to do?" I ask from behind him. He snorts but doesn't reply. I feel the phone in my pants vibrate and try to sneak a peek as we hurry along. I hold my breath, hoping it'll be an email or text from Maggie. I've been waiting for some kind of a response to the flowers I sent, but my heart sinks when I see the offer for penile enhancement. I almost laugh out loud with the irony.

"Jesus Christ, Brett, put the fucking phone away already!" Jeremy grumbles.

We walk past the concert hall, which is dark. No Bach in there. Down the long hallway of empty classrooms. No Bach there, either. Finally, we trace the sound up the rickety back stairs to the wing that houses the instrumental studios. Each professor has his own little home-away-from-home on this floor where students go for their lessons. The cello studio is all the way down at the end of the hall. Sure enough, Mr. Johann Sebastian Bach is spilling out, loud and clear, from under the door of Dr. Sam Michaels.

Jeremy puts a hand on the doorknob, turning to give me a wide, triumphant smile. Before I can insist that he knock, my brother pushes the door open with so much force that it bangs hard into the wall on the inside of the studio. He freezes in the doorway. When I look over his shoulder, I see why. It isn't Julia playing the Bach Cello Suite, it's Mila Strassman.

Unlike Mila, Dr. Sam doesn't seem at all surprised to see us. If Julia's told him half of the shit that Jeremy did to her, then Dr. Sam would've known it was just a matter of time before he showed up here looking for her.

"Jeremy!" Mila squeals excitedly, a huge, grin plastered to her face. "I can't believe it's you! Are you back from your tour already?

Oh, of course you are! That was a stupid question wasn't it? I mean you're standing right here. Was it exciting? Did you get to play for the Queen or one of those dishy princes? Oh, Jeremy, it must have been amazing..." Before she can utter another word, Dr. Sam puts a hand on her shoulder, and she stops. "Oh, sorry. I didn't mean to blabber..."

"No, it's okay," Jeremy says, affecting his friendliest expression. "It was fabulous, Mila, thanks for asking. I came back early so I can take some horn auditions. I'm sorry, I didn't mean to interrupt your lesson. I thought you might be—"

"Julia?" Dr. Sam finishes the sentence for him without so much as a trace of his normally good-natured manner.

I clear my throat and nudge Jeremy with my elbow. He ignores me, but Dr. Sam doesn't. He shoots a hard glance in my general direction, and I find myself shrinking backwards.

"Yes, exactly," Jeremy is saying. "I was sure it was Julia playing the Bach..."

"Well, you were mistaken. Now, if you... *gentlemen*... will excuse us, we were in the middle of something."

I feel the sting of his disdain dripping from the word 'gentlemen.' Dr. Sam is not someone to fuck with. But, then again, neither is Jeremy Corrigan.

"Oh, of course," my brother says, making a conscious effort not to show the irritation that I know is welling up inside him. "I'm so sorry we've interrupted your lesson. I was just wondering, Dr. Sam, have you heard from Julia, or seen her? I have something of hers that I need to return to her."

"What?" the man asks.

"Excuse me?"

"What do you have that you need to return to her, Jeremy?"

It's clearly a challenge. Dr. Sam wants to see Jeremy squirm to find a suitable reply, knowing full well there isn't one.

"Uh, a book," Jeremy pulls the answer out of his ass. "I found it the other day and thought she might like to have it back."

"Oh? Which book might that be?"

My brother doesn't miss a beat. "*In Cold Blood.*"

Holy. Shit. He did *not* just say that.

But, as shocked as I am, the expression on Dr. Sam's face hasn't shifted even a fraction of an inch.

"So... can you tell me how to get in touch with her?" Jeremy asks again.

"No, I can't," he says so flatly that Mila turns to look at him.

Jeremy decides to try his luck with her next. "Mila?"

She shakes her head. "No, Jeremy, I'm sorry. But if I see her I'll tell her you're looking for her. She hasn't been around here since...uh, well...since just after the Kreisler's I guess. She just kinda disappeared. One day she was here, the next day she wasn't. It was really strange because we had a few weeks of class left, you know? And I've tried calling her, but the number's been disconnected. Maybe if you..."

"Okay, Mila. Back to Bach, if the Corrigans will excuse us."

Jeremy waits for a long moment, clearly expecting Dr. Sam to crack under his malicious glare. But the guy doesn't so much as blink. In fact, he lifts his eyebrows as if to ask what the hell we're waiting for. I put an arm on Jeremy's shoulder.

"Come on, let's get out of here," I murmur quietly, stepping back out into the hallway and waiting for him to do the same. When he finally decides he's had enough, he follows me, slamming the door behind him so loudly that another door at the other end of the hall opens up and a curious head pops out to see what's going on.

"Rich!" Jeremy calls out to the horn professor, his demeanor flipping from incensed to casually cordial in less than a heartbeat. "Just the man I was hoping to see!"

Something inside me says to go. Just get the fuck out of here before I can get sucked into anymore of my brother's bullshit vendetta. But it's never that easy with Jeremy.

"How was the tour?" Rich Kellogg is asking as he ushers us into his studio, several doors down from Dr. Sam's. "Did you show those wimpy European horn players how we do it here in the USA?"

"Oh, well, it got off to a great start in France but there were issues in Germany. I decided to cut my losses and come back so I could get in on some of those horn auditions coming up."

"Gee, I'm sorry to hear that," he says with genuine concern in his voice. "Please, sit down. Brett, it's good to see you. How are you feeling? I heard about your accident."

I shrug, knowing that the faint outline of bruises still marbles my face. "Oh, I'm getting there little by little, thanks, Rich."

Jeremy rolls his eyes. "You're such a fucking pussy," he jabs at me while his teacher looks on, trying to suppress a smile. Jeremy has this guy wrapped around his little finger.

"So what's on your mind?" he asks, leaning forward intently.

"Well, I came home to a huge pile of mail, including letters from Seattle, New Orleans, Houston and Detroit."

"Good for you! I wish you'd told me sooner, I would have written a recommendation for you."

"Thanks, Rich, but it was a pretty quick decision, and I posted everything from Europe."

"Okay, so when's your first audition? We've got to get you ready to go. Those are some tough committees to impress."

"Thing is, all four declined my applications for an audition."

He's looking at Jeremy as if he's misheard. Obviously this guy had no idea this was coming. If I know my brother, he's here fishing to see just how much Rich Kellogg *does* know about all this.

"I don't understand. You're one of the top horn players in the country. You just took the Kreisler gold, for Christ's sake. That alone should get you a courtesy audition!"

Jeremy and I are both nodding our heads in agreement.

"And there was no indication as to why?"

"Not exactly."

"What do you mean, 'not exactly'?"

"I've already seen my attorney. He's convinced it's all the rumors surrounding Cal's death. He thinks that's why they won't even audition me."

"I can see that being the case," Rich says finally, stroking the sad little goatee on his chin. "Those orchestras are PR machines. The slightest whiff of scandal and their major donors are taking their checks next door to the opera company or the ballet."

I know I'm going to be here all day if we don't get down to the bottom of what it is that my brother wants to know. "Rich, is there anything you can do?" I ask hopefully. "Do you know anyone on the inside who might be able to help him get an audition, at least?"

He shrugs. "I can make some calls, but I doubt it will help. They're not going to admit to anything, they'll be too afraid of a lawsuit."

From next to me, Jeremy gives a heavy sigh and looks down at his hands. If he could shed a tear on cue, I'm sure he'd do that, too. As it is, the best he can manage is a troubled, disheartened expression. "It's just so wrong, Rich. I mean, how can someone get away with deliberately smearing my reputation out of revenge?"

Oh, hell. He is *not* going down this road.

"Revenge? Who do you think is out for revenge? Why?"

And Professor Richard T. Kellogg plays right into my brother's hands. Here comes Jeremy's 'pained' expression. I know it very, very well. It telegraphs to Rich that what he's about to say is incredibly difficult for him. That he really doesn't want to do it, but he doesn't see any way around it. All that in one little perfectly practiced glance.

"I... I'm pretty sure it's Julia James."

"What? You mean the little redhead cellist?" he asks in surprise.

Jeremy nods solemnly as I look down at the floor uncomfortably. "Don't let her fool you, Rich. She is the most devious, conniving bitch..." Jeremy stops and holds up a hand. "I'm sorry. I hate to resort to name-calling. Let's just say she was not happy about taking the silver medal. I think in her mind, with Cal out of the way..." he lets the rest of the sentence hang there.

"Jeremy, what are you suggesting?" Rich asks, hanging on every melodramatic word.

Next to me, my brother clears his throat.

"I don't know this for sure, but I can't help but think that she's the one who had something to do with Cal's death. Julia was there at the hall when he collapsed. She was right there on stage while the conductor and I were trying to help him. I even found her sneaking around backstage. And let's not forget that *she's* the one who was the finalist at that point! With Cal out of the picture, her odds got a whole lot better."

"Jesus Christ," Rich whispers incredulously. "Jeremy, you have to go to the police with this!"

He shakes his head. "They beat me to it, Rich. They tried to convince the police that I was involved, made up some story about me putting peanut oil on Cal's mouthpiece. And then... how convenient! I make the perfect target. The second place horn player. Of course everyone is suspicious of me! Who would ever suspect the girl they call 'The Mouse'? Hah! 'The Barracuda' is more like it!"

Now Rich is shaking his head in disbelief. I want to do the same thing but for different reasons. This really is too much, even for Jeremy.

"Jeremy, that's a serious accusation."

"You think I don't know that? You think I don't feel like a total idiot for letting her seduce me and take me in?"

And here comes the tear. Sniff, sniff. Wipe, wipe.

"Jesus, I'm so pathetic!" Jeremy says, putting his head into his hands. "I loved her, Rich! And I thought she loved me too... I was so sure we were going to have a life together."

A snort of laughter rises in my throat but I'm able to mask it as a cough. Jeremy shoots me a 'don't you fucking dare!' glare.

"Don't say that, Jeremy," Rich tries to soothe him. "You're not pathetic. And you're certainly not the first guy to be taken in by an unscrupulous woman."

"Thanks, Rich. That makes me feel a little better. I just hate that they're going to get away with it."

"They?"

"Yeah. Julia and her real boyfriend, Matthew Ayers. They masterminded this whole thing together. I'm sure of it. They set me up, and when I won the competition anyway, they hired some guy—a private detective or something—to contact all the major orchestras, all the conservatories and all the festivals. He's insinuated that I was the one who had something to do with Cal's death and suggested that any organization that hires me will suffer the fallout of the investigation."

"Okay, so you said they beat you to the police. What did the police do after they made their complaint?"

Jesus Christ, this guy is like a kid anxious to hear the next chapter of his bedtime story.

"Well, luckily, the lead detective on the case saw right through them. He went so far as to tell Julia she looked like a 'woman scorned' who was trying to blame her old boyfriend so she could ride off into the sunset with her new boyfriend."

"Matthew?"

"Exactly."

Rich sits back heavily against the couch. He looks like one of those cartoon characters who's just been hit over the head with a mallet. I can almost see the little stars and bluebirds floating around his head.

"So now you see what I'm dealing with, man. They've already taken so much from me, and this could be the thing that ends my career before it ever gets started."

"Brett? What do you think about all this?" Rich asks me. I look up, startled.

"Oh, he's been such a great support system for me," Jeremy interjects before I can answer. "My brother always has my back."

Uh-huh. I offer a weak smile.

Rich sits up again and nods resolutely.

"Okay. Now I understand. Where are they—Julia and Matthew?"

"If only I knew!" Jeremy laments dramatically. "They've gone into hiding and nobody seems to know anything. Or if they do, nobody is saying anything."

"Do you think someone is protecting them?"

My brother feigns reluctance. What the hell is he getting at now?

"It's okay, Jeremy. You can tell me. Just be honest with me. Who is it?"

I know what he's going to say a split second before he says it. Holy shit, he wouldn't! Would he? Please don't, please don't, please...

Jeremy takes a deep breath and closes his eyes as he whispers the name. "Dr. Sam."

And with those two words, my brother has lobbed a Molotov cocktail big enough to flatten McInnes Conservatory.

Chapter 11

Maggie

I'm late, as usual. And I am *so* regretting the decision to wear the heels today. What was I thinking? I was thinking I'd finish up at five and pop home to change into something more comfortable. Well, that was just a ridiculous plan. I've never once finished up at five.

"Goodnight, Lou!" I call to the security guard in the vestibule between the CPS lobby and the sidewalk.

He reaches out and puts a heavy hand on my shoulder, stopping me in my tracks.

"Hold up a second there, Miss Collins," he says, looking past me and out the front door.

I don't like that look. Lou gets paid to watch for anything or anyone suspicious. More than one disgruntled parent has come into the CPS office looking to give us a piece of their mind. And, occasionally, something a little more violent.

"What is it?" I ask a little alarmed by his concern.

"Mmm... don't know, but something ain't right with that guy across the street. He's been checking his watch and looking over here for the last half hour."

I follow his nod toward the shady character in question. The guy is faced away from us as he paces the sidewalk, but I can tell he's tall with dark hair. Maybe six foot one or two? I'm making mental notes now in case I have to describe him to the police. He walks a few more feet and then pivots to walk back the other direction. I practically choke.

"You okay, Miss Collins?" Lou asks.

I nod yes and try to catch my breath, holding up my hand in a 'hang on a sec' gesture. When I can breathe again I feel my face growing red with embarrassment. "Uh, Lou, I know that guy."

"Seriously?" he asks, looking at me and then out to the wandering figure on the sidewalk.

"Yeah, I kinda went on a date with him a couple of weeks ago."

Now Lou looks even more agitated. "You think he might be stalking you?"

"What? Oh! No, Lou, he's not stalking me! I just... He's been calling me, and I haven't returned any of his messages, so I guess he's come to find me..." Even as I say the words, I realize that it does sound like stalking. I put a reassuring hand on Lou's sleeve and smile. "He's a good guy, Lou, no worries. I'll tell him to take a hike."

The security guard doesn't look convinced. "Alright..." he says reluctantly, "but I'm going to be watching you from here. You just give me a signal and I'll be out there in a flash if you need me. Okay?"

I giggle. "Well, trust me, you won't have to come out to protect me from him, but you might just have to come out to protect him from *me!*"

Lou snorts. "The date was that bad?"

"Worse." I roll my eyes.

"Oh, yeah. That boy's gonna be in some trouble!"

I toss a smile and a wink over my shoulder at Lou as I push open the door and walk quickly, pretending not to notice the solitary pacing figure across the street. Out of the corner of my eye, I see him scurry to try and keep pace with me from the other side of Main Street.

"Maggie!" I hear him call out over the traffic. I pretend not to hear him and keep walking. "Maggie! Hey, Maggie!"

He finally catches me three blocks away, literally racing to beat me to a crosswalk and intercept me. And then he is there, standing in front of me, looking more handsome than he has any right to look. Idiot. I want to smack him.

"Maggie..." he says, clearly not sure what to say to me now that he's caught me. I raise an expectant eyebrow, but I don't utter so much as a syllable.

After dozens of phone messages, unanswered emails and texts, he's apparently graduated from cyber-stalking to real life stalking. I take note of the dark circles under his eyes and the way his brows knit together in concern. Anxiety maybe. This guy is tired and nervous. I take pity on him finally and speak.

"Brett, what are you doing here?"

"I had to see you," he says breathlessly. "You wouldn't return my calls. Can we please talk? I want to apologize for the way I acted at the coffee shop."

"You already have. About fourteen times by my count, in fact."

He looks down at the sidewalk and then back up at me. Gone now is the air of arrogance that followed him into our last meeting. Something has definitely shifted, and I think about what my mother said about him parroting someone else.

"Please, Maggie, can we just go somewhere and talk? I'd love to take you to dinner. No strings, just dinner."

"I have plans," I say flatly.

"Change them."

The earnestness in his tone takes the edge off of the command. He's pleading with me, not ordering me. He's lucky I'm good with tone and body language. Any other girl would have cleaned his clock with her pocketbook by now.

"I can't. I'm committed to be somewhere, and I'm already going to be late. So I've got to go. Now."

"Take me with you then," he blurts out before he can stop himself.

"Take you where? You have no idea where I'm headed! I could be going to yoga. I might be meeting friends. I might have a date!"

He seems to consider this and then dismisses it, shaking his head. "No, I don't think you have a date at all. But whatever it is, wherever it is, I'll go with you. I'll keep you company. I'll carry your purse... whatever I have to do. Come on. Please," he presses, not sure exactly what it is that he's pressing for.

I tilt my head to the side and look at Brett Corrigan. A fixer of hearts and a mender of souls, my mom called me.

"Okay," I say finally, raising a finger at him and wagging it. "But there's no backing out. You go with me now, you stay with me until the end of the night. There's no sneaking out early. I'll be there till after nine. Can you make that kind of a commitment?"

"I can."

"Alright then," I say, waving him to follow me down the block. "We've got to hurry.

He jogs a few quick steps to catch up with me.

"Late for what, exactly?" he asks.

"You'll see."

And so will I.

Chapter 12

Brett

I *don't* see, at least not for another five blocks, and then I can't miss it. The gothic revival church is huge—complete with stone facing, leaded windows and...are those gargoyles up there? I can't help but crane my neck as I look skyward.

"Come on," she says, beckoning me to follow her around the corner.

She's still moving quickly, and I have to hurry to catch her as she slips down a set of stairs around the side of the church. When she opens the door, I see long banquet tables and folding chairs set up in rows across the room. Dozens of people are seated, eating. Still more are lined up at a makeshift serving station on the far side of the room, where apron-clad men and women are handing out trays and filling them with food.

"A soup kitchen? We're eating at a soup kitchen?" I ask.

"No," she says slowly, as if I'm a little dim. "We're *working* at a soup kitchen, Brett."

"Okay, then," I mumble under my breath and follow her to the serving area.

Within five minutes, I am outfitted with my very own apron,

gloves and hairnet. I argue with her on the last item, but one glower from her and on it goes. Maggie sets us up at the end of this mini assembly line, so that by the time one of the diners reaches us, his or her tray is complete with a hearty slab of meatloaf, mashed potatoes and gravy, and green beans. She plops a dinner roll and butter onto every tray along with a cup of chocolate pudding. I get to hand out a choice of water, iced tea or lemonade. The biggest coffee urn I've ever seen in my life is set up on a different table for self-service.

The people who pass before me seem to come from every age, ethnicity and walk of life. Men and women of ambiguous age, worn out from a hard life on the city streets. They are the elderly, the homeless, runaways and even entire families. I'm embarrassed as I recall my comments from the coffee shop, and I have to force myself to make eye contact with each person into whose hand I place a cup.

If Maggie is monitoring my behavior, she doesn't show it. Actually, I'm the one who keeps sneaking glances at her. I'm blown away by the ease with which she interacts with all of these unique personalities. Here, in this setting, her bright smile is so much more than a pleasantry. Without even trying, Maggie Collins naturally conveys empathy, kindness and understanding. And, perhaps most importantly, she conveys respect for every man, woman and child who stands before her. There isn't even the slightest whiff of pity coming from this woman.

"Do you see that man at the end of the line?" she leans over and asks me quietly, so no one else will hear her. "The one with the blue shirt?"

My eyes skim over about twenty people before they land on a man probably in his forties with sandy blonde hair and a well-worn face. Something about him reminds me of Robert Redford.

"Uh-huh," I say, with a nod.

"His name is Will. He eats here and at the other two soup kitchens on different nights of the week. When he finishes here, he'll head over to the shelter on West Third Street for the night."

"So, he's homeless," I deduce.

She nods. "And do you know what he'll do tomorrow morning?"

"I don't know," I shrug, "find a bench in the park to hang out on?"

"Nope. He'll get up at six to wait on line for a shower that'll probably be cold by the time he gets in there. He'll shave, put on the other shirt that he owns, the one that he washes in the sink at the shelter, and he'll walk fifteen blocks to work."

I stop, holding a plastic cup of iced tea halfway to the tray it's headed for. "Oh! Sorry!" I say to the woman who is waiting patiently for her beverage. "Where does he work?" I ask.

"He's a janitor at a private school. Works there thirty-nine hours a week."

"So what's he doing living in a shelter?" I ask, clearly confused.

"He makes ten dollars an hour, Brett. That's three-hundred-and-ninety dollars a week. Not even enough to rent a room. And the thirty-nine hours? That's no accident. He only qualifies for health benefits if he works forty hours a week."

"What? That can't be legal!" I find myself suddenly indignant on his behalf.

Maggie gives me a sad smile. "Oh, it's legal. But it sure as hell isn't ethical. He's what we call the 'working poor.' He just plugs away, putting his money in the bank, hoping to save enough to share an apartment with someone."

"Holy shit," I murmur. "I didn't know that was even a thing—that you could have a fulltime job and still be homeless."

"Of course you can. Of all the people sitting here and eating right now, I know of at least six others who are in that boat. They're proud people. Hard-working people."

I look around the room, as if they'll have neon signs over their heads. They don't. I'm about to fill some more plastic cups with iced tea, when I catch Maggie slipping an extra pudding onto an older man's tray when no one is looking. She puts a solitary finger to her lips, telling him it's their little secret.

"Thanks, Maggie!" he says with a toothy grin.

"You eat all that, okay? I want to see you put on a few more pounds before winter!"

"Yes, Ma'am!" he agrees enthusiastically and shuffles off with his chocolate bounty.

It's nearly three hours until the last two meals have been served. Our meals. Maggie grabs a couple of trays for us and starts to load them up.

"I didn't realize you wanted to eat here," I say, looking down at the meatloaf. "Are you sure you wouldn't rather grab a pizza or something?"

She waves away the suggestion. "You won't find better meatloaf anywhere—except maybe in your mother's kitchen. Assuming, of course, that your mother can cook," she says over her shoulder.

"Oh, my mom can cook!" I assure her.

We join the rest of the volunteers who have also ditched their hairnets and gloves. They are as diverse a group as the people they serve, from students to retirees.

"I used to be a regular here," a woman named Phyllis tells me. "My husband...he used to get drunk and hit me. One night, he broke my arm. So I took my son and left. We spent a lotta nights sleeping in the shelter, too. But we got back on our feet. I got a job and a little apartment and now my boy's off at college on a scholarship."

"He's studying to be a music teacher," Maggie says, as she nudges me with her elbow.

"Really?"

Phyllis beams at the thought of her son. "Yeah. My Kenny plays the piano. He used to practice right over there," she says, pointing to a battered old upright in the corner. I make a mental note to ask Joe about the Walton doing a benefit concert for the soup kitchen... and a new piano.

From the end of the table, I catch the eye of a man probably in his seventies. He's dressed in what I recognize to be casual, but expensive clothes. Somehow, I don't think he's a soup kitchen alum. "How about you, sir?" I ask. "How long have you been volunteering here?"

"Oh, going on about twenty years now, isn't it, Patty?" he asks a stout, balding man next to him.

"Just about," Patty agrees. "Andy and I been friends since nineteen-sixty-nine," he informs me.

"Wow, that's a long time! You two grow up together or something?"

"I guess you could say that," Andy says with a smile. "We were in Vietnam together. Just a couple kids, really. But we were lucky—we made it back. Not everyone did."

I nod my head in grim understanding. Jesus, the things these men must have seen. But they're not done telling me their story, not by a long shot.

"Even the ones who did come back," Patty picks up, "they didn't always come back the same way they left, you know? A lot of them ended up on the streets. Back then there wasn't much help for vets. And when there was help, most of them didn't know about it or how to get it."

"Patty and I just started walking around the city. When we worked, we did it on weekends and nights. Once we retired, we were on the streets all the time. We got to know every soup kitchen, every shelter, every clinic and social services office. Then, we got to know the people who worked in each of them. Before we knew it, we had a whole network of people working together to get our veterans the benefits they earned fighting for our freedom."

"Andy and Patty are the founders of *A Voice for Our Vets*," Maggie explains.

"Hey, I see your signs everywhere! And the servicemen and women, they're always at Penn Station," I say, excited that I actually know what they're talking about.

Andy gives me a broad smile. "Grand Central and Jamaica Station, too!" he tells me proudly. "Those men and women are active military, volunteering for outreach on their off time and on the lookout for veterans in need all the time. Our organization has helped thousands of vets in New York City alone. Now they want us to help form a national center!"

I feel Maggie's hand on my forearm. She rubs my skin with her thumb. "Hey!" she says in a surprised whisper. "You've got goose bumps!"

"Tell me about it," I say with an unexpected shiver.

* * *

Maggie lives in a third floor walk-up about five blocks from the church. Not too far from my apartment, for that matter. Her one-bedroom is a lot smaller than mine, but then again, she doesn't have to live above a pizza parlor. It's just as hot as mine though, and she immediately turns on the window AC unit.

I wasn't expecting an invite up when I walked her home, but I tried not to act too surprised when she offered me a nightcap. What that means at this point is anyone's guess, so I just follow her lead.

"Have a seat," she offers, gesturing towards a big blue denim sofa. She goes into the kitchen and returns with a pair of wine glasses and half a bottle of chardonnay.

"Would you please pour those for us?" she asks as she makes her way to what I assume is her bedroom. When she emerges, her slacks and blouse have been replaced by faded jeans and a t-shirt. This time it's AC/DC.

She situates herself cross-legged on the opposite end of the couch and I hand her a glass.

"So, let me get this straight, you spend your days working to help families, and in your spare time you serve at a soup kitchen?"

"Yup," She takes a sip of her wine.

I'm awestruck—and by more than her looks. "You are amazing, Maggie Collins."

"No, don't say that," she says. "I'm not. I wish I were. This is what people are supposed to do, Brett. Helping someone shouldn't be a big deal—it should be an everyday occurrence. That's the way my parents raised me, anyway."

"Still, it's impressive," I insist, putting my glass down on the table and scooting closer to her.

"Stop it."

"What?" I ask sheepishly, thinking she's going to send me packing to the cushion that I've just abandoned. But apparently that's not what's bothering her.

"I want people to like me because of who I am, not what I do," she says firmly.

"Why can't it be both?"

She ponders for a moment. "I'm not sure. It's never come up before," she admits.

"What do you mean?"

"I don't know. The guys I date don't tend to stick around too long. I mean, at first they're all *'Wow! You're such a good person!'* and after a few weeks they're feeling more inconvenienced than impressed."

"Oh. Well, that sucks, but it also weeds out the tossers from the keepers, doesn't it?"

"It does," she agrees.

We sip in companionable silence for a few moments.

"So, what's the verdict?" I ask.

Her brows furrow in confusion. "On what?"

"Do you think, maybe, I could be a keeper? Or, at least, not a tosser...just yet, anyway?"

Her lovely, full lips twitch with the hint of a smile. "Ah, well," she begins, pretending to give the question serious weight, "the jury's still out."

"Oh." Not the answer I was hoping for.

"I have to ask, now that you've seen a little bit of my world, do you still believe the things you said to me at the coffee shop?"

Her question hits me like a sucker punch to the gut. I think about what Joe said to me about showing Maggie who I am. I guess this is my big chance. "I'm not sure I ever believed them," I confess quietly, only now realizing that this is the truth. "I've been hearing that shit for so long that I finally just started thinking it was my opinion, too. And then tonight..."

"Tonight you put a face on the problem," she finishes for me.

I nod. This is hard, admitting to her that I'm full of shit. But, to my surprise, she doesn't seem surprised. Maggie pushes the Buddy Holly's up to the bridge or her nose.

"Surprisingly, this isn't a leftwing-rightwing thing, like most people assume. I mean, I don't think *anyone* wants people to be hungry and homeless. And I'm fairly certain that's the case on both ends of the political spectrum. It just comes down to different ideas on how to fix the problem."

"And I've been acting like a jerk with lots of opinions—and no solutions."

"No," she cuts me off, shaking her head, and then she stops, rethinking her reply. "Well, actually yes... and no. In retrospect, I think you formed an opinion based on second-hand—maybe even third-hand knowledge." Maggie leans forward, her blue, blue eyes pinning me to my spot on the couch. "Tell me, Brett. Tell me what you believe in."

"What do you mean?"

"Tell. Me. What. You. Believe. In," she repeats, slowly, so I can't miss a word.

"What? Like Santa Claus and the Tooth Fairy?" I laugh uncomfortably. But Maggie's not laughing. She's expecting an answer. "Jesus, Maggie, I don't know..."

"Exactly!" she says, slapping the couch in triumph. "You don't know *what* you believe in, so you'll believe in anything."

"What? That doesn't make any sense!" I object. Shit. I'm so not in the mood for a philosophical discussion.

"Doesn't it?" she counters.

I open my mouth to give her a smartass reply, but I stop. It does make sense. I've been living with Jeremy for so long that I've just started absorbing his opinions instead of forming my own. When the hell had that happened? I can't recall.

"Do you like what you do for a living, Brett?" she asks, when it's obvious that I'm conflicted.

I nod my head slowly. "I love what I do. I love playing the viola and I love being a part of the Walton Quartet."

She gives me an approving smile. I'm like a child who's earned a gold star. "Excellent! Do you love your parents?"

The faces of Trudy and Danny Corrigan flash into my mind. They're smiling and encouraging. "Yes. Yes, I do," I confirm, and am rewarded with another double-dimpled smile.

"Do you care what people think about you?"

"No. Not usually, anyway."

"And unusually?"

"I care what *you* think of me," I say softly.

Maggie uncrosses her legs and meets me on the middle cushion of the big, blue denim couch. I can't take my eyes off of hers as she reaches out and gently runs her fingers down the side of my face and along my jaw. I'm about to say something when she puts her other hand on the opposite side of my head and pulls my face to hers.

She smells of lilacs as I inhale deeply into our first kiss. It's not that sloppy, awkward tongue-dueling thing that often happens when you kiss someone for the first time. This is soft and gentle, a flurry of tiny, sweet kisses that embrace my lips. I wrap my arms around her and pull her onto my lap. Then, we fall back onto the couch together, her on top of me. I hold her face in my hands this time, drinking in every bit of it. I hadn't realized how beautiful she really is until this very second when I am only inches from her.

"What?" she asks, obviously uncomfortable with the intensity of my gaze.

"You're beautiful," I tell her quietly.

Instantly, her cool, confident demeanor is replaced by an embarrassed awkwardness. It's clear that Maggie is used to giving the attention, not getting it. And she has no idea how sexy she looks in the midst of her discomfort.

"Can we take this someplace with a little more room to... spread out?" I ask hopefully.

"I was actually just thinking I'd love a cup of tea," she says with a teasing smile as she climbs off of me, and the couch, at the same time.

"Oh, well, yeah. Tea. Of course," I mumble under my breath.

"Would you like some?" she asks me over her shoulder on her way to the tiny kitchen.

"Sure, why not," I say, giving up on getting lucky. And, speaking of luck, I know I shouldn't be pushing mine, so I adjust the attitude before it can get me into trouble again.

"Can I help?"

"Nope. I'm just going to put the kettle on here. How do you take yours?"

"Milk and sugar, please."

I hear her opening and closing cabinets and drawers. "Mind if I use your bathroom?" I call out to her from the couch.

"Sure. It's just through the bedroom."

I flip on the light switch as I make my way slowly into the unfamiliar room. When it illuminates I find a queen-sized bed, carefully made up with one of those old quilts. Her tiny dresser and nightstand are both covered with books. No TV. I didn't spot one in the living room either.

I'm seriously out of my element in her girly bathroom with its pink shower curtain and matching towels. Even the hand soap is pink. I close my eyes, so I don't have to see it while I lather up my hands and forearms to get the last traces of meatloaf juice off of them. But it's not too bad, actually. In fact, my skin feels softer after I rinse off. By the time I've washed my face and dried off with one of her luxuriously fluffy towels, I'm thinking about doing it all over again. But, I've kept Maggie waiting too long as it is.

"You know, I was going to give you shit about the pink soap, but then I used it and..." I stop mid-sentence when I spot her, sound asleep on the couch, two steaming mugs of tea on the coffee table in front of her.

Quietly, I retrace my steps to her bedroom and pull the quilt from her bed. I bring it into the living room and drape it gently over her body, which is already pulled in tight against the chill of the air conditioner.

I find her keys on the coffee table and take off the one that fits her deadbolt, so I can use it to lock her in from the hallway and then slip it back under the door. I'm halfway out the door when I turn back on impulse. Silently, I tiptoe to the couch and look down at her, hair fanned across a throw pillow, rosy lips slightly parted. I lean down and give her the slightest brush of a kiss on the forehead.

"Sweet dreams," I whisper, just the way my mother did when I was a kid.

Maggie stirs ever so slightly before falling back into her angelic slumber. I find a notepad and pen by the phone on the end table and scribble a quick note, putting it under one of the teacups so the AC won't blow it onto the floor and under the couch. Then, I leave quietly, turning off the light as I do.

I could be wrong, but I think I might just be in trouble here. And I'm not so sure that's a bad thing.

Chapter 13

Maggie

Five days, four dates, three meals, one movie and countless make-out sessions. Had I not seen the transformation with my own two eyes, I never would have believed it possible. In under a week, Brett Corrigan has gone from being absolute nightmare date to potential man of my dreams. I have to admit I was sure he'd fall flat on his face at the soup kitchen, maybe go running from the building when I showed him his hairnet. But he surprised me.

That night, I saw a side of him that was humble, empathetic, concerned. Not even a whiff of the obnoxious bravado I saw at the coffee house. It got me thinking maybe my mother was right. Maybe Brett has been absorbing someone else's bullshit and spewing it. And maybe that someone is his brother. Before I get in a whole lot deeper, I'm going to have to do a little more investigating on the subject.

I dab at my face with a tissue. It's one of those brutally bright days without so much as the whisper of a breeze for relief, and I can feel the heat melting the makeup right off my face. Finally, I give up and toss the tissue into my purse. Well, so much for looking 'fresh as a daisy.'

Brett offered to meet me at work, but thanks to the Dynamic Duo of Marisol and Maria, my love life is the headliner at the CPS Rumor Mill. And, truth be told, all the cloak and dagger stuff is kinda hot! I want to try and keep it for myself for just a little bit longer.

"I believe in you."

Those were the four words scrawled on the back of an envelope he left on my coffee table. It took me a minute to recall our conversation from the night before when I confronted him about his beliefs... or lack thereof. How could I say no when he called and asked me to have dinner with him the next night? Or when he showed up at my door with egg sandwiches and coffee the day after that? Or when I got the text asking if I wanted to try the best chocolate pudding in town this afternoon?

When I turn the corner, he's already there, standing out in front of the diner waiting for me. He's tall. I like tall. Lean, but not too skinny. His hair is a nice warm shade of brown, threaded with bits of gold as I look at it now in the sunlight. I'm suddenly glad I got up early to iron my favorite blue sundress. The one that shows off my shoulders.

"Hey, you!" I greet him as I approach him.

"Hey, yourself," he replies with an easy smile as he meets me on the sidewalk. He bends down and I think he's going to hug me. Instead, his lips brush against mine. It's a sweet kiss with just a hint of something firmer behind it. Suddenly my temperature's going up, and it doesn't have a damn thing to do with the weather.

"I, uh, well... let's go inside, shall we?" I sound a little more flustered than I'd like. There's a difference between kissing on the privacy of one's couch and kissing on a Brooklyn sidewalk.

Brett holds the door open, and I walk past him to the hostess station so we can be seated. I feel his breath on my neck before I hear his voice in my ear.

"I'd like to nibble on those shoulders," he murmurs so no one else can hear.

Score one for the sundress!

I toss a scandalized look behind me as the waitress shows us to our booth. "You'd better watch it, buddy," I warn playfully.

"Oh, I intend to," he grins at me, looking quite a bit lower than my shoulders. "You just keep walking, baby."

We're through with the burgers and onto dessert when I finally work up the nerve to mention the subject that's been nagging at me. "I want to meet your brother," I say, looking up from our shared chocolate pudding.

He snorts with laughter.

"What?" I ask defensively. "What's so funny about that?"

Shaking his head, he pulls his phone out of his pocket and takes a quick picture of me. When he hands it to me, I see for myself the whipped cream mustache across my upper lip.

"Oh, no!" I laugh, looking for my napkin.

"Wait, wait, wait," he says, reaching across the table with his, wiping the offending topping from my face.

"Do you think we could do that soon?" I ask after we've stopped chuckling.

"What? Meet Jeremy? I guess. One of these days," he says noncommittally.

"You don't like to talk about him much, do you."

It comes out as more of a statement than a question.

"I don't know," he shrugs. "Why?"

I take a deep breath and jump in. It has to be done.

"Brett, just because I don't own a TV doesn't mean I don't keep track of what's going on in the world around me. I have the Internet. I use Facebook and Google."

"What is that supposed to mean?" he asks, spoonful of pudding paused halfway to his mouth.

I meet his eyes squarely. "It means I've heard all about Jeremy. I've read all the articles. I've seen all the headlines. I know he's an incredibly talented musician. And I know he was caught up in something really awful."

Brett puts the spoon down. I can see that he has no idea where I'm going with this.

"I know that there was... that there *is* speculation that your brother had something to do with that other horn player's death."

His eyebrows knit together for just a second and then he clears his throat. "Well, you're right. It was all anyone was talking about for a while," he says uncomfortably.

I'm waiting for him to tell me that there's no truth to the story, but he doesn't.

"Is he, okay?" I ask. "I mean, is all of that going to be a problem for him now that he's home from his tour?"

He considers me for a long moment before speaking again.

"Maggie are you... concerned by what you've heard about Jeremy?" he asks quietly. "Does it make you uncomfortable about seeing me? Because..."

"No," I interject, lying through my teeth. "I just—you know, I don't want it to be this thing between us that just gets bigger and more awkward. I thought we should just get it out there before things go any further."

"Are they?" he asks.

"Are what *what?*"

"Are things going further?"

I feel a blush creep up to my cheeks. "I hope so..." I say quietly.

He reaches out and touches my face with his hand. It feels warm and soft against my skin, and I lean into it.

"Maggie, Jeremy is a complicated guy. And I won't lie to you—he can be a real ass. But you can ask me anything. I'll tell you whatever you want to know. Although, if it's okay with you, I'd rather hold off on introducing you for a little longer. I'm enjoying having you all to myself."

I can't help but smile as he echoes the same sentiment I was thinking not an hour ago. I give him a nod that tells him I understand. "You let me know when the time is right, okay?" I suggest. "And then maybe I can cook the three of us a nice dinner. He sounds really fascinating and I'll bet he has some amazing stories."

Brett takes his hand away and sits back, shaking his head in disbelief. "How is it that you *always* look for the good in people?"

"Some people think that makes me naïve," I reply with a shrug, wondering if he's one of them.

"I think it makes you incredibly kind. And generous," he says. "And will you please stop licking that pudding spoon? You're making me crazy over here!"

"What?" I don't get it. And then I do. "Oh!" I say with a laugh, putting down the offending utensil. "My, my, Mr. Corrigan, you do have a dirty mind!"

He catches the attention of our waitress and holds up the empty pudding cup. "Can we get another one of these? Extra whipped cream, please!"

Chapter 14

Brett

I watch her walk away, blue dress swishing around her, black curls lit by the sun. She has no idea how fucking sexy she is. Maybe I'll get her an ice cream cone to lick on next time, I think with a lascivious smile.

Instinctively, I take a second to look around me, scanning the blocks in all directions, keeping an eye for shadowy figures ducking into doorways. But nothing seems out of place. No one looks suspicious. While I'm thinking about it, I take out my phone and skim through the apps to make sure nothing new has mysteriously appeared there. Maybe an app that tracks my whereabouts or mirrors my text messages. But there's nothing unusual there either. Like Maggie, I'm doing my best to keep 'us' a secret for now. Unlike Maggie, I'm doing it for personal reasons rather than professional.

If you didn't know Jeremy, you'd probably think I was being paranoid. But anyone who knows anything about my brother, who has seen past the veneer of charming civility he wears like a mask, can understand why I need to protect this relationship. The longer I can keep things a secret, the longer I have before... Before what? Before Jeremy tries to fuck it up, that's what.

There's not a doubt in my mind that my brother is going to feel very threatened by Margaret M. Collins, LCSW when he finally does meet her. Probably more threatened than he's been by any other girl I've dated. That's because she isn't like any other girl I've ever dated.

I can already see his strategy—I know it by heart. First, he'll turn on the charm, seeing if he can catch her eye, get a feel for whether or not there's seduction potential there. That's how it went when I found him in bed with my last girlfriend.

Now, if that doesn't work, he'll take a slightly different tack, appealing to her sense of vanity. Lots of flattery and ego stroking meant to plant the seeds of doubt in our relationship. He'll try to get her to see me as 'beneath' her, playing up her perfections and my perversions. That's how he got Lisa to dump me right before the senior prom. He didn't even want her—he just didn't want *me* to have her. Or *anyone*, for that matter.

Finally, if neither of those approaches work, he might go for menacing. He's good at menacing. Creepy comments uttered through even creepier smiles. Stalking her at home or work or even chasing her around our apartment. He's a master of conveying veiled...and not-so-veiled threats. That's how he scared away two or three other girls I was seeing at various points in my life.

But Jeremy will have his work cut out for him with Maggie. She's not superficial enough to be taken in by his good looks and charm. And there isn't a self-centered bone in her body, so the vanity card is a bust. No, if I know Jeremy—and I do—he'll figure out pretty quick that intimidation is his best course of action. Just the challenge of it will probably give him a boner.

What my brother doesn't know is that she's not afraid of monsters. She's seen them before. Hell, she's even gone toe-to-toe with them! So she already knows to what dark depths people are capable of sinking and very little shocks her. No, while I can see how Maggie might be disgusted by him, I don't think she'll be intimidated by him. Yeah, she'd definitely give him a run for his money. Just the idea of it makes me snort out loud on the sidewalk. Not that I want to test my theory anytime soon.

Chapter 15

Maggie

"Why don't you come with me?" he asks as I squeeze an avocado.

I put it down and turn to face him, wondering if I've heard right. "What? To Philadelphia?"

"Sure, why not? It'll be fun. I mean, I'll have to play my concerts in the evenings, but we'd have the rest of the time to explore the city."

He's holding my hand tightly as we stroll through the farmer's market in midtown. This is the third of these Saturday mornings we've shared, and we've already got a routine going. We meet up for early coffee and croissant at a little cafe. That's followed by a scavenger hunt for vintage books, vinyl and clothing—which is more my thing than his—but he's a good sport about it. Last week, I even managed to talk him into a leather jacket. Right now we're checking out all of the fresh produce and making a plan for the dinner that I'll cook for us later. It's been a nice month. Really nice, in fact.

"Oh, Brett, I wish I could. But I have to spend the weekend catching up on my case notes."

He shakes his head at me. "Nope."

"What do you mean, 'nope'?"

"I mean I don't accept that answer. It's a two-hour train ride, Maggie. Bring your case notes with you. You can work on them while we're rehearsing in the afternoons. Come on, don't think about it, just say you'll come," he cajoles, his hands holding my upper arms, his brown eyes watching my face intently.

"I know what this is!" I accuse. "You're trying to get me into bed with you aren't you? My mother warned me about guys like you!"

He throws his hands up in a gesture of surrender. "That's it! You've caught me!" he laughs. "I admit it! I'm guilty! I want to go out of town and have hours and hours of hot sex with my hot girlfriend in a random hotel."

"Dramatic much?" I ask, rolling my eyes at him.

He puts his hands down and gives me a sheepish grin. "Was that a yes?" he asks.

"That's a maybe," I say, though we both know I'm just dragging this out. Of course it's a yes. He leans down to kiss me, holding up a mob of irritated shoppers behind us.

"Get a room!" someone grumbles when our lips finally separate again.

The irony is that we've been taking things slow. Like, maybe, the speed of the glaciers. Lots of sweet handholding, lots of warm hugging, lots of intense making out. But I've been putting on the brakes after that. No sleepovers, no quickies, no anything past second base. I'll be ready when I'm ready. And I think I might be getting close to ready.

I slip my arm through his and he holds my hand as we continue along the sidewalk packed with vendors. Being with him like this makes me feel safe and cared for. I want him to hold my hand forever...at least, I would want him to, were there not a table full of beautiful pashmina scarves just fifteen feet away from me. I give Brett a tight squeeze and extricate myself so I can check them out.

"So much for romance..." I hear him teasing behind me.

"Are you kidding? This is love at first sight!" I grin back at him over my shoulder as I head to the stall.

"Fine. You go propose to your scarf, while I get us a pretzel," he mumbles as he heads to the cart across the street.

"Don't forget the mustard!" I call after him. He holds up his hand in a wave without turning around.

I really am in love with the rainbow of fabrics in front of me. Accessories are a serious vice for me, and I have an entire drawer dedicated to these little morsels of soft, vibrant color.

"How much?" I ask the small Asian woman behind the table.

"Two for twenty."

"Hmmm..." It's all I have to say.

"Two for fifteen for the pretty girl!" the woman says with a smile that's missing a tooth or two.

"Does that go for me, too?" asks another shopper at the other end of the table.

"Of course!" the vendor agrees. "Two pretty girls!"

The other customer and I smile at one another. "I don't feel so pretty these days!" she laughs and puts a hand on a large baby bump protruding from under her sundress.

"Oh, but you're glowing!" I insist. And she really is.

"Sweating," she corrects me, swiping at a rogue bit of red hair that's escaped her ponytail.

"What do you think?" I ask her, holding up a pink and green paisley scarf. "I know I want one in red, but I'm not sure about the second."

She peers at it in my hand, then up at my face, then back at the other scarves on the table. Finally, she points to one in a deep, corn-flower blue. "That one. It matches your eyes."

"Sold!" I say, picking up the scarves and handing them to the other woman along with a twenty-dollar bill. She puts them into a bag and hands it back to me, along with a five-dollar bill.

"Jeez, I leave you alone for three minutes and you're walking away with a shopping bag!" I hear Brett's voice. He comes up behind me, delivers a kiss on my cheek and squints down at all the scarves. "Which ones did you get?"

"That red one over there," I say pointing to the shade. "And this kind lady helped me to choose the blue one, too," I continue, gesturing to the other color I've selected.

"Oh, yeah, Mags. I love that blue. It's like the color of your eyes. Good choice!" he says, turning toward the pregnant woman.

He takes a breath, as if he's about to say something else, and then he stops cold. His body is literally frozen next to me. When I glance over at the redhead, she's staring at him, the color suddenly draining from her face.

She looks horrified.

He looks stunned.

What the hell is going on here?

"Brett?" I whisper up at him, the single word packed with concern and fear.

"Julia," is his breathy reply.

Chapter 16

Brett

When I turn to face the other woman, it's as if I'm watching in slow motion. First, I see the top of her head as she looks through her purse and pulls out a bill. It's a very red head of hair, and I know an instant before she looks up that it's Julia.

"Julia," is all I can think to say.

She doesn't reply, only stares at me in horror.

"Brett?" is Maggie's much stronger, louder contribution to our monosyllabic dialogue.

Julia has dropped the twenty-dollar bill she was holding, and it wafts down through the air, lilting first to the left, then to the right like a flat, green pendulum swinging back and forth. It makes the slightest swish as it finally hits the concrete. We stare at one another in wide-eyed, slack-jawed disbelief. Maggie is looking from her, to me, and back again, trying to work out what's going on. She bends over to pick up the money and holds it out for Julia to take. Julia doesn't notice.

"Do... do you two know each other?" Maggie asks slowly.

But while I can hear her, I am unable to formulate any words. My eyes have moved down to Julia's midriff, and the swell of her belly beneath the skirt.

Holy. Shit.

"Uh... yes," I say at last in response to Maggie's question. "Maggie, this is Julia, she's a cellist," I mutter, still in shock.

"Oh! You're a musician, too!" Maggie says, sounding relieved, though, I'm not sure why. Maybe she thought Julia was an ex. Maybe she thought that baby was mine.

"I–I'm sorry," Julia murmurs. "I'm not feeling very well..."

She puts a hand on the table to steady herself, looking very pale. In an instant, Maggie has commandeered a bench, evicting a couple of teenagers in the process. She takes Julia by the arm and guides her so she can sit down.

"Julia, you just sit here for a minute while I find you some water, okay?" she offers, squatting down so they are at eye level.

Julia nods blankly, glancing at me over Maggie's shoulder.

Maggie stands up and pulls me close to her so she can speak to me privately.

"I'm going to grab one of the guys at the medical station on the other side of the park. Someone should have a quick look at her. You go sit with her for a few minutes until I come back." She fishes through her oversized purse and pulls out a miniature-sized bottle of water.

"Here."

"I'm not thirsty," I tell her as I sneak glances at a glaring Julia.

"It's not for you!" She swats me on the arm impatiently. "For her! Go give this to *her!*"

I nod and take the bottle as she disappears into the crowd, then I take a deep breath and walk to the bench slowly. Now Julia is sitting, hands on her knees, face down toward the ground and breathing deeply.

"Oh. Oh, no! You're not in labor are you?" I ask, the alarm apparent in my tone.

She looks up, startled by my voice and shakes her head.

"What? No. Just a little...winded. I wasn't expecting to see you."

"Yeah, well, that makes two of us," I mumble. I hand her the bottle of water and she takes it with a soft 'thank you.'

I'm just wondering what the hell to say next when I spot it. As she lifts the bottle to her mouth, I notice the thin gold band on the ring finger of her left hand.

"Y-you got married?"

She nearly chokes on the water, and I pat her back. When she's past it, she takes a few deep, shaky breaths before speaking again. "Yes. Matthew and I were married a couple of months ago."

"Matthew? I didn't think you two were... I mean, I thought you were just friends."

She pats her large belly. "Yeah, well, sometimes things happen, and you have to change your plans."

I nod, trying to do the math in my head. "When are you due?" She gives me a sharp look as if she doesn't trust me with this information. "Julia?"

"In late September," she says finally.

The realization hits me with the force of a freight train. It takes a moment to sink in.

"Is it...is the baby Jeremy's?" I ask dropping down onto the bench next to her. But she doesn't respond, just keeps looking straight ahead. I see a tear roll down her cheek. "Don't cry, Julia, it'll be alright." I'm trying to be comforting, but I'm apparently doing a shit job of it, considering the look she's giving me now.

"Really, Brett?" she says, her voice taking on a caustic tone. "How do you figure? You're going to go home and tell Jeremy about this, and we both know what'll happen then, don't we, *Brett*?" She utters my name with such contempt that I feel as if I've been slapped by the five letters.

"No. No, that's not going to happen. I won't tell him..."

"Oh, no? You're just like him!" she spits at me. "You couldn't care less about anyone else."

"That's not true, Julia," I say, extending a hand to touch her arm.

"*Don't you touch me!*" she hisses, recoiling.

People walking by are starting to give us strange looks.

"For fuck's sake, Julia! I'm not going to hurt you—I just want to help you!"

But the words sound lame, even to my own ears.

Then she gives a laugh that makes the hair on the back of my neck stand up. This is not the sweet, shy girl my brother brought home last fall. Something has definitely changed.

Oh, who the hell am I kidding? He changed her. We changed her.

"You tell him that if he even *thinks* about coming after me or this baby I'll kill him myself," she spits with such menace that I have no doubt she means every word.

I hold up my hands in a gesture of surrender. "Please," I beg her. "Please, just listen to me." But she's shaking her head and pulling away from me on the bench. "I won't, Julia. I swear to God I will not tell him anything. Not that I saw you, not that you're pregnant. Nothing. I swear."

She looks at me suspiciously.

I can tell she wants to believe I'm sincere, but she just can't let herself do it.

"Why should I believe a thing you say, Brett? You've never lifted a finger to help me before. Not when your brother was treating me like shit. Not when he hit me."

Suddenly, I can see myself through Julia's eyes. "Julia," I begin on impulse, "that girl, Maggie? She's sort of my girlfriend, and she's made me see things... differently. She's such a good person. She cares about everyone, and she makes me want to be a good person, too."

I have her attention now, but still she doesn't speak. So I take a deep breath and continue. "I am so sorry," I say in barely a whisper. "I'd give anything to be able to take it all back, but I can't. What I *can* do is promise you that I will not breathe a word about this to him or anyone else. Please, just let me at least do this much to make it right. Please."

She's finally about to say something when Maggie walks up behind us, trailed by a uniformed EMT.

"What's this I hear about a fat lady giving us trouble?" jokes the cheery woman with a medical bag slung over her shoulder.

Julia forces a tight smile onto her face. "No trouble," she says, still looking at me as she answers. "I'm feeling much better now. Brett has been a big help. I'm relieved he was here."

That's my answer. She's sending me the message that she's willing to give me the huge benefit of this very big doubt. I close my eyes and give her the slightest gesture of a nod to acknowledge that I understand.

"You must be Maggie," she says, suddenly swiveling her gaze behind me.

Maggie steps forward with a big smile. "Hi, Julia, I'm so happy to meet you. You're the first of Brett's friends that I've met since we started dating."

I have a feeling that if I don't move this along Maggie may very well invite Julia to join us for lunch or something. Julia seems to sense it, too.

"Thanks," she says, forcing a small smile at Maggie. "You know, I'll be fine here with the medic, so you guys go and enjoy the rest of your day. I really am feeling much better now."

Maggie's about to object, but Julia doesn't give her the opportunity. "Brett, it might be a while before I see you again, with the baby coming and all," she says, patting her belly while looking me in the eye. "So, take care," she says making it clear that she'd like us to leave her alone now.

"I will, Julia. You too. Good luck with the baby...and everything," I say, getting up. The medic takes my seat and straps a blood pressure cuff on Julia's arm.

I start to turn away, but something makes me stop. "Julia?"

She looks up. "Please get in touch with me if you need anything. Okay?" I pull a business card out of my wallet and hand it to her. "This is my cell phone," I say so she'll know she won't get Jeremy if she calls that number. She nods and takes the card. If we're lucky, she'll never need to use it.

Chapter 17

Brett

Jeremy is looking at me curiously as I pack up my bag. Clothes, toiletries, music… I'm missing something. What?

"You're headed out a little early, aren't you? I didn't think your train was for another couple of hours," he comments.

It isn't, but I have to catch a cab to Maggie's apartment and pick her up so we can go to Penn Station together. But he doesn't know that.

"Joe and I are going to meet up early. Since this is my first tour with them, he just wants to go over the itinerary with me," I reply without missing a beat.

It would seem that my normally self-absorbed brother has taken notice of the fact that I'm not around nearly as much as usual. I'm also pretty vague about my plans these days. This is, of course, intentional. I've been seeing Maggie every day and it was just a matter of time before he realized something was off.

"So what's going on with you? You got plans while I'm away this weekend?" I ask, trying to deflect his attention

A broad smile fills his face. Jeremy is Jeremy's favorite topic.

"Oh, man, Rich Kellogg called me this morning with some great news," he smiles.

"Yeah? What's that?" I ask distractedly, scanning the room for whatever it is I think I'm missing.

"He did a little digging for me. Did you know there's a rule that none of the four musicians performing at the Kreisler Gala can play music by the same composer?"

"No..." I say slowly, not clear on what advantage this could possibly give him.

"If I play Bach, then Julia can't."

"Huh. Okay, correct me if I'm wrong, but Bach didn't write anything for the French horn, did he?"

"Nope. But someone was kind enough to arrange the cello suites for horn. I'll bet Julia's been working on them all spring. But now *she* can't play it because *I* am. But that's not all, the violinist and pianist are playing Elgar and Dvorak."

"And...?"

"Dude! That knocks out the two other major pieces she could have played instead. Nope, She's going to have start from scratch and try to learn something in the next ten days."

He's grinning so hard I think I can see small cracks forming in the foundation of his face. Christ, he's downright giddy with the idea of fucking over Julia and I've really just heard about all I can on the subject. Time to start my three blissful days without him.

"Okay, well, that's all very interesting, but I'd better get going," I say, slinging my viola case over my shoulder. I'm about to roll my bag out when I remember what I'm missing—my phone charger. I duck into the kitchen to grab it, and when I walk out again, there is an altogether different person sitting at the table. All traces of the glee he possessed not five seconds ago are gone. He's watching me intently, scrutinizing my face.

"Did you know?" he asks me.

"What?" I glance down at my hands as I roll up the phone cord.

"Did you know that she's pregnant?"

I stop what I'm doing, raising my eyes to meet his. I'm trying to keep an impassive expression on my face. "Who? Did I know *who's* pregnant?" I lob back at him.

"Julia," he replies flatly.

My eyebrows go up in my best facsimile of surprise. I set my case down on the floor heavily and take a few steps toward him, head tilted to one side. Yeah, my brother's not the only one who can fake it. "I'm sorry, what did you just say?"

I see Jeremy relax visibly. So, it was a test then. He sprang it on me like that to see what my reaction would be. What that tells me is that he doesn't trust me quite as much as he used to.

"Rich tells me she's pregnant. And really pregnant—like six months, at least."

I'm having a hard time gauging his feelings on this news. "Do you think she and Matthew were...?"

"Fucking around behind my back?" He waves a hand at me dismissively. "Not a chance. She was too busy following me around like a lost puppy. Besides, I made her account for every second of every day the entire time we were together." He shakes his head. "Nope, that little rugrat she's carrying is most definitely mine."

"I... uh... I had no idea," I say, sounding genuinely stunned. "What—I mean, how... Do you have any idea what you're going to do?"

He shakes his head. "I haven't decided yet," he says thoughtfully. "I just wish I'd known sooner. It's not like this hasn't happened before, but I've always been able to—you know—deal with it within a reasonable period of time."

"Huh..." is all I can think of to say. I had no idea my brother had ever gotten someone pregnant before. Probably best for the gene pool that there aren't a bunch of 'Mini Me' Jeremy's running around out there, wreaking havoc.

"But, then again, anything can happen, right?" he says with a shrug and a knowing smile.

"What is that supposed to mean?" I don't think I like where this is going. Surely he's not suggesting...

He shrugs. "Just that anything can happen between now and the time she has the brat. She might fall. She might be in a car accident, she might..."

"Stop it," I hiss at him more harshly than I'd intended.

I watch as my brother's eyes narrow with suspicion.

"Since when have you ever had a problem with *anything* I've done?"

"Since you started threatening to kill babies," I retort coldly.

In a heartbeat, he changes his entire affect, his face softening, his smile turning sheepish. "Aw, Brett, you know I'm just blowing off steam," he says, waving a dismissive hand at me. "You know I'd *never* hurt a pregnant woman."

Bullshit. He'd hurt anyone who got in the way of something he wanted. He knows it, and he knows that I know it.

"Nah, I'm just going to have a chat with Julia next week," he continues. "Rich was also considerate enough to track down her rehearsal schedule. Won't she be surprised when I show up at midnight!"

I make a mental note to get in touch with Julia. There's no way I can live with the possibility of Jeremy doing something to hurt her or her baby. I'll have to figure something out before he goes looking for her.

"Do you think that's a good idea?"

His shoulders rise in an affable shrug. "I don't see why not. I just want to talk with her. Is that so unusual? Tell me, Brett, wouldn't you want to know if *your* girlfriend was having your baby?"

The way he asks makes me wonder, for a split second, if he already knows about Maggie. No, not likely. I've been way too careful.

"I don't know," I say, feigning nonchalance. "I guess it depends on which girlfriend it was."

He throws back his head in a loud laugh as he smacks the table in front of him. "Well, you've got an excellent point there, bro," he says when he comes up for air.

But I don't respond, I'm already out the door, holding up a hand as a goodbye before he can suck me into another disturbing conversation.

Chapter 18

Maggie

When Mary Dancy tells me she's brought us some snacks for the train ride to Philly, I'm expecting a bag of gold-fish crackers and a cup of yogurt—maybe some gummy bears. Instead, she uses the table that separates our seats to set up a makeshift tapas bar. One by one, she opens containers filled with meats and cheeses, spreads and olives.

"Wow... Mary, I don't even eat this well when I go to a restaurant," I comment, shaking my head in wonder.

She smiles at me as we begin to munch. Across the aisle, Brett, Joe and the other two members of the Walton Quartet are in a huddle, discussing their itinerary for the rest of the weekend.

"I haven't been to Philadelphia since I was about ten-years-old," I tell her, popping a grape into my mouth. "My parents took my sister and me to see the Liberty Bell."

"Well, I've been there more times than I can count. It's been a regular tour stop for the Walton for the last twenty years."

"Do you always travel with them?"

She stacks a cracker with some salmon and capers and hands it across to me. I take it, trying to keep myself from licking my lips at the sight of it.

"I used to go along more when we were first married, but I got a little tired of hearing the same concerts in the same cities all the time, so I took a break. When Joe mentioned you'd be joining Brett on this trip, I thought it would be a good chance to get to know you. Also, I couldn't bear the idea of you on your own while the boys run off to their rehearsals, and sound checks, and whatnot."

"Oh, well, I'm glad you came." I force a smile, wondering when, exactly, I'm going to have time to get my own work done.

She puts a hand on my forearm. "I'm glad, too. I've been wanting to meet the girl who finally put a smile on Brett Corrigan's face!"

I feel myself blush a little. "Do you know him very well?" I ask.

"Oh, yes," she says as she fishes around in the bag again and comes up with a thermos of coffee and cups. "He was a regular substitute for the Walton even while he was a student at McInnes. I used to make up little care packages for him to take home after rehearsals. I don't think that boy eats very well."

"No," I agree, nibbling on my cracker. "He seems to think that a pizza will cover all of his nutritional needs."

She giggles as she fills one of the cups and slides it over to me. I take a grateful sip. "Well, he's been single for a while now," she explains.

I glance over at Brett. He's flipping through pages of music, intently following something Joe is pointing out. It's now or never, I decide. "Uh, Mary, can I talk to you about something?" I ask quietly.

She looks up from a chunk of Gruyere and meets my eyes.

"Yes, of course, Maggie. What's on your mind?"

"It's just that... well, Brett and I were at the farmer's market last weekend, and we ran into this girl. They both seemed surprised and uncomfortable, and he didn't want to say much about her. I'm thinking maybe she was an old girlfriend of his?" I leave the statement dangling as a question, in hopes that Mary will illuminate me. She doesn't disappoint.

"Huh. Well, you know, I can't say I've ever seen him with a girl more than once or twice. But, then again, I only know what I see at concerts and what Joe tells me, so I suppose it's possible. What did she look like?"

The woman's pretty freckled face pops into my mind. "She was small, petite with a slight build. Long red hair and light freckles on her face. Very pretty. I think her name might have been Julie..." I say, pretending I'm unsure about that last detail.

A light bulb seems to go off in Mary's frosted blonde head.

"Oh! Well, that sounds like Julia James. She's a cellist," she says.

"Yes! That's right, her name is *Julia*. And he did say they went to McInnes together."

Mary smiles, and nods, happy to have solved the mystery. After a moment, though, the smile slides from her face. "But, Maggie, Julia wasn't Brett's girlfriend, she was his brother's. She was with Jeremy for a while."

Jeremy, of course! I don't know why I hadn't considered that possibility. And why didn't Brett just say so instead of leaving it as a big mystery for me to obsess over?

"Well, I have to admit I was a little nervous. The girl must be about six months pregnant. And the way he looked so shocked when he saw her, I was starting to think maybe she was carrying his baby and he didn't know about it," I say with a little laugh.

But Mary doesn't seem to be amused by this at all. Her eyebrows have knit together, and she turns away from me to look out the window at the landscape as it whizzes by.

"Mary?"

Her head swivels back to me again. "Has Brett said much to you about Jeremy?"

I shake my head. "No, not too much. Why?"

She leans forward, so I'm able to hear her when she drops her voice. "Well, Julia was one of the Kreisler competitors. She came in second place to Jeremy after... after poor Cal Burridge died. You knew about that, didn't you?" I nod. "Joe is old friends with Julia's cello professor, Sam Michaels..." she begins tentatively. After a few seconds she continues. "Now, keep in mind that Sam is very fond of Julia. He's been teaching her since she was a child, he's like a father to her."

"Okay..."

"So, according to Sam, Jeremy was all about the romance in the beginning. He just swept Julia off her feet. But then, little by little, he started to change. He became nasty with her. He questioned everything she did, wanting her to account for every moment she was out of his sight."

"So, he was jealous?" I surmise, trying to figure out what she's getting at. So far, it just sounds like any other ugly relationship breakdown.

"No, it was more than that. Sam swears that Jeremy kept her from practicing for the Kreisler finals, and that he did his best to isolate her from him, and from her roommate, a young man named Matthew Ayers..."

"Oh," I cut in, "I know that name..."

"Yes, I'm sure you do. He's a violist, and he had Brett's job before Brett did."

"What? Wait, wait, wait, this is getting confusing..."

Mary holds up a hand. "I know. Just bear with me for a sec here. So, things get pretty bad between them, but Julia is determined to hang in there. And, when it comes time for her final recital, Jeremy is there with her, backstage, being sweet as pie. According to Sam, he got down on one knee, as if he was going to propose...only he didn't."

I can't take my eyes off of Mary as I hang on her every word. "What—what did he do?"

"He broke up with her right there, not five minutes before she was meant to perform. And he didn't just break up with her. He spewed all kinds of hateful things at the poor girl, telling her how he'd never loved her and how stupid and untalented she was. It was heartbreaking, really. Brought tears to my eyes when I heard about it. Julia James is the sweetest thing."

"What happened?" I ask breathlessly.

"Well, I wasn't there, but I understand she did manage to play, though I can't imagine how. In the end, though, it wasn't good enough to beat out Jeremy. He was awarded the gold and she got the silver."

"But why? Why would he do that to her? And how could he have chosen *that* moment?"

I hear myself ask the question, but somehow, I already know the answer. I already know this story—or at least, some variant of it. This behavior is textbook to someone in my profession.

Mary purses her lips for a moment and breathes in deep through her nose. It's as if she's trying to decide whether or not to tell me something. "Sam Michaels will go to his grave swearing that Jeremy set out to destroy Julia so she couldn't compete against him. I have a hard time believing someone could be that cunning—that hateful."

Oh, Mary, if you had any idea of what people are really capable of, you'd be horrified.

"At any rate," she continues, "I'm not sure what all happened after that exactly, but I do know that Matthew Ayers was very public with his suspicions about Jeremy being involved in Cal's death. It made Jeremy very angry. So angry, in fact, that Matthew decided it would be best if he resigned his position with the Walton and took Julia away someplace until things could blow over."

"Holy crap," I murmur.

Mary nods in agreement. "Exactly! So sordid, isn't it?"

My turn to nod. "So, that's how Brett got the spot with the Walton? His brother chased off the guy who had the job?" I don't like the words anymore than I like the thought that's in my head at this moment. Mary jumps in to quash both.

"Oh, Maggie, no. I can't say that I know Jeremy Corrigan at all, except by his reputation. But Brett, he's another story altogether. Brett is a good man and an exceptional musician. I've never even heard a whisper about him being anything but professional. But, as I mentioned earlier, he's never seemed to be especially happy. And I get the distinct impression that has something to do with Jeremy. Not that Brett would ever say a word against his brother. He just lives his life and lets Jeremy live his."

"Wow... So, this Matthew, he and Julia ran off together then?"

"Well, sort of, I suppose. He and Julia grew up together in foster care. They've been roommates for years since then, but any fool could see plain as day that he was in love with that girl. I'm sure it killed him to watch her with Jeremy."

"I'm sure he wanted to kill Jeremy after what he did to Julia," I murmur.

"I'm sure," she echoes. "All this is to say, Maggie, that I see a huge change in Brett, just in the weeks you've been seeing one another. He didn't seem to care about anything before. But now...well, you seem to be the *only* thing he cares about," she says with a nod toward Brett.

He's watching me from across the aisle, with a sweet smile on his face. Well, I seem to have most of the pieces to this puzzle. Now, I just have to start putting it together.

Chapter 19

Brett

"Okay, guys, I'll see you at the theater for sound check at six," Joe says as he and Mary head off to the hotel bar for a Bloody Mary.

Maggie and I check in and head up to our room for a rest. In the elevator, she leans into my side, and I lift my arm so she can snuggle in. "Thank you for inviting me here," she says quietly as we pass the fourth floor, then the fifth. "I'm really glad I decided to come."

"Me too," I say, trying not to sound surprised by this declaration. I am, in fact, thrilled that she agreed to join me on this trip. I couldn't take my eyes off of her the whole train ride.

The doors slide open on the twelfth floor, and we make our way down the long, orange-carpeted hallway to room 1205. After a few failed attempts, the keycard decides to allow us access to the room, and we step inside. The door to our room has barely closed when I feel her arms wrap around my waist from behind. When I turn around, she leans up, waiting for me to put my lips on hers.

"Wow, you're not wasting any time are you?" I mutter in between kisses.

"Can't help it," she murmurs breathlessly, "I've got a thing about hotel sex. I think it's the anonymity. It makes me really, really hot."

That's all I need to hear. Her getting hot has me getting hot, and we start to pull and tug at one another's clothing. Her blouse, my pants. Her bra, my shirt. I reach for my briefs, but she pushes my hands out of the way.

"Uh-uh," she says, sinking to the carpeted floor in nothing but her panties. She loops her index fingers into the elastic waistband and pulls my underwear down, freeing my newly minted erection. She smiles up at me lasciviously and, without warning, takes me in her mouth.

"Jeeeesus..." I breathe out as her moist warmth envelops me.

My sweet Maggie is surprisingly good at the oral arts, using just the right combination of suction and teeth. When I feel her cup my testicles in her hands I groan loudly, and my head falls back on my neck.

"Oh, Maggie, Maggie," I moan as I reach forward and run my hands through those soft, black curls. I can't believe how confidant she is, taking me deeper and deeper into her mouth until I feel as if I'm about to...

"Wait!" I say, putting a hand to her head to still her. "Wait, Maggie!"

She stops what she's doing and looks up at me in confusion. "Brett, what's wrong? Did I hurt you?"

I almost laugh. "What? Hurt me? No, that's the best thing I've felt in a long, long time."

"So, why are we stopping?"

"We're not stopping." I smile down at her.

Before she can say another word I bend down and scoop her up from the floor, depositing her on the edge of the bed.

"Brett..." she starts to say something, but I put my index finger to her lips and shake my head no. She nods and I push her back on the bed so that her legs are dangling over the foot. Sitting on the floor between them, I reach up and slowly peel the panties from her body, down her legs and off. I put them to my face.

"My, my, these are some very wet panties, Maggie," I murmur wickedly. She tries to sit up, but I gently push her down again. Then putting one hand on the inside of each of her thighs, I spread her legs apart widely. Before she can protest I am on her, kissing her thighs, inhaling her sweet, musky scent and finally, I put my tongue to her, snaking upward from bottom to top.

"Oh... oh... Brett..."

I can hear her but I'm too busy concentrating on what I'm doing to reply. I repeat the action, stopping just short of her clitoris. Twice more like that and she is whimpering.

"Oh, please. Please, Brett..." she moans. That's all I need to hear. With my tongue I start to slowly nudge her from side to side. Just enough for the sensation but not enough sustained contact for anything else. She starts to wriggle under me, trying to guide me to her again and again. But I hold her spread wide and firmly affixed to the bed. I am going to prolong her sweet agony as long as I can.

"Now, please, now!" she is begging so pitifully I can't resist. I start a direct contact assault on her, swirling my tongue around and around in a firm, circular motion.

"Oh... God... Brett, I'm so close..."

I stop and, in one fluid motion, I drape her ankles over my shoulders and align my rock hard cock with her entrance. She gasps when I slam hard into her. I can see her perfectly now as I look down on her beautiful body—her hair fanned out across the bed. I start stroking, in and out, in and out until she is moaning again. I take her feet off of my shoulders and pull them wide apart as I literally fall onto her on the bed.

She snakes her legs around my waist, pulling me as close to her as I can possibly get. Her head cranes up so her lips can meet mine halfway. I'm kissing her, all the while building up speed. She's moaning into my mouth and it's the sexiest fucking thing I've ever felt. I can't hold back anymore. I drive in and out more frantically until her nails are clawing at my back.

"Ahh... Brett... Brett..."

I can't even grunt at this point, let alone utter her name. When I feel her muscles starting to contract around me it's all the encouragement I need. In a matter of seconds we are one sweaty, tangled, panting mass of flesh on the bed. I don't move, kissing her gently. First her mouth, then below her ear. Then I make my way to her neck. She sighs contentedly under me until I finally pull out and off of her, rolling onto my back next to her.

"I really wish you'd said something about the hotel sex sooner. I'd have moved into the Marriott down the street after our first date. We could've been having a real good time," I tease.

"Excuse me," she says, propping herself up on her elbow. "I thought we *were* having a good old time!"

I roll over on top of her and dig my fingers into her sides until she is laughing and screaming uncontrollably.

"Stop!" she begs breathlessly. "Brett! Stop, stop, stop!"

I finally do and she smacks me hard across the chest. "You're awful!" she squeals at me.

"Well, you didn't seem to think I was so awful a few minutes ago!"

She grabs my face in her hand and pulls me closer to her for a long, slow, deep kiss. When we're done, she doesn't let go. She keeps one hand on my cheek while the other brushes the hair from my forehead. For me, this is even more intimate than the sex. I can't take my eyes off this beautiful woman.

"Maggie, I... you really make me happy. I can't remember the last time I felt this way." I say the words before I can think about it. Before I can waffle about it or ponder it or evaluate it. For the first time, in as long as I can remember, I have indulged in a definitive action in response to a specific emotion. And it feels good.

She smiles and continues to stroke my forehead, never taking her eyes from mine.

"I know, me too. This is nice."

She rolls over and nestles into the crook of my arm and I rest my chin on the top of her head, breathing in her sweet, lilac scent. We're quiet for a minute. So quiet, that I can hear the beat of my heart in my ears.

"Brett, tell me about Julia and your brother," she says, breaking the silence

I never knew your heart could really, literally, skip a beat. I thought that was just something that people said. Now I know better. I don't know how to respond, but it doesn't matter, because she just continues.

"It wasn't hard to see that you were surprised to see one another. And not pleasantly surprised, either."

Shit.

"I'm right aren't I?" she presses. "She was startled to see you."

I take a deep breath. "She was. I was. We were both startled," I begin. "She and Jeremy had a bad breakup."

"I know," she says, looking up at me.

"You do?"

"Yeah, Mary gave me some of the details."

Mary? *Really?* Is there anyone who doesn't know about the shit that goes on in my apartment?

"Huh," is all I can manage to say.

She continues quietly. "She told me some really ugly things. Rumors, really, because she only knows what Joe told her."

"Mags, I really don't want to do this right now."

"Do what?"

"My brother is a conversation we should have at home, over drinks. I've said it before, he's a complicated guy."

"Did he really break up with her right before she went on stage?" The question is just a question, thankfully, not an accusation.

"Jeremy and Julia should have never been together," I start, choosing my words carefully. "They were competitors in something with really high stakes. He could have been kinder, yes. But she should have had her eyes open. Maggie, it was just bad all around. I wish it had been different, but it wasn't."

She seems to consider this for a long moment. "And the baby?"

"She's married. To a guy named Matthew Ayers. It's their baby." I don't hesitate in repeating Julia's lie, as I promised her I would. "He's a good guy. She's much better off with him than she ever was with my brother."

"Okay," she says simply, returning her head to my chest.

"Okay?" The one word comes out sounding more surprised than I intended.

"Okay," she repeats. "It's your brother's mess. Let's try and stay out of it. Sound like a plan?"

Thank. You. Jesus.

"Yes," I say. "Yes, I think that's a really good idea."

Chapter 20

Maggie

I had no idea. It's not as if I dislike classical music, I just haven't spent much time listening to it. But now, here, tonight in this concert hall, I've been transported. In an instant, I'm swept away by this quartet of Haydn, so appropriately nicknamed *The Sunrise Quartet*. I can actually hear the brightening dawn as the first violin rises above the others. Then they swell beneath it and, suddenly, they're off on a sprint. All throughout, the two violins work in tandem, one lower than the other. And the cello, with its rich bass sound, provides the foundation for them. It takes a bit of careful listening and concentration, but after a few minutes, I'm able to discern the deep, throaty sound of the viola. Once I do, it's all I can hear. And Brett is all I can see.

I can't believe how different he looks when he plays. Brett is perched on the very edge of his chair, viola under his chin, bow gliding across it in his right hand. The music is in front of him, but he rarely looks down at it. Instead, his eyes are on Joe. And Philip. And Neville. He watches the movements of the other members of the quartet and adjusts himself accordingly. Louder, softer, faster, slower. And, every once in a while, I see him close his eyes. When he does this, his body rocks slightly, forward and back, as if the music itself is moving him.

When they finish, there's a long moment of silence. Finally, they put their instruments down and all around me there is an eruption of applause. I jump to my feet and clap as hard as I can, beaming with joy over the music I've just heard and pride for the man I heard playing it. It goes on like this for two more pieces and an encore, until the quartet finally goes backstage for the last time.

"Maggie!" Brett calls out when he sees me. His hands are full with the viola and its bow, but he holds his arms up high so I can come into them.

"Brett, that was... it was so beautiful!" I exclaim, arms wrapped around his chest, face tilted up towards his beaming smile.

"I'm so glad you came! I really wanted you to experience this with me. It's such a rush!" he says emphatically.

"Hey there, Maggie!" Joe calls out. "What'd you think?"

"Oh, Joe! I had no idea I was going to enjoy it as much as I did. The four of you are such a great team," I say to him as I extricate myself from Brett.

"Yeah, well, your boy makes a great addition," he tells me with a chin nod toward Brett. "Say, are you two going to join us at McNulty's for a late dinner? We always go there when we're in town. The sea bass is out of this world!"

I look at Brett and I can see he'd rather we were alone. "You know, Joe, I think we're going to pass if you don't mind. I'd like to have this guy all to myself tonight."

Joe gives us smile and a wink. "Ah, young love! You remember when we were like that?" he asks his wife just as she walks up to join the conversation. Mary plants a kiss on his cheek.

"Oh, I don't know, Joe, I think we're *still* like that. They just have more stamina than we do," she chuckles.

"Okay," I interrupt, before this conversation can take an awkwardly intimate turn, "I'm going to wait for you outside if you don't mind. It's such a beautiful night."

Brett nods. "Good idea. I just need to pack up and change out of this tux. Meet you by the stage entrance in ten minutes?"

I nod and give the rest of them a wave goodbye before making my way out of the concert hall. I'm surprised to find there's still a little daylight when I step outside at close to nine o'clock. It's balmy, too, and I'm immediately struck by a wall of humidity. After a moment, I notice a young woman hovering close by. Tall and thin, with dark hair cut short and blunt, she's clearly waiting for something—or someone —to emerge from the stage door.

She's wearing a long and shapeless black dress that must be uncomfortably warm in this weather. The haircut and the dress project onto her a harshness usually reserved for much older women. As I amble closer, I get the distinct feeling she's in some kind of distress.

"Hi," I say, offering her a friendly smile. She nods a hello but doesn't speak. Yes, there's something that's definitely off with her. "Are you waiting for someone?" I ask her, edging a little closer.

She nods but doesn't speak.

"Forgive me for being nosy, but are you alright?" I ask quietly. "Do you want to come into the theater and sit down for a second?"

"No," she says, shaking her head and looking alarmed at the suggestion.

"My name is Maggie," I offer, expecting her name in return. I get a question instead.

"Are you here with Brett Corrigan?" she asks. "I saw you with him before."

Aha! Maybe she's one of his fans. Does that happen? Do viola players have groupies?

"I am," I confirm. "Do you know him?"

She swallows hard and nods.

"He'll be out in just a second, if you want to wait for him..."

I can't even get the sentence out before Brett comes barreling out of the stage entrance, viola hanging over his shoulder, smile on his face.

"Damn! Now *that* was the shit," he says exuberantly. "Did you feel the electricity, Maggie? We were so..." he stops when he realizes I'm not alone. The smile on his face is replaced with a look of confusion.

"Hi," he says jovially, walking up and draping an arm over my shoulder. "I'm sorry, do I know you?" he asks the girl. "You look so familiar."

She nods, and is about to say something, but he holds up a finger.

"No, wait, let me see if I can figure it out," he says, turning it into a game.

"Have we played together somewhere? Are you a musician?"

"I used to be," she says quietly.

"Ah. Gave it up, did you?"

"Not by choice."

Now, that's a strange thing to say. It sends up a red flag for me.

"McInnes, then?" he tries, making another guess. "Do I know you from the conservatory?" She gives him a small, tight smile and a nod. "I knew it!" he says, proud of his deductive skills. "Don't tell me," he says, closing his eyes, as if trying to envision her somewhere else. "You are...Laurie! Laurie Daughtry, right?"

The girl nods, the expression on her face frozen in place.

"Wow! You've really changed your look, huh?" Now he turns toward me. "Laurie and Jeremy used to date," he explains to me before returning to her. "Jeez! It's been what? At least four or five years, hasn't it?"

"Four years, four months," she says.

Okay. There's red flag number two. People don't normally keep track of time that closely unless they're counting the days and hours since something has happened. But Brett isn't picking up on any of this. He's still flying high on his performance, and it's keeping him from realizing that something's not right here.

"So, what have you been up to?" he asks, obviously happy to take a stroll down memory lane with her.

"Not much," she replies slowly, glancing down at her feet periodically. "I moved back home with my parents. I have a part-time job in the music library at Penn State."

"And you said you're not playing anymore?" he asks with disappointed surprise. "You were such a phenomenal flutist. I was so sure you'd be playing with a major orchestra before you even finished your degree."

"No, I don't play anymore," she repeats for him, this time sounding a little annoyed.

"That's a shame, I'm sorry to hear it. Was it a medical thing?"

She tilts her head to the side and knits her brows together as if she's trying to work something out. And *that* is red flag number three. I grab Brett's hand in my own and give it a hard squeeze, hoping he'll get the hint. He doesn't. He just squeezes back as he waits for her to answer his question.

"Brett, do you remember the last time we saw one another?" she asks.

He seems to think for a second and then starts to nod, slowly. "Yeah. The night you and Jeremy had that big fight. The night you broke up."

She forms her lips as if she is going to say something but then stops cold. He stiffens a little next to me and I can tell he's starting to pick up on the fact that this woman isn't the girl he used to know.

"I'm sorry, did I get that wrong?" Brett asks. "Have I seen you since then and I just don't remember?"

She shakes her head at him, incredulously. "It was Thursday, April 24th. 7:30pm. The last thing I said to you was *'Please, help me, Brett.'* The last thing you said to me was *'Sorry Laurie, this is where I get off.'* The last time you saw me, your brother was dragging me to his bedroom, kicking and screaming. The last time I saw you, you were picking up your keys and walking out the door of your apartment. There wasn't any fight, Brett. Jeremy and I had already broken up. I just came to get my stuff."

Wait, wait, wait...

"You don't remember, do you?" she asks, without a trace of surprise in her voice.

"I—I'm sorry, Laurie, it's just that it was so long ago..." Brett offers weakly, not sure what she's getting at.

"I wish I could forget it so easily, Brett. But I remember every single second of it."

"Okay..." he starts. I'm not sure what he's going to say to try and placate this woman who's growing more agitated by the second, but it doesn't matter, because she jumps right back in again.

"After you left, he dragged me into his room, threw me down on the bed and ripped my clothes off. I struggled and he broke my jaw. Ringing any bells yet, Brett?" We're both staring at her now, mouths agape. "No? Well, after that he proceeded to rape me. And beat me. For two hours, Brett. Two hours. I *wish* it was all a blur," she repeats.

Oh, my dear good God. Either this girl is nuts or Jeremy is... Christ, I can't even finish the thought.

"He put me in a cab and sent me to the ER alone. He threatened to hurt my family if I told anyone, so I just pretended that I fell down the stairs. The doctors were smarter than that. They knew something else had happened, but I wasn't going to say a word. I denied I'd been sexually assaulted even though his fingers actually left bruises all over my body. It was obvious to anyone with eyes what had happened to me. They sent in female detectives and a rape crisis counselor. My parents came all the way from Philly and still I wouldn't admit I was raped. Do you know how banged up I was, Brett?"

Brett's hand has gone clammy in mine. He's not really holding it anymore—I'm the one clutching him, afraid of what will happen if I let go.

"Broken jaw. Five teeth knocked right out of my head. Fractured arm from where he twisted it, three broken ribs from where he punched me in the gut. A concussion from when he slammed my head against the headboard while he was raping me. Any of *that* jarring the memories loose?"

He doesn't respond, and she shakes her head at him, disgustedly.

"I couldn't play flute after that. You need teeth to play flute, you see, and a denture kind of gets in the way. And even if I could have worked around that, my jaw was never the same again. So my career was over before it ever started. Not that I ever wanted to play again."

"Laurie," Brett says softly, "I'm... sorry. I'm so sorry that happened to you..."

An angry cloud crosses her face, and the disgust turns to unmistakable rage. For a split second I think she's going to attack him, and I prepare myself to intervene if necessary.

"You should be sorry, you son of a bitch! But you aren't, are you?" she spits. "Are you?" she repeats louder when he doesn't reply.

"Okay," I say quietly, trying to be the voice of reason. "Obviously there's some history here. Laurie, why don't you come with Brett and me back to our hotel? We can sit down, and you can tell him exactly what this is all about—"

"Laurie, I don't know what you want me to say," Brett cuts me off. "I had no idea," he continues. "I didn't know that he was going to do that to you. I didn't know that he *did* do that to you. Jeremy doesn't exactly keep me in the loop on his relationships..."

"Relationships? Are you out of your fucking mind, Brett? Tell me, what exactly do you remember about that night?"

"I—I remember Jeremy telling me that you were coming over to get some of your things. I remember you coming, and the two of you arguing. That's when I stepped out. It was awkward and I didn't want to get in the way."

She just shakes her head. I can see the anger starting to drain from her face, replaced by something even more disturbing. "Wow. Absolutely amazing," she murmurs.

"What's that?"

"Your capacity to rewrite history, so you don't have to face the truth."

"Hey, hold on just a second, Laurie," he pushes back. "I think you need to be having this discussion with Jeremy."

Shit. He's sounding more irritated now. And that won't help.

"You!"

"Me what?"

"*You* did this to me!"

In her tone the five words are a supreme accusation.

"What the fuck, Laurie?" Brett demands, throwing his hands up in frustration.

She raises her index finger and points it at him, as if she's leveling a curse upon him and his entire bloodline. "You did this to me, Brett Corrigan. You could have saved me, but you didn't. And I want you to remember that every day for as long as you live."

"Hey, Laurie," I try again softly, stepping in between them so she has no choice but to look at me. "How about if you and I go somewhere alone, just us girls? We can go someplace quiet, maybe get a bite and you can tell me all about what happened to you. I think maybe you need someone to tell your story to and I'm a really good listener..."

She seems to consider it for a split second, but then the moment is gone. She shakes her head violently and stares past me to Brett. "You did this to me," she says, pointing at him one last time before she turns and starts to walk away.

"Laurie!" I call after her. "Laurie? Please come back. Please don't leave like this..."

Brett puts a shaky hand on my shoulder. "Just let her go, Mags," he says quietly. "It's just my fucking brother's mistakes coming back to haunt me. Again."

Chapter 21

Brett

I feel as if I've been hit by a truck. Again. This run-in with Laurie Daughtry has rattled me to my core and—what I find most disturbing—is that I can't really explain why. She was Jeremy's girlfriend. They were the ones who had the bad breakup. How did I become the focus of all her rage? And, my God, is it possible he did everything she's saying he did to her? Just the thought of it brings the taste of bile to my mouth.

We leave the hall and head back to the hotel, neither of us in the mood for a night on the town anymore. No late dinner, no cocktails. No set at the Jazz club on Sansom Street.

This time, we're not all over each other when we get to our room. Instead, I'm all over the minibar. I hold up a small bottle of vodka, but Maggie shakes her head no. I unscrew the tiny top, tip the bottle back to my lips and gulp. When I'm done, I reach for another. After a third shot, I take a seat next to her on the edge of the bed.

"Well, that was a little scary," I comment.

"Sure was. Are you okay?"

I nod, looking down at my hands in my lap. And then her warm, soft hand is on top of mine, her thumb stroking my fingers gently. She leans into me, resting her head on my arm.

"Brett," she begins quietly, "what she said about Jeremy—about what he did to her—was any of that true?"

"It's not how I remember it, Mags. But... I don't know what my brother did after I left that apartment."

It's hard, telling this woman that she's involved with a guy whose brother is a total douchebag. Maybe even a rapist.

"Clearly, that girl is troubled. I don't know what happened between her and your brother, but you can't be held responsible for every shitty thing Jeremy does. Listen, why don't you go take a nice hot shower? I'll order some room service for us. Okay?"

"Yeah, that sounds good," I agree, but I don't move.

"Come on, let's go," she says after a few moments, standing up and pulling me with her by the hand.

When I'm up on my feet, she leads me to the bathroom, letting go just long enough to start the water running. Then she turns around and starts to undress me. She's very gentle as she helps me out of my clothes.

"Okay, hop in there, you," she says with a gentle slap to my naked ass. "Oh, here, wash your hair, too. You're all sweaty from those stage lights."

I take the miniaturized bottle of shampoo she's holding out for me, and step into the steamy shower, giving a long, involuntary sigh as the hot water hits my chest and legs. I duck my head underneath the spray, allowing it to rain down on my head until my hair is saturated, then I pour the shampoo into the palm of my hand and start to lather. It feels good, scrubbing my scalp until I have a full head of soapy froth.

When the image pops into my head, I nearly lose my footing and fall out of the shower. In a flash I can see it, hair the color of corn silk —Laurie's hair. Jeremy is holding it. No. Jeremy is *grabbing* it. He's pulling it—pulling her to his bedroom by her hair.

The weight with which this memory hits me is so oppressive, that I feel physically unable to support it. I have to slide down into a sitting position in the tub, under the shower, streams of soapy shampoo running down my face, stinging my eyes and clogging my ears. I spit from the taste, and it burns my tongue.

She didn't tell me that part when she saw me tonight, but now it plays out in my head like a movie. I'm about to go to a rehearsal. Jeremy and Laurie are in the kitchen, fighting. No. She's silent as he's calling her a whore. She turns to leave, but he grabs her hair. The long, silky strands are wrapped in and around his fingertips and his knuckles. When he yanks, her knees buckle under her. Tears start to run down her face, and he is talking. He never fucking shuts up! He is telling her what a bitch she is. That no bitch is going to make him look bad. He drags her into the hallway and past where I'm standing. She looks at me.

"Help me," she pleads. *"Help me, Brett!"* Jeremy looks at me with that snide little smile of his.

I gasp out loud with the force of the recollection, realizing that it's just as she described it to me. Suddenly, my eyes are open, and I'm scrambling to get out of the tub, slipping and clawing at the shower curtain in my desperation to get out. When I finally manage to extricate myself, I grab a towel and run to the bed, sitting on the edge and looking back at the bathroom as if it were a chamber of horrors. Steam from the still-running shower billows out into the room.

"Brett? Brett! What is it? What's going on?" Maggie's voice is filled with alarm.

I'm trembling when she comes to squat down in front of me, her deep, concerned eyes trying to lock onto mine as they move wildly around the room. She gets up again, going into the bathroom from which I've just escaped. I hear her turn off the water and she returns to my side with another fluffy white towel. She doesn't speak as she dries each part of my body carefully. When she's finished, she pulls out some underwear and sweats for me to put on. I allow her to help me dress, just as I allowed her to help me undress not twenty minutes ago. I'm just getting a t-shirt over my head when there's knock at the door.

"Room Service!" comes a muffled voice from the hallway.

Maggie opens the door, and a young man rolls in a cart with a tray on it. She has him set the food on the desk and signs for the bill. When he's gone, she turns back to me.

"Alright. Now, tell me what happened in there."

I open my mouth to tell her that it was nothing, but then, the words just start to tumble out.

"I started to remember it, to remember Laurie that night. She broke up with him and he was so furious that all he wanted to do was get even with her."

It takes Maggie a second to switch gears and focus on what I'm telling her. "Get even how?" she asks slowly.

"I don't know," I say, shaking my head.

"Brett, how can you *not* know?"

I lick my lips and try to think of a way to say this that doesn't make me sound like the bastard that I am. "Because I left the apartment."

"Right. Before they started to fight," she says, parroting the version of events that I gave her earlier. I shake my head now.

"So... you were there when Laurie arrived... and then you left?"

"Yes."

"Was she..." Maggie closes her eyes for just a moment, as if steeling herself to ask the question. "Was she in trouble when you left, Brett?"

I take a deep breath. "I—I didn't think so at the time, but now I know she was, yes."

"When she said, *'You could have saved me'*, is that what she was talking about? That you *literally* could have saved her? Why would she say that to you?"

"Because she asked me for help, and I left her there alone with him anyway."

Maggie's eyes have grown as wide as saucers, and I don't think she's blinked in close to a minute. "So your brother actually did that to her? He beat her? He...raped her?" Her question comes out as barely a whisper.

I can't look at her face anymore, so I look down at the ugly green hotel carpet. "I left, so I can't say for sure..."

"Yes. You. Can," she says firmly.

My eyes return to hers and I see considerably less compassion in them than there was just a few moments ago. "I think he did, yes."

"And she... she asked you to help her?" she confirms what I have already told her, hoping, I'm sure, that the answer will be different this time. That, somehow, she has misunderstood me.

I nod. She's about to say one thing, when, clearly, something else occurs to her.

"Julia?"

"What about her?" I ask, confused by the sudden change in topic.

"Brett, that girl was terrified when she saw you. That wasn't surprise on her face, it was fear. Why would she be afraid of you?"

My stomach is heaving now, and I have to choke back the urge to vomit. "Because she's afraid of Jeremy."

"Why? Did he rape her, too?" Maggie asks, her voice flooding with alarm.

"No!" I say sharply. "No, I—I mean I don't think so..."

The truth is I don't really know what the hell he did to her behind closed doors. But I do know what he did to her out in the open. Maggie senses there's more to this and presses me further.

"Brett, was there a point when Julia asked you for help, too?"

"No."

"Did Jeremy hurt her?"

"Yes, he hit her on New Year's Eve."

"And you saw him do it?"

I can't say the word, so I just nod.

"And you didn't help her?"

Long, awkward pause here. Laurie commented on my capacity to rewrite history so I wouldn't have to face the truth. I can't rewrite this. Not for Maggie.

"No," I say at last.

Jesus Christ. What have I done?

Chapter 22

Maggie

"Okay, okay," I say, putting my palm to my forehead. "Let's walk this back. What, exactly, did you see?"

He clears his throat.

"Julia was angry and upset because he'd treated her badly while they were out. He flirted with a waitress and left her to pay the bill and the cab fare. When they got back to our apartment, she confronted him about it and he punched her in the face, right there in the kitchen. She hit the floor," he says so softly that I can barely hear him.

I take a deep breath before I ask the next question. The question I don't want to ask. The question that I can't *not* ask.

"What did you do?" I rise from my squatting position to pull the desk chair over so I can sit, facing him where he's sitting on the edge of the bed.

I'm expecting to hear that he beat the shit out of his brother, or called the police, or at least helped the poor girl to get up off the floor. But I don't hear any of those things.

"I sat on the couch with Jeremy. We were watching TV and drinking wine."

I blink hard. "Brett, please tell me you're kidding." He doesn't say anything, but it doesn't matter, because something else pops into my aching head. "And the baby?" The words come out so softly they're almost a whisper.

"It's his. I'm sure of it. But she wants everyone to think it's Matthew's baby."

"When we ran into her at the farmer's market, she knew you'd see her and do the math. She knew you'd realize that she was having your brother's baby."

"Yes," he agrees, looking miserable as he nods. "She was terrified I'd tell Jeremy because she knows he'd never let her have it."

"Well, she's got to be in her third trimester. It's not like he could pressure her into an abortion at this point, even if he did know," I mutter.

Brett focuses on me now, really focuses. He wants me to hear this. "It wouldn't matter to him," he says.

I feel my eyebrows draw together in confusion. "You mean he'd want to take the baby from her?" I try to clarify.

"No. Yes. I mean…" he takes a deep breath and finally spits it out. "He would never let her carry it to term. Not even at this stage of her pregnancy."

"You're saying that he literally would not allow her to give birth? That he'd do something to make her *lose* the baby? Is *that* what you're telling me, Brett?" He can only nod silently. "Holy mother of God," I murmur under my breath.

I cannot believe what I'm hearing. I've fallen for a man whose brother is a suspected killer, a likely rapist and a would-be baby slayer. I can't even tell which emotion I'm experiencing at this moment. I feel badly for this pathetic soul sitting in front of me. I'm frightened by everything I've learned about Jeremy Corrigan in the last twenty-four hours. I'm furious that Brett has allowed this to go on for…

"How long has this been going on?" I ask him suddenly. "Has your brother always been like this—done things like this?"

"Maggie, I know how bad this sounds. But, it's more complicated than you think. It's a fucked-up situation, I know, but you have to understand my brother..."

"I do understand your brother," I say in a tone that is far icier than even I expected to hear coming from my mouth. "From what you've told me, his motives are crystal clear. It's *you*, Brett, who I don't understand. How could you—how could anyone with a beating heart—walk out on someone in trouble? Laurie wasn't just in trouble, Brett. She was in danger. So what did you do?"

"Nothing," he whispers.

"That's right," I agree. "Not a damn thing. You looked the other way. You walked out the door. You could have saved her, but you chose not to."

"But I'm not the one who..." he begins some pathetic self-defense.

"What?" I hiss at him suddenly, my change in tone so abrupt that it makes him jump. "You're not the one who beat her and raped her? Is that what you were going to say?"

Another silent, sullen nod from him.

"Okay, let me ask you this—if that guy who just brought our food came in here right now and told you to go take a walk around the block so he could rape me, what would you do, Brett? Just get up and walk away and put it out of your mind?"

"Of course not!" he protests, getting to his feet now. "Maggie, that's not fair..."

"Why isn't it fair?" I counter calmly as he grows more agitated. "It's what happened isn't it? It's just that it happened to Laurie, not to me. And it was your brother, instead of some stranger off the street."

He opens his mouth to say something, but it's clear that he doesn't have any words. Because there are no words to justify that kind of apathy.

"Who are you?" I ask incredulously, getting back up so we are standing face to face. "I mean, I sure as hell don't have any idea. Do *you* even know who you are, Brett?"

"No," he says at last, shaking his head slowly.

I close my eyes and take a deep breath. There is only one thing for me to do at this point. "Okay, you know what? I need to go," I say calmly.

"What? Where?"

"Home," I say, getting up and pulling my roller bag out of the closet.

"Are you...are you breaking up with me?" he asks pathetically.

I look at him for a long moment. He's like a confused little boy. "I don't know."

Chapter 23

Brett

I walk and I walk, block after city block. I pass by stores, shuttered and barred and chained—locked up tight against the creatures of the night. The amber colored streetlights illuminate the asphalt roads, appearing to give them a glossy sheen. All around me, memorials and statues, and other mementos of our great American history stand in half shadow, seeming larger than life as they rise up out of the ground.

I'm not sure how long I've been gone, or how far I have travelled, but it's already light by the time I find my way back to the hotel around the corner from the concert hall. I'm in a daze as a doorman holds the door for me. I can see by the way he looks me up and down that he's considering asking me if I'm a guest here. That's when Joe Dancy spots me from across the lobby.

"Brett!" he calls out. I look up at him with unrecognizing eyes as he jogs over to where I'm standing. "Brett? What's up, man? Are you okay?"

I force myself to focus on him and nod. "Yeah, I couldn't sleep so I've been walking," I mumble as I start to move past him, but he gently takes my forearm and stops me.

"Brett, I heard that Maggie went home. I'm sorry. Come on with me, we'll have some coffee and talk about it. Or not. Whatever you want..."

I shake my head. "No, thanks, Joe, I can't. I just want to go back to my room and lie down."

"Okay, but I really think you should..."

Something behind him catches my eye. There's a TV on in the now deserted bar area, it's broadcasting a local news channel. I shake Joe's concerned hand from my arm and walk toward the screen. At ten feet I can confirm that I'm looking at a picture of her. At five feet in front of the large flat screen, I can hear what the news anchor is saying about her.

"...has been identified as a North Philadelphia resident. Authorities say that Laurie Ann Daughtry's car was found parked at the base of the Henry Avenue Bridge, her purse and keys still inside. Again, the Bridge and adjoining ramps are closed until further notice as police investigate what they are calling an apparent suicide. In the weather today, another scorcher..."

When I turn back around, Joe is looking from the screen to me and back again. "You know her?" he asks, quietly.

I shake my head. "No," I whisper. "But I should have."

"We have a *realllllly* sweet convertible," says the woman whose name badge reads Christine. She's looking up at me from her computer screen with a wide, pink smile. "I can get you into that for just thirty-dollars a day more...plus insurance..."

"No, thanks. The sedan is fine," I tell her, repeating the same answer I gave her when she offered me the minivan and the Town Car.

Her eyebrows shoot up in a 'suit yourself' gesture. "Now, we usually offer GPS for ten-dollars a day, but I can get it down to eight for you..."

I don't need a GPS because I don't even know where I'm going. "Just the car. Please," I say through gritted teeth.

"How about satellite radio? That's just five-dollars..."

Before I can stop myself, my arms are down on the high counter, my head resting on them.

"Please," I say softly from underneath my forehead. "*Please*, just give me the car..." My intention was to sound irritated, but it only comes out sounding pathetic, like I'm on the verge of tears. Which I think I just might be.

I feel a warm hand on my arm. It pats me gently until I look up at Christine. She's probably about my mother's age. She considers me for a long moment before turning back to her computer and entering a few keystrokes. When she's done, she picks up the walkie-talkie on the counter and presses the button on its side.

"Kato, would you please bring around..." She looks at the screen again. "Spot two-thirty-five."

"It'll be ready in five," the disembodied voice of Kato crackles in reply.

Christine folds several papers and slips them into a folio, which she hands to me. I mumble an embarrassed thanks to her, but before I can pull away, she rests a perfectly manicured hand on my wrist and leans forward across the counter so we're only inches apart.

"Listen to me," she says quietly, so the people on line behind me won't hear her. "Sweetie, you look like you just got your heart put through a paper shredder. You be careful out there on the road tonight. Okay? No one's worth wrapping yourself around a tree for. Understand?"

I nod dumbly and she sits back, adjusting her blazer and pasting the plastic smile back onto her face.

"Thank you for choosing Happy Trails Car Rentals, Mr. Corrigan. Just go through the double doors to your left and the car will be brought around for you.

I nod my understanding.

"May I have the next customer, please?" she says, looking over my shoulder at someone behind me. I take my cue and leave.

I'm waiting at the curb for a few minutes when a bright, metallic blue Mustang convertible pulls up. A young guy with a ponytail hops out from behind the wheel. He looks down at the tablet in his hand and taps it a few times.

"Okay, why don't you take a look around the car to make sure you don't see any damage that I might have missed? We're looking for scratches and dents bigger than a quarter—"

"Wait, wait, wait," I cut him off, waving my hands. "I'm supposed to have a midsized sedan."

Kato looks back at his screen. He swipes, taps and swipes again. "Are you Mr. Corrigan?" he asks.

"Yeah..."

"Then this baby's all yours!"

"But, I didn't..." I start to protest, glancing over my shoulder through the glass doors and back to the counter I've just left.

Christine turns her head slightly and I'm able to catch her eye. I raise my hands in a *'what's up with this?'* gesture. She winks and turns her attention back to the gentleman in front of her, showing him the ten-dollar-a-day GPS.

As I pull out of the airport and onto the highway, I think about the summer of my sixteenth birthday. I spent long days working in my dad's garage trying to earn some extra money... not for a car, like most kids my age, but for a new viola. I knew I'd be doing conservatory auditions and I knew I'd have to show up with something more impressive than a student instrument.

"Brett, come on out and help me with this..." my father had called to me from outside the garage. I found him underneath the hood of a battered 1965 Mustang convertible.

"Jeez, this thing looks like it's been put through the wringer," I commented with a low whistle as I walked around the rusting body.

"Yeah, well, it's just cosmetic, son. This little lady has an engine that runs like a top."

I doubted that. No way something this beat-up could be mechanically sound. Still, my father and I spent weeks restoring every square inch of the thing. By the time the summer was over, it had been transformed into a candy apple red wet dream on wheels.

"How much you gonna ask for it?" I wondered one evening as we admired our handiwork.

"Oh, it's already got an owner," my father said just before he reached into the pocket of his coveralls and tossed the keys at me.

I caught them and looked at him in confusion "I don't understand..."

"It's for you, son. It was yours from the day they towed her in here."

I couldn't believe what I was hearing. I must have looked ridiculous with my mouth open because my father gave his easy laugh and punched my shoulder. "You've earned it, Brett."

"But... what about..." I left the sentence hanging, but he knew what I was asking.

"Jeremy is too young to drive. Besides, he had the same opportunity to work here this summer, but he decided it was beneath him. If he wants a car when the time comes, he'll have to figure it out for himself. We reap what we sow in this family, Son."

Now, as my hair is blown back by the cool evening wind, the lights of the Philadelphia skyline fill my rearview mirror. I spot the sign for I-76, and I exit westbound.

They say you can't outrun your past, no matter how fast you go. I press on the gas pedal a little harder anyway. Time to find out if the past can outrun me.

Chapter 24

Maggie

The picture online looks nothing like the girl I saw in Philadelphia. Here, in the New York Herald, she has long, shiny hair, the color of spun gold. Her smile is infectious, showing off her perfect white teeth and offsetting the rosy color of her cheeks. She is, quite simply, stunning. The caption under the picture reads *"Laurie Daughtry, McInnes Conservatory student."* This picture must be close to five years old.

I think about her choppy black hair, and how painfully thin and pale she looked when I saw her last.

"Dammit!" I yell, slamming the lid of my laptop down.

I should have known that this girl wasn't just angry—she was in trouble. Why didn't I see it? She came to that concert hall to deliver a message to Brett. It turned out to be her suicide note.

I'm surprised to feel the tears slipping down my face, and I swipe at them with some irritation. But that doesn't work. In a matter of moments, they're coming faster than I can wipe them away and, before I know it, I'm sitting on my couch, sobbing into a pillow.

I'm crying for Laurie and her suffering, and the fact that I wasn't able to do anything to help her. I'm crying for Brett, who seems to be such a good and decent man on one hand, and an apathetic monster on the other. And, I'm crying for myself, because I think I'm in love with him. I know it's ridiculous. I should be running the other way, but there's something about him that's making my heart overrule my head.

"Okay, enough," I mumble, dragging myself off of my sofa and out of my self-pity. I splash some water on my face in the bathroom and, when I'm a little more composed, I pick the phone and try Brett's number. It goes directly to voicemail. I glance at my watch—he's not due to start the matinee performance for another two hours. Maybe he's still at the hotel.

"No, I'm sorry, miss, but Mr. Corrigan checked out late last night," I'm told by the desk clerk in Philadelphia.

How can that be? He's got one more concert to go. Then it hits me. I know at least one more person who can tell me what's going on.

Mary Dancy picks up on the first ring. "Maggie! How are you?" she asks, her voice filled with concern. "We were worried when you left so suddenly! Did you get home alright?"

"I'm okay, Mary, thanks. I wondered if you know where Brett is? They say he checked out of the hotel..."

"Oh, honey, he rented a car and left right after the concert last night."

"Rented a car? Where was he going? Don't they have a matinee today?"

"They do, but Brett was so upset about Laurie Daughtry that Joe called a local violist to cover for him. Did you hear about Laurie?"

"Yes, I did," I say softly. "There was an obituary in the paper today."

"Well, he decided to head home late last night. Joe tried to talk him out of it, but Brett had already made up his mind."

"Why wouldn't he just take the train home?"

"Oh, no, sorry... I didn't mean he went home to New York. He sent Joe a text from the road last night letting him know he was headed back to his *family's* home in Illinois. He said there were some things he needed to discuss with his parents. I think Joe has a phone number for them if you want it..." she offers.

"Would you please text it to me when you have a chance, Mary?" I ask.

"Of course. Maggie?"

"Yes?"

"I don't know exactly what the two of you discussed on Friday night but, based on Laurie's suicide and the talk you and I had on the train, I can take a guess." I wonder if she can. "It's none of my business. Or anyone's business, for that matter. But I want to reiterate something to you."

"Okay..."

"Maggie, Jeremy Corrigan is a very...strong personality. He's used to getting what he wants, and he doesn't take kindly to anyone who gets in his way. That includes his own brother."

"I'm sorry, Mary, I'm not sure what it is that you're getting at."

"I'm just saying that Brett has made a lot of sacrifices in his life to placate Jeremy. It's the nature of their relationship. Since you've come along, he's changed. A lot. And in ways that Jeremy is not going to be happy about. I don't doubt for a second that Brett is losing sleep, worrying about what will happen when his brother finds out how serious things are between the two of you. So, before you judge him too harshly, please keep that in mind."

"Are you saying that I should give him a pass because he's afraid of what his brother will do to him?"

There's a long, awkward pause from Mary. "I'm saying you should give him a pass because he's afraid of what his brother will do to *you*, Maggie."

Chapter 25

Brett

Just over an hour outside of the bustling metropolis of Chicago, the tiny town of Owl Bridge, Illinois is barely large enough to warrant its own zip code. It's where Trudy and Danny Corrigan raised us in the little white house with the black shutters on Cairn Road. Now, when I wake up in what used to be my childhood bedroom, it takes me a minute to remember where I am and how I got here. Then it all comes back to me in a rush.

It was nine o'clock this morning when I pulled the Mustang into the driveway, an unexpected wave of relief washing over me.

"Oh, my dear, sweet boy!" my mother said when she found me standing on the front porch. "Why didn't you call and tell us you were coming?"

"It was a last-minute decision. I thought I'd just surprise you."

"Here, let me have a look at you!"

She pushed me away slightly, her smile fading as she took me in from head to toe. "Oh, no. That's not good at all," she clucked, shaking her head, not bothering to disguise the disapproval in her voice. Before I could comment, she grabbed my hand and pulled me inside.

"Good Lord, Brett, you look like you haven't slept in ages."

"I haven't," I mumbled. That's when she sent me straight upstairs to get some rest. That was over seven hours ago.

Now, finally strong enough to make my way down the hall for a shower, I hear my father's voice in the living room below.

"But why do you think he's here?" he asks. I pause by the landing, curious to hear her answer.

"I don't know, Danny, but you should have seen him. He looks awful. He'll be down soon, and you can ask him yourself."

Under the steaming water of the shower, I wash the grime from my body, trying hard not to think about Laurie Daughtry. I brush my teeth and shave and put on some clean clothes. Now I feel a little more human, at least. It was breakfast time when I arrived, but it's the smell of a roast chicken dinner I smell as I head back downstairs. In the kitchen, my father is sitting at the table, peeling potatoes.

"You know, you can buy the potatoes already mashed," I say as I enter.

My mother scowls at me over her shoulder from where she is rinsing green beans in the sink. "As if I'd ever let such a thing into my kitchen!" she says with disdain.

My father gets up and holds me in a tight embrace. "Do you want a beer, Son?" he asks. "Or would you prefer some coffee? Your body probably doesn't know what time it is."

"Coffee would be great, Dad," I say, having a seat at the kitchen table.

"So, tell me, what's her name?" my mother asks without preamble.

I look up sharply, surprised by the question. "Whose name?" I ask.

She turns off the faucet and faces me. "The girl who sent you driving halfway across the country, no doubt like a bat out of hell."

I don't answer, I just stare at her. Not for the first time, Trudy Corrigan has startled me with her uncanny instincts.

"Maggie. Maggie Collins. She's a social worker in Brooklyn," I say.

"How did you meet her?"

"She's the girl I told you about—the one who stayed with me after the accident until the ambulance came."

My mother nods to confirm her recollection. "And this girl is special."

This is a statement rather than a question. I look toward my father who shrugs as he hands me a mug of steaming coffee. He's not getting involved in this one.

"Yes. I think she is," I say finally.

"But something's wrong."

"Yes," I agree. There's no sense trying to hide it, she'll wheedle it out of me sooner or later.

"Did you fight about something?" she asks, taking the apron off over her head and hanging it from a peg on the wall.

My turn to shrug.

"Son, I'm thrilled to see you," she begins, sitting at the table with my father and me, "but I want to know what upset you so much that you had to come all the way home when you could have just as easily picked up the phone. You know we're always here for you, day or night."

"It wasn't exactly that we had a fight... Something happened in Philadelphia. She came with me for the weekend, and everything was going great until Friday night," I pause and buy myself a couple of seconds by taking a sip of coffee "Yeah, everything was going great, until an old girlfriend of Jeremy's tracked me down after a concert. She obviously wasn't well..."

"What do you mean by that?" my mother presses.

"She was mentally unstable. She'd become so pale and thin and gaunt. She was like this... withered version of who she used to be. And she was so angry! She came there to tell me that she would never forgive me for something that Jeremy did to her," I look down into the mug, not wanting to see my mother's face when I say it. "Something horrible. And she blames me for not helping her. Maggie was there for the entire ugly conversation."

My parents take a moment to digest this before speaking again. "Did the two of you—you and Maggie—talk about it?" my father asks.

"Of course! But like I said, Maggie's a therapist. She made me peel away some of the layers and the more we talked, the more I realized that the girl was right. I just walked away because it's what I always do. It's what Jeremy expects me to do."

My mother reaches over and puts her hand over mine so that I will look up at her. But I can't. I can't face her. "You are not a bad person," she says quietly, but adamantly.

I don't respond.

"Brett Daniel Corrigan, look at me!" she snaps. I do as I'm told. "Your brother is his own man," she says. "He makes his own choices, good or bad. They have nothing to do with you."

I slap my hand on the table. "No, see, that's what I've always told myself, that it's all him. That's how I've justified it all these years."

"Justified what, Son?" she asks with some exasperation. "What is it that you're trying to tell us?"

"I was there, and I saw her trying to get away from him... but I just looked the other way. I always look the other way. And he just keeps on doing what he does, knowing full well that he can count on me to keep my mouth shut and pretend it never happened."

Now they're both staring at me with solemn faces. They're probably wondering what the hell they did to deserve two totally fucked-up kids.

"What did he do, Brett?" my mom asks finally. "Why did this girl come looking for you?

God, it's hard to say this to them.

"She says he assaulted her—raped her and beat her," I say softly. "She was obviously telling the truth. It destroyed her. And now it's too late for me to tell her how sorry I am."

"It's never too late, Brett—" my father interjects, but I cut him off.

"No, dad, sometimes it *is* too late. She killed herself yesterday."

Suddenly, the only sound in the house is coming from the old grandfather clock in the living room. I can hear its pendulum swinging back and forth with the tick of every passing second. It's my mother who breaks the silence at last.

"I'm not going to sugarcoat this," my mother says slowly. "If you stand by and allow Jeremy to do abhorrent things without intervening, then you are equally at fault, if not more so." She takes a long breath in, and I think that's the end of her thought. But it's not. "I know this because we—your father and I—are guilty of the same thing."

"What? What are you talking about?"

"Brett, you don't think any of this comes as a surprise to us, do you?" my father asks.

"Well, yeah, kinda…"

The shock must be showing on my face because they look at me and then at one another.

"Honey, did you really think we didn't know there was a felon living under our roof all those years?" my mother asks. "I gave birth to that boy. We watched him grow up every day of his life, and we saw him, just the way you did. We were waiting to see what horrible thing he'd do next. Kill the neighbor's cat. Steal someone's car. Blackmail a teacher."

My jaw goes slack with shock as she continues.

"Oh, yes," she says, picking up on my disbelief. "We knew about all of those things and more. We watched that sweet little angel face of his lie to us over and over again, as if we were imbeciles. We aren't imbeciles, Brett. So, you'll understand if we're not shocked and dismayed by what you've come to tell us. That is what you came to do, Son, isn't it? To get this all off your chest?"

I'm prepared to disagree, but then it hits me, she's right, that's exactly why I'm here. I wanted to break the news to my parents about Jeremy being a sadist and me being a fool.

I nod slowly, in agreement to what she's just asked me.

"Brett, you've let your brother control you for far too long, and I'm not sure why," my father observes.

"Because we had a deal," I say softly.

"What kind of a deal?" my mother asks with suspicion in her voice.

"When we were kids. I promised not to tell on him, or get in his way, if he promised not to do anything to me or to you guys."

My parents look at one another across the table. "But, Son," my father begins, "only one of you stuck to that deal, wouldn't you say?"

"What do you mean?" He looks at me as if he can't believe I'm serious. "What?" I insist.

"Think about it, Brett. Anything you ever expressed an interest in, your brother stole it, broke it, destroyed it or found a way to ruin it for you. And I'm not just talking about toys and sports. He did the same thing with your friends, your girlfriends even! I can't imagine much has changed. In fact, I'll bet you think long and hard about what you mention to your brother, and who you bring home to meet him."

I set the coffee cup down hard on the table as a sickening wave starts to churn in the pit of my stomach. Along with it comes a film of cold sweat across my face. I can't quite take a full breath and it's starting to make me nervous, panicky. Even my hands are trembling now as my mother watches me intently. Can't she see I'm in trouble here? Something is terribly wrong. When I open my mouth to ask her to call an ambulance I don't even recognize the sound that comes out of it. It's some cross between a gasp and a gulp and a wail. And it scares the shit out of me.

In an instant, she's on her feet, opening her arms and wrapping me inside of them. She strokes my hair and soothes me. Even as I choke on a sob, my first impulse is to resist her, to 'man-up' and suck it up. But I don't feel like a man right now, I feel like a child crying in his mother's arms. And I just don't give a flying fuck anymore.

"I don't know what to do," I say when I can finally pull my head away and look up at her again. She reaches down and wipes the tears from my face with her thumbs.

"Well, I think the first thing you should do is get out of that apartment you share with him and find yourself a place of your own. Pay his rent out for the rest of the year—I'll give you the money. But you've got to give yourself some distance."

I'm nodding.

"And go get that Maggie back," my father says resolutely.

"What?" I ask incredulously. "How can I possibly do that? The girl thinks I'm a monster!"

"Do you love her?" he asks.

I don't take even a second to contemplate the answer. "Yes," I say softly.

"Then you show her your heart. You commit yourself to her, and to being a different person. Show her the amazing man that I know you are," my mother pipes in now.

"I—I don't know if that'll work."

"Well, you won't know if you don't try. And believe me, you'll regret it every day of your life if you don't try."

"Alright, I'll try." I nod, trying to compose myself.

"Brett, if you can win Maggie back, you keep her as far away from your brother as possible," my father warns.

"I know, Dad. He doesn't even know she exists. I've been seeing her behind his back for weeks now."

My mother puts a reassuring hand on my back. "It's okay, baby," she says gently. "It's all going to be okay. I promise."

I'm instantly comforted by those last two words. Never once has my mother ever broken a promise she's made to me. And I doubt she'll start now.

"Why don't you go on up to bed, Brett?" my mother asks me after we have washed and dried the last of the dinner dishes.

"Because I just got up a few hours ago," I point out.

"Well, you've had a very long, very upsetting couple of days and I think you should go upstairs and have some quiet time for yourself. I left you some books on the nightstand."

I have to admit, a quiet night alone sounds really good right now. "Alright," I agree. "But only if you make me a cup of your hot chocolate to take up with me."

She puts her hands on her hips and raises an eyebrow at me. Wow. I never realized how much Jeremy looks like our mother. "Honey, it's eighty degrees outside. Are you sure hot chocolate is what you want?"

"Oh, yeah. And don't forget the extra marshmallows," I say with a grin.

She pats my cheek gently and gets the milk out of the refrigerator. Ten minutes later, I'm kicking off my shoes and stretching out on the bed. When I reach for my mug on the nightstand, I see the small stack of books she's left for me. A collection of Stephen King short stories, the bestseller John Adams bio, and an old favorite of mine by Nelson DeMille. All good choices. I grab the DeMille and notice right away that there's some paper sticking out of it.

Folded carefully in the book are several pages printed out from the internet. Probably recipes if I know my mother. But when I open them, I realize they're definitely not recipes. And, apparently, I don't know my mother as well as I thought. She has, in her most delicate manner, given me an article outlining the traits of a sociopath.

My first thought is that she has just done this for my benefit, but then I notice notes in the margins and sentences that have been underlined. These aren't freshly creased pages, either. No, they definitely show the signs and wear of multiple readings. Okay then, Mom, let's see what it is that you're trying to tell me.

> If they are strong enough, the sibling of a sociopath grows up developing skills to cope and adjust to the actions of the sociopath.

And, with that single sentence, my entire life, or rather, my brother's entire life begins to unfold on the pages in my hands. For every general trait of a sociopath that's listed, I can immediately think of at least one example that fits the description, and my brother, to a T.

When caught in a lie, a sociopath will continue to deny it even in the face of clear proof.

And just like that the moments of my life begin to unspool like film running across the lens of a projector.

DAD: Don't you lie to me, Jeremy. I found your mother's diamond bracelet at the pawnshop.

HIM: It wasn't me, Dad.

DAD: Of course it was! Your signature is on the receipt, Jeremy.

HIM: Someone forged it.

DAD: Son, stop it. I saw the video footage. It was you.

HIM: Lots of people look like me.

DAD: (snorting) What? You don't think I'd recognize my own son? Even if that were even remotely possible, how would this mysterious person who looks like you have gotten the bracelet?

HIM: I'll bet in here and took the bracelet and nothing else?

HIM: I don't know, maybe they didn't want to make you suspicious so they could come back and do it again.

DAD: Come back and do it again?

HIM: Sure. Wouldn't surprise me if this isn't the last time it happens.

Sociopaths are callous.

HIM: Mom! I want my dinner now! Mom!

DAD: Shhhh! Jeremy, your grandmother just died. Let your mother get some rest. She's exhausted.

HIM: I'm hungry and I want to eat now! Mom!

DAD: I'll order a pizza for you.

<u>HIM</u>: No! I want Mom to cook for me!

<u>DAD</u>: Son, you better cut it out right now.

<u>HIM</u>: Why are you yelling at me? Stupid Grandma's the one who died. It's not my fault. *Mom!*

Sociopaths are narcissistic.

<u>ME</u>: What makes you so sure you're going to get first chair in the All-State Orchestra?

<u>HIM</u>: I'm the best horn player.

<u>ME</u>: In the entire state?

<u>HIM</u>: Of course.

<u>ME</u>: Why do you think that?

<u>HIM</u>: What do you mean?

<u>ME</u>: What makes you think you're the best?

<u>HIM</u>: Because I am the best.

<u>ME</u>: Says who?

<u>HIM</u>: Says me! Who else is going to be the best?

I'd tick off all the traits that fit the bill, but someone has beaten me to it. Next to each and every characteristic of a sociopath is a small check mark in my mother's hand. At the bottom of the page she has scrawled my name and the word 'enabler.'

Chapter 26

Maggie

He doesn't notice me right away when he comes around the back of the house. And when he does, he stops short, taking a moment to put me into context. I don't belong here—not in this part of his life, anyway.

"Maggie?" Brett asks, as if he needs to confirm my identity.

I nod and give him a shy smile. I was surprised that Trudy Corrigan *wasn't* surprised by my call last night. When she told me Brett was asleep, I apologized for disturbing them and tried to hang up, but she seemed to know who I was...and she seemed to have other plans. Two hours on the phone and one flight later, I'm sitting out on the deck of the Corrigan home in Owl Bridge, Illinois.

He comes towards me slowly and I notice he's blinking a lot. The poor guy probably thinks he's hallucinating on top of everything else that's happened in the last few days.

"What are you doing here?"

"Your mom and I had a long talk last night. She convinced me I should come here and see you."

"*What?*" He sounds horrified.

"I didn't want to leave things the way they were the other night," I say. "And after I read about Laurie, well, I was worried about you."

He comes and joins me at the round glass table overlooking their lush yard and garden. His brows are furrowed together as he looks at me, trying to wrap his head around what I've just told him.

"Okay...so, are you telling me that you had a phone conversation with my mother last night and then just hopped on a plane this morning?"

I nod.

"I didn't think you ever wanted to see me again," he says softly. "Not after what you found out about me in Philadelphia."

"Did I say that?"

"Well, no, but..."

"I needed some time and space to sort through it all. I mean, suddenly I had no idea who I was sleeping with, and it scared me, Brett."

He hangs his head in disgust and embarrassment. I just keep going, talking to his scalp.

"Brett, I'm a really good judge of character. It's why I was willing to give us a chance after you accused me of holding your viola hostage, and after that catastrophic date at the coffee shop," I let a little smile creep into my voice, and he looks up at me slowly. "Right now, my gut tells me that the apathetic person who let his brother do all those awful things wasn't you—isn't you."

"Maggie, I'm so sorry," he says.

"I know."

"So...what's next then?" he asks tentatively, as if he's afraid of what my answer will be.

"Brett, I—I think I might love you a little bit."

A smile spreads slowly across his face.

"I think I might love you a little bit, too," he says.

"But your brother..."

He holds up a hand to stop me.

"Don't you worry about him. I'm going to start looking for my own place as soon as I get back."

This is big. What he's telling me is that he wants this relationship to work more than he cares about what his brother will do or say. I reach across the table and take his hand in mine.

"You're not a bad person, Brett. Somewhere along the way you just forgot that you're a good person."

Chapter 27

Brett

I'm actually pulling the clothes off of her as we stumble up the narrow staircase to my apartment above the pizza parlor. Every few steps we stop so I can pin her against the wall and devour her mouth with mine. I will never, never, never let this woman out of my sight again. By the time I get the door unlocked, she is minus one blouse, half of her bra and a sock, which I can't quite figure out, because both of her shoes are still on her feet.

"I want you so much right now," I mumble as we literally fall over the threshold and onto the floor. "I don't think I can wait to get to the bedroom," I breathe heavily as I nuzzle her throat and wrestle with her bra.

"Then for goodness' sake don't!" she murmurs.

She gasps when my hand finds her breast and gives the nipple a pinch. Suddenly she's wriggling out of her jeans and kicking off her shoes and the one remaining sock. I kick the door shut with my foot and pull my shirt off over my head. We crawl across the carpet leaving a trail of clothing behind us until we are both naked and every square inch of her is pressed up against every square inch of me. I feel her hand moving lightly, deftly between my legs.

I can't even formulate a recognizable sound as she wraps her fingers around my shaft and squeezes gently with one hand while running the thumb of her other hand around the head. This girl knows her way around a penis, that's for sure.

"Oh, Maggie..." I breathe deeply, pushing my face into her flower-scented curls as she continues to fondle me. "Maggie, Maggie, Maggie..." I murmur.

If we keep going at this rate, though, there won't be any 'after play' to go with the foreplay. I wrap my arms around her and roll onto my back so that she is lying on top of me. She doesn't need any more encouragement than that. In a second she is using her hands to position me. She runs my hard length up and down her soft, wetness, taking time to linger in a spot or two. Finally she can wait no longer, and she allows herself to sink down all the way on top of me. She puts her head back and lets out a long, satisfied sigh as if she has been waiting for this for more time than can be measured. Then she starts to rock gently, back and forth, slowly.

The sight of her above me mesmerizes me. Her alabaster skin marbled by tiny blue veins. Her perfect breasts pulled taut as she arches her back against me. I take a more active role and give her a hard thrust upward, making her gasp with pleasure. A few more of those and she leans forward again, putting one hand on either side of my head so our faces are only inches apart. Then she starts a slow, figure eight motion that makes my eyes roll back in my head.

"Ohhhhh..." I always thought it was women who were the moaners. But it just can't be helped.

With her arms still on either side of me, I reach up and run my thumbs gently along the ridges of her nipples. Then my fingers walk their way down her breastbone, across her stomach and I dip a finger into the cleft where our bodies are attached. The affect is immediate as she sits bolt upright and leans back on her knees, giving me more room to move my fingers up and down, teasing, circling and nudging her hard little bud. She moves up and down atop me, grinding herself into my hand, which I keep firmly fixed for her manipulation. Her turn to moan loudly now.

"I'm so close Brett..." she rasps. "I'm going to come, Brett. Now, now, Brett!"

I renew my thrusting with more vigor until she calls out a garbled version of my name. Once I'm sure she has reached *The Promised Land*, I grab her around the waist and buck into her again and again until I can't hold back another second. I am still shuddering as she collapses atop my chest, her head positioned just over my heart.

"You are amazing," she says hoarsely.

"Me? Jesus, Maggie, you—"

Before I can even finish my sentence, she lifts her head, bringing her mouth to mine. She kisses me with a tenderness that tells me that we'll be alright. That she's forgiven me. It is, I think, the best kiss I've ever had in my life. I'd like for it to go on forever, but it's cut tragically short by the startlingly familiar voice that comes from six feet away in my kitchen.

"Hey, Brett, you gonna introduce me to your new friend?"

Chapter 28

Maggie

"Jeremy!" Brett yells from our rather compromising position on the floor.

Ah, so this is the brother, then. *'The Psycho Brother'* as Randi calls him. I watch as he stands in the doorway to the kitchen, one palm pressed against either side of the frame surveying us with a smirk on his face.

"Wow, you two really give new meaning to the term shag carpet, don't you?" he says with a self-satisfied chuckle.

He walks over to where I sit on the floor and extends a hand for me to shake. Seriously? I've managed to reclaim my panties but I'm not even sure my bra made it out of the stairwell. "I'm sorry, I don't think we've been introduced. I'm Brett's brother, Jeremy."

I take a deep breath and put a calm smile on my own face, refusing to give him the embarrassment he's looking for from me. I use my left arm to cover my breasts and shake with my right. My, my. So this is what a sociopath looks like up close.

"Hello, Jeremy. I'm Maggie Collins. I've heard a lot about you."

His expression morphs into one of utter charm and gentility. "All good, I hope," he says with an endearing smile. I return neither the smile nor the sentiment. "Maybe not *all* good then…" he observes, his lips curling up a little more at the corners.

He's sizing me up, trying to gauge what kind of a threat I am.

"Well, if you'll excuse me, I think I'll hop in the shower," I announce, standing up, spinning on my barefoot heels and seeing myself to the bathroom. *His* bathroom. I can feel his irritation as it comes off of him in waves from behind me. He was hoping I'd be dazzled by his stunning appearance and charming wit. Barring that, he was hoping I'd be too shy and embarrassed to face him. I am none of those things.

"Glad to see she's made herself at home," I hear him say to Brett who, by now, is on his feet and looking for his own underwear. "You know, I much preferred the scenery when she was in the room," he mutters with a chuckle.

I close the bathroom door, leaving it open just a crack and start the shower before returning to hear what's going on out there.

"I cannot fucking believe you!" I hear Brett say loudly.

"What was I supposed to do? I mean, I could be wrong, but I'm pretty certain the coitus interruptus has to come from your end, not mine. I thought the polite thing to do was to let you finish. You seemed to be having such a good time. I had no idea you were into being rode hard and put away wet!"

The sneer in Jeremy's voice is palpable. I can just imagine the tide of red rising from below Brett's neck, up across his face to his hairline.

"Okay, okay! I'm sorry. My bad. I'll apologize to the lady. What's her name? Margie?"

I snort and slam my hand over my mouth, hoping they haven't heard me.

"Maggie!" Brett spits. But I know full well that Jeremy knows full well what my name is. He probably even knew it before today. It's not likely him being here, right at this moment, is a coincidence. Brett texted to let his brother know he'd be arriving home this afternoon and Jeremy responded that he had plans and wouldn't be home till late. And yet, here he is. And here I am, hiding out in the bathroom and eavesdropping.

"Seriously, I'm sorry Brett," Jeremy says sincerely.

"Seriously, we both know that's bullshit, Jeremy. How long have you known I've been seeing her?"

"Long enough. Where'd you find her?" he asks.

"She helped me after the accident."

I hear Jeremy snort while I wave away the cloud of steam that is now billowing out of the shower and surrounding me.

"So, little Meggie was there to hold your hand. How sweet!" he says in an intentionally sappy voice.

"Maggie!"

"Meggie, Maggie, whatever. Why should I bother learning her name when you're just going to dump her in a few weeks, anyway?"

Oh, now I can't wait to hear where this goes.

"It's not like that," Brett says quietly.

"What do you mean?"

"I mean I'm not going to dump her."

There is a pause so long that I think maybe they've left the living room, but then, Jeremy's voice comes to me through the bathroom door, clear as a bell. "Okay. So what're you saying, Brett? That you love that little bitch in our shower?"

Motherfucker!

"Yes, Jeremy, I do love her. And since you know about her now, I guess this is as good a time as any to tell you that I'm going to start looking for my own apartment."

"Whoa, whoa," Jeremy says, sounding very conciliatory all of a sudden. "What the fuck are you talking about? You're nuts if you think I'm going to look for some dumbass roommate off of Craig's List."

"I'm sorry, Jeremy."

"Don't be sorry, Brett. Be reasonable. Let the princess move in here if you want her in your bed that badly."

Hah! Over my dead body.

"No. Not gonna happen," Brett replies flatly.

"Why not?"

"Because we need our privacy for one thing," he says.

"So, she likes to make a lot of noise when you have sex," Jeremy jabs.

"For another thing," Brett continues as if his brother hasn't spoken, "this place is too small for the three of us."

"So, this isn't the first time you've had sex outside of the bedroom."

I can sense Brett's frustration mounting but, to his credit, he keeps right on track.

"Besides, I think it's time I give you some space, too."

"Oh-ho! *Now* I get it! You're afraid I'm going to seduce her and steal her away from you!" he declares triumphantly.

I have to bite the inside of my cheek to keep from screaming a response to that one.

I can't hear exactly what it is that Brett is saying to his brother at this point, but I can pick up the intensity of it. He is not happy and he's letting Jeremy know that in no uncertain terms. Well, I'm guessing this new, more independent Brett is quite a change for Jeremy. I'm also guessing he's plenty pissed off.

I no sooner have the thought then I hear the apartment door slam. I pull my panties off and jump in the shower.

"Mags? You okay in here?" Brett calls in.

I stick my head out of the shower and give him my sweetest smile. He's earned it. "Better now that you're here. Hey, I need some help soaping my back. Would you mind helping me?"

I don't have to ask twice.

Part Two

Chapter 29

Julia

I groan as his hands map the geography of my body. My shoulders, my arms, my breasts, hips and thighs. I gasp out loud when his mouth finds my neck.

"I love you so much..." I murmur.

He doesn't reply.

And then his lips are gone, replaced by his hands. They wrap around my neck with an immovable strength that squeezes from me any lingering passion, replacing it with sheer panic. I struggle against his grip, but it's too firm. My fingers try to pry his away, even as my mouth gapes, desperately searching for the smallest gulp of oxygen. But there is none.

His eyes bore into mine. I see clearly that what he wants is to witness my final moments. He wants to watch me—to see the very instant that I slip away. It doesn't take long for my struggling to subside. My hands drop away from his as I feel something give within me. My body relaxes and he seems so far away now, growing more dark and distant by the second. I see him smile at me. That brilliant, warm smile that stops my heart. This time, that's exactly what it does.

I sit bolt upright, covered in sweat and panting so hard that my throat actually hurts. My hand goes instinctively to my neck as I look around my bedroom. I flip on the bedside light, fully expecting to find a tousled, chestnut-haired head on the pillow next to me. But there's nothing there. Not so much as a dent in the pillow. I listen intently, but the apartment is silent, save for the hum of the refrigerator and the beating of my heart in my ears.

"Hello?" I call out into the dark.

Nothing.

"Matthew?"

More tentatively, "Jeremy?"

Still nothing.

A glance at the clock on my nightstand tells me it's ten o'clock. I'm scheduled for my first rehearsal at Carnegie Hall in a couple of hours. I guess this nap is over. I've moved back into the New York City apartment until the Kreisler Gala Concert is over. I'm comfortable here, and, more importantly, Matthew is comfortable with me being here on my own while he's working upstate.

When Dr. Sam first suggested midnight rehearsals at Carnegie Hall, I was skeptical. But the more I thought about it, the more sense it made. It's not like I sleep at night—not since I hit my third trimester, anyway. And it has the added benefit of reducing my chances of running into Jeremy—or anyone else who might alert him to the fact that I'm back in town. Alone. And pregnant

As steam fills the bathroom like some coastal fog, I consider what the recurring dreams might mean. Is it that I still love him? Is it that I'm afraid of him? It's all such a confusing jumble of emotions on top of the river of hormones running through my body. The only thing I can say for certain is that they started almost immediately after I returned to my old room, and to my old bed. Since then, there have been entirely too many nights like this when I wake with a start and find myself reaching for a man who isn't there. A man who never should have been there in the first place. And I hate myself for it.

After I dress, I fix myself a cup of herbal tea and take a moment to look around the apartment that Matthew and I have shared since the day I turned eighteen. The place has been on the market for a few months, but there haven't been any serious nibbles yet. And I'm glad about that now. For me, the fact that this place is comfortable and familiar helps me to feel secure as we enter month number seven in the countdown to Little Guy's arrival. I pat my baby bump gently and smile to myself as he turns summersaults in utero. He's a night owl, like his mother. I can be furious with Jeremy for a lot of things, but this baby isn't one of them. The simple truth is that no matter what he has done or said Jeremy gave me more than he took from me. And that includes my son.

The car service is waiting for me at eleven-thirty promptly, the driver jumping out to take my cello for me and escort me to the back seat. At this time of night, it's a quick trip to Carnegie Hall, and pulling up in a Town Car is a whole lot different from my undergrad years. I used to bribe the night guards with coffee and cookies, so they'd let me sneak in to play for a half hour here and there. Tonight, I'll have the whole place to myself.

My excited feet seem to remember their way around the intricate maze of hallways leading from the stage entrance to the stage itself. What they've forgotten is just how cold and creepy it can be down here, so they move a little quicker. And then, I pass through the darkened wings that give way to the view that takes my breath away every time.

There are close to three-thousand seats on three tiers. And if it's this impressive when it's empty, can you imagine what it looks like when it's full? Actually, I *can* imagine—and have— though I've never experienced it firsthand. Not from on stage, anyway.

It takes me a few minutes to stop my gawking and get settled on stage with my cello and music. I run some scales and do some plucking. I have to tune and re-tune a few times to adjust for this climate-controlled space. With its wood body and gut strings, the cello can be very fickle in its reaction to different environments. At last, I'm ready for Bach.

I've played the first *Suite for Unaccompanied Cello* many times before, including in the Kreisler Competition. Now I'm mixing it up a bit with the sixth of the Suites. When my fingers stretch out across the fingerboard, they take up the familiar positions of Bach. But in this piece, it's really the bow that's the hero.

Someone who's not familiar with this one might think, for a split second, that they're listening to a fiddle. A really low fiddle. The sound is open and full and my bow digs into the strings with an abandon—a freedom that I seldom have when I perform the more delicate pieces. My wrist hinges easily as the bow rocks from low notes to high notes in quick succession.

There are moments when it sounds as if there are two of us playing on stage. This is the magic of Bach, many voices that sound as one, one voice that sounds as many. Now, I'm on a rapid journey up and down the strings, up and down the scales. Here comes a juxtaposition of the florid and the frenzied, set against the rugged and the raw. The two worlds tussle back and forth, chasing one another until a series of musical slashes announces the end of the game and return to the voice of the cello.

My head drops to my chest, and I have to catch my breath. The Prelude to this suite lasts only four minutes, but it's an exhausting four minutes. Dr. Sam and I have worked very hard to bring this one up to snuff. Sure, it's Bach, again. But it's different Bach and, considering all of the drama surrounding this situation, this music will be the one thing that I can count on. The one thing that I can lean on and into.

I give my belly a quick rub and then I close my eyes and run through the rest of the Suite from memory, fingers flying and bow gliding. It's a joy to play such glorious music in such a magical space. Everything else seems to just fall away. Here, on stage, I'm not worried about the baby or Jeremy or anything else. This is what I was born to do. This is where I was born to be.

Reluctantly, I open my eyes when I've finished. I put the bow on my music stand and set the cello down on the stage so I can get up and stretch. Neck to the left and the right. Arms over my head. I stop, mid-stretch and look up into the first balcony. I use my hand to shade my eyes against the glare of the stage lights above me, and I scan from one end to the other, trying to distinguish any silhouettes in the darkened rows of seats.

Nothing. There is no movement. Not so much as the flutter of an eyelash. If I'm to believe my own two eyes, I am totally, completely alone. But I don't believe my own two eyes, because there's something else telegraphing a warning to me. I'm not quite sure how to explain it, except to say that it's as if some freaky mom-to-be *'spidey-sense'* has kicked in. Every single cell in my body is telling me that I'm being watched.

Spooked, I turn to grab my cello a little too quickly, hitting the music stand so that it tips over and spills pages across the empty stage. I survey the scene. With a sigh of exasperation, I turn toward the balcony once again and peer up into its vast nothingness.

"Well?" I call out. "You gonna come down here and help me out? Or are you just going to stand there and watch while the pregnant lady crawls around on the stage?"

In a matter of seconds, a single shape separates itself from the shadows and moves forward to the rail where I can finally get a good look at the tall, lean man who has been watching me this entire time.

Chapter 30

Julia

"How did you know?" Tony Ruggiero asks when he's made his way to the foot of the stage.

"Spidey-sense," I reply, staring down at him with irritation.

"Seriously? I didn't think that was a real thing. You know, outside of Spiderman comics."

"It's real," I grumble. "I'd ask what you're doing here, Tony, but I have a feeling I already know the answer."

He gives me a sheepish grin and hops up onto the stage with me. "Yeah, well...I do what I'm paid to do, Red."

"I should've known Matthew would have you lurking around, keeping tabs on me. You could have told me, you know."

He starts to pick up the music scattered across the stage. "I was going to tell you tomorrow," he says over his shoulder. "I just wanted to hang out this first night and get a feel for the place, for your routine."

"And do you?"

"Do I what?"

"Do you have a feel for the place and for my routine?"

He's got all the music now and is squaring it into a nice, neat pile before he sets it back up on my music stand. "Enough to know the layout of the hall and what you do when you get here. Which way you come in, that kinda stuff."

"So, does this mean I'll be seeing more of you, Tony?" I ask, not sure if I'm more relieved or irked about it.

"Maybe, maybe not. It's not like I'm going to be tailing you everywhere you go. I just told Matthew I'd stop in here and there, especially on these night rehearsals. Honestly, Red, it's more about him sleeping at night than me protecting you."

I can't stand on these swollen feet another second, so I sit back down on the chair. Tony is a good guy. He's been there for Matthew since his parents died in a boating accident. Tony works for the same law firm where Matthew's dad had been a partner...I think his official job title is 'Private Investigator,' but what he does is so much more than that.

"Tony, do you think I'm in trouble? I mean I just want to play this concert, have this baby and get on with my life."

He gives me a sympathetic smile. "I think you're fine. No one is looking for you right here, right now. The other performers don't get to use this hall until next week, so it wouldn't occur to anyone that you'd be here."

"And by anyone, you mean Jeremy."

He shrugs. "He's not a good guy, Red. You know that firsthand."

"Yes, I do."

"I think as long as you stay out of his way, everything will be fine. I keep an eye on him too, you know."

"Really?" I lean forward, suddenly more interested. I had no idea.

"Oh, yeah. I have friends in Customs who alerted me the second he was back in the country. Mostly, he's just been practicing since he's been back. I think he's getting ready to audition for some out of state orchestras."

"Well, it would certainly make my life easier if he were to relocate," I say, picking up my cello and laying it in its case.

"Anyone ever tell you that thing looks like a coffin when you've got it all zipped up?"

"All. The. Time."

* * *

"Was it really necessary to have Tony following me secretly?" Matthew is silent on the other end of the phone. "Matthew? Are you there?"

He clears his throat. "I'm here. I'm sorry. I didn't want you to feel as if you were under surveillance. I just wanted Tony to make sure everything goes smoothly. If I were there, I'd do it myself. Tony is the next best thing."

"I'm not mad," I tell him with some exasperation. "I just hate it when you do stuff like this behind my back. I wouldn't have minded having him around. He just scared the crap out of me, that's all. Anything or anyone else I should know about?"

"Nope. That's it. He's my army of one," Matthew assures from his hotel room in upstate New York.

Last year, he tracked me with a hidden app on my phone. Now I've got my own personal stalker-for-hire. He just cannot help himself!

"Alright," I grumble. "But I better not find a GPS tracker on my cello!"

"I swear," he laughs at me. "No more surveillance, I promise. Now, tell me about Carnegie."

My anger melts away when I think about the glorious acoustics and the beautiful setting. "It was like a dream, Matthew. I'm starting to get really excited about performing there."

"Good! No sign of Jeremy, or Brett, or anyone from McInnes?"

"Nope. Not a soul."

"Perfect. And how are you feeling?"

I sigh. "I'm feeling big and tired, but otherwise pretty good. How is it playing with the Gotham City Chamber Players?"

"Well, I'm still not comfortable being this far away from you, but aside from that...I'm really having a good time."

I knew he'd like it. That's why I pushed so hard for him to take the gig when it came up. Matthew gave up so much when he left his spot in the Walton Quartet. But now he's playing again, and with an amazing group of musicians. Right now they're in residency in the cozy upstate town of Rhinebeck. When he's not playing with the ensemble, he gets to teach some really exceptional teenaged viola players.

"What about the kids?" I ask. "I know you were nervous about the teaching."

"Julia, there are a couple of kids in my studio who could take my place tomorrow. Easy. That's how good they are!"

I laugh at his enthusiasm. Matthew Ayers is happy for a change, and happy sounds good on him. Now I'm feeling guilty about being so grumpy before. He's tried so hard to make a new life for us.

"I miss you," I say, realizing, suddenly, just how true it is.

"I miss you, too, but I'll be home soon."

Not soon enough.

Chapter 31

Julia

I'm standing over the brewing coffee, trying to fan its moist fumes toward me. I'm hoping to get a contact high from the caffeine, but it's just not the same. Sighing with disappointment, I pull out a large mug and put three sugar cubes in it. I remove the chilled creamer from the fridge and set it out alongside the mug and a spoon. Light and sweet, especially for Dr. Sam. I've been calling him that since the day I met him. Back then I was an eight-year-old ward of the state, living at the North Fork Children's Home.

"Hello, Julia. I'm Dr. Sam," he had introduced himself. "I've come to teach you how to play the cello. Would you like that?"

His face was so kind and soft, his eyes the warmest shade of brown. Even his voice was gentle and welcoming. How could I not want this man to teach me something? Anything?

I nodded and he stood up, held out his hand and waited patiently for me to make the decision to take it. When I did, he led me to a chair and pulled a child-sized cello from a case on the floor. He handed it to me and then took the seat next to mine, picking up his own instrument from its resting place on the floor.

For the next hour, Dr. Sam plucked strings up and down the

fingerboard, with me imitating his every move. He made it like a game. He'd pluck an E, I'd pluck an E. He'd pluck two C's and a G, I'd pluck two C's and a G. By the time the lesson was over he had me giggling with his silly faces and crazy little musical patterns.

When he returned the next week, he stood behind me and showed me how to hold a bow. Pluck, pluck, bow, bow. I was thrilled when I was able to imitate him through a round of 'Twinkle, Twinkle, Little Star.'

By the third week, I was waiting in my chair when he walked through the door.

"Well, well! Miss Julia, what a pleasure to see you today. It looks as if you're ready to play!"

I nodded with a shy smile as he set up his own instrument.

"Do you remember where the C is, Julia?"

I nodded and plucked the string.

"Wonderful!"

I was hungry for the praise. I had spent so many years trying to please a father who was never satisfied. Once I had an adult who was willing to give me his time, his attention and his kindness, I couldn't get enough of him. I only wanted to please him. It was during our sixth lesson that he asked me the question that changed everything.

"Julia, which note is this?" he asked with a pluck of a string.

Easy, it was a C. He was plucking a C. I said it in my head, but my lips just wouldn't form the words. I stared at him, and he waited. Finally I shook my head.

"Do you know which note this is?"

I nodded.

"Then you must tell me. Say it out loud, Julia. Just the name of the note, you don't have to say anything else if you don't want to."

I could feel the tears welling up in my eyes. What was I supposed to do? I hadn't spoken a single word to anyone in over a year. Dr. Sam put a hand on my shoulder and smiled down at me, even as the tears started to run down my cheeks.

"It's okay, Kiddo. Just the one letter. Can you whisper it in my ear?" He leaned down so that his face was close to my mouth. I looked at him for a long time until, at last, I cupped my hands around his ear as if to tell him my deepest, darkest secret.

"C," I said in barely a whisper.

He sat up and looked down on me. "Thank you, sweet girl," he whispered back, with tears of his own streaking down his face.

When my lesson was over, I put away my tiny cello and started toward the door. About halfway there, I set the case down on the floor and turned around to where Dr. Sam was packing up to go. Before I could stop myself, I ran back to him, throwing my arms around his waist and resting my head on his chest.

I squeezed him hard for a moment, and he slipped to his knees on the floor, scooping me up into his arms and holding me in the tightest, safest embrace I had ever felt. I don't know exactly how long we stayed like that, clinging to one another in silence, but when I was finally ready I gave him a kiss on the cheek and gestured for him to let me whisper in his ear.

"I love you."

I meant it when I said it then, and I still mean it now as he stands in the doorway of my apartment.

"Julia!" he exclaims, "You grow more beautiful with every passing week!"

"I grow more gargantuan with every passing week!" I counter with a laugh.

These days when I hug him, it's a little more complicated. But, I do the best I can with my baby bulge between us. He sits down at the table, and I serve him the coffee I *can't* drink, and don't, along with the coffee cake that I *shouldn't* eat, but do.

"I'm going to miss these at-home lessons with coffee and cake," I joke as I poke at a crumb the size of a golf ball.

"Well, there's nothing that says we have to stop after the gala. I'd be perfectly happy to come to you here or even out east, if that's where you and Matthew settle when the baby comes."

I roll my eyes. "Well, that's what he'd like, to hide me away out in the suburbs, safe and sound from the big bad city."

Dr. Sam points at me with his fork. "Somehow, I don't think it's the city that he's trying to protect you from, Julia."

"I know," I mumble and look down at my plate.

"Have you... come across Jeremy since he's been back?" he asks me cautiously.

I shake my head. "Nope. But the gala is in less than a week. Not likely he's going to miss me up on stage," I say.

He gives me a tight smile and puts a hand on my arm at the same time. Uh-oh. That's never a good sign. "I hate to add to your stress level right now, but we have a situation with the gala concert."

Oh, hell.

"When I called to file your program with the committee this morning, they rejected the Bach."

"What? Why would they do that?"

"Because it's already being played."

This makes no sense. The Bach *Unaccompanied Cello Suites* are for unaccompanied cello. I'm the only cellist performing.

"By who? Whom. Whatever."

The pause is just long enough, just awkward enough, that it gives me the answer before he does.

"Seriously?" I stare at him in disbelief. "*Jeremy* is going to play my cello suite?"

"I'm afraid so. It seems to have been quite deliberate."

"Well, no surprise there," I mutter with an irritated sigh. "Fine. We'll do the Elgar."

"You can't. The violinist is playing Elgar."

Ugh, jeez. Dvorak then..."

When he doesn't say anything, I know. "The pianist?" I guess.

He nods silently.

"Dr. Sam, the dress rehearsal is in four days! What am I supposed to play?"

"I have an idea. But it's something you've never played before. I think it will be perfect for you, Julia, though it's going to require every ounce of strength you can muster to learn it, play it and own it in time for the concert. Do you think you can trust me on this, Julia?" he asks.

I don't have to think, I know.

"Always."

Chapter 32

Julia

It was nearly one-thirty in the morning when I finally left Carnegie Hall tonight. I didn't see Tony, but I could feel him out there in the darkened seats, watching me. I'm pretty sure he followed me home, too. But what Tony doesn't know is that I took my cello up to the apartment and promptly came back down to soothe my craving for late night pancakes.

Hey, the baby wants what the baby wants!

Now, at closer to three in the morning, I leave cash on the table and waddle out of the diner. I don't worry about wandering around at this hour because I'm hardly alone out here. The cars on the street and the people on the sidewalk are proof that this city really *doesn't* ever sleep! Well, that's one thing we have in common, I think as I rub my tummy. I can't remember the last time I slept through the night.

I decide to take the long way around to our building, through Lincoln Center and past one of my favorite spots, the Revson Fountain. It's such a beautiful night that I just can't resist. Unfortunately when I get there, I find a good portion of the area blocked off for some sort of construction. The fountain's lights are off, but I can still hear the water running. I take a quick look over my shoulder. No one is paying me the slightest bit of attention. I continue another twenty feet until I find a spot where I can slip my mammoth belly past the barricade.

As I get closer, I keep an eye out for a security guard or police officer that might shoo me away, but I seem to be on my own. And then it's in front of me, sprays of crystalline water sparkling in the moonlight. It's a gift, having this place to myself. I pull out a pocketful of change and start to toss coins in, one by one, making a wish with each tiny splash.

Please, let my baby be healthy.

Please, let Matthew be happy.

Please, let me find some peace and closure with Jeremy.

Please—

I jump at the feel of warm hands over my eyes. With the sound of the water, I never heard anyone coming. It also makes it hard to distinguish the voice in my ear.

"Guess who?"

My heart skips a beat. Matthew has come home early to surprise me! I pull the hands from my face and turn around with an excited smile. But it isn't Matthew I'm looking at.

"Hello, Jules."

You know that moment? The one where everything simply... stops? Sound. Sight. Movement. It all comes to a complete and sudden halt as the moment in which you are standing becomes frozen. This is *that* moment. I can't hear the fountain anymore. I can't see the headlights of the cars that drive by. I am frozen. All I can see, and hear, and feel is him.

"Jeremy." His name is a whisper on my lips.

I'm rewarded with a smile. Not the big, glitzy one, but the sweet one. The one that he first bestowed upon me that night at the diner right across the street from where we are standing now. He is so close, I would only have to raise my hand a little to touch him. As it happens, though, he's the one to take my hand in his. My left hand.

"So it's true?" he asks, searching my eyes.

"What's that?" I ask, distracted by the changes in his appearance since I last saw him. He's different—and not in a bad way. His chestnut hair is a little longer, his coloring a little darker.

Now he wiggles the gold band on my ring finger. "You married Matthew?"

I look down at my hand as if I need to confirm it for myself before answering. "Yes."

And then, still holding my hand, he gently lays his free hand on the curve of my stomach. "And you're having a baby."

I nod. "Yes."

That sweet smile again, now with crinkly hazel eyes thrown in for good measure. He seems... Dare I say it? *Happy.*

"Why didn't you tell me?"

I am at a loss all of a sudden. Why *didn't* I tell him? Breathe, Julia. Stop, Julia. Think, Julia.

"Because it doesn't have anything to do with you," I say at last.

His brows draw together in concern. "Oh, Jules. Please don't be like that. I'm not stupid. I can do the math. This baby is mine. Yours and mine."

His words have the undesired effect of giving me goose bumps. I shake my head and start to speak, but he puts his index finger to my lips.

"You don't have to say it. But I know it. It's why you rushed to get a ring on your finger. And I'm sure it was Matthew who had that brilliant idea. But maybe if I had known..."

He leaves that thought hanging out there for me to fill in the blank. Maybe if he had known, it would be his ring on my finger, not Matthew's. Maybe if he had known it would be the two of us excitedly preparing for this baby's arrival. Maybe if he had known...

His lips interrupt my thoughts. They brush softly against mine. I don't pull away. Quite the opposite, in fact, I allow him to pull me closer to him. It's a tender kiss that holds the promise of nurturing and adoration and love. When he finally separates his face from mine, I open my eyes to find him staring down at me expectantly.

"Tell me," he says.

"Tell you what?"

"Tell me it's my baby. Tell me you love me. Tell me that it's *me* you want to be with and not Matthew."

For a split second, I am ready to blurt out an emphatic '*Yes!*' to all of those things because, for a split second, they are all true. But only for a split second, because that's all it takes for me to come back to my senses. I pull my hand from his and break the intense stare between us.

"Maybe I could have said all those things six months ago, but I can't say any of them now," I reply quietly. I reach up and put a hand to his face, stroking his cheek with my thumb. "I was so in love with you. Maybe it was a lie, but it was a lie that made me happy. You know, all you had to do was ask," I whisper.

Now it's his turn to be confused. "Ask what?"

"All you had to do was ask me not to play, Jeremy. I'd have pulled out of the competition in a heartbeat for you. It would have been such a small sacrifice, and I would have made it happily to support you."

"I don't understand..."

"I'm saying you didn't have to try so hard to destroy me. I would have done it for you willingly."

He seems to be unable to process this. It doesn't make any sense to him. Of course it doesn't. What does Jeremy Corrigan know about sacrifice?

"I'm married to Matthew now and we're expecting our first child. All I want is to live a quiet, peaceful life, Jeremy. I don't want to interfere or make trouble. And I don't want to be afraid anymore. Please, *please*, I'm begging you. Please just let me have this, and I promise you'll never get a moment's trouble from me. I'll keep Matthew out of your way. I swear, Jeremy. Please."

The transformation is at once subtle and instantaneous. And it's frightening as hell. The smile isn't sweet anymore, it's sardonic. His grip on my hand isn't delicate now it's painful. And his eyes have hardened into suspicious little slits. Ah, here is the real man, at last.

"Oh, Jules. Still the naive little rube, aren't you? No, no, no. You can beg all you want, but it doesn't change a thing." He drops my hand and jabs at my belly. "Just like that ring on your finger doesn't change the fact that that's my little bundle of joy in there."

I take a step back from him, shaking my head defiantly. "No. He's Matthew's baby..."

"*He!* So we're having a boy, then? I think we should name him after me, don't you? Jeremy Dean Corrigan Jr. I like that! Or, I *would* if I were planning on having a son."

The suggestion behind the comment is unmistakable. I turn my back on him but before I can actually step away, I feel his grip on my shoulder. He forces me back around to face him.

"I don't think we're done talking about this," he says with some irritation. "How about you and I go on up to your apartment where we can be alone?"

Before I can reply he has a hand on my elbow and is moving me in the direction of my building. I try to pull away from him, but he has a firm hold on me.

"If you don't let go of me right now, I'm going to scream my head off," I snarl as he leads me along.

He laughs and holds up his left hand, gesturing to the deserted space around us. "Jules, it's after three in the morning and you have, very conveniently for me, wandered into a deserted construction site. There isn't anyone out here. And, it would seem your bodyguard isn't around at the moment."

So he's been watching me closely enough to notice Tony Ruggiero hanging around. "Exactly how long have you been following me?"

He shrugs. "I was just waiting for the right time. I'm sure you understand that I wanted to have you all to myself."

The smile he shoots me makes the hair on the back of my neck stand on end.

He's pulling me, once again, in the direction of my building. Okay. This is going to be okay. The guys in the lobby are on notice to be watching for him. I'm certain someone will intervene once we get there. But then, as if reading my thoughts, he speaks again.

"Oh, and in case you're thinking of having one of your doorman friends call the police, you can think again."

He pulls a key ring out of his pocket and dangles it as we walk. "I have access to the back door, the basement and the service elevator. No one will even know you're home."

Shit. This is bad. This is really, really...

My thoughts are cut short by a sudden, sharp pain that stops me in my tracks. I double over and try to catch my breath. What the hell was that? When I straighten back up again slowly, he's eyeing me suspiciously.

"Really, Jules? You think I'm stupid enough to fall for that?"

I grunt when another pain strikes me in the same area. This can't be labor, it's too early. No, something is definitely wrong. My nails are digging into his forearm. I would have done that to get him to let go of me but, as it turns out, I need to use him as a way to push through the pain. I don't think he thinks I'm faking it anymore.

"Jules, you don't look so good," Jeremy says without a hint of genuine concern.

"I need to go to the hospital," I say between clenched teeth.

He just watches me. When the worst of it is over, I straighten up as best I can and yank my arm from his grip. Then I turn and start to shuffle off in the direction of the street so I can hail a cab to the closest ER. Jeremy circles around to block me.

"Yeah, I don't think so. Why don't we wait it out a little bit and see how this progresses? Mother Nature has a way of sorting things out sometimes. You know what I mean? Maybe I won't even have to get involved at all. It'd just be... one of those things."

"Get out of my way," I hiss in my most menacing tone. Unfortunately, the effect is lost when I'm hit by another jab. This one practically brings me to my knees. My head is throbbing now, and I stay hunched for a long moment, taking some slow, deep breaths. Jeremy is still prattling on above me as if nothing has happened.

"You know, I'm surprised you were able to hide it for so long. Things would have been easier if I'd known sooner, but that doesn't mean we're out of options. Still, you could have saved yourself a lot of discomfort by taking care of this right away. Now it's more... complicated. Well, nothing to be done about it now, I suppose..."

"Julia? Are you okay?"

I don't immediately recognize the voice, but Jeremy clearly does. And how could he not? The voice belongs to his brother. Brett steps out of the shadows and comes to my side, putting a gentle hand on my back.

"What is it?" he asks me quietly. "Are you in pain?"

"Yes, and Jeremy seems to think this would be a good time for us to be alone together up in my apartment."

"Is that so?" I hear him ask his brother as he turns to face him. "What's going on here, man? Did you do something to her?"

"Oh, please. I haven't laid a finger on her...yet. But you've got to admit the timing is great. I was just saying that sometimes these things work themselves out. Obviously she's not meant to have this kid..."

"What the fuck is wrong with you?" Brett spits at Jeremy.

Slowly, I unfold myself into an upright position again so I can see exactly what is transpiring here.

The two of them are less than a foot apart. With about three inches of height and thirty pounds of weight over his brother, Brett makes Jeremy seem so much less threatening. But what he lacks in size, Jeremy makes up for in venom.

"What's wrong with *me*? What's wrong with *you*, Brett? And what the hell are you doing here, anyway? You following me?"

"No, actually, I'm following her," Brett informs him, gesturing back to me, as I stand behind him.

So it wasn't Tony!

"How long?" Jeremy asks.

"How long what?"

"Stop fucking around. How long have you been acting as her guardian angel?"

"It doesn't really matter, does it, Jeremy? You're going to see it as a betrayal whether it's been two days or two months."

"Really? You know what she did to me. You know what that motherfucker Matthew did to me."

Brett shakes his head.

"No. I know what *you* did to *her*. I know what you did to Cal and to Laurie and a dozen other people." Waves of fury are rolling off of Jeremy as Brett continues. "I'm the one person on the face of this earth who knows where all the bodies are buried. That's why you like to have me close by, isn't it? So you can be certain you've got me under your thumb? Yeah, well, that's over."

"It's over when I say it's over," Jeremy grits out as he tries to move around Brett to get to me again.

Brett shoves his brother away hard enough to send him stumbling back a few feet. He doesn't fall, but he's not happy.

"You're making a very big mistake here, Brett," he warns.

"I've already made a big mistake, and I'm about to rectify it. Come on, Julia," Brett says, turning toward the street. "Let's get you to the hospital."

Before I can take a step, Jeremy reaches out and grabs my arm again. This time I don't pull away. This time, I face him full on so I can look up into his face. The handsome face with the stubble and the square jaw and the hazel eyes with the long, dark lashes. I will not be flinching or wincing or cowering or blushing this time.

"Get. Your. Hands. Off. Of. Me!" I spit each of the words with so much acidity that I can actually taste them in my mouth as I say them.

He considers me for a long moment, and as he does, I can almost see the calculations going through his head. Even in his warped, narcissistic, delusional mind, Jeremy knows that I will kill him before I'll let him do anything to jeopardize this child. And the truth is, I don't know how I would do it. It's not like I'm packing a gun in my maternity bra or anything. I can barely walk more than ten feet without stopping to rest. I certainly couldn't outrun him if he decided to come after me. And yet, somehow, we both know that I would find a way. That only one of us would come out of this altercation alive, and it sure as hell wouldn't be him.

So, while some might think it odd that he would let me go, I know that it's totally in keeping with his character. He has assessed his risk versus his reward and decided there is nothing in it for him. Jeremy steps aside as his brother, his former partner in crime, turns his back on him.

"We are *not* done here, Brett," he calls out after him. "Not by a fucking long shot!"

Brett supports me with his left hand and sticks up the middle finger of his right hand without so much as a backward glance.

Chapter 33

Julia

I wake with a gasp and a start, using my hands to shield my eyes from the brutally bright florescent lights above me. There's a needle in my arm, and the sounds of beeps, blips and whooshes surround me. When I roll over onto my back with some effort, I find a figure looming over me, blocking out the florescent sun above. I gasp in horror and try desperately to wriggle up into a sitting position.

"Whoa! Hey, Julia, calm down!"

"Get away from me!" I hiss, covering my eyes.

I hear him walk away, and then the light filtering through the flesh of my fingers is extinguished. Slowly, cautiously, I pull them away and peek out. There is a figure in the now-darkened room with me.

"So help me God, Jeremy, I will kill you..."

"Wait, wait, wait!" he says, crossing the room and turning on a small lamp over my bed. It spills a wash of soft light across Brett Corrigan.

"Julia, it's me, it's Brett. I brought you here. Do you remember?" he asks. "You were really out of it by the time we got here. They couldn't even get your name out of you."

"The baby..." I start in a hoarse whisper but he's shaking his head before I can finish.

"He's fine," Brett rushes to tell me. "You're both fine. Just dehydrated and exhausted. They're going to release you in a couple of hours."

I scour his face for any trace of insincerity, but I can't find it. I take a deep but shaky breath and nod that I am okay.

"I couldn't find your phone anywhere," he says, taking a seat next to me, "so I didn't know how to get in touch with Matthew. If you give me his number, I'll call him for you. Or get him on the phone. Whatever you want."

I wave a hand of dismissal at him. "No, I'm fine. If I call him now, he won't let me out of his sight for the next ten weeks. But I guess I'll have to tell him about Jeremy at some point. He's going to freak."

I notice him looking down at his hands in his lap before he meets my gaze again. "I'm so sorry, Julia," he says softly. "I'm sorry that my brother is such a fucking psycho."

"Well, you can't be held responsible for that."

"I *can* be held responsible for a lot of other things, though."

"Listen, you just saved my baby's life. Maybe mine, too. As far as I'm concerned, Brett, all is forgiven."

This makes him smile and, if I'm not mistaken, breathe a sigh of relief. "You were pretty impressive back there, you know. I've never seen Jeremy back down so quickly in my life. Hell, *I* was scared of you!"

I smile. "He wasn't too happy with you, was he?"

"No. He was pissed, that's for sure. When I was away, visiting my parents, I made up my mind to get a place of my own. My parents have even offered to pay out the rest of the lease so Jeremy can have some time to find a roommate, or another apartment, or get a job or whatever. I really thought he'd be okay with that."

"But not so much..."

He shakes his head. "No, not so much."

"So, how's it going with you and..." I think for a second trying to recall her name. I can see the curls and glasses. "Maggie. Are you two still together?"

The smile that immediately lights his face answers the question for me before he can. I never noticed before how different Brett looks with a smile on his face. It's a good look for him. *She's* a good look for him.

"Oh, yeah. I almost fucked it up and now that we're okay again, I'm not letting her out of my sight. She's dedicated and compassionate—*so* compassionate. I've never known anyone who cares about other people the way she does."

He loves her—that much is clear. Maybe she really *has* turned him around. The question is whether or not his brother is strong enough to turn him back.

I look at him carefully. I mean really look at him. Brett is a paler version of his brother—not in his coloring, but in his overall appearance. He's just a little less vivid. Less bright. Less shiny, maybe. That's it, less shiny, but by no means dull. Just a little more like the rest of us mere mortals than his brother.

Brett is average. He's taller and broader—and yet Jeremy gives the illusion of being larger-than-life. His eyes are simple brown unlike Jeremy's complex hazel. His hair is dark brown, but not the same rich chestnut as Jeremy's. It's as if you're comparing a bird of paradise with a pigeon. The pigeon never wins that beauty contest. And yet, in this context, far away from his sibling's exceptional good looks, I can see Brett as he really is. I see what Maggie finds so appealing.

"Thank you, Brett. I don't know what would've happened if you hadn't shown up when you did," I say and I reach out my needle-scabbed, tube-infested hand.

He looks down at it, then up at my face as if to confirm the intent of the gesture. I give him a single nod of encouragement and he takes my hand in his own. He has a big hand, warm and soft and gentle. I like this hand, and I think I like this man who is sitting with me at six o'clock in the morning. He's not the same hateful man that I knew not so very long ago. And then something peculiar strikes me... This is my child's uncle.

It is not an altogether unwelcome thought.

Chapter 34

Julia

Mrs. Doyle has acquired a dog. I discover this now, as I stand across the hallway, outside of my apartment. It sniffs and pants noisily, slipping its little white paw under the door. Finally, it gives a quick, high-pitched 'woof!' alerting her that a predator may be lurking in the sixteenth floor hallway.

"Max! Stop that this instant!" I hear Mrs. Doyle yell from the depths of her apartment.

Max doesn't have to worry about me, I'm just waiting for the elevator to open, and I can already hear its ding from the end of the hall.

Maggie Collins is taller than I remember. She's attractive in a quirky kind of a way. And those curls! What a nightmare they must be in this humidity.

"Julia," she greets me with a warm smile when she reaches me.

"Maggie, it's nice to see you again. Please, come inside."

She sets her overnight bag on the tile floor of the foyer and walks further inside, still carrying a distinctive looking orange box. "What ya got there?" I ask slyly.

She gives me that dimpled smile. "Oh, a little birdie told me you might be a fan of donut holes. After your ordeal last night, I figured you could use a little sugary treat," she explains, setting the box on the breakfast bar.

I think Maggie Collins and I are going to get along very well indeed. "I can't thank you enough for this. You've known me for about five minutes and already we're having a sleepover."

"Well, as near as I can tell, Brett pretty much blackmailed you into having me here," she laughs.

"Yeah, he may have threatened to call Matthew if I didn't let the two of you keep an eye on me for a couple of days," I say, with a smile. "But, now that you're here, I kind of like the idea of someone else around. You know, just in case..."

She nods. "I get it. Just in case you have any more scares with the baby."

"Or Jeremy."

"I wasn't going to go there, but yes, Jeremy is pretty scary, too."

"Oh, so you've met him!"

"Yes. Under some rather...intimate circumstances."

I lean across the counter. "Really? Spill it!"

She shakes her head and closes her eyes for a second, as if trying to block the memory from her mind. "Brett and I had... well, we'd just had... you know... and there he was..."

I gasp involuntarily. "What? In the bedroom with you?"

"We didn't quite make it to the bedroom," she says, color rising to her face and painting her cheeks with two perfect, rose-colored circles.

"Well, that's something the brothers have in common," I say with a wry smile.

"So the sex with Jeremy...?" she ventures.

"Was amazing."

Thankfully, she doesn't press for more detail than that. Instead, she hops off her stool and walks into the living room.

"Wow, this is some place you've got here," she marvels.

She must be spending time with Brett at the apartment he shares with Jeremy. That would definitely make this one look like the Taj Mahal.

"Thanks. Can I get you a cup of coffee or tea?"

"Oh, yes, I'll take herbal tea if you have it," she replies distractedly, walking across the living room to peer out onto the balcony. "Spectacular!" I hear her mumble to herself.

I put the kettle on and prepare two mugs with small tea bags.

"Here you go." I set her beverage on the other side of the breakfast bar. She returns to her stool and catches me shooting a not-so-discreet glance at the orange box.

Taking the hint, she pops the top open and presents me with an assortment of glazed, chocolate and jelly donut holes. Well, hello, my pretties! I pluck a jelly one out and pop it into my mouth, closing my eyes and relishing the taste.

"Wow," I mumble, mouth still full. When I open my eyes again, she's smiling at me. "I'm supposed to take it easy on the sugar," I explain after I swallow. "This is a rare treat for me. Thank you, you couldn't have picked anything better."

The smile broadens and I notice again what beautiful blue eyes she has. Their unusual shade caught my attention that day at the farmer's market, too. Not quite a sky blue. They remind me of a crayon I once had. I used it until it was just a tiny little nub. Cornflower blue, I think it was called.

She looks down at her hands for a second before meeting my gaze again. "I just wanted to tell you that I know this is all very strange. Brett's told me about Jeremy, what kind of man he is. And, he's been very honest about his role in the way Jeremy treated you. So, I'm sure this change in Brett must seem very... unexpected."

"I would have said unbelievable. In fact, I *did* say un-believable. And then he came to my rescue last night. Now... well, now I don't exactly know what to think, Maggie. But, one thing I can say for sure is that I feel better with you here. *Both* of you. And I'm grateful for that."

"I'm so glad, Julia, because he's desperate to make it up to you. To prove himself to you. And to me, for that matter."

She pauses to take a sip of her tea. "I think the two of them have had a really—pardon the expression—fucked-up relationship since they were kids. Even their parents couldn't break them out of the cycle. But now things have changed."

"Is that your personal, or professional opinion?" I ask as I rummage around the box for a chocolate morsel.

"Both," she says without hesitation.

I sigh. It's obvious that this is a bright, sweet woman sitting in front of me. It's just as obvious that she's head-over-heels for Brett Corrigan. And how could I not relate to that, having felt that way about his brother?

"I know Jeremy is the father of your baby," she blurts out suddenly, causing me to choke on my crumbs.

"Oh! I'm sorry," she says, rushing around the breakfast bar to pat my back.

When I have caught my breath again, she puts a hand on my arm and looks at me so intently that it's as if she's looking *into* me.

"This must be such a difficult situation for you," Maggie says. "Very complicated and confusing."

"You don't know the half of it," I mumble.

"Julia, did you love him?"

I have to shake my head with a disbelieving smile when she says this. "Not very subtle, are you, Maggie?" I tease.

She doesn't respond, just keeps me in her tractor beam of a gaze until I sigh and give in.

"Yes," I say simply.

"Did you believe he loved you at the time?"

"Yes."

"But he didn't."

"No."

Suddenly, there is a soft, warm hand on my arm.

"You didn't do anything wrong, you know. Jeremy, by his very nature, is wired to find what is missing in your life, what you yearn for deep down in your soul, and then he fills that void totally and completely. It's what guys like him do," she explains quietly.

Until this very second, I hadn't realized that guilt was part of this equation. But this woman has tapped something deep within me. I know in my heart that Matthew thinks I could have prevented this whole mess. On some level, he blames me, though he'd never admit it. Not even to himself. What I *didn't* know is that *I* blame me, too. I can only stare down at her hand. She pulls it back after a few seconds and I meet her gaze again.

"And, if Brett should ever even think about helping his brother again, I'll kick his ass, and then I'll kick him to the curb," she assures me with a vehemence that doesn't match the compassion she's just displayed.

I like Maggie already. I like her enough to be concerned about her. "Don't trust him," I warn her quietly.

I can see she understands that I'm not talking about Brett.

"Don't trust a thing he says or does," I continue. She may be the one with the degree, but I'm the one with the practical experience on the topic of Jeremy Corrigan. "Your safest bet, honestly, is to just steer clear of him. Get Brett the hell out of that apartment as soon as you can and keep him as far away from his brother as possible."

"Yes, that's exactly the plan," she agrees.

"And Maggie... he'll be gunning for you." That gets her attention. She waits for me to finish the thought. "It's entirely possible that Jeremy will see you as a threat to his relationship with Brett. And, let's face it, you are. He'll blame you, and then he'll do his best to remove you from the equation."

"That's what he did with you, isn't it? He tried to remove you from the competition."

I sigh heavily and swirl the tea in my cup.

"Yeah, well, it didn't help that I was a naive fool. I thought... I mean, I was so sure..."

I don't have to finish the sentence.

"He was being the man of your dreams. You just said it yourself, Julia, it's what men like Jeremy do. He *made* you fall in love with him."

"That he did," I say with a sigh as I pick a jelly donut hole out of the box.

Part Three

Chapter 35

Matthew

Rita Michelle Roberts is looking at me sheepishly over her shoulder. She has her viola case on top of the upright piano and is taking her sweet time getting it out. Uh-huh. I know what that means.

"So... late night at the bonfire again?" I ask casually.

She shrugs.

I make a point of looking at my watch. "And what time did you get up this morning? Exactly?"

Another shrug.

My eyebrow goes up and she sighs as she comes to take the seat next to mine.

"Professor Ayers, I can't help it! I could stay up all night talking to the other students. They're from all over the world and it's just so interesting to hear their stories!"

I get that. I really do. There's something so magical about this place and the young people who come here for long summer days filled with music. The kids—nearly a hundred of them in all—spend their time going from orchestra rehearsals, to lessons, to practicing, to chamber groups, to concerts. They are everywhere on this beautiful farm campus, instruments slung easily over their shoulders, laughing with other young musicians from across the globe. When they're not playing, they have bonfires and movie nights and trips into the town of Rhinebeck.

"So, no time to warm-up this morning I'm guessing."

"No," she admits sheepishly. "I'm sorry. It won't happen again."

I can't help but smile. The sixteen-year-old has long, straight brown hair that hangs almost to her waist. While the other kids are in rock band t-shirts and shorts, she's wearing a peasant blouse and faded jeans that flare at the bottom. With her hippy aesthetic and free spirit, Rita Michelle is a throwback to a different generation. She's also a spectacularly talented violist. She just doesn't know it yet.

"Rita Michelle, we've had this conversation three times already. You know very well it's going to happen again, so don't make promises you *know* you can't keep."

Her smile is broad and easy.

I soften. This music festival is just as much about the time with the other musicians as it is about the lessons and the performances. Jeez, she's sixteen years old. She should have time to socialize. It's only going to get harder as she gets further into this career she's chosen.

"Alright, alright." I give in and pick up my own instrument. "We'll warm-up together."

Oh, how Julia and I would have killed for this kind of an opportunity when we were her age. But we made do, I suppose, and I can't say I regret any of it. As heartbreaking as it was to lose my parents, had I not ended up at the North Fork Children's Home I never would have met the love of my life.

"Okay, scales by half-steps starting with C. Eighth notes up and down. Three, two, one..."

Forty-five minutes later, the girl is playing Mozart better than many professionals I know. "Excellent!" I praise her when we're done.

"Thanks," she mumbles.

"Rita Michelle, you're probably the best violist here. I know it and the other students know it. I'm not sure why *you* don't know it."

Blank stare. "Can I go now?" she asks, clearly embarrassed by this —and all compliments.

"Fine, go. But you'd better be warmed-up when you get here tomorrow. I don't care how late you're at the bonfire. Understand?"

"I promise!" she calls over her shoulder as she rushes out.

I have a half hour before my next student, so I pull my phone out of my pocket. Hmm. No messages from Julia yet today. But then, she did have a late night rehearsal last night. I decide not to bother her. I bother Tony instead.

> Hey, how'd it go last night?

My text flies off into the ether with a whoosh. I have one in return a few seconds later.

> All good. Red sounds great. She seems to be doing fine with the night hours. I watched the car drop her at your building myself.

Excellent. I probably haven't heard from her because she's still sleeping. I'm thinking about checking in with the lobby manager, just to be sure, when the studio door opens and a familiar face peers in.

"Philip!" I exclaim when I see my sandy-haired buddy from the Walton Quartet.

He slips in and closes the door after him, taking the seat that my student has just vacated. "Matthew, you are a sight for sore eyes," he says with a smile as he pats me on the shoulder.

"What are you doing here, man?"

"I come every year but this summer I had a conflict..." his voice trails off.

"You had a conflict with the Walton Quartet schedule," I finish for him.

He nods. I know this is awkward for him because it's awkward for me.

"What happened, Matthew? You quit so suddenly."

"Well, it's kind of complicated, Philip..."

"Did it have something to do with Jeremy Corrigan? You know, there are rumors flying everywhere about him."

I nod. "It did. But if you don't mind, I really don't have the energy to go there right now," I say.

He nods his understanding. "Of course."

I don't want to ask, but I have to. "How's Brett working out?"

"He's good. Really good, but really...different from you."

"Yeah. I'll bet he is." I snort.

Philip looks a little uncomfortable. "Matthew, I don't know what it is, but there's something different about Brett. He doesn't talk about Jeremy at *all*. I'm pretty sure they're not even speaking at this point. And there's this new girl he's seeing now, too. A social worker."

"Good for him," I say disinterestedly, unmoved by the *'new and improved'* Brett I keep hearing about.

"Anyway," Philip says, "that's not what I came here to talk about."

"What, then?"

He sighs, and I can see in his expression that something is really bothering him.

"What is it, Philip?" I ask again with more concern.

"I'm going to tell you something that you can't repeat. Not to anyone." I nod. "I've been having some problems that have affected my playing."

"Okay..."

It takes him a few seconds to continue. "It's my hearing, Matt. It's been a little muddy for a while, but I've noticed it's been getting worse, so I went to an audiologist last month."

"Jesus," I breathe. "What did he say?"

"Just what I thought he was going to say. I have something called Otosclerosis. It's a hereditary condition involving bone growths in my ears."

"Fuck, man! Is there anything they can do about it?"

He shrugs. "There's a surgical procedure. If I'm lucky, it will restore some of my hearing but it's entirely possible I won't be able to keep performing with the Walton."

I'm shaking my head. Philip Tonka is the flakiest musician I've ever known, but he's a damn fine cellist. He's a founding member of the Walton Quartet and it's hard to imagine the group without him.

"I'm so sorry, Philip. Is there anything I can do to help?"

"Yes, actually there is. I'm going to arrange to have the surgery at the end of the year, but it's going to take some time for me to bounce back from that, and even more to see what kind of audio range I'm left with afterwards. So, I was hoping you'd talk to Julia about taking my spot for a season while I go on medical leave. It might even be permanent, but I just don't know."

"Wow, Philip, that's...I mean, I don't know what to..."

He senses my confusion and steps in. "You do see her, don't you? I mean, I know you don't share that apartment anymore, but I wasn't sure exactly what your status is..."

I hold up my left hand and he spots the gold band. "No!" he says with a shocked expression. "No way! You and Julia?"

I nod and his face breaks into a huge grin. He gives me a playful punch on the arm. "You dog, you! And you didn't tell anyone? You didn't invite anyone? Dude!"

"Hey! Slow down." I laugh. "It happened fast. It kind of had to happen fast if you know what I mean."

I can see that he doesn't. And then, suddenly, he does.

"Wait—what? Really? You guys are expecting?"

"Yeah," I confirm with a grin of my own.

"Matthew! That's great, man. I'm so happy for you. So, maybe Julia wouldn't be interested then?"

"I don't know, Philip. She just might be by that time. I don't know if she'd want to do all the touring with the baby that young, but I'll talk to her about it."

"Yeah. You do that. I'm so happy for you!" he repeats.

As he says it, I realize for the first time that I'm happy for me, too.

Chapter 36

Matthew

"Take your places, ladies and gentlemen. Let's go, let's go!"

The stage manager is trying to be heard above the din of the student orchestra musicians who are chattering excitedly backstage. Or, more accurately, back *barn*. These weekend concerts are held in a tremendous barn and throughout the summer, music lovers from all over travel here to fill the rows of benches.

This time around, the orchestra will be performing some American music by Gershwin, Copland and Bernstein. Then it's my group, the Gotham Chamber Players. We're in-residence for the summer to teach the younger musicians, coach their ensembles and give performances of our own. I'll join some of my colleagues in a performance of Mozart's *Horn Quintet*.

The students are eventually shushed and herded to their spots on stage to tune. Normally, I'd slip into one of the back row to hear my viola students, but it's an exceptionally warm August evening and the fans aren't doing much to keep the audience cool. So most of us faculty musicians are milling around out back of the tent, hoping to catch a breeze until we play on the second half of the concert. Philip and I are leaning up against a huge old apple tree when he spots a familiar face.

"Hey, Rich, over here!" he calls out, waving to Rich Kellogg, the McInnes horn professor.

"Ahh. I was wondering who the horn player on the Mozart was going to be," I comment.

Our regular guy had to pull out of this performance after he developed a nasty case of poison ivy south of the border—if you know what I mean. Interestingly enough, a very attractive piano teacher has been reputed to have the same affliction in the same... hemisphere. Neither of them will be able to sit for a week. I suppose they'll just have to get creative if they want to scratch each other's itches again anytime soon.

Rich makes his way over to us and stops to stare when he notices me sitting with Philip.

"Nice to see you," I say, looking up at him. "It's been a while since we played a gig together. What, maybe Tanglewood a few years back?"

He doesn't respond, just glares down at me.

"Rich? Something wrong?" Philip gets to his feet.

I join him in standing. I don't like the way this guy is looking at me right now, and something tells me I should be upright for whatever's coming next.

"Well look who it is," Rich sneers, sounding more like a fourth grader on the playground than a professional musician.

I actually have to look behind me to see if he's speaking to someone else. He's not. It's definitely me who's in his sights.

"Is there a problem?" I ask.

"You're a real piece of work, Matthew, you know that? Look at you, sitting here like you're some great teacher, some great performer. Everyone thinks you're such a stand-up guy. They don't know the truth, but I do."

"What the hell are you talking about?" Philip asks, inserting himself between us slightly.

He obviously has the same sense I do, that things are about to get weird and, possibly, out of hand.

"You know damn well what I'm talking about, don't you, Matthew?" he spits at me.

"Are you out of your mind?"

I ask the question seriously because I'm thinking he actually *is* out of his mind. We've never been close or anything, but Rich Kellogg and I have always enjoyed a pleasant, collegial relationship.

"I know all about how you and your little girlfriend trashed Jeremy's reputation," he says to me now. "It wouldn't surprise me if the two of you were somehow involved in poor Cal's death. In fact, maybe I should have a little talk with the police. I'm starting to think they've been investigating the wrong person all along!"

I can't believe what I'm hearing. This little rant of Rich's is totally out of character...although I have a feeling I know where it's coming from. I gently push Philip to the side and stand directly in front of Rich, trying to keep myself composed. The last thing we want is to cause a scene in front of dozens of teenagers and their parents.

"Okay, first of all, she's my wife now, so I suggest you be very careful what you say about her, Rich," I warn him for a start. "As for Jeremy, I don't know what kind of bullshit he's been telling you, but you're being manipulated, my friend. Julia and Jeremy were dating. He dumped her backstage right before her final Kreisler recital. He hit her, Rich. And he fractured her wrist. If you don't believe me, I have the medical records to prove it. *That's* the guy you're defending."

He's shaking his head in disbelief. "Jeremy told me you'd say that."

"Do you even hear yourself, Rich?" My tone is growing louder. "Since when are you so fucking gullible? Who had the most to gain by Cal's death? Huh? It's not like Cal and Jeremy got along. If anyone should know that, it's you! I mean you were their professor. And Julia? Jesus, Rich, you've known her since she was a freshman—

she can hardly say two words without blushing. What the hell makes you think she could pull off a *murder*?"

This idiot isn't hearing a word I'm saying, so I need to change my approach. I take a deep breath, lower my voice and try to sound sincere.

"Look, man, I admit it—I was the one who put out the word on Jeremy. I truly believe that he killed Cal and got away with it. I just wanted to see him pay for it on some level."

Now I soften my tone. "But Rich, if I had it to do all over again, I would've kept my big mouth shut. All I did was piss him off. And the more ripples there are from that, the angrier he gets. He's already threatened to hurt Julia just to get back at me. That's why we took off for a while—to lay low and wait for everything to blow over. But clearly it hasn't blown over if he's got you believing his bullshit."

"Rich, he's telling you the truth," Philip jumps in. "Everybody else knows that Jeremy's a bastard. I don't know why *you* haven't figured that out by now." Philip puts a hand on my shoulder. "Matthew is a decent guy. He gave up the gig of a lifetime with our quartet so that he and Julia could just get out of town and away from Jeremy. She dropped out of McInnes and gave up her degree before she could finish. Does that sound like the behavior of master manipulators? *Murderers?* Think about it. It just doesn't make sense."

Rich is starting to look a little less convinced. "Why would he tell me that story then?"

Shit, I know why.

"What did he ask you for?" I ask slowly, almost afraid to hear the answer.

"Nothing," he says defensively. Then he backpedals a bit. "What do you mean?"

"I mean, Rich, what did he ask you to do for him after he gave you this song and dance about how wronged he's been? Because I *know* that's what he did. He convinced you that you needed to help avenge him somehow, didn't he? Or maybe he asked you to do something to avenge Cal?"

He clears his throat and glances down at the floor. "He asked me to pull some strings so he could get one of the horn auditions coming up."

I knew it. I shake my head. "Well, it's your reputation on the line, man," I reply with a shrug.

Suddenly Rich is looking much less angry...and much more guilty.

Clearly I'm not the only one to notice.

"Rich... what did you do?" Philip asks.

"I, uh, well... He... He also asked me to see if I could get Sam Michaels to tell me where Julia was."

A wave of nausea starts to rise in my stomach.

"And did you find out where Julia is?" My question comes out as a whisper.

"Not exactly."

"What, exactly, *did* you do?" Philip presses, starting to sound as alarmed as I feel.

"I found out what her rehearsal schedule was, and I gave it to him..."

"You did *what*?" I can't believe what I've just heard. "Are you saying that you told him she'd be rehearsing alone at Carnegie Hall in the middle of the night? Is *that* what you told him, Rich?"

All of the color drains from his face as he realizes the magnitude of what he's done.

"I... I... didn't know... He said..."

But I'm not listening to Rich Kellogg anymore. I pull the phone from my pocket and look at my texts.

> Going to take my nap now. I'll call you when I get up later. I love you!

That was nearly an hour ago. Okay, good. So, she's home safe. Except, she's napping so she'll be awake to go rehearse later. At Carnegie Hall, where Jeremy knows she'll be. When he knows she'll be there. Shit, shit, shit!

> Do NOT go to rehearsal tonight. Stay in. Do NOT let ANYONE into the apartment except for Tony. On my way home now.

I look at the text I've just typed. It looks scary. I backspace and start again.

> Surprise! I've got the night off. Coming home to take you to rehearsal myself. Don't leave without me. Call me if you get up before I get there.

Okay, good. That'll do. Hopefully, I can make it back to the apartment before midnight. I shove the phone back into my pocket and level my stare on Rich.

"You have no idea what you've done, you stupid fuck," I hiss at him and watch as he stares back at me in guilty silence.

I gesture for Philip to follow me to the back entrance of the barn —I get lucky with the timing, the student orchestra has just finished their Bernstein overture and the stagehands are getting ready to roll out the piano for the Gershwin piece. I slip back to the viola section and squat down next to Rita Michelle.

"Professor Ayers?" she whispers with surprise.

I hand her my music folder. "I need you to do something for me."

"Uh, okay..." she nods reluctantly.

"I have an emergency and I need to leave. I want you to take my place in the Mozart tonight."

"What? With the faculty ensemble?" I nod and her eyes get huge. "No disrespect, Mr. Ayers, but are you out of your fucking mind?"

I almost smile. Almost. "Yes, but that's beside the point. Look, I don't have time to hold your hand here. I know you can do this, and I know you won't let me down. You're going to be one of the best viola players in the world someday soon, take my word for it."

She doesn't look convinced. I put a hand on her shoulder.

"Please, Rita Michelle. Please do this for me. I can't think of anyone I trust more to cover my part."

She takes a deep breath, gulps audibly and nods. "Okay," she says quietly.

I gesture to Philip who's standing close by. "Mr. Tonka here will be there to help you if you need anything, or if anyone gives you a hard time." I give the girl's shoulder a squeeze, slip back out of the barn and head for my car.

"What can I do?" Philip asks as he rushes besides me. "Do you want me to call her or something while you're driving? Do you want me to call the police?"

Christ, I don't know. Finally, I shake my head. "No. The last thing I want to do is frighten her. I'm just going to haul ass back to the city and see if I can catch her before she leaves for rehearsal. I texted her, but she isn't always great about checking her phone."

I stop for a second to face him, putting a hand on his forearm. "Thanks, Phil. I..." I don't even know what to say.

"Go," he says, pushing me toward the parking lot. "Go take care of your wife. Nothing else matters right now."

He's got that right.

Chapter 37

Matthew

It seemed the right thing to do, getting married, but there are times when I wonder. I know in my heart that Julia isn't totally over Jeremy yet. He hurt her. He abused her. He did his level best to destroy her and still, she wrestles with her feelings for that bastard. I, on the other hand, have only ever wanted to love her and take care of her. But it's never been enough. As I drive along the Taconic Parkway faster than I should, the days, weeks and years fly through my mind like a video stuck on fast forward.

"Marco!" I remember screaming, eyes shut tight against the summer sun and the chlorine-saturated water of the pool.

No reply.

"Marco!"

Silence.

"Marco?"

I opened my eyes and squinted against the bright sunlight and the sting of the water in my eyes. My best friend, Jack, wasn't even in the pool anymore. I saw him up on the patio, his mom talking to him with a very serious look on her face. She kept glancing my way. I hung off the side of the pool until he came back.

"My mom says we have to get out of the pool now," he said.

"How come?" I asked, the disappointment evident in my voice.

"Dunno. She just wants us to get out and get dressed."

I pulled myself out and went into the house to change back into my dry clothes. When I came back downstairs, Mrs. Martin was waiting for me and there was a policeman with her.

"Matthew, come into the kitchen and sit down for a minute," she said with a smile that seemed forced to me even at nine-years-old. I wasn't stupid. I knew something was wrong, I just didn't know what it was. Jack was nowhere to be found as I took a seat at the head of the table. The police officer sat on one side of me, Mrs. Martin on the other.

"Matthew, honey, this is Officer Kowalski. He wants to talk to you."

"What about?" I asked, eyeing the beefy man suspiciously. He had sad eyes and I wondered if they were always like that, or if they were just sad now. He forced a tiny smile and put one of his big mitts over my hand.

"Son, there's been an accident..."

Those five words were the last I heard for the next forty-eight hours. I mean really heard. Processed. Because, I knew before the officer could even finish his sentence that my parents were dead. I'm not sure how I knew, I just did.

What I learned over the course of the next several days was that my parents had drowned while boating with friends. They hit some rough water and capsized. Neither was wearing a life vest.

What I learned over the course of the next several weeks was that I was suddenly, completely and utterly alone. I had no grandparents. No aunts or uncles or distant cousins. And, while the neighborhood moms clucked and shook their heads at the pitiful little boy with the dead parents, no one had a permanent place for me in their lives.

At least I had Tony, the Private Investigator from my father's law firm. They had been close colleagues and friends, and I have no doubt if he'd had a more traditional job, he would have taken me in himself. But Tony's lifestyle was hardly fit for a grown man to lead, let alone a child.

Along with the partners who managed the family estate, Tony made certain I didn't end up in some dingy foster home. He did what he did best—he investigated. And what he determined was that the North Fork Children's Home, with its dedicated, caring staff, topnotch academic curriculum and family-style living arrangements, would be the best option for me.

It was a horrible time, and I was miserable. Tony did what he could, visiting me at least once a week, making certain I continued my viola lessons and even arranging for me to visit my friends from the old neighborhood. But everything had changed. Suddenly, it was as if they were afraid I was contagious. That if I spent too much time with them, their families might evaporate, too. Eventually, the invitations stopped coming and I stopped caring.

Things were pretty bleak until the day I spotted the little redhead girl sitting on the bench. She didn't speak, so I would ramble on about the life I'd had to leave behind and the guilt I felt over my parents' deaths. She didn't judge, or try to comfort, or ask me to try and 'work through the pain,' as my therapists did. Julia just listened.

We were both alone in this world, and then we found each other. I was in love with her even back then. As we grew-up together, it became a simple fact of my existence. She knew. She's always known. But she didn't feel the same way. I knew. I've always known. And now? Hell, I'm just not sure anymore.

I'm in a trance as I weave my way through the late traffic. I seem to have lost all sense of time and place as the exits whiz by and I make my way closer and closer to...to what? I don't know what I will find when I get to the apartment. Maybe Jeremy will be there. Maybe Julia will be gone. Maybe she and the baby will be...

"Enough!" I'm startled by the sound of my own voice.

I have to stop these crazy thoughts before I drive myself into a ditch. But I can't stop. I hear Jeremy's warning in my head over and over. I cannot possibly protect Julia every moment of every day. I push the accelerator a little closer to the floor and speed toward whatever it is that awaits me at the end of this particular stretch of the road.

Chapter 38

Matthew

I don't recognize the desk attendant in our lobby tonight. That's not good. The lanky young man stands up quickly, nervously.

"Can I help you?" he asks, his voice cracking just a little bit.

"I'm Matthew Ayers, apartment 1607," I gasp out between pants. He looks at me suspiciously and then down at a clipboard.

"Oh, sorry, Mr. Ayers. I have a note here that you're away."

I look at him incredulously. "Well, obviously I'm not anymore."

"Yes, sir," he says, scratching his head.

I turn and walk to the elevator briskly, jabbing at the call button repeatedly.

"Hang on, I really should call upstairs..."

I spin on my heels. "It's *my* apartment, you idiot! Look me up in your computer. There's an ID picture somewhere in there. Could you at least make yourself useful and tell me if you've seen my wife tonight? She was supposed to be picked up by a car service about forty-five minutes ago."

He scratches his head again. "Uh..."

"Redhead! About five feet tall..."

His face lights up with recognition just as the elevator doors slide open with a ding.

"Oh, yeah! Right! No, Sir, she didn't go out..." Oh, thank God. She got the message. She's waiting for me. "But she does have some company."

I hold the door with my hand so it can't close on me and move up to another floor. "What? Who?" I demand.

"Uh...tall guy. Dark hair. Wait, I think he signed in..." he runs his finger down the register book as the elevator starts to ding incessantly. Finally he looks up with triumph on his face. "Aha! Here it is. A mister...Corrigan," he says proudly.

The elevator doors have slid closed by the time he realizes I'm gone. The ride up to the sixteenth floor feels agonizingly slow and when I finally step out into the hallway, I'm met with dead silence. Nothing. The entire floor is absolutely still. I don't have a good feeling about this as I slip my key into the lock and slowly push the door open.

The apartment is dark, save for a small sliver of moonlight coming in through the sliding glass door to the balcony. I can just make out the figure of someone sleeping on the couch. I close the door silently behind me and make my way through the foyer, past the kitchen and into the living room.

The bastard is still sound asleep when I reach down and wrap both hands around his neck. It only takes an instant for his eyes to snap open, and then he's struggling under my weight as I crawl onto the couch and straddle him. But he's in an inferior position, on his back, and all he succeeds in doing is burning through what little oxygen there is in his lungs.

He starts to kick desperately, and one of the table lamps goes flying to the floor with a loud crash. I'm trying to get a better grip when the hallway light goes on and casts just enough light for me to see that my hands are wrapped around the wrong man's neck.

"What are you doing?" screams a woman from somewhere behind me.

Definitely not Julia's voice.

I jump back, releasing my grip as Brett Corrigan coughs, sputters, gasps and grabs at his neck. The woman rushes past me to his side, helping him to sit up.

"Are you insane?" she screeches at me. "Brett! Are you alright?"

He nods, still unable to speak, glaring at me over her shoulder. She joins him in the glare.

"Who the hell are you? What is wrong with you?"

"I... I—I thought it was Jeremy on the couch. I thought..." I flounder, but only for a moment, because it dawns on me that while this isn't Jeremy, it's still his brother. And with him, some strange woman with curly hair and big glasses.

"I *live* here!" I inform the woman. "Who the hell are *you?* And what the hell are *you* doing here?" I counter.

"That's Maggie. Maggie, this is my husband, Matthew," Julia says calmly from where she's standing in the hallway, surveying the action. Now we're all staring at her. "Brett was sleeping on the couch. Maggie was in your room. I told them they could share the bed, but he wanted to be close by if I needed him," she explains.

"What are you talking about? Why is he here at all? What do you mean 'if you needed' him?"

As the questions come tumbling out of me, I'm beginning to feel as if I've stumbled into an episode of the Twilight Zone. Julia looks at Brett more closely and then glances back to me, her brows drawn together with concern.

"Matthew, did you try to...to strangle him?" she asks incredulously.

"I thought he was Jeremy!" I yell, turning defensive now. "Christ, Julia, Rich Kellogg told me that he gave Jeremy your rehearsal schedule. I was so afraid he'd be waiting for you that I came right home! I was trying to catch you before you went to rehearse at Carnegie."

"Julia, you'd better tell him," Brett says.

"Yes, Julia," I say with a caustic edge that I just can't suppress. "You'd better tell me."

She sighs, and joins us in the room, wrapping her robe tight across her belly. I think she's gotten even bigger since I saw her just ten days ago.

"Matthew, the other night Jeremy ambushed me out by the fountain."

"You were walking around in the dark by yourself?" I interject.

A guilty blush rises to her cheeks. "Well, yes. But as it turns out, I wasn't all by myself. Jeremy showed up and he got a little... pushy with me..." I'm going to kill him. Jeremy Corrigan is a fucking dead man walking. "But then, out of nowhere, Brett was there to help me. Jeremy tried to get him to back down, but he wouldn't do it."

I look at the man I've just tried to strangle. He's sitting up now, the color gradually returning to his face. I could have killed him. I *would* have killed him.

"And in the middle of all this," she continues, "I was having some pain. So Brett took me to the hospital, and he stayed with me."

I'm not prepared for the ice cold wave of fear that washes over me in this moment, but Julia is. She comes to me, putting her hands on my forearms and locking me in her green-eyed gaze.

"I'm fine," she says softly but firmly. "The baby's fine. I was just exhausted and really dehydrated. They kept me for a few hours and gave me some fluids. Brett and Maggie insisted on staying here to make sure I was okay."

"Why didn't you call me?" I'm unable to disguise the hurt that's crept into my voice.

"Because I didn't want you to come back. I was fine, and I didn't want you to leave the music festival for no reason."

"No reason? Julia, I'm your husband. I'm that baby's father. I have a right to know!" Even as I say the words, I catch Maggie and Brett exchanging awkward glances over Julia's shoulder. I know instantly what they're thinking. "Really?" I hiss at my wife. "You told *them?*"

"She didn't have to, Matthew. I can count to nine. And so can

Jeremy, by the way," Brett says, his voice sounding close to normal now. Christ, I can actually make out my fingerprints on his neck.

"Matthew, now that Jeremy knows I'm pregnant, he assumes it's his baby, even though I've insisted it's not."

"Wait a minute—did he have anything to do with you going to the hospital?" I ask, feeling my pulse quicken with the thought of it. I grab her hands now and hold them tight, scouring her face for the slightest sign of distress.

She shakes her head quickly, emphatically. "No. It was a coincidence. He wanted to... to come back up here to the apartment to... talk, but I insisted on going to the hospital."

There's more to this story, I can feel it. I rub my hand over my face. This is all too much. "I'm sorry," I say to Brett hesitantly.

He shakes his head. "Not necessary, man. I'd want to strangle me too if I were you. But I'm done with him, Matthew. I'm here for you guys until the baby comes. Whatever you need."

I consider the guy in front of me—the one I just tried to kill. So it's true, then, what I've heard. Brett Corrigan really has sprouted a conscience. It would seem that this Maggie girl isn't just a social worker, she's a miracle worker.

Funny, I didn't believe in miracles before, but I do now.

Chapter 39

Matthew

There's a bottle of vodka on the table between Brett and me. I pour us each our second shot and knock mine back hard and fast. "Damn, Matthew. Pace yourself," he laughs, not holding a grudge over the whole strangling thing.

"I, uh, I appreciate you going to the hospital," I say awkwardly.

He nods. "I wanted to call you, but she wouldn't tell me where you were."

"Yeah. She knew I'd go ballistic. Which, I guess I did anyway."

"Understandable," he says, looking into his shot glass before he downs the shot.

"So what..." I don't really know how to ask this question. But, luckily, he does.

"So what happened that made me change my attitude about Jeremy?"

"Yes. Exactly. Here, let me pour you another."

He slides the shot glass across to me and I set us up for a third round. He doesn't wait to drink this time, but tips it back quickly and sets the glass back down on the table with a thunk.

The apartment is silent now, the girls having gone back to bed.

There was no sense in asking Brett and Maggie to go home at this point. And besides, I have a feeling I'm going to get more information about what really happened from Brett than I am from Julia. Hence this little *vodkapalooza* in my dining room.

Brett clears his throat and starts to speak tentatively. "Well, there was Maggie for starters. She has really changed the way I see things. I'm amazed by her capacity for kindness and generosity. Her single biggest goal is to make life better for the people who can't do it for themselves."

"She seems pretty great," I agree. But I'm also thinking there's more to his transformation. And I'm not wrong.

"And then there was Philadelphia," he begins quietly, letting the statement hang out there a little too long.

"What about it?" I ask finally.

"When I was there with the Walton Quartet I had a visit from an old classmate of ours." I know of whom he's speaking before he even utters her name. "Laurie Daughtry came to see me after one of the concerts," he says.

I recall our trip to see her not so long ago and Julia's description of the shocking transformation she had made.

"I hear she's not the same girl she was," I say.

He just looks at me for a long moment before his eyes drop down to his hands. Something is wrong. "What? What is it?"

Brett takes a deep breath and meets my eyes again reluctantly. "She killed herself, Matthew," he says, his voice barely above a whisper. "She jumped off a bridge the morning after she came to see me." I can only stare at him in stunned, horrified silence until he continues. "I—I realized how much damage I'd done...how right she'd been about me...I wanted to make things right. I wanted to... She just needed someone to validate her, to tell her she wasn't crazy."

He puts a hand to his forehead now, covering his eyes, and I can hear the catch in his throat when he finally speaks again. "Oh, who the fuck am I kidding? I wanted to beg for her forgiveness. But I was too late."

"I... I knew she wasn't doing well," I start, "but I didn't think she was...that she'd...I mean, I never would have imagined..."

He pulls his hand from his face and looks straight at me. "Christ, I'm so glad you said that, Matthew. I keep thinking that I should have known. I should have seen it in her eyes or heard it in her voice that night. I mean, she was really intense, and she was right. She was so, so right."

He leans across the table, assuring there's no chance we'll be overheard. "I see her face when I close my eyes. I hear her voice. It's like she's haunting me, Matthew."

Okay, maybe it's time to cut off the shots. Or, maybe it's time for another. I decide on the latter and pour us each another before responding.

"Julia saw her back around New Years. She went there to talk to her about Jeremy and that's when Laurie told her what he'd done," I pause for a moment. "And what you *hadn't* done. I have to admit that I was really pretty stunned, Brett. Not so much about him, as about you. I've never liked your brother. Even before he and Julia had their...thing. But I've always respected you. I just couldn't imagine you wouldn't help her."

"Yeah, well, now neither of us has to imagine. We have the truth. The cold, hard, ugly fucking truth. Julia's the one who put her finger on it. She once pointed out that I'm worse than Jeremy in a lot of ways. He was born callous. I became callous. I made a choice, he didn't."

"But you're making a choice to change that now."

He shakes his head in disagreement. "No... I mean, maybe. Maybe I am changing, but it doesn't undo anything. That woman was brutally attacked, and I could have prevented it. And now she's dead. I could have maybe prevented that, too."

I see now why Julia was willing to give Brett the benefit of the doubt. But I can think of at least one person who I'm sure isn't happy about his transformation.

"I have to ask, how has all of this played out between you and Jeremy?"

Another shot down for Brett Corrigan. Another throat clearing and deep breath. I'm starting to see a pattern here.

"Ugh. Well, things were tense when he found out I've been seeing Maggie for a while. He didn't like that I hid it from him, and he feels threatened by her. And he should. She's helped me to break this sick cycle that he and I have going. I mean, for our entire lives Jeremy has been able to count on me to look the other way. I kept my mouth shut and just let him have whatever he wanted—do whatever he wanted. Well, now I've got something—someone—that I'm not willing to give up for him or anyone else. And he is *not* happy about it."

"I can imagine."

He shakes his head. "No, I doubt you can. Things were tense before, but the other night I crossed a line. I made a choice between him and Julia. There was no way in hell I was going to let him take her anywhere. For once, I wasn't willing to just step aside and let him do whatever crazy shit he wanted to do. I think he and I were both a little stunned by that."

"Holy shit. I can't even imagine how pissed he must be."

Brett looks down at the table as he flips the empty shot glass over and over in his hands. Finally he looks up at me. "It's the ultimate betrayal as far as he's concerned," he says with just a hint of sadness in his voice.

I nod without comment. Brett is at a point where he needs to sort it all out on his own, without input from me, or anyone else. He knows his brother best and he has to decide how to proceed. And, unfortunately for him, no amount of vodka is going to make that any easier.

Julia is asleep on her side when I finally join her in bed. I wrap myself around her from the back, sharing her pillow and resting my hand on her belly. On her baby. Our baby. I hadn't expected to be so excited by his arrival. And I certainly hadn't expected to be so terrified when I heard he had been in jeopardy just a few short hours ago. It feels as if he's mine.

As I have the thought, something strikes me. Hard. Julia and I can give this child a stable, happy life—everything that we were lacking in our childhoods. But what if, at the end of the day, he's like his father? His *biological* father? This kid may be half Julia, but he's also half Jeremy. According to Brett, they were raised in a loving, nurturing home. And still, Jeremy turned out to be a monster.

I fight back the bile that threatens to rise in my throat.

Chapter 40

Matthew

"It was the young kid, he's new, and he doesn't know you or Julia. It wasn't hard for Jeremy to convince him he was a resident who needed access to the backdoor and service elevator."

"I knew it!" I say with some satisfaction.

When I pressed Julia further about her run-in with Jeremy, she told me that he had a set of keys to our building. That was when I knew it was time to call Tony Ruggiero. And he has come through for us once again.

"Yeah, well, you won't be seeing the kid again any time soon. I had a little talk with your building manager and explained how he could have endangered the life of a resident."

"I'll bet that got his attention."

"Not as much as the lawsuit I threatened him with if he didn't fire the kid and change the locks immediately. It's true what they say, money talks louder than words."

"I think that's supposed to be 'actions speak louder than words,' Tony," I correct with a grin.

"Whatever. The guy acted pretty fast after we had words, that's all I know!" He laughs. "All of the locks have been changed and, just to be safe, we're going to change your locks again later today. I'm sending my own guy for that. Building management will not have a key."

Tony doesn't miss a detail. Ever. I'm already more at ease just talking to him on the phone. "Okay, then. So what's left for us to do before the concert?"

"Not much we can do. I'll be backstage with Julia the whole time. That way, you can be out front in the audience enjoying her performance for a change. I don't think Jeremy's going to bother her though, not there anyway. He's smart enough to know that we'll be keeping a close eye on things. And as for the dress rehearsal tomorrow..."

"Yeah?"

"Your boy Dr. Sam is fucking amazing."

"Don't I know it!" I have to laugh at his depiction of the distinguished Dr. Sam Michaels as my 'boy.' "What did he do now?"

"He got the orchestra to agree to an early morning rehearsal. They'll be there at seven."

"What? How the hell did he manage that?"

"No idea. Apparently he can work magic with the musicians and their union. But then he also had a stroke of genius. He had Carnegie Hall post the rehearsal schedule listing Julia with a four o'clock slot. The stage manager and security are the only ones who know the real plan. This way, if Jeremy decides to buy himself the info, he'll be buying the *wrong* info."

"Damn, that's brilliant! I swear there's nothing that man wouldn't do for Julia."

"I can see that. How's Red doing, anyway?"

I glance across the room to where she's fast asleep on the couch, TV remote still clutched in her hand. "She's doing fine, thanks. Catching up on a lot of sleep. Dr. Sam has come by for a couple of lessons and she seems to be playing as well as ever. Our biggest challenge for the moment is her dress. And I do mean biggest. Finding something that fits her right now has been a little... challenging."

"Ah, man, that's easy," Tony says dismissively on the other end of the line.

"Tony don't tell me you have connections in the world of maternity formalwear," I challenge dubiously.

"Matthew, I have connections everywhere," he reminds me.

"Hah! Sorry to have doubted." I laugh.

"Seriously, I've got an old girlfriend who works in a bridal shop. I'll give her a call and see what she can do."

Not for the first time, I feel like I owe Tony so much more than I can ever repay him. Good thing he's not the kind of guy who keeps score. "Thanks, Tony. For everything."

"Yeah, yeah," he says. "No big deal."

I smile to myself. Only Tony Ruggiero would consider counterterrorism all in a day's work.

Chapter 41

Matthew

He doesn't think I can see him, but I can. He's in the third tier, standing in the shadows in the corner, waiting. Well, he's got a long wait ahead of him. What Jeremy doesn't know, is that Julia had her dress rehearsal first thing this morning, not at four in the afternoon as the schedule reads.

Dr. Sam stayed in the hall during the rehearsal while Tony and I kept an eye on things from outside. It's not easy to get one hundred musicians, their instruments and one conductor into Carnegie Hall surreptitiously, but I'll be damned if we didn't manage to pull it off! The rest of the performers will rehearse tomorrow, and then the big concert is the day after, on Saturday.

Right now, I'm just sitting on the edge of the stage, my legs dangling as I look out into the vast sea of empty seats. And I'm whistling. That tune from *Bridge Over the River Kwai*. Julia once told me Jeremy hates it. I'm sure he must be watching me with interest, wondering where everyone is. I look down at my watch. Four-fifteen. Tick tock.

He's stealthier than I thought, because I never see him slip out of the balcony and I'm mildly startled when he pushes open the double doors at the back of the hall. He walks down the long, carpeted aisle toward me, as if we were about to take our wedding vows.

"What's the matter, Jeremy? You lost?" I ask when he's standing just a few feet in front of me.

He smiles, unfazed. "No, I guess someone forgot to post an updated schedule backstage. I was led to believe there would be a dress rehearsal this afternoon."

I shake my head and give him a perplexed look. "Huh. No, not *this* afternoon..."

"What're you doing here then, Matthew?" he cuts me off sharply. "Clearly Julia isn't here. And, in the absence of an entire orchestra, I'm guessing she isn't going to be here any time soon."

I shrug and give him a cluck of exasperation. "That girl just does whatever she wants," I lament, rolling my eyes. "I have no idea where she'll be or when. Maybe if you hang out here long enough, you'll run into her. I mean, you've gotten lucky with that before, haven't you?" He doesn't reply, so I keep going. "You know, out by the fountain in Lincoln Center? Julia told me you decided to surprise her there."

One of his eyebrows goes up now. "Oh, she told you about our little tryst, did she? I'm surprised she'd give you those details considering what happened."

I don't like the sudden confidence in his tone. Still, I don't stop. "Oh, yeah. She told me all about how you tried to strong-arm her into going up to the apartment with you. And she told me about how you wanted to keep her from going to the Emergency Room. Does that about cover it?"

Maybe I shouldn't have thrown that last bit in because his smile tells me that *doesn't* cover it. At least, not from his perspective. His turn to cluck—actually 'crow' would be a better description for what he does.

"Matthew, Matthew. You should know by now that our Jules is prone to the dramatic. Women in her condition often are. It's the hormones. I only suggested we spend some time alone together in the apartment because of the kiss."

Okay. Now he's just trying to piss me off. "Please. As if she'd kiss you, you psycho fuck," I sneer.

"Oh, but she did, Matthew. Just ask her. It was such a nice, tender kiss, too. I'd forgotten how soft her lips are. Yeah, the little cocktease had me good and hard before she pulled that hospital stunt. She was all ready to take me up to your place for a good fuck. We do that well, Jules and I, in case you didn't know. So well, in fact, that we made that little fleshy ball of snot and shit that she's about to saddle you with."

I struggle to keep my face immobile as he speaks. "Yeah, well, you keep on believing whatever you want, Jeremy."

He makes a big show of appearing to remember something. "Oh, say, I hope it wasn't too inconvenient for Julia that I opted to play the Bach. You know, as the gold medal winner, I get first dibs on repertoire. And I made sure to suggest the other two play composers that just happen to have major cello pieces that Julia could have performed. I guess she'll have to trot out that tired old Boccherini piece. Ah, well. I'm sure the audience won't be expecting much from second best. They might even feel sorry for the knocked-up slut."

I take a breath that is so slow and silent that you probably wouldn't notice it if you were standing right in front of me, the way Jeremy is right now. I do this because I know if I breathe in hard, the torrent of hatred that streams out of my mouth will level this building. So I go slowly, and I pace myself. I wait for my heart rate to drop and, finally, I smile.

"Well, as much as I'd love to kick your ass for that comment, I'm going to cut you some slack, considering your recent... loss."

He squints at me suspiciously.

"Your brother," I explain. "I hear he cut the cord between the two of you. But your loss is my gain...I can't tell you what a huge help he's been to Julia and me. I really believe him when he says there's nothing he won't do to keep her safe. Oh, but poor Jeremy! What will you do without an evil henchman to do your bidding?"

Now my tone is just plain obnoxious. I have devolved into schoolyard taunting, but damn it feels good! As he looks at me, he does that thing. That thing where his eyes get really squinty like little slivers, and they look all hard. He's mastered this one to a science, boy. It even gives me the creeps when he adds to it that tiny little smirk of his.

"You never learn, do you, Matty boy? I told you once before, but obviously you need a little reminder. Julia James is your Achilles heel. She is what makes you vulnerable. So don't be worried about what I'm going to do to you. Be worried about what I'm going to do to her."

I hop down off the stage, so we are standing level, face to face. I put my best sardonic smile on to match his. My menacing tone isn't quite as effective, but it's not half bad.

"Well, then you might as well get her name right, Jeremy, or you may miss her on the schedule again. These days, it's Ayers. Mrs. Julia. *Ayers*. And, if you think you scare me, or her, you should think again."

And with that, I walk right past him, my shoulder knocking into his as I head back up the aisle. I stop for a second and turn to face him again, noting that he has also turned to watch me walk away.

"Oh, and you can take your bastardized Bach Cello *Suites* and shove them up your ass. Julia wanted me to thank you, actually, because that little stunt of yours forced her to find a piece that is going to show the whole world who the *real* Kreisler champion is."

If he could eviscerate me with his eyes, he would do it in this moment. But I don't care anymore. No one threatens my family and gets away with it.

Game on, motherfucker.

Chapter 42

Matthew

It's dinnertime when I get back to the apartment to wake Julia. The dress rehearsal this morning really took a lot out of her, and she's been napping all afternoon. But I know that if she doesn't get up now, she won't be able to sleep tonight.

"Julia," I whisper, sitting on the bed next to where she's lying. Not so much as a finger stirs. "Julia? Honey, you need to wake-up," I say a little louder, running my hand up and down the arm that's sticking out from under the covers.

"Hmmm?"

"You need to eat something."

Slowly she turns onto her back and opens her eyes just a slit. "What time is it?" she mumbles.

"Almost six-thirty."

From somewhere in her chest, she lets out an extended groan, then takes a deep breath through her nose and tries her best to sit up.

"Here, let me help you. I've got a bubble bath ready for you in the tub."

Now her eyes are open. "A bubble bath?" She looks as if she can't believe her good luck. "Really? You made me a bubble bath?" she asks again, like I might be kidding her.

"I did! Now come on, let's get you up, Mrs. Ayers." I help her swing her feet over the side of the bed and stand.

Julia follows me into the bathroom. "Oh, Matthew!" she exclaims, putting a hand over her delighted smile.

A mountain of bubbles floats atop the water in the tub. Literally.

Note to self here: an entire bottle of bubble bath is *not* single use.

I have her radio tuned to the classical station, so the room smells likes lilacs and sounds like Chopin. Even *I* know I did well! I help her step over the side of the tub and slide down, most of her disappearing into its warm, fluffy, foaminess.

"Ohhhh," she moans as she sinks into the water. "I could just sit here forever."

I look at my watch. "Well, you can't stay forever, but you can stay for about forty-five minutes while I finish cooking dinner. Deal?"

"Uh-huh," she murmurs, barely acknowledging the fact that I'm still in the room.

I chuckle as I go back out to the kitchen. Julia's had a rough couple of weeks and I've been gone for all of it. Now that I'm back, I'm determined to help her get calm and centered again—to get her happy again.

When she finally finds her way out of the bedroom an hour later, the transformation is amazing "Wow, Matthew, that was so..." Both she and her sentence stop short as she surveys the apartment around her. "What did you do?" she asks, bouncing up and down on the balls of her feet excitedly.

I have turned our apartment into a sea of her favorite color, pink. Roses, carnations, lilies, daisies... I think every pink flower in midtown must be in this apartment right now.

"Thank God you're such a sound sleeper, it took three guys to deliver all the flowers!" I laugh.

Her eyes are damp with tears when they finally find their way across the room and back to me.

"Oh, Matthew," she whispers, walking to where I stand by the breakfast bar, and wrapping her arms around me tightly. She rests her head on my chest. "I can't believe you did all this for me."

I push her away just far enough so I can see her face. "There is nothing I wouldn't do for you, Julia. Nothing." I pause for a long moment. "And that includes moving back to the city."

Her eyebrows shoot up in surprise. "What are you talking about?"

"We both know that you and I have been...struggling the last few months. And there are a thousand reasons why, some of them more serious than others." She nods her agreement reluctantly but doesn't say anything. "I think part of the problem is the Long Island house."

"What? The house is so beautiful, so perfect! I can't wait until it's ready for us to move into!" she protests.

"I know. But it won't be home, will it? Julia, you're expecting a baby. We got married. We moved and you left school. That's a lot of change in not a lot of time. I'm afraid that maybe I rushed and pushed you too much. I was so excited by the idea of us being a family—of me having a family again—that I didn't stop to think about how happy you would or wouldn't be living in my little fairytale."

She reaches up with a small, soft hand and strokes my cheek lovingly. I lean my face into her touch. "You dear, sweet, boy. You have no idea, do you?"

Now it's my turn to look confused. "What?"

"Matthew Ayers, you saved me. You saved me all those years ago at the Children's Home. You saved me from a really awful situation with Jeremy. And now you've saved me, and the baby, by giving us all something I've only ever dreamed about. A family. A loving, caring, nurturing family."

Now she stretches on tippy-toes to kiss me. I meet her halfway and her lips are soft and sweet on mine.

"Matthew," she starts, pulling away just a little so that I feel her warm breath on my face as she speaks. "I don't care where we live, because as long as you're there, it will always be my home."

Chapter 43

Matthew

"Jeremy has asked if he can change the order of performance and go first."

Julia looks up sharply from the makeup mirror in her dressing room where she's been applying mascara. "What? Why?"

"I don't know. Probably just to mess with you. Also, I'm thinking that after the discussion he and I had the other day, he wants to go first because he thinks he'll make the rest of you sound worse by comparison."

"Seriously? Well that seems like pretty stupid logic," she says with a frown. "So what's the new order then?"

"You're last."

She thinks about this for a minute and nods. "I can do that."

"Are you sure? You know you get pretty tired right about that time of night. Wouldn't surprise me if he somehow knows that, too."

"Well it's not that hard to guess, I'm tired pretty much all the time!" she says with a wry smile. "No, don't worry, I'll be fine."

I walk up behind her, and we survey one another's reflections in the mirror. I lean down and kiss the top of her head.

"Hey! Watch the bun!" she says with a mock stern tone.

"Oh, sorry. Maybe I should have aimed a little lower..."

I deliver loud, sloppy kisses on her neck, knowing this is where she's most ticklish.

"Stop! Stop! Stop!" she gasps between bouts of laughter.

It takes her a second to catch her breath as I stand above her, smiling impishly.

"I'll bet that took the edge off the nerves!" I proclaim confidently.

"It did, but now you've stressed me out about my make-up. What a mess! You're awful, Matthew." She laughs, dabbing at her face with a tissue.

"And you're gorgeous, Julia. Forget about the make-up."

She gives me a sweet smile. "I love you. I love you with my entire heart. There isn't any of it left for anyone but you and our children."

"Children?"

She shrugs. "Why not? I wouldn't mind another, would you?"

"Whoa! Don't you think we should get this one out into the world before we start planning for the next one?" I laugh.

"Well, maybe. But not too long, I'd like one that looks like you."

I kiss her cheek, damp from tickled tears. "Can I get you anything?" I ask.

"Actually, I'm a little thirsty. Would you please pass me a bottle of water from the table over there?"

I walk across the small room to where they have set-up a table with water and snacks for Julia. I grab a bottle of the water and start to open it, but it doesn't feel right. It opens too easily, as if it's been opened before. Holding it up, the bottle appears to be full. I pick up another one. Same thing. And another and another all with the same results.

"Nice try, asshole," I mutter under my breath.

"What did you say?"

"Nothing. Say, have you had any of this water since you've been here?"

She looks at me over her shoulder and shakes her head.

"Okay. Do me a favor and don't touch the bottles. Understand?"

"You don't think…"

"I don't know what I think anymore, Julia."

"Now you're just being paranoid."

"I think Cal would disagree," I say quietly. Her eyes meet mine in the mirror's reflection.

"You're right," she says, looking down with a sigh.

"Okay, I'm going to go out and get you a bottle of water from the vending machine," I say, heading for the door.

"Matthew don't worry about it. I want you to see the whole concert—including Jeremy. I'll ask Tony to get one for me."

I glance at my watch. Fifteen minutes to curtain. "Are you sure you don't want me to stay here with you until it's time?"

"Absolutely."

"Okay, then. Keep this door locked when Tony's not in here with you, okay?"

She nods and uses her hands to shoo me out with a sweeping motion. "Go. I am so ready for this, Matthew. No one is going to take this night from me. Not Jeremy, not anyone."

I hope to God she's right. Either way, I guess we're about to find out.

Chapter 44

Matthew

There are musicians who see Carnegie Hall as just another venue. Then there are those who see it as a sort of Mt. Everest—a peak to aspire to, a journey to train for. Some spend their entire lives planning their ascent, while others simply take a run at it and start climbing.

I've played Carnegie a number of times as part of ensembles like the Walton Quartet, but I have yet to have the experience that Julia is about to have. When she steps out onto the stage, she will be the center of attention, all eyes fixed on her. I know she's nervous, but it's a good nervous. The kind you get when you're finally about to come face to face with your dream, your destiny. Julia is about to climb to the most stunning vista she has ever seen, and I cannot wait to watch her summit.

s I make my way from backstage out to the front of the house, I catch a glimpse of Jeremy across the stage. He's blowing into his horn to keep it warm. Since he has opted to play an arrangement of one of the Bach Suites for Unaccompanied Cello, there is no orchestra waiting for him. He can take his sweet time and step out onstage when he's good and ready.

He looks up suddenly, noticing me noticing him. I watch as he stares at me over his horn while continuing to blow into it and run his fingers over the keys. I smile and give him a little wave. He takes his hand out of the bell long enough to flip me off.

Conspicuous tonight is the absence of Dr. Rich Kellogg. He should be right here backstage giving Jeremy one last pep talk before his Carnegie Hall debut. That's what teachers do...but I guess Rich is putting a little distance between himself and Jeremy. If that's the case, then it's smart thinking on his part.

I duck into the audience via a side door and make my way up and around, snaking down one aisle and up another to reach my seat. It isn't hard to spot the space that's been left for me, because it's one of just a handful of open chairs. This place is jam-packed.

I imagine that for most of the people here, Jeremy is the big draw. Not his playing so much as the events surrounding his ascension as gold medal winner of the Kreisler International Music Competition. Did he have anything to do with the death of his competitor, Cal Burridge? The police say no. The public isn't quite so sure. And while in Europe the controversy caused audiences to boycott Jeremy's Kreisler tour, here in the US, where we enjoy a steady diet of tabloid headlines, people can't get close enough. It's kind of sickening when you really think about it. So I try not to think about it.

I squeeze past the knees of a dozen people as I make my way sideways across the row until I get to my seat. Dr. Sam is waiting for me. He hands me a program as I sit down.

"How's Julia doing back there?" he asks.

"Surprisingly well. She's very calm. And very determined to kick Jeremy's ass," I say with a smile.

He gives a hearty laugh at the idea of tiny Julia sticking it to Mr. Charisma, himself. "Here, have a program," he says.

I open it, and there is Jeremy, perfect smile, strong jaw, tousled hair. I'd rip the page out and set it on fire right now, but I don't have any matches on me. Besides, it wouldn't be nearly as satisfying as ripping the real thing to shreds and setting *him* on fire.

As soon as I have this thought, the house lights go down and I watch as the real-life Jeremy Corrigan steps out onstage. There's a huge swell of applause for the Kreisler International Music Competition gold medalist/murderer. Probably more for the former than the latter... but who knows?

The performance is a reminder to me that while Jeremy is an evil fuck, there's no denying he is a brilliant evil fuck. He puts the horn to his lips, takes a deep breath and starts to play. From the very first note, he makes the Bach sound as if it had been written for the horn rather than the cello. And that's saying something.

String players don't need to worry about when or where to breathe when they play, because they're using their hands, not their mouths. A horn, on the other hand, requires a constant, steady stream of air to be played. So when a horn player picks up this piece, originally written for a stringed instrument, there is the immediate conundrum of where to catch a breath. Not having written it for a wind instrument, Bach never took that into consideration. And since the *Suites for Unaccompanied Cello* are, as the name implies, unaccompanied, there isn't an orchestra or a pianist to provide a little cover to grab a gasp here and there.

I'm not able to tell where Jeremy is taking his breaths—that's how fast he's getting them in. This really irritates me because I would be so happy to see the son of a bitch fail. But I know in my heart he won't, he's just too fucking good. And tonight, he sounds as amazing as always. By the time Jeremy plays the last note of the last movement of the Suite, he has shown the audience a perfect reincarnation of a beloved composition. The swell of applause is huge as he takes a bow. And another. And another.

Finally, the lights come up again so that the stage can be reset for the orchestra to come out. The fourth place winner in the competition, Mikhail Fedoseyev is up next. He's a talented, but very temperamental violinist. Still, unlike Jeremy, he's been able to parlay his Kreisler placement into a slew of guest performances with orchestras around the world. His handlers must be working with him on manners, too, because I don't see any of the usual snark and sneering that comes with this guy. To the contrary, he's professional as he interacts with the Maestro and the Concert Master. And his playing is nothing short of brilliant. Oh, yeah, if this guy can keep his shit together, he's going to go far.

During Mikhail's standing ovation, I crane my neck and look around, trying to spot my student, Rita Michelle. I left her a pair of tickets at the box office. Phil Tonka told me she did a bang-up job taking my place in the faculty ensemble. I'm not at all surprised. Now, maybe next time, she'll have a little more faith in herself. Unfortunately, it's not Rita Michelle that I end up spotting. Damn it!

"I'll be right back," I say to Dr. Sam, getting to my feet and fighting my way through the throngs of people headed for the bathrooms and the lobby bar for intermission.

I'm able to catch up with her just as she steps outside of the hall, pack of cigarettes and lighter out of her purse before the door has even closed behind her. Kelly doesn't recognize me at first. It comes back to her after a minute, though.

"Martin?" she asks, returning the cigarettes to her bag.

"Matthew," I correct her curtly. "What are you doing here, Kelly?"

She looks a little taken aback by the question.

"I—uh...well...I came to see Julia play. I read about the concert in the paper..."

"Are you out of your mind?"

It's not a rhetorical question, either. I'm waiting for an answer.

"No," she replies, gathering her courage to come back at me. "I've come to see my daughter play. I have just as much right as anyone to..."

"You don't have *any* rights to *anything* that involves Julia. You gave them up when she was five years old," I hiss at the woman who bears an unnerving resemblance to her daughter.

"And who, exactly, are *you* to make that pronouncement, young man?" she hurls back at me.

"I'm the one who was there for her when she was placed into an orphanage. An *orphanage*, Kelly! I'm the one who was there when her father showed up to say goodbye before he killed himself. I'm the one who was there when..." I stop. I'm done. "You know what? I don't have to explain myself to you. You're nobody. You're just some bitch who abandoned a helpless little girl to go and start a whole new life. *That's* who you are."

I turn quickly and run right into Mila Strassman. Her face lit by a huge smile and excited eyes. "Matthew! I'm so glad I saw you! How's Julia? Is she ready to play? How amazing! And wasn't Jeremy amazing? Wow, he's *so* good! Too bad about him and Julia..."

Oh, for fuck's sake, not now! Please, not now. But it's too late. Once Mila starts there is little you can do to slow her roll.

"But you! I couldn't believe it when I heard you got married! I was so mad at Dr. Sam for not telling me! I mean, he gave her away, right? She doesn't have a father, I don't think, so that was really sweet..."

"Mila..." I'm trying to shoehorn my way into her stream of conscious ramblings, but the woman next to me beats me to it.

"I'm sorry, did you just say Julia James is recently married?"

Mila swings her gaze to the redhead, noticing her for the first time. Holy. Shit. "Oh! Oh, wow! You have *got* to be Julia's mom! I mean, who else could you be? You look just like her! Or she looks just like you, I'm never sure exactly how that's supposed to go..."

"Yes," Kelly says firmly. "Yes, I'm Julia's mother, Kelly Randall. And your name?"

"I'm Mila, Mila Strassman. I was Julia's stand partner at McInnes. I play cello, too. Wow! Julia's mom! I don't know why I thought she was an orphan..."

"Because she *is* an orphan," I snarl.

Now Mila is really confused. The smile is there, but the eyes are vacant as she processes. In another second we'll be seeing smoke coming out of her ears as she spins in circles saying *'Does not compute! Does not compute!'* over and over.

"Mila, this woman is no relation to Julia. Do *not* tell her anything. *Nothing*, Mila, you understand?"

Mila nods, though I'm not at all sure she understands what I've just said to her. So, to be safe, I grab her gently, but firmly by the forearm and start to lead her away with me. "Come on, Mila, I'll walk you back to your seat," I mutter.

If Kelly James or Randall—or whatever the hell her name is— wants the dirt on Julia, she'll have to find it somewhere else. As we make our way back through the packed lobby, I hear someone calling my name. I'm tempted to ignore it and keep going, but it's growing closer and more insistent. Reluctantly, I stop and turn to see Maggie Collins weaving through the crowd to get to me.

I hardly recognize the bombshell moving in my direction. She's wearing one of those 'little black dresses' that Julia is always going on about, and she's ditched the thick Elvis Costello glasses for contacts tonight. Somehow she's even managed to wrestle her dark, curly hair into some kind of a twisty thing on the back of her head. And damn can this girl move in a pair of heels! Brett is struggling just to keep up with her.

"Matthew!" she says, breathlessly when she finally reaches me. "I thought that was you! How's Julia holding up?"

"Surprisingly well. Jeremy switched up the order last minute, but it didn't faze her a bit. She seems very calm and excited to play."

"That's wonderful! I'm so glad to hear it," Maggie says with a brilliant, ruby-red smile.

"Oh, I'm sorry, how rude of me! I'm Maggie Collins," she holds out a hand to Mila who is all smiles, until she realizes that Maggie is here with Brett.

The smile turns into a squinty, death ray-shooting glare. Uh-oh. Now I seem to recall Julia mentioning something about Mila having a thing for Brett.

"Maggie, Mila is that fabulous cellist I was telling you about," Brett says, not missing the look, or a beat as he joins us.

So he's aware of Mila's infatuation, I guess. Well, this could get awkward. Or entertaining. Maybe both.

"Of course!" Maggie says enthusiastically. If she's noticed the girl's cool demeanor, she's not showing it. "Mila, I'm so happy to finally meet you!"

And then something unexpected happens. Maggie leans in close to Mila and puts a hand on her arm. "You know, I was hoping we'd run into you here tonight," she says conspiratorially.

"You were?" Mila asks, stunned.

"Ever since Brett told me about you, I haven't been able to stop thinking how you should meet a social worker in my office. And look at you! He'd go crazy to have a date with a hottie like you! Are you... available? Do you think you might let me fix you up on a blind date, Mila?"

Maggie's gaze is so expectant, so open and hopeful, that even *I* want Mila to say yes. And she does.

"Uh, yeah, sure. That would be nice... Maggie," she says with an uncharacteristically shy, awkward smile.

It is, by far, the shortest sentence I've ever heard the girl speak. Will wonders never cease?

I can see clearly now why Brett has fallen so hard for this woman. She is the polar opposite of Jeremy. Like him, she tries to find what is lacking in someone. And like him, she tries to fill that need. Unlike him, she does it with the purest of motives. Unlike him, she wants to lift people up, not drag them down. Maggie Collins is a study in compassion, kindness and grace. And she will be what saves Brett Corrigan from his brother, and himself.

Chapter 45

Matthew

By the time I escort Mila to her spot in the balcony and once more displace everyone in my row to get back to my seat, the intermission is just about over. I glance at my watch again and again, hoping that I can somehow make time go faster. I'm not going to breathe easy until this night is over, and we've still got the pianist's performance next. Even as I think this, the stagehands roll the huge grand piano out to center stage.

"Relax, Matthew," Dr. Sam says. "She's fine. It's all going to be fine."

He's right, I shouldn't be so concerned. Tony is keeping Julia company in the dressing room. When it's time, he'll personally escort her right to the wings, where she'll go out on stage. Nobody messes with Tony. Not even Jeremy Corrigan.

"Did you see the profile they did on Julia in the program?" Dr. Sam asks, trying to distract me while we wait for the pianist to come out.

"No, I didn't."

I thumb through until I see her. The picture is black and white, so you don't get the full effect of her hair, but her coloring looks even more alabaster here. It is a picture taken just after she became a Kreisler finalist. She looks over-the-moon happy. Of course, this was when she and Jeremy were first a 'thing.' But before I can get too far into those thoughts, I hear the chimes that beckon everyone back to their seats. At last, we're going to hear Lucy Kim play.

She's a petite young woman from China who's never without a smile on her face. And, although she practices for hours on end Lucy seems to have found some balance between her career and her life—a rarity for a pianist at her level.

Earlier this afternoon she introduced me to her boyfriend. He came all the way from China to see her perform. And who could blame the guy? As she takes the stage to play Dvorak, Lucy looks like an exotic flower in her sparkly, bright orange dress. A dress that is way, way shorter than it ought to be.

She shakes hands with the Maestro and Concertmaster before turning to toward the audience for a quick bow. Then she doesn't waste a single second. The moment the little orange dress hits the piano bench she gives the conductor the nod to begin the orchestral introduction that paves the way for her entrance. And when it comes, Lucy Kim becomes a different person.

Her hands hit the keys in short, percussive bursts and then they move together, up and down the keyboard, with a deliberate, firm touch that will, eventually, give way to a softer, more sweeping line. But right now, as these early notes of Dvorak's Piano Concerto pour from the piano, Lucy Kim reminds us that while she may be easy going and easy on the eyes, she is a force to be reckoned with behind the keyboard. By the time she finishes we're all on the edge of our seats, hanging on her every note. The girl is nothing short of brilliant.

When we jump up to applaud for Lucy, I realize, gratefully, that the time has flown by while she captivated the entire audience with her playing. The little dynamo in the orange sequins bows again and again in acknowledgement of the ongoing applause. Then, I see her boyfriend, what's his name... Wang? No, Yang. That's it. He squeezes his way past the first row ticket holders until he's standing directly in front of and below where she is on stage. Come to think of it, they're positioned exactly where Jeremy and I were just a couple of days ago.

When she spots Yang, Lucy bends down—very carefully in the super-short skirt—so he can hand her a massive bouquet of flowers and blow her a kiss. She stands and holds the bouquet above her head as if it's a trophy, and the audience cheers with renewed fervor. It takes another five minutes for the crowd to finally quiet and allow her to exit the stage.

A low level buzz fills the hall as the piano is rolled away and the crew sets up a chair for Julia. There's no music stand this time around because she's memorized her piece. The piece that she and Dr. Sam have been working on non-stop for the last few days.

Composed by Eric Whitacre, Julia only needed to hear that it was written for her cello idol, Julian Lloyd Webber, and she was onboard to play it. Unlike my wife, I needed a little more convincing that this was the right choice. After all, the others picked much longer pieces. Pieces that are more technically demanding than this one...but when I heard her play it and I was reminded that I should never, ever underestimate Julia.

Now, as the house lights grow dim one last time, a hush falls over the iconic hall. I'm holding tight to the armrests on both sides of my seat, knuckles white with tension. Next to me, Dr. Sam is staring straight ahead, hands folded in his lap. This is a deja vu moment for us—reliving the last performance Julia gave. That night when she walked out from the wings, a chalky, white, trembling shell of herself, barely able to find her way to the front of the stage, let alone play her cello.

Within a matter of moments, it is quite clear that *this* is not that night.

Julia strides out confidently, head held high, broad smile lifting all the exhaustion and anxiety that have clouded her features for months now. And whoever Tony's lady friend is, she is brilliant. I won't pretend to know anything about women's fashion, but the gown she found for Julia couldn't be more perfect. It's made of a midnight blue fabric that gathers above her baby bump and then cascades down around her. It's as if she is wrapped in the inky waters of the Atlantic. She's done away with the fussy bun and her wild red-blonde waves spill loosely down to the middle of her back. She is, quite simply, the most beautiful woman I've ever seen in my entire life.

Like the three performers before her, Julia shakes hands with the Concertmaster and the Maestro before taking her seat in front of the orchestra. As she settles in I notice for the first time just how far she has to stretch around her own girth to be able to reach the front strings of the cello. Christ, another week and she wouldn't have been able to do it physically.

When the Maestro looks at her over his shoulder, she gives him a nod to indicate that she is ready to play. I hold my breath.

The orchestra opens with an ethereal passage that's like listening to the twilight sky, complete with twinkling stars. The strings spin a cloudy bed as the entrance for the cello. This piece, called *The River Cam*, was inspired by the River Cam in Cambridge, England. But Julia told me that she hears something different in its notes and, as I close my eyes and listen, I understand.

It's as if the cello is a voice telling a story. It's an ageless and tragic tale of loss. It recalls better times. It reflects upon open fields of flowers and sunnier days. There was love and it was carefree. Then the cello's voice becomes a nostalgic reverie against the swirling strings below it, crying out. The cello holds tight to the memories, even as they are enveloped in darkness.

Little bits and pieces of the opening melody bubble up to the surface and float away into the distance. Then the twilight returns again, but for just a few measures. Suddenly, there is turbulence. A churning discord that the strings create. Now the cello comes in alone with a solitary recap of the melody. It's a soliloquy for Julia to deliver at her leisure. She stretches it, taking her time. And then the orchestra slips in beneath her, picking up speed as she drops in alongside them, and then against them. Above them, and then below them until, at last, they are one. She is riding the cusp of their harmonious wave until, suddenly, everything stops and there is perfect silence.

You might think it's ended, just like that. But then the cello—longing and wandering and searching—returns with its deep utterances and high pleas. When I open my eyes, I see Julia using every inch of her body as she reaches around and places her bow low on the strings, playing the bass—the belly of the cello. Gradually, the voice climbs its way back up before fading away into nothingness.

Carnegie Hall is completely still. Completely silent.

We are all—each one of us in this packed concert hall—literally breathless by what we have just heard and witnessed. And then, as if experiencing a collective resuscitation, we all—each one of us in this packed concert hall—gasp aloud and jump to our feet.

The reception to Jeremy's playing may have been energetic and enthusiastic, but it was nothing—*nothing*—compared to what is happening right now. This isn't clapping and cheering, this is a roar. A solid mass of ecstatic sound that rings out in recognition of the beauty we have just experienced.

It is a rhapsody.

The conductor comes off of his podium to help Julia to her feet. She sets the cello against her chair and takes his extended arm, allowing him to walk her down to the very front of the stage where she can see, clearly, the thousands of appreciative faces that greet her. She looks up and across the balconies, then down and across the orchestra seats. This time there are no tears, there is only joy.

Chapter 46

Matthew

Dr. Sam and I get backstage to find Julia surrounded by a sea of people excitedly congratulating her. I spot Lester Morgan, the Kreisler International Music Competition Director, leaning close to her ear so she can hear him above the din. She's nodding and smiling.

Tony is standing just behind Julia and to the side, out of her way, but close enough to grab her if he has to. And there, again, is Kelly, worming her way through the crowd and moving closer to her. This woman just will not take a hint.

"Goddammit!" I mutter under my breath, leaving Dr. Sam behind so I can make my way through the throng and get to Julia as quickly as I can.

But I'm not fast enough. I see the smile on Julia's face fade as she spots Kelly approaching her. The woman is speaking excitedly and gesturing to Julia's belly. Well, now she knows she's going to be a grandmother.

I catch Tony's eye and point to the mother. He nods and slips in behind Julia, putting his hands on her shoulders and guiding her out of the crowd and away. He's managed to get her back by the dressing rooms by the time I catch up with them—but I'm not the only one following. In fact, I almost have to stop and laugh at the spectacle which is unfolding in the hallway.

Kelly Randall persists in trying to get Julia's attention. "Julia! Julia, honey, please just talk to me. Julia, oh, my God, I'm going to be a grandmother…"

Off to one side is Jeremy, eyebrow cocked, smirk firmly affixed as he watches Kelly buzz around the hallway. He's fanning the flames. "Yeah, Julia, talk to your mommy. Tell her all about the terrible things big, bad daddy did to poor, pathetic, little Julia."

And, in the middle of all this, totally oblivious to what anyone else is saying, is Mila, her mouth going a million miles a minute. "You didn't tell me you're having a baby! You're having a baby, Julia! When are you having the baby? Do you know what it is? Oh, I hope it's a girl! With red hair like yours! Or maybe a boy!"

Tony is trying to swivel Julia first in one direction, then another, but no matter which way they turn, they are accosted. One estranged mother, one psychotic ex-boyfriend and one blabbermouth extraordinaire. The poor guy may have finally met a situation that even he can't handle.

The din is ridiculously loud as it echoes down the cavernous hallway. I'm just about to let out a loud whistle to quiet the chaos, but Julia beats me to it.

"*Hey!*" she shouts louder than I have ever heard in all the years I've known her. Everyone stops. Everything quiets. She points to Mila. "Yes, I'm having a baby. Go home and I'll call you tomorrow." Mila nods, wide-eyed, and turns back down the hallway.

"You!" she points to her mother now. "Please just go. If I want to see you, I know where to find you, but don't hold your breath."

Kelly looks as if she's been slapped. It also appears as if she is going to say something else, but the look on Julia's face makes her think better of it. With head lowered, she follows in the direction that Mila went. Now it's just her and Tony and me and Jeremy.

"And you," she says, voice lower, walking right up to where

Jeremy has been standing, looking on in amusement. "Really nice job tonight," she says sincerely.

I'm stunned. What the hell is she doing? Even Jeremy looks surprised by the compliment. But then something unexpected happens. A big, broad smile alights on her face, her eyes crinkle and she looks positively giddy.

"Too bad I *still* kicked your ass!" she taunts. "Too bad for *you*, that is!" She starts to turn away but seems to remember something. "Oh, by the way, Lester Morgan just offered me your recording contract. How do you like that, you stupid prick?"

The unflappable Tony Ruggiero is looking at her as if she's just sprouted an additional head. I happen to know that she's referencing the fact that he called her a 'stupid cunt' right before he dumped her at the Kreisler Competition finals. Clearly, Jeremy recognizes the sentiment, too. His jaw has tightened and he's glaring at her with steely, narrowed eyes. I'm sure if they were alone he'd...well, probably best not to think about what would happen if they were alone because that's never going to happen again. Not if I can help it. And I can.

Finally, Julia turns in my direction and beckons to me with her finger. "And you," she says. "Come here and kiss your wife."

I'm there before she can blink an eye.

Part Four

Treatise

Jeremy

Violation is a favorite weapon in my arsenal. It can be wielded the same way as a gun or a knife, but with a stealth that makes it a hundred times more powerful. Violation slips past the gates, it goes over the wall, and it infiltrates the sanctity of your target's soul, because it knows *that* is where the real damage is done. Violation shatters your victim's every illusion of safety and security by demonstrating its ability to destroy, no matter how many precautions are taken.

What makes violation such an effective weapon is its insidious nature. It delivers blow after paralyzing blow long after its initial attack. A gunshot wound can be treated immediately, but violation is a cancer that spreads throughout the mind and the body, ravaging confidence and destroying any sense of peace and security.

Violation erodes the self-confidence to such an extent, that your victim can no longer be certain of what is real and what is imagined. She can't trust her instincts because they have failed her once before in allowing this menace entry to his life. So the attack replays itself again and again in excruciating detail, well after the event has transpired. Having been forced to be, and do, and experience things against her will, violation forever establishes her as a victim—powerless against opposing forces, proving that anything may be taken away at any time. There is no such thing as safety. There is no such thing as security.

Chapter 47

Jeremy

The woman sitting across the aisle from me is staring. I mean blatantly, unabashedly gawking at me. What. The. Fuck? That's when I spot the newspaper in her hand. She's looking between my face on page 1A to my face in seat 5B. I give her my most disarming smile, but she doesn't budge. Okay, time to take another tack.

"May I?" I ask, pointing to the paper.

She's taken aback. "I—uh...well...alright..." she says reluctantly, handing it across the aisle.

I make a big show of snapping the paper open and holding its full length up so that she, and any other busybodies, can get a good look. Then I turn to her, holding the picture of me next to my face. "I don't know," I say, "Do you think this picture makes me look fat?"

Her eyes get big, and she jerks herself to face forward. Still, I can see her sneaking little glimpses of me out of the corner of her eye. It's actually not a bad picture of me standing on stage, gold medal hanging around my neck. But it's not just my picture featured in inky color. Next to it is a similar picture of Julia, with the silver medal in-hand. But it's the headline that grabs me.

*I***T'S SILVER THAT SHINES BRIGHTEST AT THE K*REISLER* I*NTERNATIONAL* M*USIC* C*OMPETITION* G*ALA.*

What. The. Fuck. The story is nothing but a glorified puff piece on Julia and her performance at the gala. She was *'sublime'* and *'nothing short of brilliant.'* Where the hell am *I* in here? My eyes move past the bullshit about Julia to my own name.

*W*HILE MAKING EASY WORK OF THE B*ACH* S*UITE FOR* S*OLO* C*ELLO,* ONE WONDERS WHY M*R.* C*ORRIGAN* CHOSE A PIECE THAT WASN'T WRITTEN FOR HIS INSTRUMENT. T*HERE WAS SOMETHING DEFINITELY* LOST IN THE TRANSLATION ON STAGE LAST NIGHT...

"Fucking idiots," I mumble under my breath.

The story goes on to recount my spectacular win at the Kreisler International Music Competition and how I got to that point by stepping in for a friend and colleague who died tragically the day before he was set to compete. All true so far if you overlook the fact that I hated Cal Burridge.

And then, the article takes a decidedly negative turn, citing unnamed sources that are convinced that Cal's death was no accident, and that I was the one to benefit most from his untimely demise. It wraps-up by saying that—while I have been cleared of all allegations—a persistent dark cloud continues to hang over my reputation and will likely continue to do so for years to come.

I smack the paper down on my tray top table, knocking my glass of champagne into the aisle. Unnamed my ass! Matthew and Julia are still at it, telling anyone who will listen that I'm a murderer. Okay, maybe I am. But that's not the point! The rest of the world doesn't need to know it.

"Mr. Corrigan, let me take care of that. May I get you another drink?"

The stewardess—excuse me, *flight attendant*—is leaning in very close to me. The spectacular view of her cleavage takes the edge off my fury. *Nice.*

"Well now, that depends..." I smile. "Would you care to join me for it when we land?"

The cleavage becomes rosy as she blushes. It reminds me a little bit of Julia, always blushing at the slightest bit of attention—even the mildest allusion to sex. What's this chick's name again? When she straightens up I see the nametag that says Suzanne. "That's very nice of you to offer, Mr. Corrigan, but I'm not permitted to socialize with passengers," Suzanne says before turning on her shiny black heels and walking back to the galley.

Bitch. She could if she wanted to. And I can tell she does. A few minutes later, she returns with a fresh glass of champagne, sets it on my tray and takes the empty away with a brief smile and a nod.

"Miss Lansing, may I get you another drink?" she asks Nosey Nancy next to me.

Ah, well, at least the booze is free. And abundant. When I pick up the champagne, I spot something on the napkin beneath it.

Motor City Lounge, Terminal B, gate 24.

I smile to myself and slip the napkin into my pocket.
Friendly skies, indeed.

I don't know who invented the Snooze Suite, but whoever he or she is, they are fucking brilliant. And I do mean *fucking*. It's a business that provides little rooms that rent by the hour for weary travelers. For forty bucks, you get use of a couch/bed, TV, computer connection and complimentary snacks. But it's BYOF. *Bring Your Own*

Fuck. Which is fine by me right now, as I palm Suzanne's perfect, alabaster ass.

There's just something about taking a girl from behind. I don't have to look at the sappy romance in her eyes. In this position, she's exactly what I think of her as—a nameless, faceless piece of ass. I don't give a shit who she is or what her hopes and dreams are. I couldn't give a shit about getting her number—unless, of course, she's a really great lay—and I certainly don't want her to have mine.

I give Suzanne a nice, hard smack on the cheek.

"Ouch!" she complains. But when I reach around and run my hands between her legs, she goes all melty again. Doesn't take much. I feel sorry for those idiots who don't know where to find the center of a woman's attention. A little stroke and suck and swirl and the world is your oyster.

"Ohhh..." she moans softly, presumably so no one will hear us through the paper thin walls.

I, on the other hand, am all about the show. So I pick up the pace and go deep until she is moaning the paint off the walls. I'm pretty sure they can hear this woman come at the food court five gates away. When we're done, we get dressed and she glances down at her watch.

"Ugh, I've got to be three terminals away in twenty minutes," she complains, running her fingers over her hair to smooth it. "Are you staying here in town or on your way somewhere else?"

"Visiting an old friend. I won't be here for long, though. Just a night, maybe two."

"Can I give you my number? I'm through this airport a lot. JFK, too. You know, in case you're ever in need of..."

"A glass of champagne?" I offer with a smirk

She gives me a dazzling, stewardess smile. "Exactly."

Usually I tell them to piss off about now, but this woman has been a pleasant surprise. Not demanding, not clingy. No pretense as to what she wanted. Yeah, I'd do her again.

"Sure," I agree, and she quickly jots down her number on a scrap of paper and hands it to me. Then she leans over and gives me a kiss on the cheek.

"It's been a pleasure serving you, Mr. Corrigan."

Suzanne clicks off in her sky-high heels, while I stop by the counter to pay the bill.

"Was everything to your...satisfaction?" asks the blonde coed manning the register.

"Why yes, it was..." I look at her nametag. "Lisa."

"It certainly sounded like it, Mr...." she looks at my credit card. "Corrigan."

When I take my receipt she gives me a wink.

Oh, I think I'm going to like this city.

Chapter 48

Jeremy

Here I am in Detroit, Michigan, once the American auto mecca. And yet, when I ask what cars are available for rent, I have the choice of a Honda, a Fiat or a Nissan. I choose the Fiat. A half hour later, I am parked across the street from my destination, a neat little house in a quiet, suburban neighborhood. I slip down into the seat and wait. And wait... And wait.

In total, it takes close to two hours for Louise Kutter to make an appearance. The last time I saw her, she was splayed out on the platform of the Lincoln Center subway station with a broken leg. She was lucky that I was feeling generous that day. She was just inches from taking a header into the uptown local 1 train.

She looks much the same now as she comes out of her front door, long, black hair up in a high ponytail. She has on tight black pants. Wait, wait, wait...are they *leather*? Someone needs to teach this woman how to dress her age. She completes her ensemble with a sparkly red tank top and matching red heels. I watch as she gets into her car, a little sports coupe with a license plate that reads **1ST HORN.** No way that thing gets her around town in the winter. Maybe she's got a monster truck sitting in the garage.

She zips out of the driveway so quickly that I almost lose her before I can even start the car. She leads me around town at a good clip, buzzing through nearly red lights and changing lanes without a turn signal. If I didn't know better, I might think she was trying to lose me. But I'm certain she has no idea I'm tailing her. She just happens to be a really bad driver.

Louise pulls into a spot at the end of a desolate block, locks up the car, and starts walking. I get out and follow her on foot—keeping a safe distance back in case she should turn around suddenly. She stops when she gets to what looks like an abandoned automotive factory.

What the hell is she doing here? And dressed like that? My question is answered the second she pulls open the heavy steel door. I can actually feel the beat and the booming bass in my chest as it spills out of the building onto the asphalt street. Some very intoxicated revelers fall outside of the building along with the music as Louise passes them on her way inside.

So, Ms. Kutter likes to go clubbing. She's a dark horse, that one. I loiter in the shadows for several minutes before I follow through the doorway. It opens into a huge, concrete space that could easily serve as an aircraft hangar. This must have been some sort of manufacturing plant for the auto industry, which once made this town thrive. But with all the machinery gone, it's a hulking, two-story-high shell.

At this moment, the vast space is wall-to-wall people. The bass that was just a vibration before practically knocks me off my feet now. The limited lighting is flashing fast enough to cause seizures in a sizable portion of the population. Somewhere, a fog machine is pumping out a hazy cloud that hangs about waist-high. Groups of twenty-something's are clustered around, trying to hold conversations above the music, but the largest concentration of people seems to be in the center of the structure, where a DJ is perched atop a stack of pallets, two tremendous speakers on either side of him.

I can't seem to pick out Louise from this gyrating, humping, bumping, ass-rubbing mass of hot young things, but then I spot her at the makeshift bar. It's constructed from large sheets of plywood propped up on sawhorses. About a dozen young men and women stand behind it, filling plastic cups from kegs and serving up some kind of special cocktail in various shades that glow in the black light.

When Louise turns away from the bar, she's holding a drink that happens to be the same red as her blouse, giving her the appearance of a vampire knocking back a blood and tonic. She takes her drink with her as she walks right into the melee of dancers. I lose her again for several minutes as she gets sucked up into the crowd, but she periodically resurfaces around the edges, rubbing herself up against someone different each time.

These guys are easily ten years younger than she is, but it doesn't seem to be putting them off any. I spot one with his hand planted firmly on her ass. A half hour later, a different guy has his tongue down her throat. And at one point, I'm treated to the very disturbing image of Ms. Kutter sandwiched between two guys—one feeling her up from behind while the other suckles his way down her neck.

Oh, Louise, Louise. Don't you know by now you can't hang on to your youth? Maybe she does, and that's why she's here. Dark lighting hides her crow's feet. Loud music negates any chance of stimulating conversation. And copious amounts of alcohol ensure that the majority of the people here have their 'beer goggles' on. She probably looks pretty damn good to these frat boys right about now.

Two hours later, when I've had enough of the noise and the flashing lights and the stifling heat, I head back outside where the world is blissfully quiet and cool. I drive back to Louise's house the way I came and park down the block. A quick little walk around her house leads me to an unlocked bedroom window. It's an easy job, popping the screen out and hopping over the sill. I return it to the way it was once I am inside.

Her bedroom is a pale lilac color with flower prints on the walls with a perfectly made bed and everything meticulously placed. I start to explore, pulling open drawers and opening closets. I find neatly folded panties and skimpy lingerie. In the nightstand I find three vibrators, a bag of large zip ties and a blindfold.

"Well, well, well! I didn't know you had *that* in you, either, Louise!" I mumble under my breath with a grin.

Out in the living room, I examine several framed photographs of Louise with her parents. No pictures of her as part of a couple, though. A few of her playing horn, one where she is receiving an award. I open various doors to find a guest room, an office and a music room, her horn perched on a chair in front of a music stand. What an orderly life you have here, Louise.

In the kitchen, the counters are spotless. There's one kitchen towel folded into a perfect square sitting next to the sink. I'm about to take a look inside her fridge when I hear the sound of a car in the driveway. I pull the curtain aside just an inch to confirm that she didn't bring one of those studs home. Nope. She is tottering up the walkway all by herself. Perfect. I take a seat at her kitchen table, and I wait.

Chapter 49

Jeremy

It takes Louise a while to line up the key with the lock on her front door and when she finally does get it, the thing swings open so suddenly that she goes tumbling over the threshold and onto the floor.

She's not hurt. In fact, I can hear her giggling from where I'm sitting in the kitchen. She gets herself up, closes the front door and staggers through the living room and down the hall to the bathroom. If she had looked to her right, she would've seen me sitting here, waiting, with a cup of coffee in front of me on the table.

In the bathroom, I hear the toilet flush and the water running in the sink. When she comes back out into the hallway, she starts to turn toward her bedroom, but then stops and sniffs. Her nose points her in the direction of the kitchen, the brewing coffee and me. She freezes in her tracks and stares—not so much in fear but in confusion. The questions are written all over her face. Who is that? From where do I know him? Why is he sitting at my kitchen table? It takes her another minute to process my presence and then I see the light of recognition in her eyes.

"Jeremy? Jeremy Corrigan?" she asks through her glow-in-the-dark drink haze.

I smile as if I'm greeting an old friend. "Louise!"

"What...what are you doing here?"

"Oh, I just wanted to have a chat, but you're a very hard woman to get ahold of. I've left you messages that you haven't returned. Finally, I decided it was time to come on out and pay you a visit in person."

"What do you want to talk about?" she slurs, her eyebrows scrunching together in confusion.

"Oh, you know, the usual. The weather, the state of affairs in the Middle East, how you owe me and I'm here to collect on the debt..."

"What? What're you talking about?"

She's swaying a little, so I stand up and pull out a chair for her at the table.

"Come and sit down, I'll pour you a cup of coffee. How do you take it?"

She shakes her head and starts to back out of the doorway.

"No..." she says. "No, you—you need to leave."

With an irritated sigh, I get up from the table and start walking toward her. She continues her backward retreat, unaware of the coffee table behind her. I don't bother to point it out.

"Get away from me," she demands just seconds before she lands flat on her ass on the oriental carpet with a dull thud.

She looks stunned as she peers up at me, hovering over her. I extend a hand, but she just stares at it.

"Come on, you can't stay down there all night."

After a long moment, she reaches up tentatively and I haul her up. And I do mean haul. At five-foot-ten, Louise Kutter is not a small woman. I take her by the arm and guide her firmly back to the kitchen table and help her into a chair.

"Now, how do you take your coffee?" I ask her for a second time.

"Cream," she mumbles.

I pull another mug from her cupboard and fix her coffee as she has indicated. When I put it down in front of her, she looks up at me.

"W-why are you here?" she asks again.

"Drink some coffee." I push the mug toward her.

She closes her eyes now, her brow furrowed. She's concentrating hard, though on what, I'm not sure. It's possible that I'm going in the wrong direction here. I thought her being wasted would work to my advantage, but now I'm wondering if I'll be able to get anything accomplished with her in this state.

"Have a sip," I coax. She brings the mug to her lips with trembling hands.

"Are you scared, Louise?"

"A little," she admits after carefully maneuvering it onto the table again.

"Good." I smile. "You should be scared. Do you remember the subway, Louise? How you almost fell in front of that train? If I hadn't caught you...well, we wouldn't be here having this conversation now, would we?"

She stares at me, eyes growing wider by the second. I can actually see the color draining from her face, leaving her cheeks white and her lips an ashy blue. I think I have her just where I want her, until the second she slams a hand over her mouth and bolts for the bathroom, knocking the chair over in her wake. The sound of her retching reaches all the way into the kitchen. Shit. It's going to be a long night.

* * *

It's half past nine when she comes stumbling out of her bedroom groggily, all of that long black hair a mass of tangles around her head. Her makeup is smudged down her face and she looks more than a little green. When she comes into the kitchen, the toast has just popped.

"Sit down, Louise." I gesture to the place I have set for her at the table. "Do you want anything more than toast? I can make you some eggs if you're up to it."

She shakes her head no.

I put the plate in front of her and join her at the table.

"How're you feeling this morning?"

"Not so hot," she mutters.

"There, I put a couple of aspirin next to your plate. And drink the glass of water, you need to hydrate."

She does as I suggest, and then takes a tentative nibble at the toast, trying to gauge whether or not it will stay down.

"Do you remember our conversation last night?" I ask her.

"Vaguely."

"You were pretty hammered. Do you do a lot of that? Clubbing?"

"It's not clubbing," she corrects me. "That was a rave."

I hold up my hands as an apologetic gesture for confusing the two forms of loud, hot, drunken gatherings. "You're a bit old for raves, aren't you, Louise?"

"Why do you care, Jeremy? And what were you doing following me? You know, I should just call the police."

"Yeah, I'm sure you already thought of that, didn't you? Notice anything missing from your nightstand? Like your phone?" She glares at me. "Come on, Louise, it's not like I stole something from your stash of sex toys." I chuckle.

She's not amused. I lean forward on the table.

"I'm here because I need something from you, Louise."

"What?" she asks suspiciously through a mouth full of toast.

"I need for you to get me on the audition roster for that third horn position you have open in the symphony."

She chokes, showering the table with crumbs. "What? What are you talking about?"

"I'm being blackballed because of the whole Cal thing."

"The Cal '*thing*'?" she repeats incredulously. "Jeremy, the guy is dead, and people think you had something to do with that!"

"Oh, please. It's not like anyone can prove anything."

"It doesn't matter! I knew there was no way our orchestra was going to invite you to audition."

"So you had something to do with that?" My tone is suddenly colder.

She shakes her head quickly and winces with the action, putting a hand to her forehead.

"No. That's HR. Human Resources. We get hundreds of applications and audition videos from people who aren't qualified. HR vets them and chooses the top candidates. The audition committee never gets to see the names of the applicants. We don't get involved until the chosen candidates come to Detroit to audition in person," she explains as she rubs her temples. "Once the candidates are in-house, they audition onstage behind a screen so no one can claim discrimination. I'm removed from the process until that point to avoid any conflict of interests. You know, in case I have a student or a friend auditioning."

"Or a fucking nut job like me, Louise? Is that what you're thinking?"

She's starting to look really scared now. "It's out of my hands," she insists.

"And here I thought there was something…special between us, Louise. Why won't you try to help me? I just want to land a gig like everyone else. Think of all the good times we'll have when we're playing in the same section! Maybe you can take me to one of those raves and introduce me to the hot coeds."

She's looking at me like I suddenly have an extra eye in the middle of my forehead. "You're wasting your time, Jeremy. There isn't anything I can do to help you, even if I wanted to. And I don't," she says with a tone that implies courage I know she doesn't possess.

I reach across the table and run the back of my hand along the side of her face. "Now, don't be like that, Louise!" My words are dripping with syrupy sweetness.

She jerks her face away from my touch but an instant later her chin is firmly in my hand, and I force her to look into my eyes.

"You are going to do this for me, whether you like it or not, Louise. Do you know why? Because your parents live at 444 West Taylor Street in Dunedin, Florida. Your dad likes to golf on Wednesday mornings, and your mom likes to play bridge on Tuesday nights. It would be such a shame if something happened to one of them," I say.

I wouldn't have thought it possible, but Louise has grown even paler. I continue.

"Did you know that falls are the leading cause of fatalities in older adults? And the leading cause of brain injuries in the ones that don't die? I'd just hate it if something were to happen to Ted and Francine. Especially with their fortieth wedding anniversary coming up next month."

Her resolve crumbles and tears spill from her eyes and down her cheeks. I rub one with my thumb and smile at her comfortingly.

"Don't worry, Louise. I'm sure mom and dad will be just fine. So, let's not worry about them right now. We need to get started on a plan!"

Chapter 50

Jeremy

My mother doesn't seem especially surprised to find me standing on her front porch. Nor does she seem especially happy to find me there. "Jeremy, what're you doing here?" she asks.

"What's the matter, Mom? Aren't you glad to see me?"

I lean down and kiss her cheek and she steps aside so I can enter the house that I grew up in. I take a look around—it's been six years since I set foot in this living room. It's still the tacky, depressing dump that it's always been.

My father comes out of the kitchen, still wearing his greasy coveralls.

"Dad!" I say with exaggerated happiness.

"Jeremy," he responds flatly with a nod.

Wow, I must really be in the doghouse if Danny Corrigan won't even extend a hand to me.

"What brings you here...Son?" he asks finally. I can tell it's hard for him to call me that.

"Can we maybe sit down? Or would you rather I just stand here?"

Never one to be rude under any circumstances, my mother waves me into the kitchen. My father follows. He and I sit at the table while she rummages around in the refrigerator.

"Beer?" she asks, holding up a bottle.

"Please. No glass, bottle is fine."

She nods as she pops the top off and hands it to me. My father already has one open on the kitchen table. We sip amiably, neither of them taking their eyes off of me for a second. It's like they think I might morph into an alien or something.

"You haven't been back this way in a long time," my mother notes. "Are you stopping through on your way to Chicago?"

"No, I was in Detroit visiting a colleague. It was only a forty-five minute flight from there, so I thought I'd surprise you."

"Uh-huh," my mother says as if she's finding that hard to believe. Which I'm sure she is.

"How have you been?" my father asks.

I practically snort. "Like you care?" He doesn't bother to respond. "Yeah. Well, I'm great, thanks. Maybe you heard I won the gold medal at the Kreisler International Music Competition?"

My mother nods. "We did."

"Oh, see I wasn't sure, since I never got a card or a call or anything."

"It hardly seemed appropriate given the circumstances, that poor boy dying and all," my father says before taking another swig from his bottle. "I mean you were just an alternate weren't you? He was the one who was supposed to be competing."

I can feel my blood pressure starting to climb. "I earned it, Dad. I played my ass off. You should have been there."

"I'm sure you played well. You always do," he says.

Then nothing. Crickets.

"Okay," I begin, putting my forearms on the table and leaning forward. "So here's the thing. I've come to ask you to please stay out of my life."

They look at one another, perplexed, because they have quite deliberately stayed far, far from my life. "What are you talking about?" my mother asks.

"I mean I'd like you to cut the shit."

"Jeremy, you know how I feel about that language in this house," she chides.

"Oh, please," I say, rolling my eyes. "That's the last thing you should be worried about right now."

"I'm not worried about anything," she informs me coolly.

I take a very deliberate, deep breath before I speak again. "I know you've been encouraging Brett to move out of our apartment, and I want you to stop. Now. And I don't want you telling him to throw me over for his little slut, either." I pause to gesture to the three of us sitting around the table. "Just because we don't get along doesn't mean you have to turn my own brother against me."

"Is that what you think we're doing?" Mom asks.

"Yes. I do."

She nods thoughtfully as she looks down at her hands on the table. I'm startled when she looks up. Something in my mother's face has changed, hardened. I can't recall ever having seen this expression on her.

"I'm glad you came, Jeremy, because it gives us a chance to clear a few things up," she begins with cool detachment. "Your brother doesn't need you dragging him into whatever sordid nonsense you're involved in. And he most certainly doesn't need you telling him who he can and cannot see. What I'm saying is that you need to stay out of *his* life. We're not the problem here, Jeremy, you are."

Oh, my. Mommy's got a bee in her bonnet.

"Now, Mother, what do you really care about what goes on fifteen hundred miles away? It doesn't affect you. I've made certain of that. Why not just leave things the way they are and let Brett and me continue the peaceful, symbiotic relationship we've always had?" I say, trying my best to sound reasonable, despite my growing irritation.

"Now, Son, you should have paid closer attention in school," my mother quips. "I think the word you're looking for is *parasitic*, not *symbiotic.* You've been using your brother since you were old enough to realize you had a brother."

"Brett benefits just as much from our relationship as I do," I reply to her accusation.

"Is that so?" My father takes up the conversation now. "Seems to me he pays your rent and utilities and groceries. He even got you into that fancy-pants conservatory you go to. Come to think of it, I can't recall a single job you've gotten without Brett pulling some strings or calling in a favor for you."

What the hell has Brett been telling these people? Too much, apparently.

"Whatever, Dad. I'm just here with a friendly little request for you to stop it. Now. Because the next request won't be so friendly."

I can tell immediately that this last sentence might have been a misstep on my part. It's as if a storm cloud has rolled right into the kitchen, casting everything into a murky darkness and filling the house with an electric tension.

"What do you think is going to happen here?" my mother asks, leaning closer to me across the table. "Do you think you're going to scare us?"

I shrug but don't say a word.

"Get out," my mother says.

"Excuse me?" I laugh. "What did you just say to me?"

My mother stands up and points her finger toward the front door. She looks me straight in the eyes. Her eyes. My eyes. They're identical. Neither of us is blinking.

"You heard me, Jeremy. And I don't want you to show your face here again. Ever."

I can't keep the stupid grin off my face. I look at my father and gesture towards her with one hand as if to say, '*can you believe this crazy chick?*' But my father isn't smiling.

I stand up and face her, not three feet separating us. Mother and son.

"Do you really think you can tell me to do anything?" I ask in a tone that is chilling to even my own ears.

Still, she doesn't flinch.

"Sweet Jesus help me, I brought you into this world. But that doesn't mean I have to love you. Or give a tinker's damn what happens to you. Now get out of my house before I throw you out."

"I'd like to see you try."

My father gets to his feet and takes a step to intervene. She can't see him behind her, but she knows what he's going to do before he does it and holds up a hand to stop him. She's telling him she has this—she has me—under control. Oh, how very wrong she is.

"Would you, Jeremy? Would you really like to see me try? It seems to me that you only pick fights that you know you can win. What on earth makes you think you'd win this one?"

I cannot believe what's going on here. And she's actually waiting for an answer!

"You mean aside from the fact that I've got eighty pounds and a six inches on you?"

Now she's smiling back at me with her smile. My smile. They, too, are identical. She takes a step closer and uses her index finger to poke me in the chest, the way that she did when I was a kid. But I'm not a kid anymore.

"Stop it, Mom."

"Or what?"

"Or I'll make you stop."

"That's quite enough, Jeremy," my father barks.

Neither of them is even trying to disguise their disdain for me at this point. Suddenly my mother reaches up and slaps me hard across the face. I'm so surprised that I nearly fall backwards.

"Get. Out."

I had no idea such a slight person could affect such a threatening demeanor. It's pretty impressive. I start to take a step towards her, but she beats me to the punch, so to speak, pushing me this time.

"Stop it, Mom," I warn again, my own level of menace ratcheting up to match hers. "Dad? You wanna step in here before she gets herself hurt?"

She pushes me again, harder this time, and I'm shocked when my father disappears into the kitchen pantry. What, is this a good time for Chips Ahoy or something? I stand firm, and when she comes at me a third time I grab her wrists before she can touch me again. She tries to pull herself out of my grip, but I'm so much stronger than she is. And now I just can't help myself.

I'm thinking about every little thing my mother has done to piss me off over the years and I start to squeeze her right wrist while turning it. She lets out a gasp of pain, but I just keep twisting. Maybe a broken arm will teach her to mind her own fucking business.

I'm about to send her sinking to her knees when my father comes around the corner into the living room holding his pump action Winchester shotgun. He chambers a round for my benefit, letting me know there is live ammunition pointed in my direction.

"Get your hands off of her. Now," my father commands. He knows to stand far enough away so that I can't grab the muzzle out of his hands. Come to think of it, he's the one who taught us that bit of shooting wisdom. How *not* to have your own gun used against you.

"*Now*, Jeremy. If you don't think I'll shoot you, then you're about to find out how very wrong you are. I won't say it again."

I let her go, putting my hands up in a gesture of surrender and fixing a snide smile to my face. "Yeah, Dad. You do that. I'd like to see you explain it to the police."

"You'll be dead, so I don't think it'll make much difference to you either way. Your mother has asked you to get out, twice now. There will not be a third time."

A big part of my everyday life involves gauging the state of the people around me. I pride myself on knowing exactly whom to push, when and how hard. This situation is now out of my control and pushing will only make it increasingly unstable for me. Ergo, I need to get out of here before I have a chest full of buckshot.

"Okay, okay, I'm going. Nice to see you guys! I'll be looking for that Thanksgiving dinner invitation in the mail, okay?"

I laugh as I turn my back and walk out the front door, wondering every second if my father is going to shoot me in the back.

Chapter 51

Jeremy

"Yo, Jeremy!"

The sound of Sal's thick Brooklyn accent is like nails on a chalkboard. I stop where I am, on my way up the stairs and turn to find him at the bottom, wiping his floury hands on his apron.

"Hey, Sal!" I force a big grin onto my face. "What's up, man?"

He raises his palms up to the sky in a 'What the fuck?' gesture. "You tell me!" he bellows in his obnoxiously loud tone. "I'm here, in the restaurant yesterday morning, making dough for the day when I seen a moving truck pull-up in front of the building. Next thing I know, they're taking all your brother's shit out of the apartment! You got somethin' to tell me?"

He's looking at me as if I'm going to sneak out under cover of darkness without paying him the highway robbery he calls rent.

"Sal, I don't think it's what it looked like," I assure him. "I'm expecting to have a new job in Detroit soon, but that won't be for a couple months yet. Brett will be sticking around to cover the rent, though." I'm lying through my teeth of course, but my landlord's not an idiot, as much as he sounds like one sometimes.

"Maybe you should tell him that! I saw them boys loading up a shitload of boxes, a bed, a desk..."

He's using his fingers to tick off the items that came down the narrow staircase and out into the truck. Fuck me. This doesn't sound good at all.

"You know what, Sal? I'll bet it's just a misunderstanding. Let me give my brother a call and see what's going on. But don't worry, we're not going anywhere..."

"You better not be! Not without paying out the lease, Jeremy!" he's yelling as I turn my back on him, continuing up the stairs.

"Don't worry about it, Sal!" I call back down over my shoulder.

"Don't worry about it, he says! *'Don't worry about it, Sal.'* Yeah, don't worry about it, my ass..." he's still talking to himself when I unlock the door and take refuge inside.

I drop my bag on the floor and feel around for the light switch. When I find it, I flip to reveal a living room that looks much the way I left it. That is, except for the missing television.

"What the fuck," I mumble under my breath, making my way down the hall to Brett's bedroom. When the door swings open, the hallway light spills across a dusty, hardwood floor. Sure enough, his bed is gone. The dresser and desk, too, just like Sal said. I walk inside and pull open the slatted closet doors to reveal a naked wooden rod. He didn't even leave a single hanger behind.

"What. The. Fuck!" I repeat, yelling it loudly this time.

I stomp out of the room, slamming the door behind me as I extricate my cellphone from my pocket. Did I miss a text? An email? Did the fucker leave me a voicemail? But there's nothing. I punch in his number and wait while it rings. Once. Twice. Three...

"Hello?" Brett's voice sounds cool and calm on the other end of the line.

"You seem to have moved out of our apartment while I was out of town," I say.

"Oh, hello, Jeremy."

"Fuck you. What, are you staying with Margery?" I spit. He doesn't bother to correct me on her name. In fact, he doesn't bother to say anything. "Well?"

"Well what?" he asks innocently.

"You've got some fucking nerve. What, were you too afraid to do it while I was home? Are you really such a pussy that you waited until I was out of town?"

"Don't flatter yourself, asshole," he replies flatly. "I moved out on my day off. You didn't tell me you were going out of town, so I didn't know where the fuck you were."

"Oh, right. And I suppose mommy and daddy didn't call you whining about big, bad Jeremy showing up either, did they?" I snarl.

There is an immediate and palpable shift in the silence between us. It takes him a few seconds to draw a breath and formulate a sentence. Shit. I think I may have just shown my hand.

"Why would they do *that*, Jeremy? Is that where you were? Paying them an unexpected visit?" he asks with a chill that I seldom hear from him.

"I told you this wasn't over."

"You'd better watch yourself, motherfucker. One of these days you're going to go too far. And then, God help you."

I laugh. "Seriously? And when will that be, Brett? How much shit have you let me get away with? Some pretty ugly stuff, right? Not that you did a damn thing about it. If I haven't crossed that line into 'too far' yet, then you obviously don't *have* a line. So, stop acting like you're such an honorable guy. You're just like me," I hiss into the phone.

He's silent for so long, I'm thinking he hung up on me. But then, his voice comes down the line, not much more than a whisper.

"Oh, no, Jeremy. I have a line. And you *just* crossed it."

And then, he really is gone. "No, no, no, no," I mutter to myself. "This does *not* end like that."

I spend the next hour cleaning my brother's vacant room. When

I'm done, I drag a music stand and chair into the middle of the floor and bring in a lamp from the living room. In my own bedroom, I find my horn and music folder and bring them in there as well. This is my new studio. This is where my training begins. I've got an audition to win so I can get the fuck out of this shithole Once. And. For. All.

Chapter 52

Jeremy

The phone rings. And rings. And rings. I'm about to hang up when I hear a soft, tentative voice on the other end.

"Hello?"

"Louise, you're home! I've been trying to get you for days. I was just thinking that I was going to have to pay you another visit. That was not a happy thought for me, Louise."

"I'm sorry," she says in the same quiet tone. "I-I just needed a couple of days to get my head clear, Jeremy. You really rattled me, showing up here the way you did."

Her admission pleases me—something I'm sure she is counting on. She knows better than to piss me off.

"Good," I say flatly. "Next time, pick up the goddamn phone."

"I will. I promise."

"Alright then, as long as we're clear. Where are we with the audition plans?" I ask, my voice lightening considerably.

"Well, I did what you said and dug around. It's a woman named Amanda Talbot who gets the first round of applicants. She examines their credentials on paper and, if they're suitable, she asks them to send an audio sample of their playing."

"Okay, then what?"

"Uh, well, once she has all the audio files, she assigns a number to each candidate on a list that only she has access to. She labels their audio files with that same number and passes them on for the next level of evaluation."

"Which is?"

She clears her throat. "Me."

"You?"

"Yes. Well, me, the principal trumpet and the principal trombone. We listen to each of the audio files and whittle the candidates down to the best dozen or so. Sometimes, there are more who are worth hearing, sometimes fewer. We submit our choices to Amanda who takes out her list, matches the numbers we've chosen to the names of the performers and invites them to come and audition in person."

"An invitation that I never received," I say thoughtfully.

"Apparently."

"So it was Amanda's decision?"

"Yes...and no," she says reluctantly.

I'm losing my patience. "Louise..."

"I know, I know, I'm not trying to be difficult. Yes, it's Amanda who does that initial assessment, but I was able to find out that occasionally she receives instructions from the management to keep an eye out for specific performers...and to flag them if they should apply. Amanda told me that your name was on that list."

"I fucking *knew* it!" I mutter with satisfaction. "So they *are* black-balling me!

"When she got your application, she alerted management and was told to shred your paperwork without passing it on to the committee. You were automatically issued a rejection letter."

I take a long, deep breath and think for a second before speaking again. "Alright, now I know what we're dealing with. Louise, you have to find a way to pull some poor sucker's audio submission and replace it with mine. Then you have to get into this Amanda chick's computer and assign *my* name to *that* guy's number."

"But what if she looks? She'll know you're not supposed to be there."

"Why don't you keep the other guy's name and change the contact info? That way when she sends the audition information, it'll come to my address."

"But— "

"But nothing, Louise. All I need is a chance to audition. You and I both know that I'll blow away the competition. Once I win the spot, we can say it's a clerical error. A simple mistake in the data entry. They'll be stuck with me—unless they want a very messy, very public lawsuit."

She's silent on her end. She knows this will work, she just doesn't want to do it. Maybe she needs a little reminder of what's at stake?

"I was sorry to hear about your dad's hip."

"What? What about my dad's hip?"

"What, you don't know? Huh. I'd have thought they would have told you by now. Oh, well, maybe they didn't want to worry you. Like I've said before, once an older person breaks one of those big bones, they don't always bounce back."

I hear her breathing pick up pace on the other end of the line. The money I spent on a private investigator in Florida is paying off. He's been keeping close tabs on Louise's parents for me. And how convenient that Papa Kutter is as clumsy as his daughter.

"What did you do?" she hisses at me.

"Nothing, Louise. Not a thing. Dear old Dad slipped at the pool in their condo complex and popped it out of place. He'll be fine. This time. I'll be waiting to hear from you tomorrow night."

"Tomorrow night? I don't think I can—"

"You can. I know you can. Do it, Louise. Your parents are counting on it."

I hang up the phone before she can say another word.

Part Five

Chapter 53

Julia

I start to push the RETURN key, then pull my hand away quickly, as if it's blistering hot. Oh, hell. I rub the bridge of my nose and take a slow, deep breath in.

"It's okay. I'm okay. I can do this," I murmur to myself then sit up straight in the chair at the teahouse where I've been trying to push this one button for the last half hour.

"More hot water for your tea?" I'm startled by the voice behind me, a young girl with blue hair and a pierced brow.

"Uh...yes, please, I smile up at her and push my mug closer to the edge of the table.

"You should just do it," she says, close to my ear, as she leans down to pour from her carafe.

"Excuse me?"

"Just hit the key and see what happens," she says, nodding toward my search engine screen with her chin.

I offer her a small smile. "Yeah, well, maybe I'm not so sure I want to know."

She shrugs and smiles back. "You'll never know what you're up against until you do."

I watch her cute butt walk away to another table and wish I could still fit into *my* skinny jeans. She's right. I hit the button before I can waffle for another second. When the page reloads, it comes back with over six-hundred-thousand results for the name 'Kelly James.' Ugh. No way I can sort through that many. I add the word 'Montauk' to the search. That knocks it down to three-hundred. Much more manageable, but still none seem to fit the bill.

I sit back in my chair and take a sip of the herbal tea this place is known for. It's the only palatable brew in town, as far as I'm concerned. How is it possible that I can't find anything about her anywhere? It's like she doesn't exist. And then it hits me. Maybe Kelly James doesn't exist. She has a new daughter. That means a new husband and, most likely, a new last name.

What was the name of her shop in Montauk? Special Memories? Memorable Moments? No. *Lasting Memories of Montauk.* That's it. My fingers fly across the keys and suddenly there is the website. In the background is a picture of the shop with its green and white striped awning in the summer sun. She is standing outside with the girl I saw there, Corinne, and a tall, bearded man. I click the website for the shop and follow the links to the About Us page.

KELLY RANDALL OPENED LASTING MEMORIES OF MONTAUK OVER A DECADE AGO AS A PLACE WHERE LOCALS AND VISITORS ALIKE COULD FIND SPECIAL TREASURES FOR THEMSELVES AND THEIR LOVED ONES. ALONG WITH HUSBAND DREW AND DAUGHTER CORINNE, KELLY HAS BEEN AN ACTIVE MEMBER OF THE MONTAUK COMMUNITY FOR CLOSE TO TWENTY YEARS...

So, my mother's name is Kelly Randall. I'll bet she dropped the name James the first chance she got. Put all those bad memories behind her. Just traded in her tawdry old life for a bright, shiny, new one. I wish I'd had that luxury. Instead, I got to pick up the slack after she left. The anger my father had towards her was suddenly redirected toward me, the smaller, weaker version of the woman he both loved and loathed.

I was already asleep the night that he dragged me out of bed to go next door to get a six-pack from Creepy Neighbor Guy. It was dark and cold outside, and I was frightened by the way he leered openly, taking in every inch of me from head to toe, like he wanted to drink me or something.

I ran quickly across the yard where he was waiting for me with his slimy smile. He held the six-pack over my head and made me jump for it. I couldn't get away fast enough. But I was so small, and the bottles were heavy. When I stumbled over a tree root, they went flying. The sound of the glass smashing on concrete sent a wave of nauseating fear through me. I knew immediately that this was not going to end well for me. I couldn't have been more right.

My father was deathly quiet when he came out and surveyed the situation. That was my first indication that this was going to be really, really bad. He watched, without comment, as I desperately tried to clean up the mess. I cut my hand and the blood ran down my wrist, making a bright red plume within the foamy lake of Budweiser that was pooling on the sidewalk. I noticed a few curtains moving in windows as curious neighbors peeked outside briefly before going back to their business. This was nothing new. Rex James was always after his daughter about something.

When I had picked up all the glass, I rescued the two remaining bottles from the grass and handed them to him, praying he wouldn't slap me. He just looked down at me for a long moment before taking them and putting them on the front stoop. Then he grabbed me by the scruff of the neck and marched me over to our beat up, old pick-up.

"Get in," he barked, opening the passenger side door. I had to scramble up to reach the seat. He closed the door behind him and came around to let himself into the driver's side.

"Where are we going, Daddy?" I asked in barely a whisper.

"Nowhere."

I watched in confused silence as he pushed the cigarette lighter into its socket and waited for it to pop out again, indicating it was hot. But I didn't see his pack of Lucky Strikes anywhere.

"Do you want me to get your cigarettes from the house, Daddy?"

"No, I want you to shut the fuck up, Julia," he snapped at me, grabbing my wrist and dragging me closer to him. He pulled the lighter out and held up its glowing, orange coil for me to see.

"You broke four bottles, Julia. And now I'm gonna punish you so you never do that again," he said in a matter-of-fact tone.

"I won't do it again, Daddy. I promise," I said, trying to wriggle free.

"Sit still, girl!" he shouted. I stilled.

He pulled my arm taut.

"It's for your own good, Julia. You have to learn to be more careful with other people's things," he was saying. But I had stopped listening to him at that point. I was too focused on the lighter coming closer to my skin.

"Four bottles, four burns. That sounds about right to me," he said.

It wasn't until that instant that I knew what he intended to do.

"No, no, please, Daddy!" I begged. "I learned, Daddy. I learned. I won't do it again!"

He shook his head.

"Daddy—"

He pressed the white-hot cylinder into the flesh of my upper arm.

A chill runs down my spine with the horrific memory. My hand is drawn to the spot under my sleeve where the remnants of my childhood live. I know these scars by heart now and I'm hardly aware of my fingers as they run along the familiar dips and ridges. Without thinking, I put a protective hand over my tummy, as if I can stroke the baby through the layers of flesh and bone. No one will ever hurt this child. Not like that. Not as long as I walk this earth.

I'm pulled from my dark thoughts by the distant ding of my phone. Damn thing is somewhere at the bottom of my bag, and I have to dig to find it. Finally, it comes out, along with a crumpled tissue and half a pack of Lifesavers. I dust off the screen and hit the home button to see my message from Matthew.

> Where are you? Almost time to go!

I close the lid on the laptop and stuff it back into my bag. Enough of this. Enough of my morbid curiosity. Enough of her. I swipe at the tears that have slipped from my eyes and down my cheeks and, with great effort, get up from the seat I've been occupying for hours now. I toddle outside and hail a cab headed back toward our apartment at the Strathmore Building, where I know my husband is waiting impatiently.

Matthew has spent the last several months carefully and lovingly restoring his childhood home on Long Island for us to live in. And somewhere in this process he's begun to restore his childhood memories carefully and lovingly. It remains unspoken between us, but what he's after is clear. Matthew hopes to recapture some of what he lost when his parents died all those years ago. The happy memories of the happy family. That's what he wants, and who could blame him? The only question now is whether or not it's true that you can't go home again. For his sake, I hope not.

Either way, we're about to find out.

Chapter 54

Julia

"Go ahead!" he encourages.

I look back at him over my shoulder like a sheepish little kid.

"Really?"

"Really."

I slip the key into the lock and push the heavy door open to reveal the two-story foyer. I gasp softly as I take a few tentative steps inside, my eyes roaming up to the open landing, right to the staircase and left to the long hallway. I choose left. The first door I open is his father's study—Matthew's study now. The big mahogany desk is polished, and books line the once-empty shelves. He once told me he used to hide under that desk, and I can't help but touch my belly—I can already imagine our child playing here.

The next room is flooded with sunlight. Formerly his mother's sewing room—it'll be our shared music room. Now there is a piano, a bookcase crammed with our sheet music and some chairs and music stands. I can hardly contain my glee. In fact, I can't contain it. I'm bouncing up and down on the balls of my feet and grinning like a fool. A very, very happy fool.

He follows me silently as I explore further, around to the back of the house where the kitchen has been updated and a breakfast nook built in, overlooking the vast back lawn. It's perfect for a family. Den, dining room, living room... I get more excited with every room we pass through. Once we have made our way completely around the first floor, I stand at the base of the huge staircase, hand on the banister. Looking back at him for his permission.

"Julia, it's your house," he laughs. "Go!"

He doesn't need to tell me twice. I take off up the stairs, my exuberant steps carrying me up to the open landing where I peer down at the foyer we've just left. "Go right," he suggests, gesturing to a door at the far end of the hall.

I follow his suggestion and my heart skips a beat as I walk into our bedroom. The king-sized bed is covered in an ornate blue and white quilt with matching shams and small accent pillows. Nearby are a dresser, vanity and armoire. Two overstuffed chairs are tucked into a corner by one of the huge windows looking out over the Long Island Sound. It is absolutely perfect.

"I suppose you picked out all those pillows?" I ask over my shoulder with a smile.

Matthew shrugs. "I *paid* the person who picked out all the pillows," he replies sheepishly. "Does that count?"

I shake my head and smile before disappearing into the huge bathroom with its claw-foot tub and glass-encased shower. I'm so excited when I emerge, that I grab his hand and pull him along with me to explore the guest room and bath. Finally, I make my way down to the other end of the hall. I know what this is, and I can tell he's dying to show it to me.

He does the honors, opening the door slowly to expose the blue-walled nursery with its bright white trim. My hand flies over my mouth as I gasp. Murals of Winnie-the-Pooh have been painted onto the walls and matching Pooh-themed accessories are scattered everywhere—from the lamp in the dresser, to the nightlight, and the mobile which hangs over the big white crib.

Oh, my God. The crib.

I walk to it and gently run my hand along the rail, trying to imagine the tiny human who will soon occupy it. Matthew has placed it with a perfect view of the cherry tree outside and, for two glorious weeks each spring, it will burst into a mass of fluffy pink flowers. I look back at him and point to it.

"That's the tree, isn't it?"

He nods. I've heard him describe this tree. Actually, I've heard him describe every square inch of this room in such great detail that I feel as if I've been here before. I walk to the middle of the floor and turn slowly, around and around, drinking in every nook, every cranny. When I circle back again to where he's standing, watching me, there are tears running down my cheeks.

"Oh, Julia! What? What is it?" he asks, alarmed.

I just shake my head and smile.

"I'm happy, silly! You did this for me. For us."

"I did."

I close the distance between us in a second, throwing my arms around his waist and nearly knocking him to the floor.

"Hey!" he laughs. "Careful or you'll crush me with your hormone-fueled strength!"

With my head on his chest, I sniff and giggle at the same time. "He's ours, Matthew. Yours and mine," I say, knowing exactly what thoughts are going through his mind right now. They're the same ones going through my mind, too."

"You seem awfully sure it's a boy. Will you be disappointed if it's a girl?"

I pull my head away from his body and look up sharply. "Of course not! I would love to have a daughter. But she'll have to come a little later because this one is a boy."

"Well, you're the one who didn't want the doctor to tell us the sex, so if we're surprised, it's on you—blue nursery and all!"

"No surprises. It's a boy, Matthew," I smile up at him. "A daughter—our daughter—still to come."

He smiles down at my damp, freckle-spotted face, then leans in and kisses the tears away, one by one, until he finds my lips. I return his kiss hungrily, wrapping my arms up and around the back of his neck. Suddenly, he's scooping me up in his arms like a newlywed, his mouth never leaving mine even as he carries me back to the master bedroom.

"I think we need to christen the house, what do you think?" he murmurs between kisses.

I nod enthusiastically, and by the time we pass the guest room, I've somehow lost my blouse. And then the bra manages to make its way over the railing and onto the stairs. Between us you'd think we had eight hands. He's still kissing me when we hit the bed, stopping just long enough to pull the t-shirt over his head and step out of his jeans.

"Off," he says as he pulls my skirt off roughly, then he gets behind me, his back against the headboard. He helps me to scoot back on the bed so that my back is pressed up against him. All of him.

I have to say, everything I'd ever heard about pregnant women and sex has proven to be absolutely true. I can't get enough of it. I want him morning, noon and night and he's been quite accommodating. I reach back with my arms, stretching them around his neck so he has unfettered access to my breasts. He cups them in his hands, thumbing my nipples slowly. They're so incredibly sensitive right now. I gasp involuntarily when I feel his mouth behind my ear and on my neck. Yes, this is how I like to start.

I sigh contentedly as he switches it up and starts to tweak my nipples until they are hard little peaks under his fingers. And then, with his left hand securely tending to my left breast, his right hand snakes its way underneath me. I spread my thighs for him and cry out, throwing my weight back against him when he dips into my wetness. I feel his breath close to my ear as he starts to work me in a circular motion.

"There is nothing that makes me harder than watching you come," he whispers.

"Ohhhhh, Matthew," I moan loudly. I love it when he talks like this during sex.

"I'm going to make you come so many times today," he continues to whisper between nibbles on my earlobe.

I'm squirming under him now as he picks up the pace.

"I'm going to finger your clit. I'm going to fuck you from behind. You're gonna ride my cock until you scream. And then I'm going to start all over again..."

"Oh, Oh! Oh, Matthew!" I cry out as he checks off the first item on his sexual to-do list.

My head drops back against him, and I am panting as he swirls slowly until I am trembling with sensitivity.

"Wow. That was fast," he says with a satisfied smile in his voice. "All done?"

"I don't know, am I?" I ask breathlessly.

In a flash, he's helping me up onto my hands and knees—my new favorite position since I've been pregnant. I back up toward the edge of the bed so he can stand and position himself behind me. Then he slams into me so hard that I have to brace myself to keep from falling flat on my face. He grabs my hips and pistons in and out quickly.

"Ohhhhh..." I moan. It's all I can do at the moment. And I know he loves it. The louder, the better.

When he reaches around to rub me with his fingers, I'm done. I utter something unintelligible and feel myself convulsing around him as he slams into me harder and faster, working himself up to a grunting frenzy until I feel him empty himself inside of me.

We collapse onto our new bed, and I turn onto my side, slipping into the crook of his arm and draping my leg over him. And the belly. Matthew reaches over and rubs it tenderly.

"How's he doing in there?"

I grin up at him sheepishly. "Ah, well, I think all the action woke him up. Here, feel." I take his hand and place it where I've just felt a kick.

"I don't feel—Oh my God! Was that *him?* Did he just do that?" I nod and smile at his wide-eyed astonishment.

"Wow," he says, moving his hand all over my belly trying to feel it again. "There!" I could watch him do this all day. "Hah!" he laughs from above my head. You can already tell he's Corrigan's kid. Kicking a guy when he's down..."

But I'm not laughing and, just like that, the lovely, lazy afterglow goes up in smoke. I adjust myself so he can see my face very clearly.

"Matthew, you can't even joke about that. I mean never. You have to swear to me that he will never know that you aren't his father. Never, Matthew. No matter what."

He sobers up quickly and nods. "I know. You're right. I promise. I can promise you that, Julia," he says as he takes my hand.

"He's our son, Matthew. David is our son."

He cocks his head. "David? You...you want to name him David?"

I've been waiting for the right time to tell him. "David Matthew Ayers."

"My father's name," he says quietly.

"And yours. He'll be named after his father and his grandfather."

With his hand still on my belly, he leans down to give me the most tender of kisses.

Chapter 55

Julia

The gifts have been arriving for weeks now, giving me a chance to get to know our FedEx, UPS and Postal delivery guys by first name. In just the last few days, they've collectively hauled a ton of onesies and burp cloths, three baby blankets, four teddy bears, one silver rattle and a very fancy stroller. That last item came courtesy of Dr. Sam.

"Just one today, Mrs. Ayers," says Craig, the UPS carrier as he hands me a stylus so I can sign his tablet.

"Well, at least I can carry this one in myself," I note as I scrawl my name and trading it back for the small rectangular package.

Inside, I go to the kitchen where I've left my latest cup of twiggy herbal tea steeping and find a knife to cut through the packing tape. When I finally manage to jailbreak the well-sealed parcel, I find a beautifully wrapped package inside. It's covered with pale blue and yellow polka dots and there's a huge bow with matching blue ribbon curls that stream across the gift.

I didn't have much growing up. Not for Christmas or birthdays...or anything else, really. Nearly every gift I've ever received has been from Matthew. So, to get so many beautiful things from so many

304

thoughtful, loving people has been a little overwhelming. And incredibly touching.

Using the same knife, I slice gingerly through the tape holding the paper together. I want to add this to the wrapping paper from the other baby gifts so I can make a collage or something later on. I've never been crafty before, but apparently pregnancy brings out the Martha Stewart in me.

With the paper safely removed, I pull the cardboard lid from its bottom to expose a cloud of blue and yellow tissue paper. When I peel the layers back, I find a pale blue onesie covered in characters from Winnie the Pooh. Along with it, a tiny matching hat with bear ears knitted on the top. I pull both items out and press the soft fabrics to my face, inhaling their fresh cottony scent. I set them aside and look further into the tissue for a card, but there is none.

"Huh. Now who am I supposed to send a thank you to for this?" I murmur to myself and pick up my quickly cooling mug of tea.

I take a sip and, still holding the cup, pick up the box the gift came in to look for a clue of its giver. When I do, I realize the cardboard box is too heavy. There must be something inside that I missed. I stick my hand down deep into a sea of Styrofoam packaging peanuts and pull out a small book. On the front cover is a drawing of Winnie and Christopher Robin. A photo album maybe?

"So sweet!" I say to myself as I flip the cover open.

My suspicion is confirmed. This is, indeed, a photo album. I know this because there are already photos inside of it.

When the mug hits the hard tile floor, it shatters into a thousand tiny shards. The hot tea coats the lower cabinet doors, running down them to form small herbal rivers in the grout lines of the kitchen.

"Julia?" Matthew has come running from his office. "Julia, what is it?" he asks, looking very alarmed when he sees me.

But I can't answer him. I can only look down at the book in my hands, then up at him and then back down at the album. Finally, I pass it to him with trembling hands. He examines each glossy page, one by one. When he raises his face to me again, I see what must be a mirror image of how I look to him. Pale face, terrified eyes, confused brows.

"But how?" he asks in a whisper.

I shake my head silently because I have no words. He puts the photo album down on the counter between us, still open. I can't help myself—I have look at it again. And again. And again. Then, I start ripping the glossy prints out of their plastic sleeves and tossing them onto the counter.

The crib. The Winnie the Pooh border and mobile and matching lamp. The white rocking chair and the Piglet nightlight. Even the dresser has been captured, its drawers opened to reveal all the tiny items of clothing folded neatly within.

When I flip to the final page, I find what I'm looking for. As far as selfies go, this one is pretty spectacular. Jeremy is sitting on the window seat in the nursery, curtains pulled back to reveal the stunning view of the Port Jefferson Harbor behind him. He's holding a teddy bear and offering his wide white grin to the camera. When I bring the image closer to my eyes, I realize it's a bear that arrived only a few days ago.

For the first time, I notice raised lettering coming through the image from the back. I flip it over to reveal the message written with ballpoint pen.

Anytime. Anywhere.

I let the picture fall to the floor as I spin around and retch into the sink.

Chapter 56

Julia

It only takes Tony Ruggiero an hour and a half to make what should have been a two-hour plus drive from New Jersey to our kitchen in Port Jefferson. The first thing he does is to wrap me up in his barrel-chested embrace.

"Red," he whispers as he holds my trembling body tightly. I start to cry all over again. He pats my back. "I don't want you to worry about this douchebag, Julia. I'm going to take care of this once and for all. By the time I'm done with him, he'll be too scared to even say the word 'baby' let alone come anywhere near yours."

These are the words I want so desperately to hear, and yet they don't have the impact I was hoping for. They don't bring me any comfort because the damage is done. I've been violated. Jeremy Corrigan crossed the boundaries of my home and, with very deliberate intent, invaded the sanctuary of my child's nursery.

When the tears have finally stopped and my trembling has subsided, Tony pushes me away slightly so he can look down into my puffy, damp face. "I mean it," he says, putting his hands on my shoulders for emphasis. "Okay?"

I sniff loudly and nod as he helps me to one of the chairs at the kitchen table. Matthew sets down a fresh cup of steaming tea for me. From where I'm sitting, I can still see yellowy rivulets of the last cup stuck to the cabinet faces. I wrap my shaking hands around the mug as if it will somehow keep me from sinking into the abyss.

They sit down on either side of me. In the middle of the table lies every last Styrofoam peanut and curled bit of ribbon from the offensive package. Matthew and I watch as Tony sorts through it all. First he examines the mailing box itself and its labels. After that he empties the packing peanuts and inspects the inside. Then come the wrapping paper, decorations and the box.

He holds up the onesie and matching cap, inspecting both carefully—reading their labels and turning them inside out. Finally, he picks up the album and flips through the pages. Most of them are empty since I pulled the pictures out, but he removes the few that remain and flips them over, looking for another message. There isn't one.

"And these are all the pictures that were inside?" he asks me. I nod silently and watch as he picks up each one in turn, scrutinizing every detail of each image. He sighs heavily and sets the stack down again on the table.

"Okay, so, you're sure this is the bear that you received from your friend Mila on Tuesday?"

"Yes." My voice is a hoarse whisper.

"I was here when she opened it," Matthew offers, as if I might need an alibi witness.

"Okay, well that's good. It narrows our timeline considerably," Tony says. "This picture was taken during the day—midday, by the looks of the sun behind him. And look, there," he says, pointing to something in the background. "That's the Pt. Jeff ferry pulling out of the harbor right there behind him. They run a three-boat schedule this time of the year, so I'm guessing that's either the noon or the one-thirty."

Matthew clears his throat and thinks for a second. "Well, we were here all day yesterday. Julia was really tired, and she slept most of the afternoon."

"And Wednesday?" Tony presses.

"Dr. Sam was here," I whisper before Matthew can answer.

"What, here in the house?"

"No," Matthew says. "Well, yes. And no. He took a cab here from the ferry in the morning. He and Julia had a lesson then the three of us drove out to Greenport for lunch. We were gone from about noon to four."

As Tony seems to consider this, I get up from the table.

"What do you need, Julia?" Matthew asks, jumping up.

"Nothing. I just want to stretch. This straight-back chair is killing my back," I mumble and start a slow pace from one end of the room to the other, my hands reaching behind me, massaging my aching muscles as I do.

"I'm going to guess that Jeremy was keeping an eye on Dr. Sam and followed him out here. Then, when you left, he found a way inside the house."

"Goddamn it!" Matthew slaps his hand on the table so hard that I jump where I am standing. "When will this guy ever give up and leave us the fuck alone?"

"That's not who he is, Matt. That's not what a guy like Jeremy Corrigan does."

"So what should we do?" I ask, trying desperately not to tip into the downward spiral of panic.

Tony sits back in his chair and taps the table with his fingers. He looks as if he's playing the piano.

"First thing is we're gonna go through every room of this house to check if anything is out of place or missing. We'll also see if we can figure out how he got in. Then, I'm going to call a couple of friends to help me track this son of a bitch down and keep an eye on him."

"Do you think we should get the police involved, Tony?" Matthew asks hesitantly.

Tony shakes his head no. "Uh-uh. He'll be expecting us to do that and I'm sure he's covered his tracks well. If you file a report, it'll just make you look paranoid and then they'll be skeptical next time you need them."

"But we have a picture of him!" Matthew protests.

"Trust me on this, Matt. Getting the police involved now will only cause trouble down the line. Let me do this my way. I've never steered you wrong before have I?" Matthew just shakes his head. "When the time is right, I'm going to let Jeremy know in no uncertain terms that he has made a very big mistake. A mistake that just might be his last if he's not careful."

Neither of us needs to ask Tony what he means by that. I'm certain Matthew already knows...and I really don't want to know.

"Alright," Matthew says at last. "Where do you want to get started? Upstairs or down?"

"Before we get to that, Matt, there's one more thing," he says. "That horn player from Detroit, Louise Kutter? She's been trying to get ahold of you through the law firm. We've done a damn good job of keeping your phone and address out of any public records, so she had to work pretty hard to get as far as she did to get a message to you."

"Okay," Matthew says slowly. "Any idea what she wants?"

"Nope. All she'd say is that she needs to speak with you as soon as possible—and that it's a matter of life and death. I guess she's a little dramatic, this one," he says.

"Maybe not," Matthew replies. "If it's what I think it is, she might be right."

Chapter 57

Matthew

There was a time when I was desperate for Louise Kutter's help. It was after Jeremy 'helped her' to fall on a subway platform before 'saving her' from the oncoming train. Julia and I were trying to make a case to the police for an investigation of Jeremy after Cal Burridge died, thinking that another suspicious incident involving him and one of the Kreisler judges might help our cause. But she refused because she was terrified. Just like she is now.

"Louise, this is Matthew Ayers. I heard you've been trying to reach me."

The relief on her end of the phone is palpable. "Oh, Matthew, finally! Thank God! Yes, you're a really hard man to get ahold of."

"What can I do for you, Louise?"

"I want to help. I want to go to the police with what I know about Jeremy," she says excitedly.

I sigh. "Louise, it's too late. If you're talking about the Kreisler stuff and how he may or may not have pushed you on the subway platform, it's just too late for all that. The police have closed the case and it would probably take a miracle to reopen it."

"But—but I need protection, Matthew!"

"Why do you need protection?" I ask, suddenly more interested.

"Because he's been here."

"What? In Detroit?"

"In my house."

Shit. That's not good.

"He showed up a few weeks ago and followed me around. Then he was waiting when I came home from a night out."

"Did he do anything, Louise? Did he hurt you?" I ask, Laurie Daughtry's face springing to mind.

"No. But he wasn't about to let me out of the house until he was done."

"Until he was done with what?"

"He was rejected for the horn auditions happening later this month here in Detroit. And he's furious. But I didn't have anything to do with that—it was all orchestra management! They just couldn't take the risk of having someone associated with a controversial situation like his. But it wasn't my decision..."

She's starting to get worked-up.

"Slow down, Louise. So, he showed up at your house and said what, exactly?"

"He wants me to get him an audition."

"But you just said that's out of your control."

"I know. He made me snoop around and find out the administrative details of the audition process. Then, he told me how to fix it so he could take the place of someone who *was* invited to audition."

Jeremy Corrigan just will not stop until he gets what he wants. And now, Louise is going to find that out the hard way.

"Did you do it?" I ask.

There's a long pause on her end. So long, that I'm starting to think we've been disconnected. But then I hear her voice, soft and small.

"Yes."

Oh, hell. "And now what? What's next?"

"Now he comes here to audition. At first he said all I had to do was get him that far. That once he got to play for the panel, he was certain he could win it. But he called me a few days ago and told me that he's counting on me to make *sure* he's the winner. He said my parents are counting on me, too."

"What do your parents have to do with it?" I ask the question, although I'm pretty sure I already know the answer.

"He's been making all kinds of veiled threats about hurting them. He knows where they live. He must be watching them because he knew my father hurt his hip before *I* did. He knows their routines—everything, Matthew. He's going to hurt them if I don't help him, I just know it!"

'I could see it in his eyes,' that's what Laurie Daughtry told Julia about Jeremy threatening her family. She was right. So is Louise. But there isn't a whole lot I can do and she must know that. I'm probably her last-ditch effort.

"Louise, I'm not sure what to tell you. Can you get your parents out of town for a while?"

"No," she starts, her voice choking with tears. "No, my dad will be laid up for at least a month and my mom would never leave his side."

"Okay, so have you done anything yet?"

"Yes," she sniffs. "Yes, I swapped out addresses for him and another horn player so that Jeremy would get the invitation to play, and the other guy would get a rejection letter. The auditions are coming up in about three weeks, Matthew, and I don't know what to do."

Well, I'll be damned if I know. I offered Louise an opportunity to help me get Jeremy Corrigan nailed on Cal's murder, but she was too afraid to act then. It's a little late now and, honestly, my biggest concern—my highest priority has to be Julia and the baby.

"I wish I had an answer for you. You could go to the police and file a blackmail complaint, but if there isn't any proof in writing and you didn't record him, then I doubt anything will happen. You could go to management and tell them what you've done. If you get fired or resign, that will put you out of the position to help Jeremy... but it also puts you out of a job."

"Oh, no..." she moans all the way from Detroit. "Are those really my only choices?"

"Louise, I'm not a magician. I've got my own Jeremy issues to deal with here. What happens if you let him audition?"

More sniffing and a nose blow. Lovely.

"Uh, well, if he plays the way he usually does, I don't see how he couldn't win. But he'll be auditioning behind a screen, so there's no way I can tell for sure if it's him that we're selecting. And if he's not the best player, I'd have to find a way to convince the rest of the hiring committee to select him anyway. And then, God forbid I can't get him in..."

"Or, God forbid you *can*, Louise. How do you think that scenario would play out? My guess is he'd have you resigning the principal horn spot in under a year so he could have it for himself. No, if I were you, I think the first thing I'd do is make some calls about the other spots that are open and see if you can line-up something before they hold auditions."

"And then what? He's not going to let this go, Matthew!"

"Once you've got another gig you can tell management you're resigning to take another post, but you'd like to stick around to help the committee find your replacement. Work with Jeremy to get him one of those spots, Louise. He goes to Detroit, you go somewhere else. I mean, I hate to give the asshole what he wants, but, honestly, I'd be happy to have him out of New York and away from my wife and me. And you should get as far away from him as possible."

She's quiet for a long time on the other end of the line. I wait patiently for her to process what I've just suggested.

"I—I'm finally happy. I'm finally playing with an orchestra I love, living in a city I love. I've worked so hard to get here and along the way I've gotten a reputation for being a difficult bitch. Even if I were willing to give up the life I've built for myself here, I don't know that another orchestra would take a chance on me."

"Louise, I've given you the best advice I can," I say, rubbing my temple absently. "If you want, I'll give you the name of my private investigator. He can maybe help you get your parents more secure. Then you have to decide... are you going to stay and fight for what's yours? Or are you going to choose a safer, albeit less appealing route? Only you can make that decision."

She's stopped crying now and I hear her take a long, shaky breath. "If you'd give me your friend's number I'd be grateful. I think I'll have a clearer perspective when I know my mom and dad are safe."

"Good plan," I say, knowing that this woman is totally and completely fucked no matter what she decides to do.

Chapter 58

Matthew

I'm dreaming about bananas. And sailboats. And Mickey Rooney. What the hell?

"Matthew," she says softly besides me, her voice barely registering in my subconscious. "Matthew?" Louder this time. "Matthew Ayers, *Wake. Up!*"

That gets my attention, and I sit bolt upright, breathing heavily. "W-what? What is it?" I gasp.

"It's time. Come on, we have to go to the hospital."

That's it, that's all I need to hear. I'm in motion before she can utter another word. Her overnight bag is by the front door. I pull on jeans and a t-shirt then help her to put on a loose-fitting dress and sandals. It's one o'clock in the morning. What is it with these babies coming in the middle of the night? You never hear about someone leaving a lunch meeting to go have a baby.

By the time we get downstairs to the lobby, the car is already waiting for us. Forty-five minutes later, a gowned Julia is in active labor. Unfortunately, she stays that way for another four hours. It breaks my heart to see her in so much pain, but she's determined. She's waited the better part of a year to meet her son, and she's not going to wait another minute. Then, with one final push, David Matthew Ayers comes into the world.

As I make my way through the maternity ward, I notice how different it is from the other floors. I've been exploring the entire hospital for over an hour now, while mother and baby are thoroughly checked over by the doctor. In this particular wing, the lighting is softer, and Brahms' Lullaby is piped in through the PA system. Door after door has a big bow affixed to it. Blue for the new baby boy arrivals, pink for the girls. A few doors have two, indicating twins. One has three, all pink. Good luck to that couple! The nurse has informed me that Julia is ready in Room 164. I rap quietly and pop my head in.

"Julia?"

"Matthew! Come in! Come!" she calls out excitedly.

I enter slowly, tentatively, not quite sure what I'm going to see. Ridiculous, of course. It's not like she's got Rosemary's Baby in there or anything. At least I hope not...

Julia's sitting up in the hospital bed, a swaddled blue bundle in her arms. Her long red hair hangs around her face and shoulders softly, the smattering of freckles across the bridge of her nose appearing clearly without the makeup she usually wears to camouflage them. I don't think I've ever seen this woman look so happy, so beautiful, so at peace. For the first time in all the years I have known her, Julia seems complete.

"Come and meet your son!" she coaxes.

I suddenly feel shy, bashful, even, as I inch closer to her. To him. When I'm by her side at last, she looks up at me with her perfect, shining, emerald eyes. She holds the baby out a little from her chest so I can get a good look at him. And there he is. All squishy faced, chubby cheeks and perfect, rosy little lips. There's a tiny blue knit hat on his head that looks like one of those old time sleeping caps people used to wear. The thing makes him look like an angry garden gnome. Forget about Rosemary's baby, man, the cap is even creepier!

Julia holds him out to me, but I just shake my head. "Take him," she coaxes.

I look at her and then back at him. She smiles and nods. Reluctantly, I take him into my hands. He's so small, I'm afraid I might crush him. She reads my thoughts.

"He won't break, Matthew!" she giggles.

"Wow."

It's the only thing that seems even remotely appropriate to say as I grasp him more tightly and pull him against my chest. He nuzzles his little head against me and works his mouth, as if he's chewing gum. I'm mesmerized by this tiny human, and I drink in every last detail. He has Julia's milky white skin, and, under the cap, I can see the barest of fuzz. It's perfectly auburn. This makes me smile.

And then, something interesting happens. This little boy, not even two hours old, raises his eyebrows into two perfect arches. When opens his red-lashed eyes, they're a muddy green-brown. Even I know a baby's eyes will often change color, but there is no mistaking the effect of the brows and the eyes. There is no mistaking whose child this is.

I pass him back to Julia a little too abruptly and she looks at me in confusion. Then she looks down at her son. Jeremy's son. And she sees it, too. She's about to say something when the door opens and a young nurse with a long brown ponytail shuffles into the room. She's wearing teddy bear scrubs with bubblegum pink clogs and a nametag that reads DEBBIE.

"How ya doing in here, Mom?" she asks Julia cheerily as she makes a notation on a clipboard.

"We're doing great," Julia says, clearly reluctant to halt the discussion we were about to have.

"Wonderful! And who's this?" Nurse Debbie asks with a nod in my direction.

"This is my husband, Matthew. David's father."

"Oh." Debbie stops what she's doing and looks at me with clear confusion on her face. "Is he... the baby's step-father, then?" she asks.

Julia's brow furrows. "No. Matthew is his father. Why?"

Now the nurse appears to be alarmed. I don't like this look one bit.

"Uh, well, I—I...there was just a man in the nursery rocking him. He said *he* was David's father and he looked so much like him..."

I see the color drain from Julia's face. "I'm sorry, are you saying you allowed a strange man into the nursery to hold our baby?" she asks in a whisper.

Now it's Debbie's turn to grow pale.

"Yes... I mean... no... uh... well... he was so, you know, so... I never thought he would lie..."

I'm on my feet and moving to the door. "How long ago?" I ask over my shoulder.

But Nurse Debbie isn't listening. She's trying to piece together what's just happened.

"How long ago?" I repeat louder, forcing her to focus on me.

"Uh... he left just a few minutes ago. I asked him if he was going to join you in here, and he said he had to go, but to let you know he'd be back very soon to see you and the baby. I just assumed..."

I'm sprinting out into the hallway, looking left and right. Nothing. I run around the corner to the nursery. Nothing. And then I glance far down the corridor to where the elevator is. The doors are just sliding closed as I spot him, smiling at me, his hand up in a little wave. I'm running before the last crack of light can be seen between the connecting doors. Looking up, I see the lit arrow indicates the car is moving downward, toward the lobby.

I fling my body through the heavy door of the stairwell and race down four flights. When I come flying out into the lobby, the elevator is just gliding open and I'm waiting in front of it, fists balled at my sides, panting and sweaty from the exertion. But the elevator only carries a couple of lab techs and a woman clutching a *'get well!'* balloon. And then it dawns on me what has just happened.

Holy shit, I am such a fucking idiot!

Back up the stairs I run as fast as I can, returning to the maternity ward and practically wiping out on the slick, polished tile floors as I slip and slide my way back to Julia's room. It's like I'm trapped in a nightmare, trying to get to her as obstacle after obstacle slows my progress. When finally I burst through the door, Debbie is gone. Julia is still holding David, but she is visibly shaken.

"He was here," she whispers to me, her face ashen, lips trembling.

"What? What happened?" I ask between panting breaths.

"He just came in, walked right up to me and gave me a kiss on the forehead. Then he told me I'd done a good job, and not to worry, he was going to take care of David and me. Then he rubbed the baby's cheek with this thumb, and he left. Matthew—it was the way he said it. The way he said he would 'take care' of us. He didn't mean it in a supportive way. He meant..."

I want to run back out into the hallway, but I know it's no use. That son of a bitch is gone, though not for long, I'm sure. I don't bother saying this to Julia because I don't need to. It's already in her eyes.

Chapter 59

Julia

"I don't think he's breathing," Matthew says, peering over the crib rail.

This has been our favorite pastime over the last four months—hovering over the baby and watching him sleep. He snuffles and sighs and works his little mouth, his tiny pink tongue making an appearance periodically. David Matthew Ayers is the most beautiful thing I have ever laid eyes upon. And I know he's breathing because his every breath resonates within me. I never knew it was possible to be this connected to another living thing.

"Come on, we're going to give the kid a complex if we keep staring at him all the time." Matthew chuckles softly.

"Are you sure we can't wake him up and play with him? Just for a little while?" I ask, only half kidding.

He rolls his eyes and shakes his head as he grabs my hand and leads me out of the nursery. Once we're out in the hallway, I take one last long look over my shoulder. When I turn back around, my husband is watching me.

"What?"

He smiles and shakes his head. "It's just that I don't think I've ever seen you so happy in all the years I've known you."

I consider this for a moment. "That's because I've never been this happy before."

"He's pretty great," Matthew says with a nod back toward the nursery.

"Yeah, he is. But it's not just him, Matthew. It's us. You and me, too. You know that, don't you?" It's something that's been nagging me since the day our son was born. But I already have the answer. He doesn't know, not really.

"Let's open up a bottle of wine," he suggests, dodging the question.

"Ugh, seltzer for me or I'll have to 'pump and dump' before Little Man has his two a.m. snack."

The doctor says it's time to start preparing him for weaning but I'm resistant. I dread the thought of losing those precious moments that we share, just the two of us.

"Seltzer it is," he says, as I follow him downstairs and to the living room.

With a sigh, I sink into the sofa and put my feet up on the coffee table. I am so tired I doze anytime I stand still for more than a minute or two. I'm just slipping into a dream when Matthew returns with my wine glass of clear bubbliness. He joins me on the couch, stretching an arm across the back of my shoulders as if we're a couple of kids on a movie date.

He holds up his glass to toast. "To the Ayers family, happy at last."

"I'll toast to that," I agree as we clink. Then I allow myself to fall into his embrace—my ear to his chest so I can hear his heartbeat. We sit like that for what feels like a long time.

When Matthew finally speaks again, it comes to me as a rumble from deep within him.

"Brett says that Jeremy left for Detroit yesterday."

I pull back and sit up so I can see his face. "So...he did it? He actually conned his way into the Detroit Philharmonic?"

"I don't know that 'conned' is exactly the right word. He strong-armed, blackmailed and threatened his way in, though."

"I can't believe his plan worked!" But, even as I say the words, I know that's not exactly true. These days nothing Jeremy Corrigan does is beyond my sphere of belief.

"Oh, it worked alright...though not exactly as he intended."

"What do you mean by that, Mr. Cryptic?" I ask with a poke to his ribs. He smiles—very briefly—and then his face grows serious again.

"I spoke with Louise Kutter earlier today. As soon as the orchestra's legal counsel told management they didn't have a choice—that they *had* to hire Jeremy or risk a devastating lawsuit—she resigned.

I slap a hand over my mouth, wide-awake now. "No!"

He nods. "It was her only option, Julia. You know what he'd have done to her. Poor Louise would have been bullied into giving him the first horn spot eventually."

I shake my head in disbelief. "I suppose... Still, to give up her seat so he could take it..."

"Oh, no," Matthew corrects me with a wave of his index finger. "Jeremy didn't take her spot. He auditioned for *third* chair and that's what they gave him. Even with Louise gone, there was no way in hell they were going to reward him with the first horn position—no matter how well he plays. I'm guessing that came as a surprise to him."

It's actually a surprise to me, too. "But, surely if the principal chair was available, Jeremy would be the best player..."

"I'm sure he was the best player," Matthew agrees. "But, I'm telling you, Julia, they are fucking furious at having been tricked into hiring him in the first place. There was no way they were going to give him that satisfaction."

"Okay, so...who *is* going to replace Louise if not Jeremy?"

Matthew snorts. "You're going to love this...they gave the principal chair to a 21-year-old woman, fresh out of Juilliard. Can you imagine? Jeremy must be spitting fire!"

But I can't laugh at her expense. "Matthew, he's going to make her life a living hell."

He shrugs. "Maybe. Maybe not. There's nothing we can do about it, Julia. And all I know is that I'm relieved to have the son-of-a-bitch six-hundred miles away. Let him torment the state of Michigan for a while. We've had more than our fair share here in New York, don't you think?"

My turn to shrug. How can I be happy about someone else's suffering? Still, he's right. We've been walking on eggshells for the last twelve weeks, wondering if he'd show up here at the house again. Would he try to take David? Would he demand to be named his father? Would he hurt our family? There's just no telling what he might do, and yet extra security and hyper-vigilance have done little to make us feel any safer. If anything, we feel more vulnerable with the baby to protect. Matthew reads my thoughts.

"I'm done waiting for the other shoe to drop, Julia. We both know he'll get the first chair spot at some point. And I think that as long as things continue to go his way Jeremy will be content to stay in Detroit. He has nothing to gain by tormenting us if he has what he wants. He won't make the effort if it won't benefit him in some way. So, I believe—and Brett agrees—that we won't be seeing him for a while."

And yet, I sense that my husband isn't totally at ease. There's something else troubling him and I have a feeling I know what it is. It's the issue that I wrestle with in the small hours of the morning as I feed my son and rock him.

How can I *not* think of Jeremy when that little angel stares up at me with his perfectly arched brows and vibrant hazel eyes? Jeremy *is* his father, but with my coloring and my red hair. And he is stunning.

I take Matthew's hand and hold his gaze steadily in mine. He has got to hear this and believe it once and for all.

"Matthew, I knew. I knew that first day I held David in my arms that I was done loving Jeremy. Just like that. It was as if someone flipped a switch. Once, I *did* love him. But not anymore. Not ever again. When he showed up in my hospital room there wasn't an ounce...not a single drop of anything even vaguely resembling love in my heart. There was fear... and that was swiftly quashed by fury. How dare he think he can take my happiness away!" I take his hand and squeeze it tight, shaking my head adamantly. "No, my love, you don't ever have to worry that I might have some residual feelings for Jeremy Corrigan," I say firmly.

He doesn't look completely convinced. "I know you don't love him, Julia," he begins softly then takes a moment to clear his throat. "I —uh...what I don't know...is if you love *me*. If you're *in* love with me."

The wave of emotion that fills my heart gives me the answer to that question in an instant. I don't have to wonder about that, either. Not anymore. I smile and move my hands to either side of his face, holding his cheeks so he can't look away. "I wasn't," I admit. "Not at first. I mean, I loved you so much... but you're right, I wasn't *in* love with you. But to be fair, Matthew, I didn't know the difference at the time."

"Didn't," he echoes.

"Didn't—as in past tense. I know now because, since we've been married, I have fallen more and more in love with you every day. You're still my best friend, and you always will be. But you come into the room and..." I pause, thinking of how best to describe it. "You come into a room and my breath hitches involuntarily. When I see you holding our son, my heart swells in my chest. When you touch me, an electric current rushes through my body." Now I turn my lips up into a naughty smile. "And, when you make love to me, you can never be too close, too deep, too intimate. It's as if you can crawl into me...as if my body was made for you."

I've known all of these things for months now and I'm not sure why it's taken so long to verbalize them. Maybe I wanted to be sure they were real and not just some remnant of pregnancy hormones or gratitude that he's taken David as his own child—that I wasn't just feeling intense friendship for the only person who has been there for me in my entire life.

Matthew stares, looking into my eyes for confirmation of everything I've just said. And he finds it. Faster than I can process, he sets his own wineglass down and then grabs mine, setting them both roughly on the coffee table. Before I can even comment, he's cradling my face. He kisses my forehead. My eyelids. He kisses the tip of my nose and each of my cheeks. When his mouth finally makes its way back to mine, I am hungry for him. He's surprised when I push him back onto the couch and lay over his body, kissing him with every bit of love and joy and ecstasy that I can muster. I want this man to *feel* how much I love him.

"I want you," I murmur between kisses. "I want you and only you. And if you don't make love to me right now, right here on this couch, I can't be held responsible for what I'll do, Matthew Ayers!"

He stops and pulls his head back, surprise etched across his face.

"Well? What are you waiting for?" I giggle.

Before I can even blink, he's flipped me over onto my back, so that I'm pinned under him. His lips latch onto mine and he doesn't lose contact for an instant as he hikes up my skirt until it's bunched around my waist. I squeal when he tears the panties off of me.

Holy crap, this is hot!

I devour his mouth hungrily, even as he's unbuckling his belt. I hear the pull of his zipper and find myself whimpering into him. Matthew breaks our lip lock to kiss his way behind my ear and to my neck. My body arches back with the jolt to my core and that's when he thrusts.

"Matthew!" I gasp.

He groans atop me, his mouth moving to my nipple. I tense for just a moment, afraid that he'll hurt my tender flesh there, already so sore from the breastfeeding. But he is supremely gentle, first licking it into a hard pebble and then blowing on it with his warm breath.

"I love your breasts like this," he mumbles. "They're so full, so much more sensitive." His thumbs begin to gently circle the points of each breast.

I don't think I can take this for another second. "Just... oh, Please, Matthew! I need you. Now!" I don't even recognize my own voice at this point.

His elbows fold in under him and he blankets my body, suffocating me with the feel of his flesh. Time to take matters into my own hands. My legs snake around his hips and my arms under his so that my hands are free to feel the ripple of muscle under the smooth skin of his back.

"Your wish is my command," he whispers, thrusting forward so hard that it takes my breath away. *He* takes my breath away and I find that I can only stare at him, wide-eyed and open-mouthed.

With every forward motion I am awash in indescribable pleasure. He finds my hands and pushes them above my head, holding them there as he picks up the pace. I struggle to match him, but he's carrying my body along with his, building a wave of intensity that I am powerless to stop. Harder. Faster. Harder. Faster. I can't even moan. I close my eyes and find my head is turning from side to side, and breath is coming in quick pants now.

"Oh, Matthew.... Jesus, Matthew..."

That's all I can get out, my voice starting to splinter with my desperation. Every thrust is accompanied by a primal grunt. His eyes are closed, brows furrowed together in concentration as he pushes us further and further. I feel it. The tingling. I whimper as it turns into a building pressure. When his free hand moves between our bodies to stroke me, I erupt, shattering into a million pieces.

I scream as my body tenses, my back arches, and my toes curl—my orgasm ripping through me like a tidal wave.

Matthew is right behind.

"Julia! Julia... oh, fuck, Julia, I'm gonna come... Julia..." His face grows red with the supreme effort, and he finally lets go of my wrists so that he can hold my head in his hands, kissing my lips ferociously.

After a very long, very intense moment, he collapses on top of me in a tangle of limbs. Our bodies are drenched in sweat and we're panting so hard that we can't even speak for close to a minute. We just lie there, feeling one another's heartbeats, listening to one another's raspy inhalations. His forehead is pressed against mine for several long moments until each of us has finally caught our breath.

"So...how's your energy level?" he asks sheepishly. "Think you can manage to stay up for a little while longer if I promise to make it worth your while?"

"What?" I practically shriek. "You cannot be serious! No way you're ready to go again so soon!"

He's pulled up a little so that I can see him clearly as he looks down on me, a crooked, mischievous smile on his face. He shakes his head.

"Not exactly...I was thinking we could go watch David sleep some more," he says.

I don't need to pause for even a second. "Well, what are you waiting for? Get off me!" I say, giving him a playful push. He rolls off the couch and collects his pants while I standup and pull my skirt down, scouring the floor for my rogue panties.

When we're finally put back together again, my husband grabs my hand and together we thunder up the stairs excitedly, doing a terrible job of not waking the baby as we shush and laugh and thump our way to the nursery. I can hear David's cry before we even reach the end of the hallway.

"Oh, no! He's awake!" I say with faux alarm. "Whatever will we do?"

Matthew shrugs as he pulls me along.

"Well, I guess we'll just have to take him out of the crib. Maybe rock him. Possibly feed him. Worst case scenario, he's going to have to come back to our bed so we can all scrunch up together."

"Like we're in a nest!"

I'm delighted with the image.

He stops, turns and pulls me into a tight embrace, even as our little boy is bellowing louder.

"Yes," he says solemnly. "Exactly like that. Our family is together —warm, safe and happy—in our nest."

I put a soft hand to his cheek and nod. Then we run the rest of the way down the hall and throw open the door to the nursery and to the overwhelming love that awaits us.

Epilogue

Maggie

They call it The Magic Hour. It's that glorious sliver of time just before sunset, when the world is cast in an amber glow. Everything is softer, more romantic and nostalgic. Right now, this golden aura is cast across the backyard of Matthew and Julia's home on eastern Long Island.

Brett has gone to find me another glass of wine and I'm enjoying a quiet moment, wandering along the back of the property, where the earth falls away into a steep bluff with a staircase down to the private beach below.

What an extraordinary place to grow-up. And grow-up little David Ayers has! Barely nine months old and he's already toddling around after his mother as she sets more food out on the tables. He has her red hair and fine coloring. Oh, I can see the Corrigan in him too, but it's nowhere near as prominent as we all feared it might be. I watch as Matthew sneaks up behind the small boy and, in one swift movement, scoops him up and places him high atop his shoulders. David throws his little head back and laughs and laughs. Julia turns around to see them and Matthew delivers a kiss to her lips. They're a beautiful, happy family.

"What are you looking at?" Brett asks as he walks up beside me.

"Julia and Matthew. And David."

"I know, they're pretty amazing together, aren't they?"

I nod and smile, tearing my gaze away from them to regard the handsome man next to me.

"Hey, where's my wine?" I ask, noticing his empty hands.

"I couldn't carry it," he says.

"What, was it too heavy for you?" I tease.

"No, but it would have gotten in the way."

He's not making any sense. I'm thinking maybe he drank the wine himself.

"Get in the way of what?"

In a split second, Brett is on the ground. On one knee.

Holy crap, this is it!

"In the way of this," he says, pulling a small blue box from his pocket and holding it out toward me like some kind of a sacrificial offering.

I put a hand over my mouth as he flips the top open to reveal a spectacular ring. It isn't one of those big modern monstrosities. The perfect diamond is nestled in a filigreed white gold setting that looks like something from the turn of the century. The previous century, that is. How well he knows me already, this man.

He's smiling at my stunned expression. "Margaret Mae Collins, will you marry me?" he asks quietly, earnestly.

I'm speechless. I can only nod as the tears start to roll down my cheeks.

"Is that a yes? I have to hear the yes, Maggie," he teases me, still on the knee.

"Yes," I whisper. And then I shout. "Yes! Yes! Yes!"

He stands up, slips the ring onto my finger and gathers me into his arms. As he kisses me, he starts to spin me around, so that my sundress flares out around me. From behind us, there's an eruption of cheers and applause.

When Brett finally sets me down on the ground again, I see that they have all been watching the scene on the bluff unfold. Julia and Matthew, Dr. Sam. The rest of the Walton Quartet. That sweet girl Mila and her boyfriend, my colleague, John. Obviously they were all briefed in advance because they are raising their glasses to us now.

"You are *so* lucky I said yes!" I mumble under my breath, poking him in the ribs gently.

"Yes. Yes, I am," he says, kissing me again.

My mother once told me that when you marry a man, you marry his family. And if I am to hold to this sage bit of wisdom, then I have just made both the best and the most terrifying decision of my life. I have committed to marry the only man I have ever loved. But when I say 'I do' to him, I will also be saying 'I do' to his brother.

"What're you thinking?" he asks, catching my eyes with his.

"How happy I am." I smile as I tell the half-truth. Because right now, in this perfect moment, my love for Brett outweighs my fear and disdain for Jeremy.

I throw myself into his arms, almost knocking him over with the force of my affection. More cheers from the crowd. Somewhere, deep in my heart, I know this won't be the last time I weigh this decision. I can only hope and pray that my conclusion will be the same then, as it is right now, in this magic hour.

About the Author

Lauren Rico has earned a reputation as one of the top Classical music broadcasters in the country—introducing listeners to the stories of the great composers. But there came the point when she wanted to start writing some stories of her own, and in less than a decade, she's turned a hobby into several award-winning romance novels. By expanding into the world of Women's Fiction, Lauren hopes to create relatable characters and compelling storylines that will keep readers up all night turning pages. When she's not talking on the radio or tethered to her laptop, Lauren enjoys a quiet but crazy life in a lovely but messy home on Long Island with her husband and rescue pup, Sandy.

Lauren is represented by Jill Marsal of Marsal Lyon Literary Agency.

Acknowledgments

Thanking people isn't nearly as easy as you might think. Like so many emotions, gratitude is difficult to convey on the page... but I'm going to give it a shot

Tom, my partner and my best friend. Thanks for keeping me sane and for worrying about me.

My sister Vanessa, thanks for reminding me that I could do this. This would have been a much harder journey without your words of encouragement.

Janet and Kwaku, you've been a part of every major life event that I can recall... from the fourth grade play to grad school graduation to my wedding. And, here you are again, to share this accomplishment with me. Thank you for ALWAYS being there.

As always, thanks to my family- sometimes chaotic, occasionally dramatic, always loving and supportive.

A special thanks to my newfound friends who came to me through the world of writing, they've proven that you don't need to meet someone to care for them: Terez Mertez, Jeanette Cornforth, Snow

As with Reverie, my editor Jennifer Mishler helped me to transform my first draft into a finished novel. Thank you for your gentle guidance, your honest opinions your unwavering support.

A new addition to Team Reverie, "Book Mechanic." Thank you for making sure I put the best possible book out there into the world. I cherish our new friendship!

To Ernie who has done his best to keep me centered, balanced and on firm ground.

Thank you Dear Lord for the blessings you shower upon me everyday.

Dear Reader...

Thank you so much for taking the time to read Rhapsody*!*

If you enjoyed it, I hope you'll leave a review on GoodReads and wherever you purchased this book. I'm so grateful for your support— you have no idea how much an endorsement from you impacts the authors whose books you read every day.

I hope you'll check out of my other titles on the next page as well the free sneak-peek of the final chapter in the Reverie *trilogy,* Requiem *at the end of this book. And be sure to sign up for my newsletter at LaurenRico.com so you never miss a giveaway or the latest news.*

With all my very best wishes,

Lauren

Also by Lauren E. Rico

This is book two in the Reverie Trilogy. Be sure to scroll down for a sneak-peek of the final installment, *Requiem*!

Other titles by Lauren that you might enjoy...

The Whiskey Sisters series (Written as L.E. Rico)

If you're a fan of Hallmark Channel movies, then you'll love the sweet and sassy O'Halloran girls of Mayhem, Minnesota! These PG romcoms are funny and quirky—but don't let the humor fool you! There's a lot of depth to these characters, and a lot of love for family and friends up there on the Iron Range.

Reading order:

Blame it on the Bet

Mischief and Mayhem

Mistletoe in Mayhem (double novella)

Mismatched in Mayhem

The Symphony Hall series

Looking for something that's fun and flirty—but also has some dramatic teeth? Don't want to get invested in an ongoing storyline or cliffhangers? Check out these one-and-done New Adult romances featuring characters you won't soon forget and set in the world of Classical music.

Solo

Graduate conducting student Kate Brenner has been on her own for a very long time. Daughter of the most detested senator in America, the press won't leave her alone and her classmates won't give her the time of day. It's hard and it's lonely but she just has to hang on until spring when she graduates. *If* she graduates. Because there's one professor who seems hell-bent on seeing Kate fail.

Drew Markham knows he hasn't treated Kate fairly, but he just can't seem to stop himself because Kate Brenner is a dead ringer for the woman who left him a broken, angry shell of the man he used to be.

Now, trapped together for the foreseeable future, Drew has to set aside his painful memories of the past while Kate has to relinquish some of her fierce independence. Torn between desire and duty, loss and loyalty, the notes they play may change the course of their lives forever.

Counterpoint

Brilliant young pianist Alexandria was poised for classical music superstardom...until the night she unraveled in front of thousands at her Carnegie Hall debut.

Brilliant young pianist Nate was poised for classical music superstardom...until the night a horrific accident took away everything—and everyone he loved.

Now fate—and a wily cowboy pianist named Wyatt—have brought them both to Texas for a summer of intensive study and healing. And, while neither is happy to share the spotlight with the other, it soon becomes clear that, together, Alex and Nate possess a dazzling chemistry that eclipses anything they might have done alone.

As Nate wrestles with the gut-wrenching guilt of his past, Alex is forced to confront the grim prospects for her future. Each must decide if there is enough power in their music and enough courage in their hearts to breach the chasm between them.

The Reverie trilogy

If you didn't think Classical music could be riveting, think again! The *Reverie* trilogy is a suspenseful rollercoaster ride that's titillating and terrifying by turns. Set at a prestigious conservatory in Manhattan, the stakes are high, and some people will do anything to get their shot at the top. Highly addictive and deliciously dark.

For mature readers only.

Requiem

Sneak-Peek

Prologue: Jeremy

Watching my father die isn't nearly as entertaining as I'd hoped it would be. It's kind of cliché, actually. Even in the throes of death, the stupid son of a bitch is underwhelming. He's clutching at the collar of his shirt, trying to pull it free of the buttons that are causing it to strangle him. His face is a darkening red, and his frantic eyes are getting larger by the second. His breath is coming in labored wheezes.

The one thing I do find interesting is the fact that not once has he reached out to me, mouthed to me, or begged me with his eyes to help him. That's probably because he knows I'd laugh in his oxygen-deprived face. He won't give me the satisfaction. Oh, he did try to get to the phone on his own, but he just couldn't quite crawl across the floor. Gee, too bad. I could have reached it just by stretching out my arm.

I must admit I didn't come here looking to kill the guy. But when I realized he was headed toward a heart attack or stroke or whatever the fuck this is, I was only too happy to help him along. I have a way of getting under people's skin when I want to. And I *really* want to.

He's squirming now and his lips are starting to look blue. When I see that his eyes are starting to roll into the back of his head, I squat down beside him. I can tell there isn't much time left and I want to make sure the last words he hears on this earth come from my mouth.

He gasps in one last breath as best he can and tries to focus on me. I smile and put a hand on his shoulder, as if to comfort him.

"Don't you worry, dad. Mom won't be too far behind you. I promise you, I'll make sure of that."

And then he is gone.

Chapter One

Brett

The car is silent, save for the gentle swish of the wipers on the windshield. It's raining just enough that I have to use them, and not quite enough so that they don't make that dragging rubber noise as they squeegee across. Next to me, my mother is staring out the passenger window, watching the world fly by in a blur.

"Trudy, why don't you let me cook for us tonight? I'd love to make a big pot of minestrone," Maggie offers from the backseat.

My mother turns toward her with a faint smile on her face. "You're so sweet, Maggie, and I would love that, but why don't we just heat up one of the casseroles that the neighbors have dropped by? I really don't have room for all of them in my freezer."

"Okay, maybe I'll just fix a salad to go with it then," Maggie suggests, determined to be helpful in some regard, no matter how minor.

"That would be lovely, dear," Mom agrees, turning back to the window.

Ralph Fourquet has been our family attorney since before I was born. So, when we walk into his dark mahogany and leather office, he's quick to pull my mother into his arms for a tight hug. He murmurs something into her ear that I can't hear. She nods and wipes the tears that have sprung to her eyes.

Ralph shakes my hand, and I introduce him to Maggie. He ushers us to a sitting area on the far end of his office so that we are on couches, facing one another. He opens up a leather-bound pouch and produces some official looking documents.

"Okay, well, Trudy, you and Danny were very good about keeping your affairs in order so, thankfully, there isn't much to be dealt with at this incredibly difficult time."

He skims through the pile of paperwork and produces what I recognize to be a last will and testament. "As we discussed last year, Trudy, you are the beneficiary of Danny's life insurance policy, and all joint savings and retirement funds will revert to your sole control. There is no mortgage on the house, and no outstanding debt to be paid, so this is all fairly cut and dried. As you know, Ray Page, Danny's friend from Chicago, has made an offer to buy the business."

"Wait, what?" I ask, leaning forward so fast that I nearly slip right off my tufted leather chair. "When did this happen?"

"A few days ago," my mother replies quietly. "Ray and Pam would like to get out of Chicago and move here, to Owl Bridge."

"And you agreed?"

I feel a little hurt not to have been consulted. She smiles at me sadly. "Sweetheart, if you had even the least bit of mechanical inclination, I would have given the business to you in a heartbeat. But you don't want it. And Ray has always been a good friend to your father. Honestly, I rather like the idea of him and Pam being close by."

I consider this for a second and realize she's right. Ray and my father go way back to their days together as mechanics in the Navy. That was even before my father met my mother. And now that she says it, I also like the idea of the Pages moving to town. They can be another source of support for Mom when I'm not here.

"I'm sorry. I didn't mean to be..."

She waves a hand at me. "No, Brett, I'm sorry I didn't mention it sooner. I didn't mean to exclude you from the decision, it just slipped my mind."

"Brett, you don't have to worry. The Pages are in fine financial shape, and have offered full value for the business. We'd be hard pressed to find a better buyer."

I nod. It's just so strange to hear them talking about my father's life's work this way.

"It's just a place. It's not *him*," Maggie offers quietly, as if reading my mind. She takes my hand in hers and squeezes hard.

"So," Ralph continues, looking at me, "your mother and father discussed what might happen in this event, and they made the decision—which your mother still holds to—that you should be the beneficiary of any funds collected from the sale of the garage."

I look at him, then my mother, and then back at him again.

"But, Mom, you need that money..." I start to protest, but that waving hand goes up again.

"I have more than enough with the life insurance and our retirement savings. And I plan to keep working, Brett. Once I decide to retire from the school system, I'll have a very generous pension and healthcare. I have more than I need."

"Mom..."

"No." She's shaking her head firmly. "You and Maggie are getting married soon. You're going to need that money to buy a house."

"Okay, first of all, we just moved into the SOHO brownstone, so nobody's going to be looking at houses anytime soon. And how much money are we talking about here, anyway?"

Ralph consults one of the papers in his stack. "Just shy of eight-hundred-thousand dollars."

My mouth falls open. I know it's not a good look, but there's nothing I can do about it. I can't even speak, but my mother is amused.

"Careful, Son, or you'll catch flies in there," she chides.

"I can't take it, Mom," I protest.

It's my mother who leans forward this time. "This is what your father wanted, Brett. And it's what I want, too. Please, I don't need to be worrying about you. This will put my mind at ease."

"Jesus, Mom, it's not like I'm a substitute music teacher. I play viola with one of the biggest string quartets in the world. I do just fine..." I stop abruptly when I see the look she's leveling upon me.

Trudy has decided. Period. End of discussion.

Ralph starts to go through the details of the sale when something occurs to me.

"Wait, wait, wait...what about Jeremy?" They both look at me as if I've started speaking Swahili. "You know, Jeremy? Your *other* son?" I remind her, which doesn't go over so well.

"I'm well aware of who he is, thank you very much, Brett," my mother snaps.

Shit.

Ralph steps in and tries to smooth things over. "Brett, your parents changed their will about a year ago to name you as sole beneficiary of the business. You're also your mother's sole beneficiary and will receive the balance of the estate after her passing."

"Mom, are you sure about this?" I ask with more than a little doubt. This is harsh. *Really* harsh for Danny and Trudy.

"I have never been more certain of anything in my life," she declares flatly.

Ralph seizes the moment to jump back in and redirect the conversation. Or, at least that's what he thinks he's doing. "Alright, then, with the autopsy results back, I assume you're ready to make the funeral arrangements?"

"Yes, please, Ralph. You have the prepaid plan that we purchased from the funeral parlor. Please just ask them to follow those instructions. The church will take care of the service itself."

"Whoa, hold on a sec..." I break in, shaking my head in confusion. "What are you talking about?"

"Your father and I preplanned our funerals..."

"Not that!" I cut her off. "Why was an autopsy done? I thought it was a heart attack. Since when do they do autopsies for natural causes?"

My mother meets my gaze squarely. "I requested the autopsy, Brett. It may have been natural causes that killed him, but I don't think there was anything natural about the way he died."

Now it all makes sense. The business, the will, the inheritance. She thinks Jeremy had something to do with my father's death, and I have no idea why, other than that my brother is a bastard. But I know my mother well enough to know that wouldn't be enough reason for her to make that assumption.

I'm missing something here. Something big. But, I won't be for long if I have anything to do with it. So I try to engage my mother repeatedly on the drive home, but she shuts me down every time. "Mom, it's just that..."

"Stop it. Right. Now," she cuts me off sharply, turning to face me from the passenger's seat. I almost pull off the side of the road.

"What?"

"How your father and I decided to divide our assets is up to us...*was* up to us," she corrects her use of the present tense, my father being dead and all. "I don't want to hear about this again. Do you understand me?"

She waits for an answer, and I feel as if I'm a naughty schoolboy again.

"Yes."

We spend the rest of the ride in an awkward silence. I sneak a glance back at Maggie. She's stunning, with her wild black curls pulled back into a severe bun at the back of her head. Even in the head-to-toe black that is the universal uniform of mourning. She catches me watching her and offers a sympathetic smile.

All I can think about is getting back to the house so I can spend some time alone with her, talking through all of this. She'll give me some perspective. I pull my mother's sedan into the driveway, and we all climb out into the crisp fall afternoon. I notice that the gutters need cleaning, and the leaves need raking and add them to my mental

'To Do' list. With my father gone, the 'man of the house' duties now fall to me.

Maggie and I trail behind her on the walk up to the porch, the three of us still silent. Mom gets the door unlocked and we follow her into the house.

"Honey, I need to lie down for a little while," my mother is saying even as she's crossing the living room. "I'm going to make a quick cup of tea and go to my room. Maggie, there are salad fixings in the fridge. I'll be up to make dinner at about—"

My mother stops cold. Stops speaking and stops walking, standing rooted and staring into the kitchen from its doorway.

"Mom?"

I'm so busy looking at her, that I don't immediately see *him*.

The Reverie Trilogy comes to its devestating conclusion in Requiem by Lauren E. Rico!